I0523869

Sonder

Janie's Story

Sonder

Janie's Story

Maureen Morrissey

Printed by Amazon.com, in the United States of America.

First printing, 2022.

Indie-published
New York, N.Y.

https://maureenmorrisseysauthorsite.wordpress.com/

This book is dedicated to the people closest to me, my wonderous and expanding family. It is also for friends who have been around for part or much of the trip; my journey is richer for having you all in it.

Table of Contents

Passing by unseen
Chimeras
Shimmering on the periphery
Fringes of perception

Occasional fragment
Of a conversation
Or accidental touch
Brings cognizance
Opens awareness
Scratches at understanding

A man dressed in rags
A child with tear-stained cheeks
holding a blue balloon
Three girls, heads together,
speaking the secret language of teenagers
A woman walking six dogs
with leashes of different lengths and colors,
trying to cross the street
before the light changes.
A couple holding hands,
in intimacy
or in distress

Who are they
Where are they going
What life do they lead
Do they love
Are they loved
What will happen to them when they walk on
Are they even real
Or
Are they ghosts passing through fabric
Like extras in the movie of your life

And you
An extra in theirs

A Brief Introduction

This book is a sonder.

Sonder is defined in the Dictionary of Obscure Sorrows as *"The realization that each random passerby is living a life as vivid and complex as your own—populated with their own ambitions, friends, routines, worries and inherited craziness—an epic story that continues invisibly around you like an anthill sprawling deep underground, with elaborate passageways to thousands of other lives that you'll never know existed, in which you might appear only once, as an extra sipping coffee in the background, as a blur of traffic passing on the highway, as a lighted window at dusk."*

It is a fascinating idea for a writer that every single human has a story to be told, with lessons for all of us in each other's lives. A few minutes of listening can yield a rich, engaging tale that gives me insight into my own journey or offers me a glimpse into experiences that are just not in the cards for me.

As I am gifted these stories, my imagination takes me from their starting point and spins yarns that keep me up at night. My dreams become epic full-length feature movies starring the people who have passed through my sphere. Some of their littlest anecdotal gems wind up in my writing, and I wonder if, one day, they will read my books and recognize their contributions.

<u>Sonder</u> is a tribute to the epic stories of the lives in that "sprawling underground anthill," zooming in on just one and following her as she makes her way.

This is Janie Thompson's story.

Part 1

It's not about what it is, it's about what it can become."
-Theodore Geisel

Introducing Janie

The squeal of screeching tires nearly drowned out the dull *thump*, but Janie felt it in her bones as the world froze in front of her. Liliana's father stood across the street with his hand up, but Janie could not tell if he meant "Hi!" or "STOP!"

As she stood on the cement step in front of Liliana's first floor garden apartment still holding her dolly, Janie could see her friend's black Mary Jane shoe lying on the sidewalk, and the edge of her pink dress on the ground in the street.

The noise brought her friend's mother, Mrs. Rodriguez, out of the open door, where she took a moment before asking in a puzzled tone, "Where is Liliana?"

Then a cacophony of sound descended on them all. Liliana's father let out a bellow as he dove into the middle of the street in front of a station wagon skewed across the road. The cars trapped behind, whose drivers could not see from their vantage point the broken little girl on the ground, honked in rage. And, finally, a shriek from next to her as dawning comprehension overtook Mrs. Rodriguez.

Still, Janie stood without moving. The two girls had been sitting on the stoop in the warm June afternoon, talking their dollies. Janie had named her new doll Liliana because she thought it looked just like her three-year-old friend who lived up the hill and around the corner; and Liliana had been delighted. Just as Janie was making the doll dance around, her satin dress swishing and long hair swinging, Liliana had spotted her father's car coming down the street, searching for a parking spot. The cars where they lived, at the far end of Forest Hills, were always parked bumper to bumper along the curb. Liliana had jumped up, yelled, "Papa!" and darted out into the road to greet him.

Then suddenly the world went silent; and then it roared.

Forgotten and unnoticed in the commotion, Janie stuck her thumb in her mouth, a habit she had quit when she turned four a year ago. She walked around the corner to her own apartment, the Liliana doll held loosely by the dress. Tears streaked her pale cheeks by the time she reached the front door of her own garden apartment and walked up the stairs.

"Janie! Just in time, come help me set the table for dinner. Dad will be home any second. Here, put the milk bottle on the table…oh, what happened now? Why are you crying?"

"Liliana is on the street and her shoe is on the sidewalk," the little girl answered, sniffing.

Her mother crouched down, wiping a bit of flour off her face with her apron, to talk directly to her daughter. "What do you mean, Janie? Tell me what happened."

"We were playing and Liliana's daddy came home in his car and she ran to say hi and then there was a lot of noise and her daddy and mommy were screaming and so I came home."

"Stay right here, young lady," her mother said, turning off the stove and hurrying around the corner.

When she returned a long while later, Daddy was with her. Her mother's eyes were swollen, and her mouth was turned down. She went into the bathroom for several moments. When she came out, she had fixed her face, and busied herself getting the now-cold meal reheated and placed on the table.

"Can I go see Liliana?" Janie asked, still standing in the kitchen where her mother had told her to *stay right here*.

"No. Now leave your mother alone. She is trying to get dinner on the table." Her father spoke in a sharp tone, turning the television on and sitting in his place at the head of the table to wait.

Her brother Greg, older by three years, came home sweating and filthy and was sent to wash up. Janie followed him into the small bathroom and tearfully retold the story. With one look at his baby sister, he squatted down and gave her a tight long squeeze.

"Oh, Janie! It's not your fault, you know. It was an accident. I'm so sorry about your friend. Just remember what I always say to you: Janie, never forget, I loved you when you were brand new, and I will always love you."

She nodded her bowed head, letting Greg's words make her feel better, as they always did.

Greg had, in fact, fallen in love with his sister as soon as she had come home from the hospital. Even though he was only three, he sat with her through the day, showed her toys to entertain her, and later helped her learn to walk and to eat with a fork. He read to her and sang nursery rhymes to her.

"Baa black sheep have you any wool? Yes sir, yes sir, three bags full," Greg would enunciate the words carefully while Janie listened with fierce concentration.

Then she would parrot back, "Baba back seep havoo nee boo, lether lether free bazoo!" and he would hug her tightly so she could not see him holding back delighted laughter.

He was more patient with her and gave her more attention than their parents; and when she was sad, scared or hurt, she always went to him; and he always said those same words: *Janie, never forget, I loved you when you were brand new, and I will always love you.*

As usual, the family was silent as they ate that night, while Mr. Thompson watched the news. Mrs. Thompson's stern expression told the children clearly and plainly they were not to ask about what had happened.

Her mother disappeared into the bedroom after clearing the table and tidying up the kitchen; and Janie put herself to bed. The little girl sat on her bed, hugging herself and rocking, repeating Greg's words *I will always love you*; until, exhausted, she lay her head on her pillow and slept.

The next day, Janie's father put on his suit, pinned on his name tag, and left for his walk to the department store, where he stocked shelves and helped on the floor. Her mother got busy dusting the knickknacks on the bookcase and coffee table. Greg woke up late, played Legos with Janie until he got bored and then left the apartment to meet up with his friends. After lunch, her mother began to vacuum the shag rug in the living room, the high-pitched racket precluding conversation. Janie spent most of the afternoon watching cartoons, which she could hear intermittently between the Hoover's din and the rumble of the airplanes landing at La Guardia or JFK airport.

For the rest of the summer, Janie's repeated requests to go see her friend were denied with no further discussion, and after her parents became irate with her pestering, she stopped asking. At night, she cuddled the Liliana doll, whispering to it, "Don't worry, I will see you soon."

On an afternoon when her mother was preoccupied, Janie left the apartment and walked around the corner. Halfway down the block, she hid behind a large tree that she could peak around to watch Liliana's door. She stood there for a long time, and just as she was about to give up and go home, the door to Liliana's house opened. A woman stepped out to shake the dust off the welcome mat, an old woman, bent and thin. As Janie watched, puzzled, the lady turned towards her to finish her chore with a couple of last good shakes. Janie gasped; *it was Mrs. Rodriguez!*

If it were not for the familiar apron, which she always wore when she served the girls sweet arroz con leche and café con leche in little china cups, Janie would never have recognized her friend's mother.

Janie jumped back behind the wide trunk, heart pounding and hoping she had not been seen. When she heard the door close, she ran home and sat in her room for hours, trying to fit the young and beautiful Mrs. Rodriguez onto the destroyed old woman she had seen; and found she could not. It haunted her dreams for the rest of the summer.

Playing in front of her apartment with her best friend Deidre, who lived down the hill and around the corner, Janie told her the story.

"They won't let me go see Liliana, Deidre. I want to play dollies with her, she loves my new doll that looks just like her."

"Maybe she's dead," Deidre said, in her matter-of-fact tone. She was the youngest of four and the only girl in her family and had seen and heard much more than her best friend. Janie soaked up Deidre's stories of her brothers' adventures, especially the oldest, Bobby, whom Deidre worshipped as only a baby sister can. "You know, dead like that rabbit Bobby found in the park that I told you about. If she is dead, you can't see her anymore."

Janie pondered the thought of Liliana being like a dead rabbit, and it made her very sad. She cried a bit, and Deidre put her arm around her.

"It's okay. You still have me!" Deidre said in her cheerful voice.

"I do, and you still have me!" Janie said and dried her tears. She caught the red rubber ball that Deidre bounced to her and bounced it back. They played until lunch time, giving each other a hug and yelling, "See you later!"

Janie asked her mother just once about that day.

"Mommy, what happened to Liliana?"

"Janie, you can see that I am in the middle of this pile of laundry. Now is not a good time to ask me anything. Besides, some things are just better left alone and not brought up again. Am I making myself clear?"

"Yes, Mommy," she said, walking away with her head down.

Just before the beginning of the school year, her mother told her that Mr. and Mrs. Rodriguez had moved away.

Janie took her Liliana doll off her bed and pushed it to the back of her clothes closet, covering it with stuffed animals.

"Come on, Janie, time to go. Are you ready for your big day?" Greg said, giving his sister a once-over to make sure her shoes were tied, and her barrettes were straight in her pigtails.

They could hear their mother scrubbing at the rusty stains in the tub as Greg opened the door and let Janie out. At eight years old, he was quite lanky, towering above his sister who was about to start her first day of kindergarten.

The walk to P.S. 220 was over half a mile and across the busy 108th Street, but he was used to it. He had been doing it on his own for two years already. Janie might have been nervous except for her absolute trust in her big brother. She did not even take his hand as they went out onto the sidewalk.

By the time they had gone two blocks, they were joined by a long stream of kids, who poured out noisily from the garden apartments and six-story buildings lining the neighborhood streets.

Janie was absorbed in the sights, sounds and smells on their way to school. The odor of onion blowing out the vent from the bagel bakery mixed with the pungent smell of the storefront fish market and the chemical scent pouring out the open door of the Chinese laundry as they walked up the avenue. The incinerators of the taller apartment buildings were already at work burning the residents' garbage and spewing soot into the air. Janie kept brushing black bits off her dress; and when several larger pieces fell on Greg, she laughed and brushed him off too. The sun, on this warm September day, was veiled behind brown haze. Janie took it all in with an excited smile as they went.

The hooting, hollering, chattering mass of children arrived at the corner next to the Long Island Expressway. The oldest of them, sixth graders, stopped traffic so they could stream across the avenue to the large open space in front of the school. Life at the far end of Forest Hills was in full swing. Traffic on the Expressway was stop-and-go, cars beeping with rage; as the fire department, on 108th Street just beyond the underpass, came to life with wailing sirens and strident honking horns. The Q38 bus made tire-squealing stops on every block; and the loud, long, jangling school bell warned there were only five more minutes until line up.

A few matronly women moved among the children, encouraging them to begin finding their class line spots. They were mostly ignored until the actual line-up bell sounded, and then the children obediently moved into their places to begin the day. Greg dropped Janie off on her line.

"See the sign? K-1, that's your class. You'll line up here every day, okay? Have a great first morning, I'll meet you right here so we can walk home for lunch. Love you, Janie."

He gave his baby sister a hug which she returned, her arms trembling with a bit of first-day jitters. She watched her big brother walk to his own class line in front of a sign that read 3-1.

From an objective outsider view, should any of the adults hurrying to work or to complete their lists of errands have stopped to view, it was obvious the children were grouped with a purpose. Each grade had five sections: five separate lines of boys and girls from shortest at the front to tallest at the back. The first class was all white and, judging by the Stars of David hanging around their necks, mostly Jewish. They were dressed up in collared shirts and pressed pants or party dresses, with their Buster Browns freshly covered in shoeshine to hide scuff marks. The second class had one or two light brown children mixed in, and were also dressed in clean, neat attire. The third class had more than a sprinkling of brown-skinned children, and the fourth class had many more, along with white children dressed in worn frayed clothing and shabby cheap shoes. The fifth class was filled with dark brown children and those who did not speak English, and a few children who did not seem to know what was going on around them.

Janie, on her line in the first class, turned her head to look for Deidre. She spotted the large dark eyes and wide smile easily because her friend, in the fourth class, was jumping up and down and waving at her.

A monitor came up behind Deidre, yelled, "Eyes front, absolute silence! This is your first day of school, and you are already trouble;" and hit her on the back of the head with a binder she was holding. Janie, eyes tearing in sympathy, turned her gaze to the front of her line.

Once inside the classroom, Janie was so busy painting on the easel, playing in the kitchen center and putting on costumes at the dress-up corner, she did not want to stop for their morning break.

The teacher called out, "Clean up now, it's milk time!" and within minutes, the thirty-five children had everything back in order.

They sat in rows at their desks as she passed out miniature milk cartons from the metal carrier left outside their door. The room-temperature white milk was nearly spoiled, but the teacher checked to make sure the containers were empty before she allowed the children, some of whom were still gagging, to toss them in the wastebasket. They then began their counting and handwriting practice.

Janie, her tongue tucked between her teeth, held her pencil carefully and traced the letters and numbers with care. The only sound in the room, other than the teacher's soft footsteps as she walked around checking their pencil grips, was the scratching of thirty-five pencils on paper. Janie found it comforting and knew after just two hours that she was going to like school.

At ten o'clock, the nearly one thousand children were led

out to the play yard for morning recess. The oldest kids had the swings, and Janie watched as they played Spiderman, swinging as high as they could and then leaping off the seat at the downward part of the arc to land clinging onto the chain-link fence. She saw one of the sixth graders overshoot the four-foot-high fence, landing on his face on the concrete. He sat up, bleeding from the nose and lips, but no one paid him any attention; so, he wiped his bloody face on his shirt and ran back around to try again.

Greg was not on the swings, so Janie wandered over to the enormous blacktop play area behind the school building to look for him or for Deidre. She found her friend in line for Double Dutch with other girls much bigger than her, who were chanting as their feet moved in quick and graceful jumps:

Down, down, baby, down by the rollercoaster. Sweet, sweet baby, I'll never let you go. Shimmy, shimmy cocoa pop, shimmy, shimmy pop…

The bell rang after fifteen minutes, before Deidre had her turn to jump in. She and Janie hugged, and Deidre said, "Let's walk home at lunch time together!" before they ran back to their lines.

When the noon fire bell sounded, the school doors burst open and the children poured back onto the streets to head home for lunch hour. At the Formica table in their small kitchen, Janie and Greg chatted about the morning with their mouths full of grilled cheese and tomato soup, while their mother gossiped on the telephone, stretching the coiled line of the handset as she moved around the room. When they were done, the kids watched cartoons for the rest of their lunchtime. By one fifteen, they were all back in the classroom for the afternoon instruction.

At the end of the day, Greg met up with Janie in front of the school. Deidre and her three brothers were waiting with her. One of the boys was wearing a tee shirt that said "1966 New

York Mets." Snoopy and Woodstock slouched on top of the doghouse wearing blue caps with the orange NY, looking depressed.

They started to walk, but Janie stopped short to stare at a line of children waiting at a food truck parked on the street. Painted against the yellow and red backdrop next to the selling window, two cartoonish Chinese girls in black pigtails and coolie hats sported huge inviting grins.

"Chow…Chow…Cup," Janie decoded the truck logo slowly. "What are the kids getting, Greg?"

"Mostly French Fries," her brother responded.

The tall boy at the front of the line walked away from the window, carrying a newspaper cone drenched with grease. The salty fried potato odor wafting to her made Janie's mouth water.

"Come on," Greg said, pulling at her arm. "We don't have any money anyway. You spent your six-cent allowance already, remember? Besides, the fries are fifty cents. How many weeks would you have to save up to get Chow fries?"

Janie spent the walk home trying to figure out the answer.

The next day, as Janie was building a block tower in her classroom, a quiet voice at her elbow said, "Hi, Janie."

She turned and saw Benjamin Whitman, who lived across the street in one of the private houses, looking down at his shoes. His cheeks and the tips of his ears were bright red.

"Hi, Ben, want to help me? I'm making the Empire State Building." They worked together, Janie chattering away.

As they placed the last block, Benjamin said to her, "You should come over after school. I got the new two-hundred-and-five-piece Lego set for my birthday and we could make the whole city."

Just after walking in the door that afternoon, Janie dropped her schoolbag, changed out of her school clothes into her play clothes, yelled to her mother, "I'm going to Ben's house to play

Legos!" and ran across the street. She could not reach the doorbell, so she knocked loudly. Ben's brother, short, stocky and already fifteen years old, opened the door.

"Hello, Janie from across the street," he said with a friendly smile.

"Hi. Benjamin wants to play Legos," she said, looking up at him as she did her own big brother, only a bit higher. He stepped aside to let her in. This was the first time she was inside one of the private-property houses; she and Ben had played together outside in his driveway before, but not very often. Benjamin's mother seldom allowed him out of the house. Janie stared at the stairs with their wrought-iron railings leading up to the bedrooms, the fancy living room with its sparkly chandelier, plastic-covered gold fabric couches and baby grand piano, the large sunny kitchen at the end of the long hallway where she stood.

"He's upstairs," the teen said. "But I have something cool to show you, too. Come to my room."

Janie followed him up the stairs and into a bedroom painted black. She walked over to the desk and stared at the weird posters on the walls and did not hear him close the door behind her. He sat on the low single bed and patted his lap. "Come sit here, little Janie. I want to show you something you're going to like a lot."

She smiled and climbed onto his lap. He put his arms around her middle in a tight hug and began to wriggle around underneath her. She was puzzled; he did not seem to have something to show her in his hands. He pushed her down against himself and began to moan.

Just as Janie was about to ask what he wanted to show her so she could go play Legos, the bedroom door opened. Benjamin's mother walked in saying, "Did I hear you open the front door, Stephen? Is someone here?"

She froze as she took in the scene in her son's room.

"What is going on?" she asked, directing her angry stare at Janie. "What are you doing here?"

Stephen roughly pushed Janie to the floor, and Mrs. Whitman pulled her arm to stand her on her feet. Before Janie could begin to explain, Mrs. Whitman dragged her down the stairs, pushed her out the front door and slammed it shut.

She could hear Mrs. Whitman yelling inside, and Stephen shouting back at her, as she stood on the porch for a moment, confused. What had she done wrong? Benjamin invited her over, Stephen let her in and then Mrs. Whitman got mad and made her go back outside. Bewildered, she shrugged her little shoulders and went to sit on the cement steps outside her front door.

After a few minutes, Ben came out of his house and walked to the sidewalk; he was not allowed to go any further. Janie crossed the street again.

"Why didn't you come in and play?" he asked.

"I did. I think your mother doesn't like me. Your brother does, but she made me leave. Do you want to play outside instead? I could get my pinkie ball and we could have a catch or a game of Stoop Ball."

They played until Janie's mother called out the window that it was time to come in for dinner.

Janie and Greg's father sat at the table still wearing his suit jacket with the name tag from Alexander's Department Store fastened to the pocket, waiting to be served. On the RCA television in the living room, just a few feet away from the kitchen table, NBC announced the six o'clock news. Black and white scenes broadcast live from Vietnam showed dead soldiers, punctuated by the sound of rapid gunfire. The only talking allowed at the dinner table was their mother offering seconds, as the family sat and ate. Janie watched the scenes on television for a few minutes and then sang songs in her head to while away the time until she could leave the table. Even a peep coming out of her accidentally would earn her father's mad look; and she did not want that.

After the requisite hour, Greg asked to be excused to finish his homework and work on his model airplane. Janie helped her mother carry the dirty dishes into the kitchen. She dragged the wood step stool over to dry as her mother washed. Afterwards, Janie brushed her teeth, gave her parents a kiss goodnight and went to her bedroom. From the doorway, she could secretly stand and watch the prime time shows her parents put on every evening. Gilligan's Island, I Dream of Jeannie, The Monkeys, Let's Make a Deal, My Three Sons, and her favorite, Mr. Ed the Talking Horse; and if she stayed up late enough, the Newlywed Game came on. She did not understand the questions and randy chuckles at the answers, but she liked how the ladies who won got so excited over their new stereophonic set or Philco refrigerator or Fuller Brush Company Electrostatic Carpet & Floor Sweeper.

She watched until her eyes struggled to stay open, and her legs did not want to stand anymore; then she closed the door silently and crawled into bed. She whispered good night to her dolls and stuffed animals before falling asleep.

Janie, like many city kids, became a member of the neighborhood pack once she began school. In all weather on Saturdays, the children burst out of their apartments as early as eight o'clock in the morning and began their street games. Janie and Greg stayed in their pajamas to watch Rin Tin or Davy and Goliath cartoons or Bozo the Clown, until their father woke up around ten and threw them out of the house.

Waving at Ben, who was not allowed to join the games and was watching out the window, Janie followed Greg to the common backyard behind the apartments, where a dozen kids were in the middle of an intense game of Ring-a-Levio.

"How do you play, Greg?" Janie asked, hiding behind him. The yelling and wrestling of the kids, mostly bigger than her, was intimidating.

Greg put a reassuring arm around her shoulders as they watched the game.

"Don't worry, you'll be on my side for your first game. One team is hiding, and the other team is looking for them. When they find someone, they have to hold on to them and yell, 'ringalevio one two three, one two three, one two three, ringalevio one two three.' If they can say the whole thing without letting him get away, the one they captured goes to jail. See, jail is the old sandbox there. When they catch the whole team, they switch places. But if one of the hiders can sneak in and tag the jailed ones, they can escape and hide again. Got it?"

She did, and the game went on for over an hour until they all got tired of it. Janie had caught on quickly. Tackling one of the bigger boys, she wrapped her arms around his knee and her legs around his ankle, hanging on for dear life and screaming the entire Ringalevio call Greg had taught her while the boy, laughing so hard he almost wet his pants, tried to shake her off his leg and finally gave up, falling to the ground. Both teams cheered as she triumphantly led her captured enemy to the jail.

After the game, the whole group trouped around the neighborhood for a while, and then ran down to the Grand Central Parkway side road. At the foot of the overpass into Flushing Meadow Park, they pushed aside a broken chain-link fence and entered a garbage-strewn area. They took turns climbing into a tree with an old piece of plywood jammed between lower branches that served as a treehouse; and played pirates.

When the noon fire bell went off, they split up, yelling, "See you after lunch!" and ran back to their apartments. Gulping down peanut butter and jelly or grilled cheese or rice and beans or Pop Tarts and milk, they were back out running the neighborhood in under an hour.

Janie loved being a big girl and loved going to school every day. She leaped out of bed with the sun, ate her Apple Jacks or Cocoa Puffs cereal sprinkled with extra sugar, and was dressed in her light jacket, hopping up and down by the front door while Greg was still slurping the milk out of his bowl at the kitchen table.

"Come on, Greg! We're gonna be late, hurry up!"

"We are not going to be late, Janie. Hold your horses, I'm coming."

"Mom, can I walk by myself? Greg is taking too long!" she called.

Their mother had the window screens leaned up in the bathtub, working to remove the brown crusty filth caked on them since she had cleaned them just a month ago.

"Not until first grade, dear. You won't be late, give Greg a few minutes."

When he finally led her down the stairs, she zoomed around the corner and found Deidre waiting on her cement stoop. They grabbed hands and skipped ahead of the boys, singing nursery rhymes as they went. When they got to the corner of the busy 108th Street, they did not pause to look for traffic as they began to cross.

"Janie! Deidre! Stop! Stop!" Greg and Deidre's three brothers screamed as they raced towards the girls, who did not hear them through their singing.

Just as they stepped into the street, the boys reached them and roughly pulled them back onto the sidewalk. At that second, a large sanitation truck was backing up at the intersection to empty the overflowing trash cans, right where Janie and Deidre had been standing.

"And this is why you won't be allowed to walk yourself until next year!" Greg yelled into Janie's shocked face, while Deidre's brothers gave her a few solid smacks on the arms and bottom. The tearful, shaken Kindergarteners held their brothers' hands for the rest of the walk.

At school that week, Janie's class made Halloween decorations and the teacher read them *Georgie the Ghost* by Robert Bright, *Trick or Treat* by Louis Slobodkin, and Janie's favorite, *It's the Great Pumpkin Charlie Brown!* She could already read the simple text of *Gus the Friendly Ghost* by herself. The whole school quivered with excited energy about the approaching holiday, and Janie and Greg were no exception.

Even the adults seemed enlivened by the upcoming fun. Mrs. Thompson, whose social life consisted entirely of other mothers, bake sales, and block parties, got busy making cupcakes for the Halloween fundraiser at the school. In a rare display of warmth, and with an even rarer smile, she had Janie help her measure and mix the ingredients, fill the metal baking tin with its Halloween-themed paper cupcake liners, and place the pan into the oven.

As soon as the first batch went in, she poured herself a cup of coffee from the Farberware percolator and pulled a pill bottle out of her apron pocket. Janie read the label, *Lib..ri...um*, as she watched her mother shake one of the half-black half-mint green capsules into her hand and swallow it with a mouthful of coffee.

"Are you sick, Mommy?" Janie asked, watching her mother drop the pill bottle back into her apron.

"What? Oh no, dear, these are just mother's little helpers," she responded, patting the apron pocket.

A few minutes later, her mother seemed to suddenly relax; her frenetic wiping of the countertops became slower and calmer.

"Two more batches, and then, after they cool, I will frost them, and you can put the orange and black sprinkles on them. My cupcakes always sell out first. The secret is adding a box of vanilla pudding to the mix, Janie. These are important things to remember for when you are a mother; you always want to have a secret ingredient, and you always want to sell out first."

Janie had no idea what her mother was talking about but enjoyed the unusual attention and nodded her head.

When Halloween arrived that year, they came home from school, put on their store-bought costumes, and grabbed two large brown paper grocery bags. Greg's pirate outfit and Janie's princess both came with a plastic mask that could easily be pushed up to eat treats as they walked.

First, they circled their block, knocking on doors and yelling "Trick or Treat," while a rowdy swarm of kids echoed the demand up and down the street. They waved at their friends as the grocery bags were filled until they were brimming. They ran home, dumped the candy onto their beds and went back out.

This time, they walked several blocks to the taller apartment buildings. Running past the eight doors on each floor, they knocked and yelled and collected until the grocery bags were full a second time. After lugging the bags home and dumping them out, they went out into the dark early evening, and walked around to the private houses, filling their bags one last time.

Then the horse trading began. Sitting on the floor in Greg's bedroom, they bargained back and forth. Their mouths full, teeth brown or blue, the exchange went on for an hour: two Maryjanes and a Bit o' Honey for a large box of Good n' Plenty; one tube of Necco's for all the Sugar Daddies; Pixie Stix and wax lips for Lemonheads and SweetTarts. The ones they did not like, Swedish Fish, candy corn and Chuckles, went into a pile for UNICEF along with the pennies people had thrown into their bags for charity. Both kids slept surrounded by empty candy wrappers, their masks forgotten under their beds.

Two days later, on their way to school, Deidre's oldest brother began to cough. The nine-year-old, athletic and quick, had been showing off his sprint to the others. He was midway up the block when the hacking choking cough racked his lean body. In the smoggy brown morning, with the soot raining down on them from the incinerators, they could hardly see him. He was bent over at the waist, trying to catch his breath, when the other kids caught up with him.

"Are you okay, Bobby?" Deidre asked, patting his back. He could not respond for several moments, and then hawked up a gob of discolored phlegm and spit it out at his feet.

"Ewww!" the others yelped in unison, jumping back.

Bob coughed up more phlegm before he was able to catch his breath so they could continue on their way. Through that day and the next several weeks, more and more of the children, and some of the teachers, began coughing to the point where they could not speak. It was an unusually warm November and the children played outside as before, but the brown air that settled down on top of the neighborhood began to affect them all.

"New York City is under a smog alert," announced the nightly news, as the family ate their supper in the usual silence.

The photographs taken from the observation deck of the Empire State Building showed only the top half of the tallest buildings nearby; the rest of the city was hidden underneath a layer of filth.

"Hospitalizations of adults and children suffering with emphysema-like symptoms are increasing alarmingly through all five boroughs. Cases of chronic bronchitis are on the rise as well, according to several doctors we spoke to. Here to comment is our city medical examiner. Sir, what can you tell us?"

The bespectacled man in a white lab coat held up two x-rays. On the black and white television screen, one appeared very dark gray and the other very white.

"On the autopsy table it's unmistakable," he said, in the

matter-of-fact tone of one who sees death for a living and is immune to it. "The person who spent his life in the Adirondacks has nice pink lungs. The city dweller's are black as coal."

"There you have it. Stay tuned for more news after a word from our sponsor, Kent King Size cigarettes. Your taste buds will tell you why you'll feel better about smoking with the taste of Kent. Your taste will become clear and alive because Kent, with the micronite filter, refines away harsh flavor, refines away hot taste, makes the taste of a cigarette mild and kind!"

The news announcer shook a cigarette out of a pack and lit it, breathing in with a satisfied smile.

"Can we go out to play?" Janie said. "There's no school tomorrow because of Thanksgiving Day. Please?"

"Be back by eight," their mother said, lighting her own Benson and Hedges cigarette. "Greg, make sure you wear your wristwatch."

They could not find other kids to play with and were back in a half hour.

The next morning, Janie and Greg, sitting on the couch in pajamas and passing a box of Lucky Charms cereal back and forth, enjoyed the annual spectacle of the Macy's Thanksgiving Day parade. Televised from midtown Manhattan, in shades of gray on the screen, the show went on for three hours. They were waiting for the grand finale, Santa and Mrs. Claus atop their sleigh with Rudolph leading the reindeer pack, when there was a rapid repeated knock on their apartment door.

"Somebody get that!" their mother called from the kitchen, wrestling a large turkey into the oven.

Janie jumped up, and with her eyes still on the screen, opened the door. Standing just outside was Deidre, in her pajamas and bunny slippers, weeping.

"Who is it? Oh, Deidre. Janie, talk to her outside on the stairs. I can't have people tramping all around on my freshly washed floors."

"Bobby is in the hospital," Deidre whimpered. "He was choking and couldn't breathe. Momma and Daddy called a ambulance, and they took him away. What if he dies??"

She crumpled to the top stair and Janie sank down next to her, putting her arm around her friend's shoulders in sympathy. She imagined what she would feel like if this happened to Greg; the thought alone made her cry along with her friend.

For the next two weeks, Janie asked about Bobby every day. Deidre was not allowed in the hospital due to the age limit for visitors of twelve, and did not have any information except that he was still alive. She told Janie how her whole family cried and prayed together every night; and it must have worked because Bobby finally came home, weak and thin, but recovering. He was one of the lucky ones, Deidre had told Janie after overhearing her parents talking; a baby from the projects near their school had died, and a teacher's helper was still in the hospital and might die, too.

The winter was uneventful. It was frigid and frosty throughout much of the season, but that did not stop the children from their outdoor play.

On a day when two feet of snow fell and closed the schools, unheard of in those days, Janie and Greg pulled on their snowsuits, hats, mittens, scarves, and boots; and joined the group already tramping around the backyard. Snow covered the sandbox, brushed the bottoms of the metal swing seats, and came up well over Janie's knees, causing all the kids to laugh as she tried to negotiate through the drifts and keep up with them.

When one of her feet came up bootless, they turned it into a treasure hunt; unsuccessful as it turned out, and Greg had to piggyback her all the way home. Their mother was none too pleased about having to go up to the five-and-dime store on the avenue to get Janie a new pair.

An ice storm, covering everything with a thick, glittering coat, gave them another entertainment. The street they lived on was at the bottom of a long, steep hill. When the road was icy, Janie and Greg watched the cars come sliding down out of control and hit one of the parked vehicles with a satisfying bang that made them clap. They made a game of counting the accidents; and were delighted when the number grew to two digits in just a couple of hours.

Through the rainy and warm Spring, Greg and Janie pulled their galoshes over their Buster Brown shoes and splashed around the neighborhood until mud plastered their hair and filled their ears and noses. Their mother, grumbling about having more laundry to wash, made them strip to their undershirts and underpants in the stairwell, put their muck-covered clothes in a hamper, and go straight into the shower. Watching the mud slide off them and swirl down the drain never failed to entertain Janie and made risking her mother's ire worth going out the next rainy day and doing it again.

That summer was a very exciting one for Janie for one reason: her mother was allowing her to have a birthday party. Their parents did not believe in wasting time or money on such fuss, but Janie had worn her mother down with her constant jabbering about a party, *just this one time? Pretty please, with sugar on top and whipped cream and a cherry?? I'll never ask for anything ever again, please??*

Greg sided with her, offering to set everything up in the backyard and chaperone so their mother would not have to attend the party herself. With considerable resignation, their mother at last nodded her head, adding, "I will bake a cake and give you two cans of Hi-C, and get plates, cups and party hats at the five-and-dime. If you want to play Pin the Tail on the Donkey, you can make the game and figure out the prizes yourselves.

"Yay! Thank you, thank you, thank you!" Janie squealed, hugging her mother around the knees, and then turning to jump on Greg, almost knocking him to the ground. He laughed, nearly as excited as she was.

On the day of the party, a bright, still July afternoon, Greg dragged a folding table and eight metal chairs out of the common basement room and set them up in the backyard. He snuck one of their mother's twin-sized bedsheets out of the closet, choosing a dark-colored one in case there was a juice spill; and laid it out as a tablecloth. Janie, dressed in her favorite yellow party dress with plastic rainbow barrettes holding her hair back, helped him put out the plates and cups and hats, all decorated with dancing clowns, at each chair.

At one o'clock, Deidre and four children from Janie's class were dropped off by their mothers. They each carried a birthday present wrapped neatly in balloon or cake themed paper and placed them on one end of the table. Greg helped each of them put on a party hat and lined them up for the game.

Just as they were about to begin, Benjamin arrived with his big brother, Stephen. All the other children ran over to drag him to the hand-drawn donkey picture taped to the wall so he could join the game.

"Well, happy birthday, little Janie," Stephen said, opening his arms to her.

"Hi, Stephen!" Janie exclaimed, as he lifted her up, hugging her close and tightly; too tightly for Greg, who pulled her out of his arms and pushed her behind him. He stood almost face to face with the short but stocky teenager.

"Aren't you a bit old to be at a birthday party for little kids?"

"What, your sister and I are good friends. What can I say, she likes older men," Stephen said, leering at her and the other girls. "When I heard Janie was having a party, I told Benjamin, 'Don't even bother telling mom, she won't let you go. I'll take you and you can buy her a present out of your piggy bank.' So, you should be thanking me, little Greggy."

"I will thank you to stay over there, or else..." Greg said, putting his nose close to the teen's face.

"Fine," Stephen said, laughing and holding his hands up. "I don't want to upset my little birthday girl. Maybe next time she comes over to play..."

"There won't be a next time," Greg retorted; and walked over to help the little ones play the game.

****

Janie enjoyed first grade, especially the Dick and Jane reading series. She loved that the girl in the books had her name and a nice older brother, just like her. The books made her want a puppy and kitten like Spot and Puff, but she knew better than to ask her parents.

She read the series in less than a month, and moved on to the SRA reading box, its color-coordinated cards filled with stories and questions that were meant to challenge the children. She finished the whole first grade set by March and started the next level. Benjamin kept up with her, and they often sat together with the box between them.

"You should come over after school, Janie," Ben said to her one day. "My mom ordered the whole set of World Book Encyclopedias from the salesman who came to the door, and it's really cool. Lots of pictures and really big words, too."

"Greg said I should only play with you outside from now on; he didn't say why, but maybe you could bring some of them to the porch. I'll bring my notebook to write stuff down, okay?"

They spent the afternoon with the *P* book, gabbing about plants, planets, and porcupines. Stephen came out to invite

Janie in for a minute.

"Greg says to stay outside, but thank you, Stephen. Do you want to learn about pandas with us?"

With a sour look, he went back inside and slammed the door. The first graders looked at each other and shrugged.

"Teenagers," Benjamin said. "That's what my mom always says about him. Look, Penn-syl-vania; we went there once..." and they spent another hour leafing through the book.

In second grade, her beloved young teacher got fat around the middle and disappeared halfway through the year. The new teacher was a mean old thing with a hump on her back. She set out independent activities and yelled at the children if they chatted too much. Janie did not like her but was only called out once for talking and learned quickly how to stay out of the teacher's way.

Now in September of third grade, Janie and Deidre walked to school carrying their paper bag-covered textbooks held together in a rubber strap. Janie's bundle was heavier than Deidre's, filled with more challenging books than her friend's, but neither seemed to notice.

"I'm so excited about our field trip to the Museum of Natural History tomorrow!" Janie said.

"My class is not going to the museum," Deidre responded with a pout, her dark eyes unhappy.

"Maybe you'll go later in the year," Janie said. "Don't worry, I'll tell you all about it!"

The next morning, sitting in traffic on the school bus, the children passed the time singing.

"Ninety-nine bottles of beer on the wall, ninety-nine bottles of beer! If one of those bottles just happens to fall, ninety-eight bottles of beer on the wall! Ninety-eight bottles of beer on the wall..."

The thirty-five children in Janie's class walked into the

museum and stood around the dinosaur skeletons in the lobby in wonder. They moved through each of the rooms, absorbed in asking questions, pointing and chatting with unbridled curiosity. The teacher was holding a clipboard, observing the children and taking notes. Janie returned to her repeatedly to query about one thing or another, and as soon as the third grader ran off, the teacher wrote more on her pages.

Janie and her classmates ooh-ed and aah-ed at the giant blue whale suspended above them in the Hall of the Ocean, were fascinated by the meteorites from outer space, and became so engrossed in the Hall of Eastern Woodlands Indians they did not want to leave when the teacher told them it was time.

"We may return later in the year," the teacher said as they made their way to the exit. "I can see how much you enjoyed the museum, and I cannot wait to see your project ideas. You should start thinking about your options now, while it is fresh in your mind. Remember on the contract you each signed, you committed to completing a project for every study we did. Is anyone planning on writing a skit or making a diorama for this one?"

Hands shot eagerly into the air, accompanied by enthusiastic shouts of "Me! Me!" and the happy hum of children planning.

It was a worn-out crew of kids that boarded the bus on 81st Street to head back to Queens at the end of the day. Janie sat with one of the other girls, looking out of the bus window at everything they passed in the big city. The group was quieter on the way home, but suddenly a girl in the seat just in front of Janie began to giggle and point at something. Janie looked at the people rushing in all directions along the crowded streets, at the tall buildings, at the long lines of yellow cabs with the drivers honking their horns and yelling out the open windows, trying to figure out what the girl was laughing about. Then she looked down at the car driving alongside the bus in the heavy traffic.

A man, alone in his car, had one hand on the steering wheel. The other hand was in his lap. His pants were open, and he was touching himself, looking up at the children with an intense stare. As they watched him and he watched them, his hand went up and down faster and faster. After a moment, the bus pulled ahead of him. By then, all the children had come over and squished into the seats on that side of the bus to laugh and point, while the teacher sat in the front of the bus, dozing.

Janie sat back as soon as the bus started moving, wondering why the man would touch his penis in his car. It seemed silly and weird, but soon all the children settled back in their seats for the rest of the ride. Janie started chatting about the Egypt exhibit with the girl next to her and did not give it another thought.

She walked home from school with Deidre, telling her all about the exhibits they had seen. When they arrived back at Deidre's stoop, they dropped their books and sat.

"I think I will probably write a poem about each of the things we saw for my class project. That was one of the things I agreed to on my Study Contract with Mrs. Mast. Or maybe I'll do a poster, but I'm not so good at drawing things. Maybe you could help me!"

Deidre looked at her like she was speaking another language. "My class isn't doing projects; what's a Study Contract? Why don't we do stuff like this, all we do is workbook pages and Spelling tests."

"Maybe you'll do it all later in the year," Janie said with a shrug. "Hey, are you hungry? I am."

The girls went inside, Deidre walking behind Janie with a crestfallen look on her face. She did not even dunk her Oreos in her milk as she listened to Janie prattle on about the poems she might write; but she did come up with great rhyming words for creatures and dinosaurs, earning her an enthusiastic hug.

Just a few weeks later, unbeknownst to Janie, her mother was called into the principal's office. There was a lengthy meeting that included the teacher, who held her clipboard filled with notes.

The principal, a short, serious man in a gray business suit and dull tie, looked over his spectacles at this mother in her nice dress and shoes and matching handbag, obviously chosen especially for this meeting. He doubted she got many chances to wear such an outfit if she was like most of the other bake sale and P.T.A. fundraiser moms whose lives revolved around keeping house.

She seemed a bit uneasy sitting in the principal's office. He never failed to be amazed by how nervous parents got when called in to see him, like they may have done something wrong and were about to be scolded. He smiled to put her at ease.

"Mrs. Thompson, I called you here today to share with you a very exciting bit of news concerning the education of your daughter, Janie."

His eyes flicked down to his desk to make sure he had the name correct; it would not do to say the wrong one, especially since he had to convince this mother to go along with the plan.

"District 28 is one of the best in the New York City school system and we have been chosen to participate in a special groundbreaking new program. Due to the changing nature of our communities and an eye towards the future, we will be putting together groups of children from very...*different* neighborhoods and, using the best and most modern education methods, will offer them the opportunity to expand their horizons and work with children from, as I said, very *different* backgrounds."

He knew he had to be more specific, so he continued carefully.

"Your daughter, and other specially chosen students from Public School 220, will be working alongside children from

Jamaica, Queens, which is a neighborhood we serve that has less...fortune, less, shall we say, opportunity than we do here in our little corner of Forest Hills. Part of the experimental program will be to try the latest teaching methods, as I said. Another part will be to have students from different types of families, specifically white children, and carefully selected black children of reputable backgrounds, work together in cooperative groups where each child's strengths are tapped into; so that, together, they will all benefit from the interaction, and grow in new ways and be prepared for life in the latter part of the twentieth century."

He took an imperceptible deep breath after this runaway explanation, praying that he had done enough to convince her without scaring her off. The last mother had said she needed to consult her husband, and almost immediately called to say they would not be allowing such a thing under any circumstances.

Janie's mother listened and nodded her approval and agreement. The principal seemed assured with his assertions that this was a special opportunity not offered to most children; and that was enough for her to consent.

That afternoon when Janie got home and was about to change out of her school clothes, her mother told her to sit for a minute.

"Janie, it's very exciting. You have been chosen to attend an experimental school for the rest of this school year. You will still walk to P.S. 220, but then you will be picked up by bus with other children who were selected and taken to a classroom at the school district office. You will be meeting children from a very different neighborhood, which I think may be good for you. Not very many children were chosen for this, which means you were singled out to participate. Wait until I tell the other mothers, they will be so envious! The program begins next week."

"But I don't want to go, what about Deidre and Ben and my other friends? I like my school."

"It's settled, dear. Now go out and play. Be back for dinner at six."

Janie ran around the corner and banged on Deidre's door. Deidre took one look at Janie's tear-filled eyes and put her arms around her. They sat together on the stoop, while Janie filled her in. For the rest of that week, they played together at recess every chance they had.

The following Monday, Deidre waited with Janie for her new school bus and, just before she boarded, the two friends hugged tightly and tearfully. Deidre watched the bus go and was late to line up, which earned her recess detention for the week.

Janie wandered her new classroom to take it all in. It turned out to be an entire floor of the School District 28 building, a very large open room. It was filled with third and fourth graders, most of whom were also wandering. In one area she found speed reading machines, which she stopped to try; in another, a shelving unit full of jigsaw puzzles. She lifted up a few to see the cover pictures and thought she might try the thousand-piece puzzle showing forest animals. There were tables everywhere, and a few movable blackboards with yellow and white pieces of chalk and black erasers, and bean bag chairs strewn about the room. Along one wall was a bank of mirrored windows. Janie watched the reflection of the roomful of kids for a while, and spotted a tiny red light, barely visible, in one corner of the mirror before she moved on.

Janie took several slow walks around while waiting for a teacher to come in and give them instructions. A teacher never came.

She did the speed-reading machines for an hour, with phrases zipping by on the screen as she looked through the viewer; but got tired of it and roamed the room again. Other kids were sitting and chatting or rambling around like Janie. An observer from the other side of the mirror might have noticed that most of the white children were on one side of the room, and the black children stayed on the opposite side. Janie was oblivious to this divide.

She found a girl with a warm smile sitting alone on a bean bag chair.

"Hi, I'm Janie."

"I'm Sarah. Want to sit with me?"

Sarah, who was bussed in from Jamaica, became her first new friend. That morning, they read together, Janie helping Sarah with the harder words; and did puzzles together and drew pictures on the flimsy manila paper left in piles with crayons and colored pencils. Sarah helped Janie with the harder details on her drawings.

At noon, the large group was taken by bus with their lunch boxes to the blacktop of the school yard at the Russell Sage Junior High. Unsupervised, the children were left in the yard until the buses came to take them home. Janie and Sarah skipped rope and watched the girls from Jamaica spend hours in Double Dutch competitions, while the boys from their neighborhood played basketball all afternoon. A few of the children from Janie's school joined these games, but most stayed to themselves in the shade.

Day after day was the same; Janie became bored and spent much of her morning using the speed-reading machines or paging through books. In the afternoon, she played jacks or skipped rope with Sarah. Oblivious to the fact that, within a month, many of the other white students had begun to leave the program, Janie continued the routine she had plotted out for herself.

Her mother never asked about the program, other than, "How was school today?"

Janie's attempted answers were usually interrupted by the

phone ringing or Greg's arrival, to which her mother would say, "How was school today?" before getting busy with some housework or cooking task.

Sarah invited Janie to her house after school one day, and she could not wait to tell her parents about the plan as her mother was bringing the food to the table.

"Doesn't she live in Jamaica?" her mother asked in a tone of voice Janie had not heard her use before.

"How would you get there and how would you get home?" her father asked.

"She said I can take the school bus home with her," Janie responded.

"I don't know, it's not a good neighborhood," her mother protested. "I'm not going to take the subway out there to come and get you."

Her father turned to her mother. "Isn't this why you signed her up for this program, Debra? So she could mix it up a bit? Fine, I'll borrow the neighbor's car and pick her up. Call the school and get the girl's address; you can figure out the route using the Rand McNally Road Atlas. Make sure you write it all down in detail, so I don't get lost in Jamaica." He shook his head as he glared at her and forked a meatball into his mouth.

Her mother nodded, looking down at her plate. She seemed put-out about the whole thing and took this assignment from her husband as punishment. Janie clapped her hands in delight, while Greg was quietly amused by the whole exchange.

She ran to her room to choose a couple of toys to bring with her. Tossing aside her trolls, her Etch-a-sketch and her Chatty Cathy doll, she went into the closet. In the corner was a pile of stuffed animals that she had not played with in years. She rifled through the well-worn plush toys: a Winnie the Pooh, four teddy bears, a white cat missing most of its whiskers, a spotted dog, two organ grinder's monkeys, a Scooby Doo, a

Smokey the Bear and a Minnie Mouse. Her hand reached deep into the pile and froze.

Her fingers felt satiny fabric and the hard plastic it covered. She felt around it: long curly hair, little fingers, bare feet. Her heart remembered before her brain did. Slowly, she pulled her hand up through the stuffed animals, clutching the Liliana doll as it emerged from the pile.

When it was out, its brown eyes looking directly into hers, she sat for long minutes, holding it on her lap and remembering. She had put this sad memory in a box almost as soon as it had happened. That her little neighbor had died that day was never talked about by her parents, but she knew now it had to be true.

In her mind's eye, Janie saw it all again; and for the first time, she truly grieved the loss of Liliana. Tears came so quickly, they squirted from her eyes, soaking the pink unicorn on her blouse. She was quiet about it, not sobbing; but she could not stop the tears, either. They came and came and came, until she had no tears left. Then she sat for another moment, tenderly running her fingers over the doll's miniature features. After a long while, she stood cradling it in her arms and placed it lovingly on her desk where she could see it from everywhere in her room.

"I promise I won't forget you again, Liliana," she said to the doll, adding something she had heard on television: "Rest in peace."

Janie went to her toy box, pulled out her favorite Barbie doll, and put it by her bag to take to Sarah's house.

On the afternoon of the visit, Janie walked to the school bus with Sarah instead of getting on her own. The children from Janie's neighborhood were pointing at her and nattering to each other in confused consternation, while the children getting on the Jamaica bus gave her and Sarah wide berth as they boarded. The girls went to the back of the bus still chatting excitedly, but as soon as the bus drove off, the other children began to harangue them. Sarah shrank into her seat, taken aback by the pestering and harassment; and both girls had tears in their eyes.

Janie walked to the front of the bus and told the driver, "Those kids are being mean to us."

The older man emitted a deep sigh and shook his head in irritation. "Just sit up here with me until we get there," he said, indicating that the kids sitting on the front seat should make room for her. They reluctantly did, and when the bus stopped in front of Sarah's house, one of them gave Janie a solid shove as she and her friend got off.

Despite the bus ride, the girls enjoyed playing with their Barbie dolls in Sarah's room.

"Let's go to the beach in your convertible," Janie held her doll facing Sarah's and talked in a high-pitched voice.

"Okay!" Sarah's Barbie responded. "I'll get us something to eat, and you get your sunglasses!"

Sarah ran into the kitchen and grabbed two cans of Hunt Snack Pack butterscotch pudding. They peeled back the aluminum tops, licking the excess off the sharp-edged circle, and laughing at their yellowish mustaches.

After a couple of hours, Janie's father came to pick her up. He did not say a word to her on the ride home, ignoring her chatty retelling of the bus ride and the playtime at Sarah's house.

It was the only time she was invited to her friend's place; and when Janie wanted to invite Sarah home with her, her parents both said a firm, "No."

Months into the program, Janie and Sarah sat on the blacktop of the school yard, playing jacks. As Janie was just completing sevensies, a girl came up to them and handed her a note. Sarah leaned over Janie's shoulder to read with her:

Dear Janie,

You can't play with Sarah anymore. You are a white bitch and you need to leave our fucking school. If you don't leave, we will kick your white fucking ass.

Love,

Janice

Janie read the note over twice. It was the first time she had seen bad words in print, and it shocked her. It was the first time she had been threatened, and she did not know what to make of it. And it was the first time she had been called white.

She looked at her thin arm, still holding the paper, and then at Sarah's. She had never paid attention to the difference in their skin color, and she could not comprehend what the problem was.

Then she looked up at her friend's face. The horrified look in Sarah's tear-filled eyes startled Janie. Sarah rose, looking sorrowful, and walked over to stand with Janice and her group of friends. None of them spoke, but Janice's clenched fists were message enough.

Janie rose off the blacktop, trying and failing to catch Sarah's downturned eyes. Leaving the pile of jacks and the little rubber ball, she turned away from the small group of girls with her head down and walked into the building. Still bewildered and very sad, she handed the note to the secretary, who read it, grabbed the handset on her desk and made a phone call. Janie was picked up by the principal of P.S. 220 and brought home.

"Why didn't you tell me that all the white children had left the school except for you, Janie? Why didn't you tell the teacher?" her mother asked when she walked into the apartment.

"I really didn't notice, and there were no teachers," she responded.

"No teachers? I don't understand."

"We just did whatever we wanted all day," Janie explained. "It was really boring."

Her mother shook her head in irritation and went back to vacuuming. Stopping for a moment, she took the brown vial out of her pocket, shook a pill into her hand and dry-swallowed it. She began pushing the Hoover in jerky back-and-forth movements, while Janie stood there waiting for her to say something else. When she didn't, Janie left the apartment and went to wait for Deidre to get home from school.

As she sat on the stoop, her thoughts swirled. Her mother had put her in a class that made no sense, and what happened with her new friend made no sense. Why did they not learn anything and why did Janice get so mad about her playing with Sarah; and why did it matter what color their arms were? After several minutes, she saw Deidre walking down the street, and her friend's familiar face pushed aside the confusion in an instant.

Despite what had just happened, the best part was, she was back. Back to walking with her friend every day, back with the rest of her class, back to her normal life. When Deidre saw her sitting there, she broke into a gleeful gallop, dropped her books on the sidewalk and threw her arms around Janie. Her brown arms, Janie had a second to think, before they both squealed and hopped up and down, talking over each other elatedly.

"What happened? You're back, I'm so happy!" Deidre yelled. Her braids jumped erratically, beads clacking in happy music.

Janie did not know how to answer her question, so she just didn't. The girls clasped hands and ran into Deidre's apartment to play.

It took Janie the rest of the year to catch up academically with her classmates. Her first test, just a week after she returned, was to list all fifty states and their capitals. She had studied, but knew she was not ready. She watched the teacher fold the writing papers in half the long way, running her finger over the crease before taking her shiny large scissors and cutting them in two. The teacher walked up and down the rows, placing each paper exactly in front of each student. The classroom was silent, and Janie's paper sat on her desk, taunting her. She carefully wrote her heading, *name, date, Class 3-1*, and numbered the paper to calm herself and focus: one through twenty-five on one side, twenty-six through fifty on the other. Then she wrote all the states she could remember, adding their capitals as they came to her.

When the teacher collected the test, Janie lay her head on her desk and took a deep breath. For the first time, the answers had not come readily. The graded tests were waiting on their desks when they came to class in the morning. The red seventy in its angry circle at the top of her lined paper made her cry. It also made her work that much harder; and soon she was back in her groove.

And no one ever spoke of the experimental school again.

That June, the two friends got their report cards on the last day and opened them as soon as they met up in front of the school building. They did not even glance at the C's on Deidre's report, but went straight to the line that said, "Teacher Assignment," as they did every year, hoping the same teacher's name would be there; and as they did every year, hugged in disappointment.

As Janie handed her mother the report card, she asked, "Why is Deidre never in my class?"

Her mother responded with a scornful laugh as she looked briefly at the row of A's and tucked the folded card stock into the stack of unopened mail on the kitchen shelf to show her husband when he came home.

She was reaching for a coffee mug when Janie, still standing there, repeated her question. Sighing in irritation, she responded without looking at her daughter.

"The IGC class is for smart kids. That is not a word I would apply to her or any of her brothers, or, for that matter, to her parents. Because of who we are, you will have opportunities that she never will; nor should she. Get used to the idea that other people just aren't as good as us, and appreciate what you have, Janie. Your life will be a lot easier that way."

She did not see the tears well up in Janie's eyes as she poured steaming coffee from the percolator. "Deidre is good! And she is smart! And so is her whole family! I love them and they love me, too!"

Janie stomped into her room to cry bitter tears as her mother made a dismissive wave towards her.

Afterwards, Janie was more careful to rein in her enthusiasm for the activities her class did, at least in front of her best friend.

Now in Fourth grade, Janie and Deidre often walked a block out of their way in the morning to stop at the junior high school yard and wave at Greg and Bobby, who played handball before their first period. Janie thought she would feel nervous with Greg moving on but found herself connecting even more than before with her friends and school activities.

That year, Janie's class put on a play for the entire school. The teacher announced, "We are doing a new show this year, children. It's called Camelot, the story of King Arthur and the Knights of the Round Table!"

The eager buzz among the children stirred up a shared enthusiasm; and when the class walked up to the theater on Queens Boulevard to watch the movie, the spectacle on the big screen lit Janie on fire. As soon as the teacher handed out the scripts, Janie began studying the part of Guinevere, the woman pledged as King Arthur's wife. The more she read about Guinevere's untamed spirit, the more badly she wanted to play the role.

Janie took four quarters from her Raggedy Ann coin purse

and begged Greg to lend her four dollars. With her weekly allowance now up to fifty cents, she could pay him back in just two months. Delighting in her eager wheedling, he happily gave her the rest of the money she needed. He even walked with her up to the Sam Goody's record shop by the movie theater. While he thumbed through the rock and roll records, she went straight to the Musicals and Show Tunes section and found the soundtrack LP of Camelot. Greg could barely keep up with her as she ran the whole way home.

Janie spent the next few days singing along with the record and bugging her brother to help her practice Guinevere's lines. On the day of the tryouts, her nerves got the better of her and she could not stop shaking long enough to read the lines. Janie was sorely disappointed, and mad at herself that she wound up being an extra in the play, but at least she got to paint all the sets. She even snuck Deidre in one afternoon to help.

The next year, the whole fifth grade learned to square dance. Janie dreaded the walk from their classroom to the sweltering gymnasium, where a hundred and fifty kids stood in groups of four to form the squares. Sweat pouring down their faces, the children followed the calls of the vinyl record that the gym teacher played, holding the microphone close so the tinny voice and country music could be heard throughout the space.

Grab your partner, do si do! Circle left! Circle right! Promenade; now pass through and go home!

Twice each week for six weeks, the children were made to practice the dances, and at the end of the unit, perform them for the rest of the school. Janie was relieved when it was over.

Had she known that the next unit in Gym was going to be calisthenics, led by the teacher's record of the exercise song "Chicken Fat," she might have felt better about square dancing. The gym teacher made them sing along as she walked around, correcting their posture, and coercing greater effort. Janie often could not fall asleep at night because the song echoed in her head:

Go, you chicken fat, go away!
Go, you chicken fat, go!

She was even more relieved when they began the basketball unit. Even though she could not, for the life of her, get the ball through the hoop, at least they all had fun trying.

And finally, sixth grade! The oldest kids got the swings, wore the orange Safety Monitor belts with the tin badge and bossed the others around; and fell in and out of love every few days.

Janie blushed every time she looked at Benjamin, and at Barry, and at Richie, and Jeff and Joel and Mark and Bruce. She and Deidre giggled over photographs of T.V. and pop music heartthrobs, penning *Mrs. Janie Cassidy* and *Mrs. Deidre Jackson* all over their notepads.

One morning, midway through the school year, Janie found a composition notebook sitting on her desk. On the cover, large letters handwritten in red ink spelled out SLAM BOOK!!!! Leafing through it, she saw that each page had a different girl's name in neat script on the top blue line. Written below in flowery pen or flaring colored pencil, she read the anonymous comments: *She's fat like a slug...Ugly clothes...Nobody likes her...* Even the most popular girls had remarks, and some of these were worse still: *Hate her!...So mean...Thinks she is perfect but she is NOT...* Janie found her own page and saw that only one comment was written there so far: *So skinny her pants might fall off.*

Looking around to make sure no one was watching, she slipped it into her desk. She did not say anything to the other girls, even when she overheard whispers wondering where it was.

The next day at morning recess time, the teacher stood in

front of the class, her mouth set in a firm frown. "Boys, you may line up and walk yourselves to the playground. Girls, you stay right where you are."

The tall, thin woman crossed her arms, a severe look on her face. She waited until the boys had walked out, whispering among themselves in bewildered tones at the turn of events. As soon as the door had closed behind them, she waved the Slam Book in front of the stunned and guilty faces before her.

"I know better than to ask who started this," she began with a glare at each of them. "But I will tell you this: I am ashamed of you all. I will be giving this disgusting display of nastiness to the principal, and I can guarantee he will be calling every one of your mothers."

Tears began to fall on reddened cheeks.

"If I ever..." She slammed the notebook on her desk so hard, they all jumped. "...*ever* hear of anything like this again, you will be barred from the field trip to the Hall of Science, graduation and the sixth-grade dance. Am I making myself perfectly clear?"

With one last scowl, she made them put their heads down on their desks and wait for the end of recess bell.

Despite the chattering among them for the rest of the day, none of the girls knew how she had gotten hold of the Slam Book; except one.

The night before graduation, Janie went in her room to try on her cap and gown and look at herself in the mirror. With mixed feelings, she placed the mortar board on her shiny long hair and tried on a nervous smile. She was leaving the safety of the elementary school and going on to the junior high. Every time she thought about it, her stomach flipped, and she had to force herself to stop hyperventilating, especially late at night; and even more so because Greg would not be there to reassure her. He was graduating this year as well and moving on to high school.

She went into his room and found him listening intently to WNEW on his clock radio. Alison Steele, the Nightbird, was spinning the newest Jefferson Airplane tune.

"Let's both put on our graduation caps and gowns, Greg. Maybe Mom will take a picture. Please? It's the first time we are graduating at the same time."

He was about to refuse but looked at her imploring eyes and melted. He could never say no to her, and he got up and threw his gown over his tee shirt and jeans.

"I'll go get Mom!" Janie said and ran down towards their parents' bedroom.

She had her hand on the knob when her mother's voice came through the thin door.

"I don't want to go. I can't be bothered either; I have things to do too, you know. It's so stupid to make such a hoopla about any of it. Everyone moves from school to school; I don't know why there has to be such a fuss."

"Then don't go." Her father's voice.

Janie could hear him hanging up his suit and pulling his pajamas out of his chest of drawers. She could picture him with his back to her mother, barely listening to her.

"I can't do that. I didn't go to Greg's and the whole P.T.A. was up in arms. That Sheila Goodman even called me to tell me that everyone was talking about me. She has some nerve; her husband doesn't even come home at night. Everyone knows he is sleeping with his secretary. They should all just mind their own business; every one of them has secrets that everyone knows. I should stay home if that's what I want to do. Bunch of squawking hens. But I have to go." The resignation and bitterness in her mother's voice, made Janie's eyes well up.

Janie walked back to Greg's room. "I didn't go in. I heard Mom say she hates graduations. She doesn't even want to go."

She burst into tears. Greg put his arm around her and gave

her a hug; then dragged her to his mirror.

"It doesn't matter. Let's just take a good long look so we will remember this moment for ever. That's even better than a picture."

Janie dried her tears and gazed into the mirror at the two of them for a long time.

Janie began seventh grade, and a whole new world opened. Halsey Junior High was filled with thousands of kids from the larger neighborhood. They quickly formed cliques, and Janie found herself in two groups: the handball-playing, late-night marauding kids who were, like her, mostly unsupervised and independent. This group included Deidre and kids from the projects down the street. The other group was comprised of academically advanced kids who joined after-school clubs and then went home to do homework and extra credit projects.

Janie was part of an honors program at Halsey, but she realized quickly that some of her teachers were real winners. Her Honors English and Math teachers had high expectations, and the kids learned quickly to pay attention in these classes. Her other teachers were a completely different story.

The seventh grade Social Studies teacher kept a small bottle in his desk drawer and hid behind his newspaper, leaving an assignment on the board for the students to complete. Most days when the bell rang to end class, he was passed out sitting up in his chair as the kids left the room.

Her eighth grade Science teacher was handsome and young, causing many of the thirteen-year-olds to become giggly when he stopped to chat with them out in the school yard. Janie watched the interactions without participating. She found him overly friendly and was wary of him; especially on the day he walked over to her group of friends and, smiling broadly, asked them to read the word written in gray letters on his tee shirt.

"Therapist," all the girls read aloud, a bit puzzled.

Janie looked closely and noticed that the first three letters were just a tiny bit lighter in color than the last six.

"Ewww! The rapist!" she exclaimed. "That's not funny."

She walked away in disgust, leaving the other girls to get closer to him to see what she was talking about.

Through Junior High, Janie found most of the schoolwork easy; and found a lot of free time on her hands. During the day and into the late afternoon, she worked on projects and homework assignments. She did not need to study for tests. Along with most of her honors' classmates, she scored excellent grades without trying very hard.

The evenings she spent with her other friends, hanging out until late on the dimly lit handball courts in the schoolyard. When they were not playing, the other kids were chugging beer and talking about the groups of teens from the Bronx who came down looking for trouble, or about their older brothers and sisters: who was pregnant, who got arrested, who broke night or got thrown out of the house for good.

Janie listened but could not relate much to these stories. She was just glad they let her hang out with them, keeping her from sitting alone at night in her room. It made her feel cool for the first time in her life.

Janie guzzled her first quart of Colt 45 beer on the handball courts, on a warm October night of eighth grade. The other kids gathered around chanting her name as she upended the bottle in a chugging race with the neighborhood champion, Fernanda, finishing a close second.

"Not bad for a white girl," Fernanda said, laughing and wiping the froth off her lips with the back of her hand.

Janie was also not bad at handball, playing for hours until her hand swelled painfully. One Saturday night, Fernanda noticed her rubbing the puffed-up tender palm and said, "I have the cure for that. Do you have any money?"

The two girls walked to the liquor store on 108th Street and Fernanda pulled a bottle of Bacardi 181 off the shelf. At the register, one of the older boys from Janie's block sat on a stool, his eyes bleary and his head nodding a bit.

"Hi, Joey," Janie greeted him.

"Little Janie! You're growing up fast! Who's your friend?" Joey said with a slight slur, eyeing the petite Puerto Rican girl with her.

"This is Fernanda. How much for the rum?"

"For your cute friend, two bucks."

Without another word, Joey took the money from the young teens and shoved it into his pocket.

The girls walked to the backyard behind Janie's apartment and sat on the wooden edge of the sandbox. They took turns swigging on the bottle until it was empty. In the moonlight, the swing frame, now devoid of swings, showed signs of rust and decay; and, slurring, Janie told Fernanda about Ring-a-Levio and her birthday party and snow that almost buried the swings that used to hang there. Fernanda was too inebriated to respond; and after she stumbled, weaving, back towards the projects, Janie decided she wanted ice cream.

She made her way back to 108th Street, laughing out loud when her legs went left instead of straight or crossed over themselves and nearly made her lurch into the street. At one point she reeled into one of the large trees lining the sidewalk. Giving it a tight hug, she looked up and said, "Thank you, tree," before pushing off and moving on towards the avenue.

It was a warm night and there was a line inside the Carvel ice cream shop. The bright fluorescent lights made Janie squint, scowling; and the slow ordering of the people in front of her made her fidgety. After just a minute at the back of the line, Janie staggered ahead of the others to the counter, elbowing aside a mother with her little boy who had just stepped up. She ignored their complaints and tried to order but mangled the words and laughed at herself.

After several attempts, she got it out: "Black cherry vanilla with hot fudge in a cup."

The young man behind the counter gave the mother a helpless shrug and made Janie's order. Shoving her hand into her jeans pocket, she pulled out a fistful of change and dropped it on the glass counter over the tubs of ice cream. Several pennies rolled onto the floor, as she tried to count out the correct amount. When the young man placed her order in front of her, she took both hands and shoved all the coins toward him, grabbed the cup of ice cream and lurched outside.

As she made her way back home, she shoveled the gooey sweet coldness into her mouth with the pink plastic spoon. By the time she reached the apartment, she was licking the inside of the cup, which she then tossed into the curb. Once in her room, she lay down in her narrow bed.

Now wanting to sleep, she did not welcome the sudden swinging of the ceiling above her. When the walls began to sway, Janie knew she was in trouble. Trying hard to ignore the movement, she kept her eyes closed, clutching the sheets as the bed lurched underneath her. She spun over and rolled out of the bed, and almost fell trying to get her window open. Leaning out as far as possible, she vomited rum and fudge and black cherries and vanilla out of her mouth and nose until she felt weak, but somehow better. At least the room stopped spinning. With the nasty taste still in her nostrils, she fell onto her bed and slept until almost one o'clock Sunday afternoon.

An hour and a cup of coffee later, she dragged herself out of the apartment to get some fresh air. Opening the front door, she was met with the sight of three police cars blocking the street, blues and reds spinning silently. A couple of unmarked cars were double-parked just beyond them. For a heart-stopping moment, she thought they might be looking for a young drunk girl who had ripped off the Carvel's; then she saw them going up the stairs of the garden apartment right next door.

They did not seem to be in much of a hurry as they sipped coffee out of blue and white paper cups from the deli. Janie walked over to the downstairs neighbor, a middle-aged lady who was always friendly.

"What happened?" Janie asked her.

"That Joey boy upstairs," she answered in a heavy Indian accent. "He is dead. He went to buy some huh…heh…hehr…some of that bad drug on the overpass to the park and they stabbed him with a big knife POW."

She made a stabbing motion over and over again, until Janie turned away, feeling the last dredges of ice cream and rum tangling in her stomach and threatening to make an appearance. She took a short walk to settle herself out and spent the rest of the day in bed. Before she fell asleep, she wondered if Joey had used her two dollars to buy his drugs that night.

She awoke to the sound of yelling that pierced the thin walls of her room.

"You're becoming a lazy bum! What kind of man acts like you do?!" Her father's fury directed at her brother made her pull the blanket over her head.

Greg had picked up a guitar at the Salvation Army Thrift Store, and spent much of his time in his bedroom, strumming along to the rock music on his bedside clock radio. With his shoulder-length hair, peach fuzz mustache, bellbottom jeans and skin-tight tee shirts, he became a constant source of irritation for their father.

In exasperation, Mr. Thompson raged about his clothes, his music, and his attitude. He told Greg to throw out the guitar and get a job or he would wind up like the loser drug addict, Joey, from next door. He threatened to turn Greg in to the police for disobedience and truancy.

Greg ignored him or gave him a peace sign and said, "Relax, dad; I'm gonna be a rock star one day. Have a little faith, man."

Their father would become infuriated and shout louder. During the worst of the arguments, he would throw things like a two-year-old having a temper tantrum; and it did not help the situation when Greg laughed at him. Janie would peek out from behind a door until it was over, usually when their father stomped away. Greg would go back into his room, take "Belinda," as he lovingly called his guitar, and work on a new riff.

Janie loved to watch her brother strum and listen to the words he sang. She sat on the floor at his feet, while he looked down at his fingers on the strings, plucking out songs he heard on the radio. She waited for the satisfied look on his face when he finally got a run he had been practicing; and he would look down at her eager adoring eyes with a smile. She hoped he would be a rock star someday, and that she would be at his side, his number-one groupie.

In December, Greg came to Janie's room with rare excitement. She sat on her bed absorbed in Beverly Cleary's newest book for teen girls, <u>Jean and Johnny</u>, but put it down when she saw his face. In his hand he held two small rectangles of paper, which he waved around in front of her nose.

"Merry early Christmas, little sister! I am taking you to your first rock concert! Hall and Oates are playing at Queens College, and we are going to be in row twenty-two, dead center! I might even spring for a concert tee shirt for each of us if I'm flush!"

He swept Janie right off her bed in a bear hug, winging her around in circles. She laughed in joy, not knowing who Haul in Notes was; but catching his excitement as her own.

The night of the concert, they took the city bus over to the college and walked into the packed lobby of the venue. Janie stopped in awe at the energetic buzz of the other teens, who were lined up to buy merchandise or milling around in anticipation; but her brother tugged on her arm and dove them right into the middle of it.

Greg bought them each a concert shirt, which they pulled on, and they made their way to the seats. As soon as the house lights went down, a funky odor wafted through the space, making Janie wrinkle her nose.

"It's pot, Janie. Lots of kids smoke it to get a buzz. I don't do it; I get high on my music. You don't need it either. You have me," Greg said, with a hug.

The houselights went down, and spotlights wove around the stage where a full set of band instruments seemed to be waiting in anticipation. The audience began to call and then cheer and then scream; and finally, the musicians ran out onto the stage, grabbed their instruments, and began to play. Janie could barely hear them, until the shrieking of the crowd faded back a bit. The music went on for hours, and the audience sang along to every song. Janie found, to her delight, that she knew one or two from listening to Greg's practice sessions. They never sat down the whole time, bopping and dancing with the sold-out crowd. When the stage went dark near midnight and the band walked off, waving to the crowd, Janie got ready to move out of their row.

"Not yet, little sister. We didn't get our money's worth yet. Start screaming!"

All around them, Bic lighters went up, small flames swaying by the thousands, accompanied by shouts and screams of "More! More!" Carried along by the exhilarating energy, she joined in.

They were rewarded for their efforts. After several suspenseful minutes, the band came running back onto the stage, accompanied by a wild light show and three of their most famous songs, to end the night with a grand finale. Janie could not wipe the smile off her face for the whole bus ride home.

Far from being tired despite the late hour, Greg grabbed his guitar and began to pluck out one of the songs they had just heard, "Sara Smile."

Janie, sitting on the bed next to him, was delighted at how quickly he picked up the song, and felt like he was singing directly to her heart.

"*God damn it,* I'm going to throw that guitar out the window. It's two o'clock in the morning, go to bed! NOW!!" came a raspy threat from their parents' bedroom.

After a tight hug tinged with silent laughter, brother and sister slept until early afternoon.

A few days later, on a rare temperate evening in December, Janie sat on the blacktop at the handball courts. Since her rum and ice cream event, she had stopped binge-drinking; but she still loved the nights with her group of friends.

"Yo, Janie, get the fuck up here and play."

"What asshole dumped out my Mad Dog 20/20? I'mma kick his fucking ass."

"My moms is such a bitch, said she's gonna ground me if I get home at sunrise again. Fuck her, she don't get home 'til sunrise neither."

Every time they cursed, she felt an impish tingle; and occasionally tried it on for size. After a while, she became more comfortable with dropping random f-bombs, but it did not seem to come organically, until one night in Spring.

Sitting on Deidre's stoop on an April evening, chatting about nothing in particular, the girls were startled by the sound of running and sobbing coming down the block towards them. It was one of their friend's younger sisters, and when she saw them, she stopped.

Trying to catch her breath, all she could manage was, "You have to come with me! Hurry!!"

Deidre shrugged and said, "I'm not going. If it's such a big emergency, call 9-1-1."

"Please! Hurry!" the sobbing girl pleaded, giving her attention to Janie, and pulling on her arm.

Janie sighed and stood up. She followed the young girl, trying to keep up as she raced down the street towards Flushing Meadows Park. As they headed up the stairs of the overpass, Janie saw the plywood sheet, dark brown and crumbling on the corners, where she and Greg used to climb into the "treehouse" and play pirates. It showed signs of being well-used by other neighborhood kids. Brown paper bags holding cans or quarts of beer lay around the tree base like a dead garden. A few white paper Carvel cups, residual slime holding pink spoons fast, kept them company.

They headed up the concrete steps to the highway overpass. The yelling and laughing of a small group of kids, and the sudden high-pitched shriek of the girl tugging on her arm, slapped Janie to attention.

"What are you doing?! Stop, come back here!" the young girl yelled.

She let go of Janie and raced towards a boy who had one leg around the top of the low fence and was trying to climb over. She grabbed a fistful of his shirt and held on, her thin arms tight with the effort.

The other kids were holding their stomachs and doubled over in laughter. Around them, more brown paper bags were scattered on the ground with an empty nickel bag and a wrinkled package of Zig Zag rolling paper. Janie recognized the kids from the neighborhood. How old could they be? Ten, maybe eleven?

Another shriek made her sprint towards the boy, who now had his other leg over the rail and was hanging off with his feet kicking. Underneath him, the rush-hour drivers on the Grand Central Parkway seemed oblivious to what was happening fifteen feet above them.

"What the fuck?" Janie yelled, as she reached the girl, who was now standing back and sobbing.

"He's drunk," she sputtered out. "We were in the treehouse after school, and he got really drunk and said he was ready to show the world his true superhero powers and he jumped down out of the tree and ran up here."

The boy began to yell in inebriated ecstasy. "I can do anything! I am super-strong! I am super-invincible!"

"You are super-stupid!" Janie snarled at him, as she leaned over the rail, becoming dizzy from the roaring of the traffic that moved just below them. She grabbed his skinny wrists in an iron grip.

"Release me! Unhand me, you mere mortal! I can fly!" and the boy let go of the rail with one of his hands.

"Shit," Janie breathed, as she braced her feet against the concrete lip of the walkway. The racket around her became a buzzing sound in her head; the moving cars became a shifting pattern of light and color. All her energy focused on her hands, her arms, her shoulders, as she gave a strong tug on those bony wrists.

The boy let go with the other hand. The sudden added weight pulled her to the rail up to her arm pits. He would not stop kicking his feet and Janie knew she might only have one shot. Her face contorted and she let out a growl that became a scream. She hauled as hard as she could, and that scrawny boy came flying over the rail. She fell flat out onto the concrete walkway, and he landed on top of her.

"Get off me, you fucking suicidal idiot!"

Now the sounds came back, especially the laughter of the other drunk kids. Furious, Janie pushed him off and stood, brushing the nasty layer of soot and trash off her Chino pants and jean jacket.

"What a bunch of stupid shits. You!" Janie said, pointing at the girl that had found her on the stoop, who seemed like the most sober of the group. "Show me where he lives."

Janie cuffed the boy a good one on the back of the head and said, "Stand up, asshole."

He needed help, and Janie and the girl each took an arm and hauled him up, stumbling. They made their way back to his apartment, right around the corner. The door was unlocked, and the place was dark and empty. She flicked on a light and cockroaches scattered. The boy was rambling on and muttering nonsense as Janie dragged him into the bathroom and unceremoniously dumped him into the tub.

"Go make him a black cup of coffee, really strong," Janie barked.

Then she turned on the cold water in the shower. As soon as the icy stream hit the boy, he jerked and let out a scream and tried to scrabble out of the way. Janie easily pushed him back down.

"Stay," she commanded, as if he were a dog; and he complied, whimpering and shivering. The girl came back with a large, steaming mug. "Watch him. Don't let him out."

Janie went into the living room and found the stereo receiver behind a sliding door of the T.V. console cabinet. She switched on WPLJ, and rock music came blasting out of the four-foot-high speakers. She turned it up until the bass thumped through the walls.

"Sing," Janie said to the boy, pushing his nodding head roughly a few times. He joined the Rolling Stones' praise of Honky Tonk Women, but three bars behind. It was a pitiful performance. The boy's goofy smile and jerking prone pelvis showed that he thought he was giving Mick Jagger a run for his money. If she were not fuming and shaken, Janie might have laughed.

"Make him stay here until he finishes that coffee, and he can sing on time with the radio. What a bunch of morons."

She shook her head and walked back to Deidre's stoop to tell her what happened.

"I guess it's a good thing you went, or we would have been hearing about that idiot on the nightly news," Deidre said.

"Fuckin' A," Janie exhaled in agreement.

Towards the end of that summer, after a game of handball which Janie lost by two points, several kids sat around the court talking about what to do next.

The boy who had just beaten Janie, full of his win and cocky, said, "I'm gonna jack a car and take it for a ride. My brother showed me how to do it. Who's in?"

All three of the others stood with him. They turned to look at Janie, who still sat on the blacktop, leaning against the chain-link fence, massaging her hand. She felt them waiting, felt the challenge, felt their brimming anticipation; and was torn. These kids accepted her, liked her, and now wanted her to join them in doing something that crossed a line for her.

With high school beginning soon, Janie had felt pulled in different directions for quite a while. Between her parents, Greg, school, friends, and raging hormones, she sometimes did not know which way was up and who she was. That night, she discovered who she was not.

"Yeah, you know, I think I'm going to head in for the night. Gotta put some ice on this puppy," she said, holding up her swollen hand.

She stood and walked away as the group whooped and hollered and headed towards one of the side streets where the cars were parked in a long line against the curb.

It was the last time she hung out with them; a good thing since just two years later she heard that this same group committed gang rape of a local teen with Downs Syndrome and pulled the first robbery murder of a cabbie in New York City; and were all sent to Riker's Island prison.

Once high school began, Janie got busy with yet a new group of friends. Some of them lived in the private property houses across the street, and all were involved in academic clubs and advanced courses. Janie did not see Deidre often at Forest Hills High School, with its four thousand students; but they had both moved on from the childhood they shared and still waved at each other from afar.

It was even more fun to see Greg in the hallways again. He made it a point to leave funny notes on ripped pieces of paper jammed into the vents of her locker or drop in at her table in the cafeteria for a quick hug. When she found him leaning against the brick wall outside during her free period, strumming his guitar with a couple of the other boys in his grade, she would ask, with worried eyes, "Shouldn't you be in class right now, Greg?"

He would just smile at her and say, "It's all good, little sis," and keep jamming with his friends.

When Greg's grades in school dropped, the fights with their father became vicious. Greg had always been at the top of his class with little effort. His complaints over the years about his boredom at school had been disregarded by both of their parents; and his attempts to join the school music program had been flat-out rejected.

"A real man does a real job, Greg. Music is just a distraction," their mother told him.

Their father was less patient, harassing Greg daily at dinner time until Greg stopped asking to be excused and just walked away to his bedroom. Janie sat watching their father's face turn nearly purple, hoping he did not turn his rage on her.

When their mother tried to get involved in the arguments, their father told her to shut up and stay out of men's business. She sat on the sidelines yelling at Greg about being a responsible man of the family. Their father asked if he wanted to wind up like that Joey loser from next door who had been knifed to death buying drugs.

Greg responded in a calm voice, "I don't do drugs, dad. It's just music for Christ's sake. What is your problem?"

The fights became physical in his senior year of high school, with thin, lanky Greg taking the brunt of punches from their bigger, stronger father. Janie got between them only once and was rewarded with a blow on the cheek meant for her brother.

"Get out of here, Janie," Greg said as the clenched fist sailed towards him again. Holding her hand on her reddened face she left the apartment and took off running. She had no idea where to run to, but her feet took her to Deidre's, whose horrified reaction, baggy of ice and hug while Janie sobbed reminded them both of their early friendship.

As Janie calmed down, Deidre spoke. "What are you going to do, Janie? Do you want to stay here? You can, you know."

"I don't know what to do. It's getting worse at home every day with Dad and Greg. Thank you for offering, Dee; and thanks for being here for me, it means a lot."

They sat without talking, each of them lost in thought. After a while, Janie gave Deidre another hug and said, "I guess I'll go home. The fights don't usually last that long."

She took the long way around the block to catch her breath before opening the door to a thick silence left behind in the empty apartment.

After each of these fights, their father would either storm out the door, or plant himself on the sofa and turn the volume on the television set up so loud, it competed with the constant roar of airplanes landing at the nearby airports. The walls and wood floors throbbed with the rumbling bass as if they, too, were furious, making it impossible to hear anything else, or to think.

After a particularly brutal row, Greg went out back with Janie and sat on the edge of the crumbling sand box where they used to play Ring-a-Levio.

"Our parents are selfish assholes. They just don't give a shit about us as long as we toe the line and stay out of their way. Janie, we are on our own in this world, we really are."

Janie, who for the most part did toe the line and stay out of their way, listened to his words as if they were a new song he was learning.

"They just don't see me at all, man." Greg's voice cracked in a rare display of open rage, and he wiped at his eyes with the palms of his hands.

She put her arms around his waist and leaned her head on his shoulder.

"I don't know about you, but I am about done taking this shit. From them, from school, from the fucking world."

She gave him a squeeze, not having words to comfort him. He turned to look into her worried face.

"Janie, you are the only light in this life for me. You always have been, and I will always love you for that, no matter what happens."

He put his arm around her shoulder, and they sat in silence together for a long while.

She came home after chess club on an afternoon in June and found Greg in his room, where he was placing folded clothes in his olive-green army backpack. His tall, awkward body moved from dresser to bed with thoughtful deliberation; his cheek was dark red from the punch his father had landed once again.

Behind him, tacked onto the wall, was his Bob Dylan calendar. She noticed today was Friday the 13th and got a sudden bad feeling.

"What are you doing, Greg? Where are you going? What happened now?"

"I've had it, Janie. I don't belong here; Dad has made that perfectly clear."

"You can't just go. Take me with you, don't leave me here,"

she begged. "It's only two weeks until you graduate, just hold on for a little while longer. Things could get better. I will talk to him."

"It doesn't matter. It could be any day, any month, any year. Talking to him will not work, I've tried. He is not going to change, so I guess I have to."

He sat on the bed and patted the spot next to him. She sat; and he took her hands and looked into her shiny brown eyes. She was alarmed at how tired his looked and realized he had not been sleeping.

"Janie, our paths are different, yours and mine. I don't even know where mine is taking me right now and it would be irresponsible..." He paused, his smile tinged with irony at the word his mother often threw at him like a weapon. "...to take anyone with me. They pretty much leave you alone, and I know that's tough on you, but you're tougher than you think. You have to understand, it's dangerous for me to stay. Maybe things will be better for you if I leave. I really hope so."

A tear drew a line down Janie's face and Greg had to look away. He stood, put his arms through the straps of his backpack, and picked up his guitar case. He turned and looked into his sister's distraught face; and saw the shadow of that little girl whose adoration had kept him sane all these years. It almost broke him. Almost.

His shoulders straightened as he steeled himself to finish what he had started.

"Janie, I need to leave here to find my way, I see that now. If I don't, my soul will shrivel to nothing, and I will be dead inside. I would be no use to you, little sister; or to myself. I'm terrified; but I'm more terrified of what will happen if I stay. I will let you know as soon as I can where I wind up, Janie."

To punctuate this statement, he pulled his house keys out of his pocket and placed them on the nightstand. Greg's face was reconciled to his decision and resolved to follow it through.

Janie walked behind him as he went past the vacant living room, where the overturned side table and smashed vase on the floor told the story of what had happened.

That was when he opened the door and turned to her and said those words: *"Janie, never forget, I loved you when you were brand new, and I will always love you."*

With a last long hug, he walked out the door and was gone.

"Good riddance to bad rubbish," her mother said, when she came out of her bedroom to find Janie still staring at the closed door. "At least now I can tell the neighbors that there is something wrong with Greg, a screw loose in that weird head of his. I really don't think anyone will be that surprised. He never fit in with the other kids anyway. Janie, go get ready. Remember? It's Friday. We are in charge of the block party dessert for tonight. I think we will pick up some of those cookies at the Jewish bakery, and maybe some eclairs from the Italian on the corner. I..."

"Are you kidding me?" Janie finally found her voice. She stared at her mother, incredulous. "Greg just left for good, and you are worried about *cookies*?"

Her mother scoffed at her. "Oh, goodness, we should be so lucky. He'll be back. Where is he going to go? He has nothing, he never could hold onto a job because he was too 'sensitive' to deal with the expectations; who is going to take him in but us? He ran away from home like a four-year-old. I should have made him a peanut butter sandwich for his backpack before he left. Now, again, go get ready. I want to get my hair done and you know how crowded the beauty parlor gets on Friday. All those Jewish women have to get their color-and-cuts done before their Sabbath starts."

Janie and her mother stared at each other. Mrs. Thompson's gaze was steady, expectant, and unwavering. Janie's eyes smoldered with loathing and incredulity.

But she lost. Her shoulders dropped, and she turned with a

defeated look to go get her shoes and sweater. She just hoped her mother was right and he would be back soon. Even beaten down and resigned, at least he would be here with her to buffer the pressure, as he always had been.

But her mother was wrong.

Days went by, and there was no word from Greg. Janie, in a quiet moment alone with her father while he drank his morning Chock-Full-of-Nuts coffee and read the Daily News, had asked him in frustration, "Aren't you worried about him at all? He has never run off before; and he had plenty of opportunity. And reasons."

Her father, ignoring her pointed jibe, said, "He is probably sleeping on someone's couch half a mile from here. Let him sulk for a few more days. Smart ass."

Janie was not sure if he was talking about Greg or her, because he did not say another word.

A week went by. Then two, then three. Life was weirdly routine, as if Greg had not walked away from this family, as if he had never existed. Her parents went about their summer days working or watching Mets games on the television, cleaning or cooking or shopping, and attending neighborhood barbecues. Classes began again, and Janie attended her chess and word-scholar clubs and worked on the latest feel-good volunteer project with her school groups.

But she did not feel good.

Janie kept herself busy and away from home as much as possible, as the school year raced by. She stopped in Greg's empty room every day to talk to him, imagining that he was sitting on the bed next to her. If she turned on his clock radio to his favorite station and closed her eyes, she could almost feel him there. She kept her eyes shut as long as she could, because opening them meant re-opening the wound in her heart.

As if time had folded, the school year went by. Greg's calendar hung open on last June. Janie stood in front of it, absorbing the red circle she had drawn around the 13ᵗʰ, emotions brimming.

With the summer looming, Janie felt a void that she did not know how to fill. She began to walk dogs or babysit for the neighbors. She walked a mile to the Lefrak City neighborhood pool and obtained her junior lifesaving card, thinking she could work her way up to lifeguard in a year. She occasionally took the subway into the city with friends and walked around Central Park; but was overawed by the visual, auditory, and emotional noise and did not make the trip very often. It was a relief when school started up again, keeping her absorbed and distracted.

Early in October, Janie was invited to the Bar Mitzvah of one of her friend's younger brothers. Mrs. Thompson seemed strangely excited about it.

"This is good, Janie. Rubbing elbows with people like that can open doors for you. If you marry one of those Jewish boys, your life will be a lot easier. They usually become lawyers or doctors or dentists and make a lot of money. Of course, their mothers will call you "goy" and "shiksa" and treat you like a maid; but it will be worth it not to have to worry about paying bills. And if your first baby is a boy, their mothers will get over it. I will bake my best chocolate chip cookies for you to take to the party."

Despite Janie's protests, Mrs. Thompson baked three dozen cookies, plated them on a decorative platter, and covered them with Saran Wrap on which she placed a large blue and white bow. Mortified, Janie seriously considered tossing the whole platter in the trash can on her way to the temple but felt guilty about it, and had to sit next to it through the service. When she arrived at the family's house after the ceremony, Janie handed the celebrant's mother the tray and shyly said, "My mother made these for the party."

The woman took the tray with her fingertips as if it had

bugs on it, and with a forced smile said, "Thank your mother for me. The teenagers are down in the basement."

Janie watched her carry the platter into the kitchen and leave it on the counter in a corner, far away from the catered repast.

Janie walked down the stairs and found it full of kids she did not know. The Bar Mitzvah boy's older sister, who was in her Chem class, was nowhere to be seen. She wandered the room for a bit, looking at the albums queued up by the record player, watching a vicious ping pong game in progress, and finally sitting in an open spot on the plush couch. She felt alone in a crowded room and thought she might just go home.

Someone passed a lit joint to Janie, and she took it without thinking. She had always felt sorry for the kids who did drugs. She did not judge them and was not above drinking a beer now and then. But she always thought "those grass-smoking freaks," as her social circles called them, were sad and lost, and looking for something. She remembered Greg saying, at the Hall and Oates concert, that she did not need to smoke pot, because she had him. But now, she did not have him.

Now she held the joint in her hand and watched the smoke curl lazily from the burning end. The odor, pungent and skunky, suddenly appealed to her.

The boy next to her leaned over and said, "You better hit that before it goes out. I don't have a book of matches."

She put it to her lips and took a long, deep drag, holding it the way she had seen the others do. It exploded inside her and she coughed violently, bent over and trying not to puke.

The same boy said, "Rookie mistake. Don't take such a big hit. It's potent stuff, Sensemilla. You don't need to get it all in with one drag."

He took the joint, smoothly and expertly inhaled, held it in for a beat, and slowly let it out. He handed it back to her and she did the same. This time she shuddered a bit to keep from coughing and was successful.

"Thanks," she said, laughing at herself, a bit embarrassed.

They passed the "doobie," as he called it, back and forth. When it got too short to hold, he pulled an alligator clip, a *roach clip* he told her in an almost teacherly tone, out of his pocket and attached it.

As she took a hit and handed the clip back to him, she noticed her hand: so white, so smooth, with perfectly neat fingernails and cuticles. She brought it close to her face and flexed it, watching the skin ripple and stretch. She turned it slowly, looking at the lines on her knuckles from both sides, scrutinizing how they changed as she bent her fingers. She observed, as if for the very first time, delicate blue-purple veins on the inside of her wrist running up and down her arm. It was like a blood superhighway, and the blood cells traveled back and forth in rush hour traffic like miniscule delivery trucks with her heart being downtown and the roads going on forever, and that meant she was a city! Welcome to Janietown!

This made her laugh out loud. She pondered why she had never noticed her hand before; why she had never really *looked* at it. With wonder, she wiggled her fingers and saw the lines on her palms dance with the movement; and then thought about which line on her palm was the lifeline and which one was the love line and why there were lines at all and why her thumb only had one knuckle instead of two like the rest of the fingers, and what a thumb would look like with two knuckles.

She heard, as if from far away, the boy next to her chuckle as he watched her. Still turning her hand over in wonder that she had never noticed how very *cool* a hand was, she heard him say, "Pot gives you cotton mouth. I'm going to get a drink. Want one?"

She nodded absently. By the time he got back with the two cups, she was staring at the table. With its vein-like wood grain it was so much like her wrist! Then she looked up.

The music boomed from an invisible source, like it was part of the very air. It synchronized weirdly with the shifting mass of kids in the room. The colors of their clothes seemed to move on their own in the dim light.

She took the offered cup and sipped it: sweet, sparkling, fizzy, with a dark undercurrent of chemically medicinal taste. She took another sip and stared at the cup. It fit her hand perfectly, fingers wrapped around and almost touching. It was so comfortable, she smiled at it.

Now the boy was laughing madly at her, but she thought it was funny too, and began to join him.

"Vodka and Mountain Dew. It's called Rocket Fuel. Drink a few of those and you will be up all night."

"It's so good," she said, marveling at the lime green bubbling liquid surrounding the oddly shaped pieces of ice floating in her cup.

"It's all so good," she repeated, looking around again.

He smiled and nodded in agreement. "I'm Jerry, by the way. I've seen you around school, you're Janie."

"Jerry. Janie. J-j-j," and they both laughed for a long while.

She did drink a few more, and she did stay up all night. And, she thought, as the sun came up, that it was the best night she had ever had.

That evening with Jerry was the fork in her rail tracks, when her life split in two and continued on both ways at the same time, at least for a while. Through Jerry, she met a new crowd of kids that she had not even noticed before; but now she related to them better than to her other friends. They were mostly members of the local temple with families in good standing, high-performing students who, from outside appearance, dressed and acted like everyone else.

At home and even at school, she continued to be obedient, straight edged, on the trajectory that she was expected, by her teachers and parents, to follow. She went to class and after-school activities, excelled in tennis to the point where her coach thought she might have a shot at the Forest Hills Region Team, and aced New York's challenging annual High School Regents Exams.

Underneath the façade of Janie Thompson, smart and on-her-way high schooler, lurked a different girl: one who whispered her brother's name many times a day; who walked inside a gray cloud; who numbed that other Janie into submission with alcohol or grass or whatever the kids were passing around at the nightly gatherings that took place under the radar.

Like her, they had developed two lives to hide their truths from the outside world. But here, at night, together, getting as high as they could and still function the next day, they bonded over their feelings of being disenfranchised from the values of their families and community. The marginalization of these kids would have astounded their parents, their teachers and coaches, the Rabbi, the youth group leaders. The kids knew it, and kept it hidden until night fell.

Sitting in a basement of one of their large brick houses that lined the streets between the rent-controlled apartment buildings and the high school, called "Private Property" by the apartment kids who were rarely invited to such gatherings, they met under the guise of being a study group.

"I found these in my mom's drawer," one of the girls said one night, handing out white oval pills stamped with a number: 714. "Quaaludes. She says they help her sleep, so let's take them right before we go home."

Janie palmed hers with her left hand while sipping straight vodka from the cup in her right. She only put the drink down to take the wrinkled joints that were being passed around. Just after ten o'clock they all popped the pill into their mouths, clinked their cups in cheers and swallowed. Then they walked into their homes and crawled into bed without being noticed.

The waves of deep relaxation floated Janie into oblivion until morning.

Another night, one of the boys threw a plastic baggy containing something that looked like dried shit onto the table.

"Mushrooms," he said. "They take a while to kick in and the high lasts hours, so I think we should save them until Saturday night. We should be fine for Sunday Hebrew school, since it doesn't start until ten."

Nearly every night, a different drug made an appearance.

"Valium, from my aunt's medicine cabinet, ten milligrams; the good stuff."

"Bennies, these are uppers so let's take them in the morning. My dad uses them to stay up for when the Japanese stock markets open."

"PCP, you lace a joint with it. My boss at the hardware store gave it to me for after work." The kids all agreed they did not enjoy the brain-fog from this one.

Janie tried to get her mother's Librium, but Mrs. Thompson kept it in her apron pocket, close at all times. Janie had done some research to find out what pill her mother was popping like candy. She had discovered that it was prescribed to calm anxiety but was also given to recovering alcoholics. Her adolescent opinion of her cold, unfeeling, uncaring mother became even harsher and more cynical: her mother was a hypocritical drug addict. If Janie were more like Greg, she might have called her mother out on it; but she was not. And she could not.

Sometimes, the pills the other kids brought were wrapped in tin foil scrunched up in a pocket; other times they came in a sandwich baggy folded over so the pills would not escape. Without knowing what half of them were, the kids ingested them anyway.

In the summer between Junior and Senior year, one of the girls took a small, folded piece of tin foil out of her backpack.

Inside was a light-orange circle about the size of a dime stamped into a paper with an odd texture.

"Blotter acid," she explained. "My brother says it's eight-way, which means each circle is enough to get eight people really high."

They cut it up and put the LSD-infused bit of paper under their tongues. It took so long to kick in, Janie forgot she had taken it until she reached for her cup of vodka and saw that it was glowing.

As she watched in awe, a rainbow of brilliant sparkles shot out of the cup, making her jump. It streamed up and flowed until the entire ceiling was covered with a coursing, cascading blanket of tiny stars in colors she had never imagined existed. Some of the stars grew bigger and began to float around her in the dark room. One became as large as a baseball and sat directly in front of her face with a warm light that seemed friendly, benevolent, loving. It glowed and dimmed with a rhythm that matched her heartbeat, which she could clearly hear.

She knew in her bones and blood that it was Greg, come to tell her that she would be all right. Once she realized that, the light grew larger and dimmer until it faded away and left her feeling peaceful.

The river of brilliant colors began to beat in time to the Pink Floyd song coming out of the stereo speakers.

As the music flowed into a spacey instrumental section, Janie felt herself become ephemeral, incorporeal, part of the sound that floated around the room. She drifted above the others, momentarily watching them, mouths open in awe on their own trips.

When, seven hours later, the effects began to wear off, they looked at each other in emotionally and physically drained wonder.

"WOW!" Janie breathed, and they all agreed.

The group tried every drug they could get their hands on, but had an unwritten code, a line they would not cross. Big H, horse, junk, smack, as it was called on the streets; the kids all knew someone who had gotten addicted, or had overdosed or, like Joey, had been killed trying to score Heroin. They believed that as long as they did not cross that line, they were in control; and they had no desire to lose control in that way.

During the day, by mutual agreement, this little group did not acknowledge each other in the hallways or in class. Theirs was a secret society; and they liked it that way. They kept their "study group" exclusive and clandestine through the last two years of high school, dubbing themselves "Eraserhead Society," after the campy, gleefully gory, black and white horror movie that was an underground hit of the time.

To stay away from home, and to begin planning her own escape, Janie took a job at the Mini Mart on 108th Street. She worked evenings at the register, often with another girl named Tina who lived down the street just past the fire station in Corona. She had never met anyone like Tina, who entertained her every night in her tough New York accent, with stories about her group of friends and their crazy adventures in the Italian neighborhood where they lived.

One shift, Tina came in with a black eye and a big smile. She did not wait for Janie to ask her what happened.

"Man, last night was fuckin' crazy! Me and my fuckin' girls were hanging out at Spaghetti Park shooting the shit and looking for trouble. A bunch of dirty fuckin' *fricchettones*, all long-hair and beards and shit, came up to us and asked where they could score some pot. 'Grass' they called it; what a bunch of *jamokes*. Then one of them started hitting on Theresa. That was mistake number two. Angie and her sister Anna got in his face. Then all hell broke loose, and we kicked their *stunad* asses right back to Rego Park. Toni Marie was swinging her baseball bat, and I got hit in the eye, that's how I got this fuckin' shiner."

Other nights, Tina told stories about Toni Marie using her bat on Theresa's boyfriend's windshield after hearing rumors of him cheating; or chasing a bunch of *boombots* from Jackson Heights who were harassing the kid working at the Lemon Ice King.

At Janie's puzzled look, Tina exclaimed, "Boombots? *Disgratziats? Girdrul? Maron,*' you don't know nothing about nothing!"

Tina was as awed by Janie as Janie was by her. They lived a mile and a world apart. On the nights they went out to the Justice bar or the Hilbar after closing up the Mini Mart, Janie could not get enough of these tough girls and their stories, and secretly wished she could be more like them.

Janie worked most nights until closing, stopped to party with her friends, and then walked to the darkened apartment, slipping into her room. She avoided any conversation with her parents. They seemed content to avoid her just as much; she assumed they were just glad she was not Greg.

She was haunted on her walks home from work by the headlines in the Daily News: *Forty-four Caliber Killer to Cops: I'll Do It Again.* In the New York Post, known to be a sensational yellow rag of a newspaper, the headlines screamed, *"No One is Safe from 'Son of Sam."*

One of the articles had a frightening paragraph that caused Janie to consider staying home until further notice: *"Detectives said the ballistics tests indicated that the .44-caliber bullet used to shoot the couple had come from the same old-fashioned Western-style gun that killed three young women and wounded four others in Queens and in the Bronx. Two blocks away from Sunday's murders, Donna Laurie, 18, was ambushed on July 29 while sitting in a parked car in front of her home. Virginia Voskerichian, 19, was slain by the same weapon in March while walking near her home in Forest Hills, Queens. And in January, just a block away, Christine Freund, 26, of*

Four victims with long brown hair like Janie's from her own neighborhood splashed across the evening news; and yet her parents went on with their routine as if oblivious to the dangers their daughter feared. They watched the news as if it was happening on the moon, and not in their own backyard. They did not seem to put together that the victims resembled their own daughter, and when, on one occasion, Janie blurted out, "That guy is killing girls that look like me! I feel like hiding in my room!" her mother responded without even looking up from the television screen, "Don't be dramatic, Janie; you'll be fine."

It was only when the killer was caught that Janie felt she could breathe again.

Janie, through her school, participated in the Midnight Run, preparing hundreds of bag lunches, and traveling in vans to homeless shelters in the city. As they carried the trays of brown paper bags filled with apples, ham sandwiches and chips, Janie furtively stared at every young man to see if Greg might be among them.

"What are you looking at?!"

The angry timber of the voice at her elbow made her jump. "Are you a narc? No drugs here, can't you read the sign?!"

The disheveled woman who was yelling at her pointed towards a piece of paper taped to the wall that said, "Please throw your trash in the bins."

Janie was about to offer a flustered apology when a large man came from behind the serving table and stood between Janie and the irate woman and ushered her away.

On summer nights, the Eraserhead Society took the party outside to Flushing Meadow Park, which would have given her mother apoplexy had she known her daughter was hanging out there. It was the only place that Janie's mother absolutely forbade, mainly because she herself would never venture there, especially after sundown. Her mother's fears were justified; the park, with the vestiges of the World's Fair fifteen years deteriorated, was dark, and not policed, and was often the site of rapes, murders, robberies, and muggings. It was on one of the walking bridges to this park that the neighbor boy, Joey, had been killed.

The kids went anyway.

They were sitting on a bench under a dim yellow light near the boat lake passing a joint, when Jerry pulled Janie aside to go for a walk.

"Hey, Janie, I just want to know if maybe, I don't know, like if you would want to...like go with me, you know, go out with me, maybe, sometime?"

Janie was a bit surprised; she had never thought of Jerry as anything but one of the gang. Then, again, she had never really felt that way about any boy in school, and decided; why not Jerry?

"Sure, Jerry. That sounds like fun," she answered him. In the dark, she could not see him release the breath he had been holding.

"Hey, kids." The deep whisper came out of the night, somewhere just ahead of them.

Janie and Jerry looked at each other, whispered, "*shit*" at the same time and went running back to the group, laughing all the way.

That week, Jerry called Janie and told her he had gotten tickets to the Mets game for Wednesday. She found herself looking forward to it; her father was a huge Mets fan, listening to every game on the transistor radio. But he never once took the family to an actual game.

It was a steamy night. They took the bus up 108th Street to Roosevelt Avenue and walked under the 7-train tracks to Shea Stadium. Their seats were in the last row of the upper deck.

The climb up the concrete steps was scary, but when they turned around to look through the opening at their backs, they could see the city lights all the way to New Jersey. Way off in the distance, sporadic lightning turned the cloudy night a warm faint yellow. The players looked like ants on a green field, and the crowd was wild, screaming and cursing at the Chicago Cubs when they scored two runs in the second inning.

The sea of blue and orange Mets jerseys swept Janie up in the excitement; and she found herself yelling along with the crowd for Jerry Koosman or Ed Kranepool to kick some Cubby ass.

A vendor, carrying a heavy cooler and walking the steep stairs with practiced skill, called in a loud voice, "Getcha beeah heeah, cold beeah heeah! Miller, Schlitz, Schaefer, Rheingold!"

Another cried, "Popcorn, peanuts! Popcorn, peanuts!"

And still another yelled, "Getcha red hots, Nathan's hot dogs, get 'em while they're hot!"

Jerry ordered them each a hot dog, and Janie thought a frank had never tasted better.

An hour and a half into the game, with the Mets getting a run in the fifth and trying to tie the game before the seventh inning stretch, the lights went out. For a few moments, the crowd went silent, sitting in pitch black darkness. Then yellow and blueish lights came on slowly, giving the stadium an eerie glow. The players all scampered back to their dugouts. There was a smattering of cheering from the stands, as Janie looked around to see what was happening. The smell of pot drifted through the air and Janie laughed.

"They're all lighting up!" she said to Jerry, who was also looking around, trying to figure out what was going on.

For long awkward minutes, there was nothing. A few of the Mets' players ran onto the field. They started doing flips or racing along the foul line, trying to rally the crowd into a cheer. As quickly as they came out, they ran back to the dugout, and it became weirdly quiet again.

Janie happened to turn around to look out towards the city. It was gone. She blinked hard, but it was still gone.

"Hey, Jerry, look. The city is dark. I think there's a blackout."

Everyone nearby heard her, and the chatter swept through the stadium. Just as they were getting riled up, a tinny voice came through a megaphone. Up at the top of the stadium, they could barely hear what he was saying.

"There is a city-wide blackout. We are asking you to leave the stadium immediately in an orderly fashion. Please walk down the ramps, the elevators are not working." He repeated the statement four or five times, while the fans began to make their way down.

It took over an hour to clear the thousands of spectators out onto the street. Once Janie and Jerry made it outside, they stood on Roosevelt Avenue, as uncertain as everyone else what they should do. The people who had come to the stadium from nearby neighborhoods began to walk off. Those who had ridden the subway or bus, neither of which was running, milled around, confused.

"Come on, let's walk, Jerry. It's only a couple of miles. I know the way; my friend Tina from work lives there. We head down to 108th Street and then straight back home."

"No way, that's a dangerous neighborhood. We should definitely not do that."

"Do you have another idea? The bus is not running. Besides, if you just hold it together and act like you own the place, nobody is going to bother you."

"I could call my dad to come and get us," Jerry said.

But the line at the phone booth was already two blocks long.

"I'm not waiting," Janie said, getting a bit exasperated with him. "I'm walking. You can come with me or stand on this long line to call your dad. You might be waiting hours. Up to you."

Jerry unhappily agreed to walk. In the darkness, he squeaked in fear at every noise and hid behind her when a group of people approached. Janie, remembering her friend's stories of nights in Corona, tried to appear confident even though she did not feel it. Channeling her inner Tina, she walked with her head up and a bit of a strut; and no one paid her any attention.

At one point, she turned to Jerry, who was quaking with anxiety, and hissed, "You're going to get us killed, stop acting scared!"

When they passed the Lemon Ice King, Janie knew they were close to home. They got to Janie's apartment first, and Jerry became chivalrous, holding the apartment door for her. Janie was having none of it and swept past him without a word. It was their only date, and they went back to being friends. But Janie thought she had learned an important lesson about boys: find one that isn't afraid of the dark.

Through their senior year, Janie's secret group got together as often as they could; but they were all buried under the process of applying for college. Following the advice of her guidance counselor, Janie sent applications to Princeton in New Jersey, Boston College, and New York University in the city. She could not afford to apply to more places; the fee for sending in the form was twenty dollars, a small fortune that she did not even bother to ask her parents for.

Boston was the first to send her a letter. She could tell before she ripped it open that it was not good news. The envelope was light, containing a single sheet of paper that told her she was wait-listed for a spot. She threw the letter in the trash, disappointed. She wanted to get far away from her parents and had had high hopes for Beantown. Princeton's envelope came next, just as light, an outright rejection.

She stopped sleeping. Tossing and turning with the

possibility of a third and final rejection, her mind reeled with other options and gave her no peace. She would leave, as Greg had; just pack a bag and take off for parts unknown. She would get a job somewhere, anywhere, and move into an apartment with other failures; and figure it out from there. She would go to a trade school or take night classes or anything that would get her out of here. Janie went to class and her after school clubs and the basement parties, but every day she would come home and rifle through the mail; and come up empty.

Days went by and Janie felt like she might go crazy. It did not help that her friends were getting acceptance letters from at least one of their top schools and going on about plans for Freshman year.

Very early one morning, still dark, she got up to use the bathroom, and then went to get a drink of water from the kitchen sink. She reached for a glass, and her hand brushed paper tucked in the cabinet. Puzzled, she drew out a thick manila envelope, clearly cut open with a letter opener.

In the upper left corner: N.Y.U. It was addressed to Miss Jane Thompson.

Her hands were shaking as she spilled the contents onto the counter, already knowing what she would read: *Your application to attend N.Y.U. has been approved. Welcome to the Freshman class! Enclosed please find all the information you need to...*

Janie sat, stunned, her thoughts spinning. She had been accepted! But her mother, knowing this, had tucked the envelope in the cabinet to keep it from Janie. She knew it was her mother that opened the envelope. Her father never got the mail, and her mother always sliced open the envelopes with her personalized letter opener, a gift from her grandmother when she had married.

But, why? Why had she hidden it? What on earth would make her bury Janie's future on a kitchen shelf? A million explanations, each more implausible than the last, tumbled through her frazzled mind: her mother was afraid Janie was expecting them to pay for school and was just not going to tell her she had been accepted; her mother wanted to keep her here as a prisoner forever; her mother had some secret hate for her, for N.Y.U., for college in general. They all seemed, in Janie's overwrought, worn-out state, feasible reasons for this treachery.

Janie was still sitting at the table holding the letter when her mother, the curlers she had slept in tightly wrapping her hair and wearing a nightgown and matching slippers, came into the kitchen.

"Oh!" Mrs. Thompson said, sounding disappointed. "You found it. It came yesterday and I was going to bake you a cake and give it to you tonight after dinner to celebrate. Now you spoiled my surprise."

"Your..." It took Janie a moment to collect herself. "Mom, do you have any idea how nuts I've been, waiting to hear back from N.Y.U.? I have been checking the mail like a crazy person every day and crying myself to sleep. And you hide it from me to surprise me? Do you understand, even a little bit, how I must feel right now? No, you don't, you couldn't, you would never get it, you do not understand anything that has to do with me. You never have."

"There is no need to be rude, Janie. I was doing it for you." Her mother, obviously upset with her daughter and done with the whole thing, busied herself adding coffee to the percolator basket.

Janie wanted to scream. She wanted to yell and throw things and shake her infuriating mother. For a moment, she allowed herself to fantasize it, picturing the whole satisfying thing: shattering glass, flying utensils, the percolator hitting the wall, her mother, finally, showing some emotion, *any* emotion: remorse, embarrassment, even just some hint of awareness of what her daughter was feeling.

Shaking her head in complete frustration, she stuffed everything back in the envelope and stomped to her room. She shook the papers onto her bed and destroyed the envelope in a fit of rage, screaming silently inside. When manila shreds littered her bed and the floor, she felt better. She sat on the bed and began to read the packet.

As she did so, it sank in that she had done it. *She had done it*; and now she had her ticket out of here. It was the happiest she had been since before Greg left; and trepidation of the big change she was about to make took a back seat to unbridled joy. She could not wipe the grin off her face for the rest of the week.

When the members of The Eraserhead Society had all been accepted to various Ivy League and private colleges, they gathered for one last all-out all-nighter. They pooled their graduation gift money and some of the wages Janie had saved up before quitting her job at the Mini Mart, toasted the end of an era, and snorted a thousand dollars' worth of excellent cocaine.

Part 2

"People come into your life for a reason, a season or a lifetime."
-author unknown

Janie, Interrupted

As soon as New York University's dorms were open to incoming Freshmen, Janie packed her suitcase and backpack. Refusing her mother's offer to accompany her, much to Mrs. Thompson's relief, Janie thought, she took the bus and subway to bring her to her new life.

Although she and her friends had occasionally taken the graffiti-covered, rat-infested subway to the city to wander Central Park or see Times Square, this was the first time she really *felt* New York City. She was on her own, away from everyone who knew her, away from everything she knew. Walking towards the university, her stomach knotted. She was impossibly alone in the middle of a human, concrete, steel, and glass melee. She felt insignificant, like one solitary part of a million-piece jigsaw puzzle whose cover picture she could not see.

Greg's voice in her mind, full of love and support, now comforted her as she made her way into the towering dorm building lugging her suitcase and backpack through the meandering crowd of long-haired students. She found a place to park the bags where she could keep an eye on them and got on line to register.

Amidst the racket and hum of activity, she found herself, after forty-five minutes, standing in front of an indifferent girl not much older than her, who was asking questions she could barely hear. She could tell that the girl had her script down as she went through her list of queries: name, birthdate, home address, phone number, parents' names and work phone numbers, copy of a birth certificate to keep on file. It took fifteen minutes of back-and-forth before she handed Janie a room key and a folder marked *Incoming Freshman August 1979* stuffed with information. The girl only acknowledged that she was done with Janie when she called out, "Next in line…"

Janie made her way to the elevator and was jammed in for the ride up to the fifth floor. She found her roommate stringing lights around the room, and hanging posters of Janis Joplin, Peter Frampton, and Jimi Hendrix with duct tape on the white plaster walls. More posters were rolled up waiting on her bed. There was a lava lamp on the nightstand, bright red goo floating and swirling; and Garbage Pail Kids stickers plastered all over the dorm room refrigerator. A pile of National Lampoon, Rolling Stone and Mad magazines lay strewn on the floor. A cigarette burned in an aluminum ashtray, filling the air with a smoky screen. A macrame wall hanging covered the opening of what passed for a closet, and a clock radio at full volume played Led Zeppelin's *Stairway to Heaven*. The girl was singing along as she worked, until she noticed Janie standing in the doorway.

"Oh, hey! Roomie? Come on in! I've been here for a few hours, so I am just getting started doing a little decorating." She took a deep drag of the cigarette and offered the pack of Winston's to Janie, who shook her head.

"I'm Rhonda. From right here in the Village, although I was born in Harlem, and we moved here when I was four. But I didn't want to live at home, you know? Freedom, Independence, Autonomy, Liberty! It's our time! What's your name?" Rhonda's feather earrings dangled behind the curtain of her dark brown hair, as she leaned in for a hug.

"Janie. I grew up in Forest Hills. I like what you've done with the place."

"Yeah? Cool! Put your bags down and help me finish with these lights. Then we can unpack your stuff. There's a mandatory meeting in the Commons at three, but after that I can show you around the Village if you want."

She did want. Rhonda, she decided instantly, was going to be the perfect roommate.

They put the finishing touches on the room after the meeting and were out in Washington Square Park just after dark. Teenagers and college kids crowded the concrete steps that formed the inside of the dry round fountain. The very air vibrated with their chatter and laughter and guitar strumming and singing; the odor of marijuana permeated the scene. Rhonda led her around the fountain to give her a good look. Under the marble arch, a man, so thin and stretched so tall he looked like a cartoon character, sat on a folding chair in front of a baby grand piano banging out a rousing classical piece Janie did not recognize.

"Ha, good one!" Rhonda said. "Ligeti Etude 13."

Janie looked bewildered at this.

"The Devil's Staircase?" Rhonda told her, amused at her ignorance. "Man, your parents neglected your music education. Lucky for you, that's my major. Come on, let's head back down McDougal."

"*Nickel bags? 'Luudes, bennies, coke?*" Voices came out of the dark as they walked through one of the paths towards the street.

"I don't know if you're into drugs, I'm not, but in any case, don't buy from these guys. The grass is oregano, the coke is corn starch and who knows what's in the pills. I can get you whatever you want. The best pot is from Sergeant Mosca's dresser drawer. I went to school with his daughter, and she says he always keeps the best stuff when he busts someone."

Janie felt overwhelmed, by the scene, by her sudden independence, by Rhonda's self-assurance. It was an amazing feeling, a high she had never reached in those basements back in Queens; and she thought she might never do drugs again.

Once out of the park, it was still crowded but much calmer and quieter.

"Are you hungry? Mamoun's has the best falafel sandwich you can get and it's only half a buck. Can't beat it for the money. Cheaper than a pack of cigarettes by three cents!" Rhonda laughed as she shook one of the Winston's into her hand and lit it.

"I almost quit when cigarettes went up to fifty-three cents a pack, fuck that, can you imagine? If they go up anymore, I swear I'll just be done."

They stopped in at the tiny dark shop, filled with the odor of exotic spices frying in oil, and ordered two falafel sandwiches. Janie took her first bite and thought she had never eaten anything so delicious. The cold lettuce and yogurt sauce and spicy harissa melted onto the steaming fried balls of garbanzo, all barely held together by a fresh pita. Rhonda laughed at the white and red sauces dripping out of Janie's overstuffed smile. They walked over to Bleeker Street, taking bites, and licking sauce off their fingers as they went.

"We don't have classes for another week, and this place starts rocking around midnight. The Village Gate is the best place on Bleecker. Jimi Hendrix played there. I was still in elementary school, but my parents took me. Man, I think that was the night I woke up, musically. My parents are both jazz musicians, they mostly play small scenes. You would never have heard of them, but they're friends with everyone! I'm pretty lucky, although it was probably abuse how late I stayed out most nights, ha! Maybe next weekend we'll hit up the places on the Bowery. CBGB's is cool."

They turned onto Bleecker and crossed over Sixth Avenue. It was lined with girls in tight miniskirts, their own age or younger, calling to the men who walked by. One overly made up and extremely busty girl saw them and called out, "Yoo hoo, Rhonda! Hi, doll!" Rhonda waved back as the girl blew her a kiss.

"That's Jinxy, my favorite drag queen. She claims to have competed in Crystal LaBeija's Drag Queen Balls in the early 70's, but she also claims to have slept with JFK. He died in

1963, so that would make her like thirty-five, so I don't think so."

Janie did not know who Crystal LaBeija was, but she did not want to ask. She was busy absorbing everything she could from her sophisticated roommate and trying to hide her own unworldliness at the same time.

They passed John's Pizzeria, which had a line down the street, Murray's Cheese Shop, Faicco's Italian Specialties; Porto Rico Importing Shop with overstuffed giant brown bags in the window and the sweet-bitter odor of roasted coffee beans wafting onto the street; record shops with rock and roll posters, and head shops whose windows were packed with bongs and pipes and shiny silver oversized marijuana leaf necklaces. Janie's senses were on overload, as she took it all in.

They walked past Max Umanov's Guitar Shop. A group of young men were sitting outside on folding chairs strumming guitars. Rhonda greeted them by name; and they hailed her back.

"A lot of people play in front of Max's, but if you're lucky sometimes Bob Dylan hangs out. Even Janis Joplin and Jimi Hendrix joined in occasionally before they died. What a serious waste!" Rhonda shook her head with vehement emotion, grieving the loss of these great musicians as if they were personal friends.

Janie became even more awed by her new friend as they continued the tour. *How could anyone be so cool,* she thought to herself; and hoped Rhonda would not quickly tire of her inexperienced, boring roommate.

The girls turned onto Christopher Street. Young men in hot pink short shorts or black leather vests and matching pants gyrated in front of dive bars that blasted Disco music. The revolving lights from the darkness inside flashed over them all, and the energy made Janie's heart pound to the beat of the music.

They turned on West Fourth Street to head back, and Janie stopped short in front of a storefront with blacklights glowing in the plate glass window. Giant dildoes in dark and light skin tones stood on the bottom of the display along with large purple and silver vibrators. Whips and chains and leather and lace hung suspended from the ceiling. Rhonda laughed at the look on her face.

"Pink Pussycat Boutique," she said. "Are you into this stuff? Want to go in?"

"I don't know. I don't think so, but I've never seen this stuff just so...out there, you know? Not in Forest Hills..." Janie shook her head. "I guess I was pretty sheltered out there in Queens."

"Not anymore, city girl! Come on, let's head back. Can't do it all in one day."

Janie lay in her bed on that first night, exhilarated and exhausted, unable to turn off her careening thoughts. One of her last, before falling into a deep sleep, was that she had not thought about her parents and her old life even one time the whole day.

On Saturday night around ten, after scarfing down steaming, crispy-crusted slices from the corner pizzeria, Rhonda said, "Come on, roomie; we're going out."

"Where to?" Janie asked, but she did not really care. Anywhere Rhonda took her was an adventure.

"We're going to stop first at my parents' place, it's right on the corner of Houston and Sixth."

The apartment was in a brick post-war building, seven stories tall, with a red fire escape zigzagging down the front. The awning stated that it was called "Congress House."

The girls walked into the unassuming lobby and took the elevator up to the fifth floor. Rhonda unlocked the door with a jangling set of keys and Janie stepped into her first New York City apartment. The living room was larger than she expected, with shiny wood floors and bookshelves that rose to the ceiling. While Rhonda disappeared down the narrow hallway, Janie walked to the shelves and saw that most of the titles related in some way to music. *Perfecting Sound Forever* by Greg Milner caught her eye because of the author's first name; *Lady Sings the Blues* by someone named Billie Holiday; and the oldest book on the shelf, *The Music Master* by Charles Klein. She leafed through the yellowed, brittle pages to find it had been published in 1909.

She put it back in its place, wondering how many of these Rhonda had read, and then wandered over to the far corner where a grand piano, dark walnut brown and flawlessly gleaming, stood surrounded by a cello, several violins and at least five saxophones. She sat on the bench and plinked out the first few notes of Heart and Soul.

"You play?" Rhonda asked, crossing the room and walking into the kitchen. She had changed into a pair of black shorts and a rainbow-colored sequin top. Fishnet stockings covered her legs, she had painted her face in exaggerated make-up and a gold lamé top hat sat on her head.

"Oh God, no." Janie responded, not sure what to make of Rhonda's outfit. "My music career ended in fourth grade on my first day in band. The teacher told me after about twenty minutes that I would never be a musician and needed to find a different hobby."

"That's horrible!" Rhonda sounded genuinely outraged.

"And then, because I sing in the shower, I decided to get into the Glee Club in fifth grade. My friends and I were going to do a dance routine to *Black and White* by Three Dog Night. I love the message it gives about people just getting along. But the teacher thought it was too controversial, so we switched to Carly Simon's *You're So Vain*. I guess she thought a song about sex and drugs was more appropriate for ten-year-olds. Anyway, I wouldn't stop laughing and fooling around during practice and she kicked me out. I always thought that was ironic: I got thrown out of Glee Club for having too much glee."

Laughing at the memory, she wandered into the kitchen to see what Rhonda was up to. On the table she saw a folded newspaper, a baggy of uncooked rice, a roll of toilet paper and a squirt bottle filled with water. Rhonda had just pushed two pieces of bread into the toaster and was waiting for them to pop.

"Not for me, thanks, still full of pizza," Janie said.

"Oh my God, it's not for eating. You really are sheltered," Rhonda laughed and shoved everything into her army green backpack.

They walked two blocks north on Sixth Avenue and got on a long line. Janie looked up and read the marquee of the movie theater they were apparently going into: *The Waverly*. And under that: "Rocky Horror Picture Show, every Fri. and Sat. at midnight."

"Oh, fun! I heard of this, but never went."

"I could tell you are a Rocky virgin. Well, we are going to pop your cherry tonight!" Rhonda almost cackled.

Janie was momentarily terrified, but she trusted Rhonda implicitly, so she began to look around at the other people on line. About a third of them wore some kind of costume: glittering gold lamé top hats identical to Rhonda's, black feather boas and corsets, and lots of fishnet stockings and sequins. The odor of marijuana floated through the crowd, and Janie recognized the dilated black-basketball pupils of people high on LSD.

Just before midnight, the line began to move into the theater. Rhonda led her to the middle section about midway back from the stage. A man walked down the aisle to the open space in front of the seats to loud cheering and hooting.

"That's Sal. He runs the floorshow," Rhonda yelled to be

heard above the ruckus.

"Where are the virgins today?" Sal called. "Come on virgins, stand up and show yourselves! Don't be shy, it only hurts the first time!"

Slowly, half of the audience stood. Rhonda prodded Janie until she joined them.

"We're going to pop your cherries good tonight, virgins! Ready? 1-2-3!"

At this the costumed regulars, pointing at those standing, screamed in unison: "*Fuck you!*"

"Okay, sit down. I hope it was as good for you as it was for us! Give me an R! Give me an O! Give me a C!" The audience, including all the former virgins, repeated back the letters Sal called out to spell *Rocky* with wild caught-up enthusiasm.

For the next ninety minutes, with the audience screaming hilarious responses to the movie dialogue, singing along with newspapers covering their heads to protect them from the water being squirted through the theater, and throwing toast, rice and toilet paper at each other, Janie was swept up into a wonderful, weird alternative universe. When it ended, she wanted it to start all over again.

Once classes began, Rhonda and Janie met up mostly at night and on weekends, and for an occasional falafel sandwich at the fountain in Washington Square Park. On a Saturday afternoon in September, they walked down to Mulberry Street in Little Italy.

Green, white, and red glittered decorations had been strung over the road, which was closed off to traffic. On both sides of the street, vendors sold Italian specialties, the sizzling odors competing and making Janie instantly hungry.

"The Feast of San Gennaro," Rhonda explained. "It's a religious thing and later there will be a procession with a really heavy statue being lugged down the middle of the street. But for most of us, it's about the food."

She ordered a sausage, pepper, and onion on a roll for each of them and squirted a thick line of brown mustard down the middle of it. They chewed with big smiles as they walked among the other people relishing their own Italian goodies. As soon as they were done, Rhonda walked to another vendor and returned with a brown paper bag covered in greasy spots. Sticking her hand inside, she pulled out a steaming ball of fried dough covered in white powdered sugar, and handed it to Janie, who stuffed a big bite of the amazing thing into her mouth.

"*Zeppole,*" Rhonda said. "You can get it during the year in other places, but I always wait for San Gennaro's." She licked the powdered sugar off her fingers and added, "Want to try a fresh cannoli? They stuff it with cream to order, that makes the shells stay really crunchy."

Janie did. She was so full after that, she was relieved when Rhonda said it was time to head back. She felt she could not eat another morsel, no matter how delicious.

Classes and homework and studying took up most of their waking hours, but she and Rhonda always made some time to hang out on weekends. Each time they did, Janie saw, ate, heard, or tried something new. She stayed with Rhonda's family over Thanksgiving, and they went to the Macy's Day Parade. The spectacle in living color reminded her of pajama-clad Thanksgiving mornings with Greg, slurping Apple Jacks cereal and milk on the couch, watching it on the television for hours. When the reindeer brought Santa on his sleigh to end the parade, Janie cheered and waved as enthusiastically as any five-year-old standing nearby.

When she went home for Winter Break that first year, she felt like a completely different person. The apartment in Forest Hills seemed oddly smaller than she remembered, the neighborhood felt foreign, shabby, and isolated, and her parents looked older.

They, however, picked up her sudden reappearance as if she had never left.

"I don't know why you need to go to college at all," her father said one night as Janie and her mother cleared the table. "Your mother and I never did, and we are fine."

"You could find a nice man and settle down. Don't feel like you have to finish school, Janie. That is not really a priority for people like us."

"People like us?" Janie asked.

"Working class people, Janie. We learn to be satisfied with our lot in life and stop banging our heads wishing for something else," her mother explained.

"That did not work out so well with Greg," Janie said.

Bitterness welled up in her, and rage grew against these two people who had raised her. *Raised* might be too strong a word, she thought. Rhonda had been *raised*; she had just been allowed to grow up at their table.

"Sometimes, things just don't work out well," her mother said. "Did you hear about that boy named Jerry? He was in your grade. The one who lived in one of the private-property houses up towards the high school?"

"Wait, did you say 'lived'?" Janie asked.

"Yes, well, for all of their airs and riches they couldn't stop him from doing drugs. Apparently, he was sent home from college, Ivy League college, mind you, because he spent all day doing that drug where you smoke cocaine out of a pipe. Freebase, I think they call it. At least that's what the neighbors said. He passed out in his basement and the pipe was still lit and it caught the whole room on fire. He burned up right in his own house. Of course, his mother is saying she had no idea that he was doing such a thing, but I say of course you would know your own kids were into things like that..."

Janie did not stay to hear the rest. She hurried out of the apartment, working to keep her dinner down, and went for a long walk. Horror and sadness fought inside her head. Jerry had died a terrible death, and it took a long time to stop visualizing it and calm down. She was so grateful she had escaped this purgatory. Janie was coming to appreciate for herself why Greg had left and never returned.

On New Year's Day, Janie called Rhonda and asked if she could come crash at her place until the new semester started. Thank goodness, she said yes. Janie packed her things and left while her parents were out. It would be the last time she came home from school.

The second year at N.Y.U., Rhonda moved into the music dorm. Janie went over to meet her new roomies, and although Rhonda introduced her as her best Freshman friend, Janie felt out of place. They asked her about her music background, and Rhonda and Janie laughed at their private joke about Janie's aborted foray into the music world.

"I love listening to all kinds of music," Janie responded. "I am the best groupie you'll ever have."

The others did not seem amused by this and gave her a dismissive nod.

Her own new roommate was a quiet girl from Oklahoma City. Alison was a Literature and Culture major, with an emphasis on women's studies. Janie thought that was an interesting choice for a midwestern small city girl, and she liked Alison; but there was no spark of potential best Sophomore friend, and they both kept to themselves much of the time.

Janie became a world-class people watcher that year. In between classes, and late into the evening, she would sit on a bench and just look at the others who strolled by, sat around the fountain, slept in the scrubby grass, played chess at the concrete tables at one end of the park, came and went out of the dark, scary bathroom building, or sold drugs. It was like she was an audience of one, and they were all in a stage production for her entertainment.

She began to relish this time much more than she looked forward to her classes. Still taking her required courses, she felt no pull towards a major. She had expected that to happen naturally; and as the other students began to fall into their career paths, she felt more and more alienated from the scene at school.

She was watching a middle-aged man chatting up some high school girls when a voice next to her said, "Obviously a perv."

She startled at the sudden remark, turning to see a guy a couple of years older sitting right next to her on the bench. He had long dark hair and wore a David Bowie tee shirt. A Nikon camera hung around his neck.

"Wedding ring on his fat finger, ironed shirt collar, scuffed leather shoes, slight paunch under the cheap belt. He is from Staten Island, probably born and raised. Married his high school sweetheart who turned out to be a demanding bitch and made him get a job in the city that he fucking hates. His revenge is trying to get into the panties of teenagers."

Janie did not respond immediately, so he continued: "He was happy being a Fuller Brush door-to-door salesman out there in old Richmond County. *'A brush for every need. I will be courteous; I will be kind; I will be sincere; I will be helpful.'* He even won Employee of the Month when he sold the largest number of the new bath brush for ladies, the one that hooked up to a hose nozzle? Revolutionary; the secret behind the women's lib movement, unbeknownst to the general public."

"Wow, you're a master," Janie breathed in awe.

"I don't just watch. I take it to the next level. See that couple over there, sitting on the grass and hugging? She just found out she is pregnant. They have been trying for a while and it was really stressing them out to the point where he thought their marriage was over. He even thought maybe she didn't want kids after all and was doing something to prevent getting pregnant. He found an old birth control package at the bottom of her underwear drawer and confronted her. She just screamed at him about trust and dumped the whole drawer of granny panties over his head. Turns out she was overly emotional because of the hormones and now they will live happily ever after with their two point five kids in a house with a white picket fence. You try it."

"I don't think I will be as good at it as you. You do realize that both of those stories involved panties, right?"

He laughed out loud.

"Fine," Janie said, looking around at the hundreds of options. Kids, teens, college students, adults in suits crisscrossing the park on their way somewhere important, elderly women with shopping carts full of overstuffed garbage bags, a homeless man lying on a bench masturbating inside his pants; she was overwhelmed with the choices.

Across the fountain under the arch, was the tall, achingly thin man playing gorgeous melodies on his baby grand. *Go big or go home*, Janie thought.

"The piano player comes here every day, dragging that piano from his basement apartment over on Fourth Street by the Pink Pussy Cat Boutique. He plays here because he has no other place to go. He was fired from his very prestigious position at Lincoln Center for showing up drunk too many times. He was always drunk because his wife, a prima ballerina with the New York City Ballet Company, left him for their doorman."

Janie looked over to see how she was doing, and her fellow storyteller had a look on his face that said he needed just a little bit more, so she added, "He figured out she left when he found a pair of her panties hanging on the doorknob of the building."

"And there you go! Not bad for a rookie. I like making up stories about everyone I see, but I always think it would be way more interesting to ask them their real stories. I think about taking a photo of each of them and writing down their story. I bet you could publish a book like that. Call it Stories of New York People, or something like that. My name is Taylor, by the way."

"Janie," she responded.

They spent the next hour taking turns making up stories about the people around them. A teenaged boy was planning to drop out of school and join the Navy and see the world, and his mother was dead set against it; two men walking out of the bathroom and going their separate ways had just had their weekly liaison and were heading home to their wives; the homeless masturbator on the bench was formerly a rich businessman from Greenwich, Connecticut who got caught embezzling from his own company to finance drug deals in Colombia, and had skipped town before his court date.

Taylor's stories were very entertaining; and Janie's were not too bad, Taylor said, for a beginner.

"Well, I gotta go, Janie," Taylor said, standing and stretching. "That was fun, though."

She watched him walk away, thinking it was nice to have someone to people-watch with. She looked out for him every day after that, but never saw him again.

She also never looked at people the same way again. Now every time she sat to observe, she tried to guess people's real-life stories. That one hour with Taylor had opened her eyes; and it was if she was now truly *seeing* for the first time.

Janie began to wander further from the Greenwich Village area in her spare time. She spent one day standing in a doorway on Broadway at Times Square, marveling at the commotion before her. The energy alone was so different than what she felt sitting in Washington Square Park, but the *people!* Young men in jeans and button-down shirts open to the navel lined the sidewalk in front of fold-out T.V. dinner tables, hustling three-card monte games. Scruffy men stood in front of plate glass windows spray painted with the titles of peep shows, hawking the acts occurring twenty-four/seven inside. Every marquee on the street advertised XXX movies and Girls; Navy sailors in dress whites and men of all ages milled around trying to choose one.

Up and down the street, very young women in skintight mini dresses and sparkly high heels called out to men as they went by. Janie zoomed in on one, standing on a corner, that seemed new and unsure of herself.

She is just fifteen, Janie thought, *and from Bumfuck, Indiana. Had a fight with her single mom, who is only thirty years old herself, and hitchhiked to the big city to start a new life, with nothing but her Penelope Pitstop backpack and the ten dollars she saved up babysitting. Wound up meeting someone who told her he knew a great way to make some money, and now here she is on her first day.*

The story made Janie very sad, so she searched for someone else to watch. From her position in the doorway, she spotted two girls, even younger than the new prostitute, crossing the street and looking, for all the world, very at home here. They were all but skipping in their ankle high Keds sneakers and knee-high tube socks, chatting with bubbly adolescence.

They go to school somewhere near here, Janie thought. *They're in seventh grade, maybe eighth, and they are cutting class to come to Times Square. It looks like they are on a mission of some kind.*

Janie watched the girls open a blackened door between peepshow storefronts and head up the steps. A small sign next to the door, easy to miss, said "Tannen's Magic Shop."

So, they are budding magicians; on their way to buy a new deck of cards for the card tricks they are learning. Back at school, they usually entertain the other kids in exchange for snacks.

Janie stayed in her spot for hours and had a field day telling herself stories about everyone she saw.

Another day, she wandered down to the business district

and sat in the shadows of the Twin Towers. Although they had been completed seven years earlier, Janie had never been close to them in person. For several moments, she sat on a bench, her neck craning to see the tops of the towers, imagining what it might be like to work there every day. A different type of energy, again, accompanied the people she watched here.

A family, whom she decided was from Arkansas, had saved up for years to come visit New York City and were blown away by the noisy, trash-strewn streets filled with rushing people, and the skyscrapers they had only seen in travel books. The husband took copious photographs of them with his Kodak Instamatic camera, its Magicube flash popping in the overcast day.

She watched a man in a disheveled, poorly tailored business suit that, she thought, was on his way to interview for a job that would be a huge step up; out of his working-class existence and to the next level, if only he could land it. The pressure he put on himself, as he imagined telling his wife they could finally move out of their crummy basement studio apartment in Brooklyn, made him walk into gawking tourists and drop his suitcase on his way into the building.

She got lost in her storytelling and stayed until dark.

Back at school, Janie continued losing interest in her classes. Her grades began to slip. She found herself spending more time people-watching than completing assignments; it was the only time she felt truly engaged.

On a warm day in April, Janie wandered down St. Mark's Place towards Thompkins Square Park. The street was packed and noisy with chatter, and the odor of marijuana pervaded the air. She passed groups of long-haired people wearing patched dungarees and feather earrings, and others with colorful mohawks, black leather jackets, facial piercings, and black fingernails. She wondered what these people did for money, and then decided it was not a priority for them; they seemed happy and carefree.

Thompkins Square Park was another world, again. Homeless men and women of all ages slept on benches or large patches of grass. Dozens of bearded young men strummed guitars, humming, or singing softly. Women, some holding babies, danced barefooted, their long skirts swishing around their braceleted ankles.

She could not figure out why it had taken her so long to make it just a few blocks east, but now that she was here, she had only one thought: *Greg!* She had packed away the sadness and pain of him leaving deep in her heart, but now hope soared.

Slowing down to look at each of the men she walked by, Janie made her way around the park, which took up three city blocks. Her first pass yielded one possibility, but then the man sitting next to him snuggled up, called him "Jerome" and gave him a lingering kiss on the mouth. Janie still thought it could be her brother; after all, she had not seen him in four years.

After watching them for another minute, she walked up and tentatively said, "Greg?" That was when she saw his brown eyes, instead of her brother's gray-blues.

For the rest of the afternoon, she asked everyone she could if they knew a Greg who played guitar, had grown up in Forest Hills, and was in his early twenties. She had no luck and made her way back to her dorm with her head down.

Saturday night before finals, Janie put her textbook down on the bed and rubbed her eyes. The names and dates in the American History 101 course swirled around in her head, making no sense, and finding no home in her memory. The dorm building was hushed with the studying and cramming of ten thousand other students. To Janie, the silence was a distracting roar. She needed to get outside and regroup.

Washington Square Park was quiet and low-key, with high schoolers and the homeless oddly affected by the seriousness of final exams radiating from the university into the neighborhood. Janie turned right instead of entering the park, made her way down to Bleeker Street and then towards the Bowery, an area she still had not explored. She needed an all-encompassing brain hijacking to give her mind a break and reset it to prepare for next weeks' finals and hoped to find it along the seedy boulevard.

As she approached the corner where Bleeker ended at the Bowery, she heard people conversing in loud voices on the street, and it drew her in. She passed closed storefronts, with their graffiti-covered metal gates drawn down tight against the night. Crossing over the busy road, Janie stood for a moment in front of a white awning overhanging the door of a club. Live music floated out to the street, where a crowd of black-leather and blue jeans-clad men and women held bottles of beer and smoked cigarettes and pot.

CBGB, she read on the awning; and below that *OMFUG*. Remembering that her roommate Rhonda had mentioned this club as "cool," she smiled to herself and entered the fray. The vibe, carried by the live music and the crowd, welcomed Janie; and she made her way to the bar and ordered a bottle of Budweiser. From her spot, she could watch the band and the people dancing on the floor and sip her cold beer. She found herself moving to the beat and when she felt someone tap her on the shoulder, she turned with a smile.

"You look like you could use a friend, it's never as much fun to dance all by yourself!"

A young woman held out her hands to invite Janie to the floor, and several of her friends nodded and said, "Come on!" Janie set her beer down and bopped with them towards the stage. They danced to the rhythms as a group, moving around and through the crowd, Janie losing herself in the moment. When, after an hour, the band announced a short break, they trooped back to the bar. Janie lifted her beer and the brew, now lukewarm, did not quite quench her thirst.

"I'm Gretch," the young woman said, "And this is Sam, Donald, Betsy, Windy and... What's your name?"

This last she directed at a young man that had joined their group on the dance floor.

"I'm Denny," he responded. He had his hands shoved into his jeans pockets and leaned heavily on the bar.

"I'm Janie," she said, waving at each person in turn, repeating their names so she could remember.

Just as she was about to order another beer, Gretch said, "Hey, how about we head over to this other place not far from here. I hear they are having a big party tonight!"

The group of friends all loved the idea, Denny nodded his head, and Janie said, "Sounds good to me!"

When they were still a block away, Janie could hear the roar of riotous hammering bass from live music. There was a crowd on the sidewalk in front of the club, as Gretch led them inside.

"Let's get a drink!" She yelled to be heard over the thrashing arrhythmical beat of the punk music coming from the stage.

The crashing resonance reverberated the very air, instantaneously enveloping Janie's blood, bones, and limbs, searing her. The darkness, broken in epileptic fits by white pulsing strobes and brilliant flashes of blue, red, green, and yellow assaulted her eyes with blinding erratic explosions. Dense smoke, mostly cigarette with the underlying reek of pot, overwhelmed her vision and sense of smell, lambasting and excoriating her ability to think. The moving, throbbing mob swept her in, and she gave herself over to it.

She was carried along to the front of the club, where she could see the low stage and the band jamming on guitars and drums. The front man was screaming out incomprehensible agitated lyrics, juxtaposed against the rapid chords of the leather-jacketed woman playing guitar and the irregular beats of the drums that jangled the nerves.

Janie was stunned and dazed, paralyzed by the assault on all her senses at once. A teenaged girl wearing a Sid Vicious tee shirt and doing a pogo dance banged into Janie, turned, grabbed her hands, and screamed, "Come on!" in her face. Janie smiled and began to hop up and down. As quickly as she came up, the teen sprang off and Janie began to move wildly, letting herself go, arms flailing in abandon with the rest of the horde.

Dancing like a single organism, the crowd's frenetic movements inspired the musicians to put their souls into their performance in a burgeoning symbiosis that left time and space outside this swelling, intensifying sphere.

A young woman, her eyebrow pierced and connected to her mouth with a chain of metal diaper pins, lips painted black and eyes wild and shiny, came up to Janie and grabbed her hands. They hopped up and down and swung around in tight circles until the girl whirled off to disappear in the crowd.

Three long-haired, bearded men surrounded Janie, gyrating against her, and throwing her long hair up and around her head in a frenzy, and Janie, with abandon, moved against them. Then they, too, disappeared into the crowd and she became one with the whole moving mass, ecstatically losing herself into the mad commotion.

Gretch and the others appeared in front of her, jumping around with uninhibited joy. Janie was as glad to see them as if they were long lost friends.

Just when she began to feel faint from the sweaty heat and high energy and closely compacted crowd, Denny appeared at her side holding a cup filled with electric blue liquid that could only be Kool-Aid. Gratefully, she took the cup and upended it, pouring it down her parched throat and shaking the cup to get every drop.

"Thank you, Denny!" she yelled, the watchful look on his face not registering as she kept bopping wildly to the music.

He stepped back in the crowd, but not too far back; from where he stood, he could keep his eyes on Janie, and wait.

The lights flashing around Janie became momentarily brighter, then began to move in slow motion. The discordance of the punk song grew exponentially, and Janie felt something go very wrong. It became hot and close, and she knew she had to get out of the place. Pushing her way through the crowd towards the door, which was weaving and jerking in front of her, she made it outside. The fresh air awakened her for a moment, and she started to run. Crossing streets without looking, not seeing anything but blinding lights and dark black spaces, not hearing brakes screeching and horns honking and angry drivers cursing at her, her legs began to feel like they were moving through sludge. She ran her hand along the walls and metal gates to keep from wobbling over.

Something grabbed her from behind and she screamed.

"Shhhh, stop yelling."

She turned and saw a face that scratched at her brain; but the face was foggy and wouldn't stop undulating, swelling and shrinking in her line of vision. Just as it opened its mouth and started to say, "It's just me, Denny," she began shrieking again and a group of people crossed the street and said, "Hey, is everything okay? Let go of her, man," and she bolted away into the darkness.

It would be the last thing she remembered from that night.

The feeling of being cold, too cold, brought Janie to sluggish consciousness. Shivering and hugging herself close, she rolled onto her back and worked to open her eyes. Dim, hazy light made it hard to see her surroundings, but she felt weak and unable to do anything about it. A dead silence met her low moan as she lay there. She called out feebly; her unanswered "Hello?" disappeared into the wide shadowy space around her.

After a few minutes, Janie put her hand down next to her, and felt the rough, hard, chilled surface on which she lay. She put both elbows down and tried to push herself up but was too shaky. She was still lying there when she heard a metal door squeal open, and the sound of several animated voices approaching.

"Jenny! You're up again! Just in time, we got soup and sandwiches at the mission. You should eat something; it's been a few days."

The mention of food caused Janie's stomach to lurch. With all her strength she rolled onto her knees, scrabbled a few feet away, dry-heaving until the urge subsided. The others sat nearby, unwrapping the food noisily, and dug in with hunger. The smell of chicken noodle soup wafted over to Janie, and she gagged again for several minutes.

"Hey, are you gonna eat yours?" a boy's voice called out. "If not, we'll split it."

"She needs to eat something, you guys, come on, you know how it feels. Just give her a minute." This from the same girl's voice who had called her "Jenny."

After another few minutes, Janie had enough strength to crawl back closer to the others. She saw a long piece of cardboard, which she realized was where she had been sleeping, and made it back, sitting up and rubbing her face with both hands. She opened her eyes again and saw that her feet were bare, white-cold, and filthy. Her jacket was gone, as were her bag and the bangle bracelets she had been wearing.

"Here, eat something, Jenny," the girl said, and lifted the paper cup with lukewarm soup up to her lips. The odor of greasy cooked animal hit her nose, and the sight of fat white noodles floating in the yellowish oily liquid threatened to roll her now painful insides; but she cautiously took a sip, then another. She made it a couple of feet away before puking it all up. She crawled back and collapsed onto the cardboard again, curling onto her side and hugging herself.

The other kids wound up splitting the food they had gotten for Janie, with the girl saying, "We'll get her more tomorrow."

When they finished eating, they tossed the wrappers and cups into a corner of the warehouse, where they fell among heaps of other trash. Janie watched a large rat that had been rifling the pile get spooked and scurry away.

One of the boys took a glassine envelope, on which was printed "blue angel," out of his underwear while the others searched the floor for hypodermic needles and a rusty spoon. He injected a bit of the liquid into his arm, and as he passed out, the same girl said, "Give Jenny a pop, poor thing, it will make her feel better."

They rolled her onto her back. She objected weakly as they strapped a rubber thong around her upper arm and slid the needle into a vein next to several other marks on the inside of her elbow. Then they all took their hits and passed out until night fell.

When Janie opened her eyes again, early morning light was trying, but failing, to illuminate the cold littered interior of the warehouse. She could see the prone forms of the kids she barely remembered from the day before. As she sat up, she shook her head to reach for some explanation, some reason, some sense of what had happened to her. She was shivering, and this time it felt more like a slight fever than just the cold humid air around her.

Janie stood, wobbling, and put out her arms for balance. Lurching over to a corner far from the others, she pulled her jeans down, squatted and let out a very small stream of pungent, brownish urine. She made her way to the door of the warehouse and stepped outside. The bright morning light blinded her and gave her an instant headache. She stepped back inside to find the kids all sitting up.

"Hey, Jenny. Fun night, huh? I felt like I was floating above my body. I could see you laying there all peaceful. You were smiling and laughing at something. Inside joke?"

Janie had no idea whether it had been a fun night and what the joke could have been. She was having difficulty thinking at all.

"Where am I?" she uttered through the throbbing in her head.

"Wow, Jenny, you really don't remember anything? Wild! Well, I'm Debbie, and these are Nicole, Matt and Will. We found you wandering down Elizabeth Street Saturday night, Sunday morning really, and invited you into our place here. You were pretty loopy, and a girl can get in trouble wandering all messed up like that. Right, Nicky? You know all about that."

The other girl nodded, then shook her head at the thought.

"But you sure can hang!" The one named Matt spoke up. "We did skin pops and that was it for you for days! I thought maybe you were a goner, but Will checked your pulse every once in a while, and he kept saying, 'faint but still with us!'"

The others laughed as if it were a fond memory they shared.

"Skin pops?" Janie was having trouble tracking the conversation through the fog in her brain.

"You know; Horse...H...Junk? Funny, I did notice your arms were all virgin, but you said you wanted some, so we strapped you up," Will chimed in.

"I wanted some?" It was all she could manage, to parrot back what they were saying. It was not computing, and she shook her head in an attempt to focus. "I shot up? Heroin?"

She looked down at the inside of her elbows and got the answer.

"I swore I never would," she spoke in a soft, despondent tone; but they all heard.

"Yeah, it's a bad scene, that's why we stick together, you know?" This from Debbie. "It'll be okay, you hang with us.

We'll show you the ropes. I remember when I started out; it's good to have people on your side."

Janie sat for a moment, working to absorb what had happened. She went out to distract herself so she could re-focus on finals; she had met the group at CBGB and they had trouped over to another club, with its extreme lights and sound and she had lost herself in the excess. Then the one guy, the one who kind of glommed on to the group, had brought her a cup of Kool Aid, and it had tasted so good. But it did something to her and she had left the club and ran and there was noise and faces and...

And that was it. Blank; nothing; empty. And now.

Now, she was apparently living in a warehouse with four junkies, who had rescued her from maybe a much worse fate. In her addled state, she found herself grateful to them; but, at the same time, so very lost. She needed to figure it all out as soon as her head stopped swooning.

Janie looked down again at her bare cold feet. "Where are my shoes and my bag?"

At this, there was silence for a moment, and then, again, the shared laughter.

"Forget all of that, Jenny. We need to get some food in you. And judging by the shakes and the look on your face, we need to get you another pop. We are pretty much out of money, but we can talk about that later. Can you walk?"

Janie took a few steps, wobbled violently, and sat down hard.

"Okay, just stay here, we'll be back."

They were gone for a while, but Janie could not pull her thoughts together. Her back and legs were achy, her heart began to race with anxiety, the shivering intensified, and her stomach spasmed, convulsing until she did not know if she was going to throw up again or shit herself. She was still sitting, weak and hunched over, when the others returned.

"Whoa, Jenny's in bad shape. Nicole, get some soup in her, and Matt get the junk ready. She is going to need it ASAP."

Janie submitted to all their ministrations and passed out for another day.

When she came to, the others were sitting in a tight circle nearby, talking intensely. As soon as she noticed Janie was awake, Debbie began to speak towards her.

"We need some money, Jenny. Any ideas? There's a coffee next to you, it's cold but it should help you wake up a bit."

Janie shakily sipped at the cup and shook her head in answer to the question.

"Jenny's cute," Matt said. "I'll bet people will give her money. Maybe you girls hit up Houston Street where all the businesses are. Will and I can work the weave by Washington Square Park, although the students who usually give have left since finals are mostly over."

Janie's cup of coffee slipped out of her hand. "Finals over?"

Matt's words got through the haze in her head, and jarred her memory, shocking her.

"Yep, and the Village is a ghost town again, at least until tourist season starts," Will replied. "Actually, that's the best time to ask for dough, the suckers from the Midwest are notoriously sappy and charitable to poor hungry homeless kids."

Janie put her head down and cried into her hands. Her brain was still murky, but she knew this much: She had fucked up. Big time.

She remembered leaving the dorm to get some fresh air and regroup before trying to hit the books again. CBGB, the other club, dancing, lights, music; and then *blank*. She had gone to take a walk, her life had suddenly veered left; and she had no idea what to do now.

The shakes hit her hard and suddenly. Janie felt like she was having a seizure and panicked. She rose unsteadily to her feet and stumbled towards the door to get outside. Stopping to gag and retch, her empty stomach cramping tightly, she doubled over gasping in pain and fell to the ground. The group watched unemotionally as she rolled and rocked, trying to get a grip on the convulsions and the pain.

"Better give her a little pop," Will said.

"That's the last of our stash," argued Nicole. "If she uses it, we have nothing for later."

"If she takes it, she can get out with us and get some money for more," responded Will. "We could leave her here and go now, but you guys know how miserable that feels. I think we should help her. Then she will have to help us."

Agreeing reluctantly, the other kids scrounged up the works they needed and approached Janie, who was still writhing on the warehouse floor.

"Jenny, lay still for just a minute, you'll feel better as soon as we get this needle in you," Debbie said.

"No! No more, I don't want it. I never wanted this," Janie protested, tears leaking down both sides of her face. "I just want this to stop. I want to go back. This is not okay; I want to go back."

At this the group's laughter was tinged with irony.

"Who doesn't?" Matt said. "But honestly, you'll feel better and then you can figure it out. Up to you, though. More for us if you don't."

A particularly strong tremor earthquaked inside Janie and she screamed. Everything hurt at once. Her arms, hands, feet, back, neck, stomach, legs, all cramped brutally, relentlessly clenching and causing Janie to leap up and dance around like a cruelly maneuvered marionette, trying to end the shooting pain.

She fell gasping at their feet, moaning, "Please make it stop," and held still long enough to get the needle into her arm. The spasms eased rapidly, the convulsions stopped, and Janie lay in a heap, breathing hard and crying with relief. The group left her there and went out the door.

When she came to a few hours later, the others were back and sitting around looking worried. They had not been able to get enough money to buy their fix for the day. Nicole and Matt were shivering slightly, sweat beading at their hairlines.

"Jenny's back," Debbie said. "You have to get up and help us now. We helped you and if we don't get some smack soon, Matt and Nicky will get sick."

Janie sat up, rubbing her face, and looked at them. She saw the beginning signs in the other two of what she had just gone through.

"Okay, what do I have to do?" she said.

Janie found that she was very good at panhandling. She had gone that day with Debbie to the mission and gotten some food, a comb, a pair of Keds sneakers that were just a bit big, a fairly new top and jeans in her size, and an olive-green army jacket that would have fit a medium-sized man.

In the church basement bathroom, she looked in the mirror. A horrified scarecrow with dark bags under her eyes and wild unkempt hair stared back at her. Janie started, at first not realizing this was her own face; until she reached up to brush a strand of hair out of the way and the scarecrow did the same.

She turned on the hot and cold-water faucets, flipped her hair over and put her head into the sink. The warmth flowed over her scalp and neck, giving her comfort and relief. She grabbed the bar of soap from the counter and rubbed her scalp with it until suds and lather built up. After rinsing her hair and combing the painful tangles out of it, she scrubbed her face and worked at the filth crusted under her fingernails.

As she lathered her arms, the reddened needle marks glaring on the insides of her elbows gave her pause.

She had crossed that line, Janie realized; the one line her friends had all said they would never cross. And they had been right; but now she was in it and could not yet see her way out. Now she was "Jenny," who "sure can hang," according to Matt; and this group had taken her in when she was wandering in a fugue on dark and dangerous streets. She still had no clear idea what had happened to her that night. But right now, at this moment, she was here, with them; and getting money was the only thing she needed to focus on. The rest would come, eventually. At least she hoped so.

Feeling refreshed and better than she had in days, Janie and Debbie made their way over to Houston Street. Debbie walked up to a man in a business suit with her hand out.

"Can you spare some change, sir?" she asked. "We haven't eaten yet today."

The man brushed by without acknowledging them in any way. Debbie walked up to an elderly woman and said the same thing.

"Neither have I," the woman snapped at her. "Do you think you're the only ones having a hard time? I have been eating cans of cat food for a week. My son won't return my calls and my welfare check is lost in the mail again. I…"

The girls walked rapidly away from her in mid-rant.

"Wait a minute, Deb. Come over here with me. Give me a minute."

Thinking she might be wimping out, Deb became irritated but followed her to stand in the doorway of a closed-down dry cleaners.

Janie scouted the people walking by. At first, they were a seething colorful mass of shifting shapes; but after just a minute she really began to *see* them.

Most of the passers-by were men in business suits in a hurry. A few women wearing boxy blazers with shoulder pads, high-waisted jeans, and white sneakers strode by, obviously on their way somewhere important. More women, sporting scrunchies holding up high ponytails, ambled by pushing baby carriages. There were a few other teens asking for money, and homeless women and men wearing many layers of clothes pushing overflowing shopping carts.

"Come on, Jenny. We're not making any dough just standing here," Debbie stepped away and began to walk down the street.

Just then Janie spotted a woman, dressed in designer jeans and a flowy top with dangling hoop earrings, crossing the busy avenue towards them. She was walking a Lhasa Apso, with a pink bow fastened on top of its head, on a sparkly leash.

"Wait," Janie said, pulling her back. "See that lady there? She is the mistress of a wealthy Wall Street banker. He has a family out on Long Island, but he rents an apartment down in SoHo and spends most of the week there with her. Her name is Tracy and he bought her the dog, who she named Trixie, after that girl in the Speed Racer cartoons. It's late Thursday afternoon, so she is on her way to pick up a cute little sexy dress, with his business credit card of course, to put on for their last night together of the week, before he goes home for the weekend. She is in a very good mood because on the weekends, she goes out to clubs with her girlfriends, which she doesn't tell him about..."

"What the hell?" Debbie said to her and watched in surprise as Janie walked up to the woman.

Janie asked her about the dog and crouched down to scratch the little furry ears with murmurs of how adorable she was. After a moment, she stood up, and Debbie could hear what she said.

"It makes me a little sad. I have a dog at home just like her, but the vet found a lump on her neck and says it's cancer. The treatment is four hundred dollars, and my mom says we just don't have it, so we will probably have to put her to sleep." A tear traced Janie's cheek as she spoke, and it was not fake, exactly.

"Oh no!" the woman said, and digging into her Gucci shoulder bag, she took out a twenty-dollar bill. Handing it to Janie, she said, "I know it's not enough, but I hope it helps your poor little…what did you say her name was?"

"Trixie," Janie responded, taking the twenty from her.

"Oh, that is so cute! Poor Trixie, I hope she will be okay." She walked away, waving tootle-loo with finely manicured fingers covered in rings.

"Are you fucking kidding me? You're a panhandling savant!" Debbie crowed, throwing both arms around her in a bear hug. "Do it again, come on, I need to see this."

Janie quickly spotted an elderly man who was smiling and whistling to himself as he walked by. She knew she could get money from him by playing a scared girl with an abusive father and a mother who was afraid to tell her parents about being broke and homeless; but his eyes were just too kind and open, and she could not bring herself to approach him.

She looked around some more. This time Debbie gave her all the time she needed, beginning to relish the game.

"There! That couple over there, they look not much older than us, but check out their Ray Bans and Calvin Kleins. I bet they are from Long Island, some fancy neighborhood where they both belong to the tennis club and their daddies own yachts. Wait here."

Janie handed Debbie her Army jacket. Underneath was a fairly new long-sleeved top with a pretty pattern. She approached the couple from behind. "Excuse me, are you two from around here? I'm trying to get back to the Upper East Side where we are staying with my dad's business partner, and I am completely lost. I took the subway down, but I was not really paying attention, you know?"

"We're from Scarsdale, and my father's chauffeur brought us down," the girl answered in a snotty tone.

"We came down to see what all the fuss was about in

Greenwich Village," the boy answered. "It's cool but it's pretty seedy."

"I know, it's my first time in the city, we're from out on Long Island, and I won't be hurrying back here. It's definitely nicer where I live. I am kind of scared to take the subway back, but I left my wallet at Mr. Debber's place and all I have is a token. So stupid. Well, I hope you get home okay. I guess you will get a ride back from the chauffeur."

"Wait, take a cab, here's five bucks. I wouldn't feel right," the boy said, handing her a bill.

As they walked away, Janie and Deb could hear the girl whining to him, "You're too nice. Or maybe you like her, is that it? You think she is prettier than me?"

The girls spent another hour on the street and had enough money for the night, even bringing home a pizza to celebrate.

Over the next few months, Janie brought home enough money to keep all the kids high. She took as little of the drug as she could to keep the shakes away, while she tried to figure out what to do with herself. Returning home was not an option; returning to school was also out.

She pondered getting a job, and even went to apply at the Crazy Eddie's store on Sixth Avenue. In the plate glass window, a television played the store's singular commercial, the announcer at full volume screaming manically over the speakers hung outside; "*Crazy Eddie's is going computer crazy with an incredible selection of home computers- Atari, Texas Instruments, Commodores! Crazy Eddie's has got them all with guaranteed lowest prices! Shop around and then go to Crazy Eddie's and he'll beat their prices! Crazy Eddie's computer prices are INSANE!!*"

The loud music and high energy in the place drove her out before she could begin to fill in the application. Besides, she realized later, she had no address or phone number to put in those spaces on the form.

Not for the first time, she felt completely untethered and helpless. That night, she shot up a large dose, and slipped into unconscious bliss for a few hours.

On a late September afternoon, Janie and Nicole were working Bleeker Street. Janie had successfully gotten a few dollars off the students that were back for the fall semester. Like Debbie, Nicole was awed by Janie's natural ability to pick out the people she could get money from and delighted by the stories that Janie told her about each mark before hitting them up.

Janie was wearing her oversized Army coat, an old Mets cap and a pair of sunglasses that afternoon, and as she turned to head back to Nicole waving a fiver, she walked directly into a chatty group of girls heading towards the University.

"Oh! Sorry," Janie mumbled, backing up.

One of the girls looked up and said, "No problem!"

Rhonda! Janie realized instantly. She turned her back quickly, but saw, out of the corner of her eye, her freshman roommate stare back at her with a vague, puzzled look of recognition.

"Let's go," Janie said to Nicole, hurrying in the opposite direction.

She heard Rhonda call, *"Janie??"* as she moved quickly away, leaving Nicole to jog to catch up with her.

That night Janie was in a clear funk. After they had all taken their turns with the needle, she wandered off to a far corner of the warehouse, moved a pile of trash out of the way, brushed the rat droppings to one side, and sat down against the wall, hugging her knees to her chest. She stayed in that position until she came to in the morning, stiff and cramped.

The first sound to pierce her consciousness was a moaning that swelled and dwindled without rhythm, coming from the other side of the room. A low series of careful coughing to clear a sore throat was followed by more moans. Standing slowly on painful legs, she made her way towards the sound. Three of the kids were still passed out, but Matt was stirring, hugging himself in feverish arms, sweat pouring down his neck.

"Are you okay?" Janie asked, still not one hundred percent awake herself.

"My throat is on fire, my whole body aches, I'm freezing…" Matt whispered in raspy tones through lips covered in sores. He could barely turn his head; under his chin and his ears, swollen glands pushed alarmingly at the thin skin.

Janie nudged Will and the girls to wake them. "Something is really wrong with Matt, you guys. I think he needs to see a doctor."

"Probably caught something from the guy he sucked off last night outside the club on Christopher Street," Will said, not sounding in the least concerned. "I told him so many times he was going to catch the clap or something, but he wouldn't listen."

The others did not get up, so Janie helped Matt stand and they walked to the door, stopping every few steps for him to take shallow, pained breaths. The morning sun was warm, but he shivered uncontrollably as they slowly walked the six blocks to the hospital emergency room.

Just outside the entrance, stew bums littered the sidewalk, leaning up against the wall and drinking Thunderbird from brown-bagged bottles. Some of them were bleeding from sores on their bare feet and legs, and others were crying dry tears, toothless mouths open and wailing.

Janie helped Matt over to the only open space in the room, where he leaned on the wall hugging himself tightly. The seats were mostly filled with young men not much older than them. They seemed to be in couples; one gaunt, haggard and in pain, the other holding his hand with worried looks and anxious words of comfort. Many of the sick men had the same swollen necks and sores encircling their mouths as Matt.

Janie went over to the harried woman at the front desk. She was busy writing furiously on a sheet of paper, pushed it over roughly on top of a messy pile when she was done and continued on a new sheet. She did not look up, even though the dim light threw Janie's shadow over her desk.

"Hi," Janie said to get her attention. The woman did not acknowledge Janie in any way.

"Hello. Good morning. My friend needs help."

The woman, unbelievably, still acted as if she did not hear. Janie took a frustrated breath.

"*Hey!!* My friend needs help! He needs a doctor; he is really hurting. Hello?? Doctor?!" Janie lost her patience and pounded her fist on the counter.

Slowly, the receptionist lifted her gaze, looking at Janie like she was a pest to be swatted away. Staring unemotionally at Janie's face, she waited for her to speak again.

"He has a fever, really bad. His throat is really sore, his neck is swollen, and he feels terrible. He needs to see a doctor. Now."

"Is he a homosexual?" the woman asked.

Janie was taken aback; these were not the words she was expecting, and she did not know how to respond.

"There is some kind of virus going around the homos in this area," the woman said, pointing with the end of her Bic pen at the other patients crowding the room.

"I don't know and what difference does it make? How long until he can see a doctor?"

Pointing at the room again, the woman answered, "I'd say it will probably be sometime tonight. We are short staffed, as usual, and all of these…men…are ahead of him."

She flipped her pen around into writing position, pulled a blank form out of a folder and asked, "Name?"

"Matt."

The woman looked up at her as if she were stupid. Slowly

she enunciated in a sarcastic tone, "Does he have a last name?"

Janie ran over to Matt. He had slid down the wall and was sitting on the filthy floor, head lolling, and eyes shut tight in pain.

"Matt, what is your last name?"

There was no answer. She tried again, shaking his shoulder very gently; still no response.

Returning to the front desk, she said, "I don't know."

The woman rolled her eyes. "I can put John Doe for now. Birth date?"

"I don't know."

"Home address? Home phone number? Medical history?"

"I don't know!" Janie snapped.

"Do you know anything about 'your friend' at all?" The woman was barely fighting the sneer threatening to curl her lip.

At this, Janie's shoulders slumped in defeat. "No," she said. "I just know he is sick and needs help. Isn't that enough?"

"I guess it will have to do. A nurse will call you when it's his turn."

Janie went to Matt. She slid down next to him on the floor, gently wedging herself between him and another shivering young man and put her arm around his shoulders. She was alarmed at how thin he was under the oversized sweatshirt and pulled him close to warm him while they waited.

At some point, she dozed. At another, she whispered "I'll be back" into his ear and went to stand in line at the mission to get them soup and a sandwich. He sipped and nibbled at his, then shook his head and pushed it away.

The sun was well-set when a nurse came out into the room and hollered, "John Doe?"

Janie helped Matt up and walked him to the door. "I'll be back to check in on him in a bit," she said to the nurse.

She watched them go down the hall before turning around

and walking back to the warehouse. The others were sitting around and chatting, just about to shoot up when she walked in.

"Where's Matt?" Debbie asked, seeing that she was alone.

"Hospital. He is really sick, and the weird thing is the lady said there is some virus going around with gay guys. I hope he is going to be okay."

"I hope it's not contagious to straight people," Nicole said, taking the hypodermic needle they all shared and pushing it into her arm.

Matt did not return to the warehouse. After a week, Janie and Nicole went to the emergency room at the hospital to check on him and were told only that the staff had gotten in touch with his family, and they were not allowing any visitors.

"Well, one less person to help us, but also one less to use our stuff," Nicole said, as they walked away.

Janie shook her head but did not say a word as they walked over to Houston Street to begin begging for the day's money.

The usual work rush and shoppers and baby strollers and students and dog walkers and kids as young as five walking by themselves crowded the sidewalks.

Janie had thought, when she first started panhandling, that more people meant more money. She quickly learned that she was wrong. It was more difficult for her to find a mark who stood out from the masses; and more difficult for them to stop long enough to make their donation. She and Nicole stood in a doorway amid the McDonald's wrappers and brown-bagged empties, searching for their first contribution.

After fifteen minutes, Nicole became impatient and walked among the people with her hand out, repeating the standard, "Can you please spare some change? We haven't eaten today."

She was given a quarter by one of the mothers pushing a stroller; and that was it.

"Let's try somewhere else," Nicole said in frustration.

She was beginning to get jittery and irritable; signs Janie knew well. They walked up LaGuardia Street past the Italian pastry shop. The rich smells of espresso, frothed milk and sugary sweetness making Janie's mouth water and her stomach rumble, but Nicole did not seem to even notice.

As they passed the newspaper stand on the corner, the bold headlines on the New York Post and the Daily News screamed out at her, making her stop short.

"STUDENT SUICIDE!"

"SWAN DIVE AT NYU LIBRARY!"

Janie picked up the Post and read the column quickly, before the grizzled man at the stand could yell at her, "No free reads! Pay up or put it back!"

> *Alison Brennbecker, a third-year student at New York University, committed suicide last night at the Elmer Bobst Library. She leaped to a bloody death from the tenth story balcony in the controversial building, which was completed in 1973 amid protests from community activists.*
>
> *Miss Brennbecker was originally from Oklahoma City, Oklahoma. She was majoring in Literature and Culture, and she had joined the N.Y.U. Women's Studies Center, according to her mother, Marjorie Brennbecker, who added that there had never been any indication of major emotional problems. "She was a happy, well-adjusted girl," Mrs. Brennbecker said, and was "an avid reader."*
>
> *The city medical examiner's office*

"Hey, put that down, you street rat!" the man behind the newsstand bellowed at the very same time as Nicole came back, whining, "Come on! Let's go, I don't feel so good. What are you doing?"

"My roommate killed herself," Janie said aloud, as Nicole hurried her towards 8th Street.

"I might kill myself eventually," Nicole said to her. "I'm going nowhere fast and getting tired of this shitty life. Don't you ever think about it?"

Up until that point, Janie hadn't. Now, suddenly, it loomed as a viable option. She, too, was tired of this shitty life. She did not seem to be good at anything except begging for money, and saw no avenues that led her out of this hole she was in. She had crossed her own line, even though she had no recollection of making that decision. Still her own choices had led her here, and now "here" was the only thing she had. Her only friends were as lost as she was; and were they really friends? It seemed to Janie that they were just using each other as they steamed towards a mutual dead end.

She was deep in these spiraling thoughts when Nicole stopped short. Janie did not notice and walked full on into a large man who had stepped out onto the sidewalk, blocking their way.

She backed up to where Nicole was standing. The first thing she noticed was the way he was dressed: dark sunglasses, a felt fedora hat with a band that matched the yellow button-down shirt opened to his broad chest, brown plaid suit, overly shiny platform shoes. He smiled widely, showing big white teeth under his tightly trimmed mustache, and spoke.

"Well, hello ladies! How are you beautiful ladies doing on this fine, fine day?"

Neither of the girls answered him, but he kept on smiling, like a friendly shark, Janie thought.

"And where are you headed today? Dressed like that, I'd say you're on your way to the avenue to ask people to make a donation to your cause, am I right? Well, if that is the case, then this is your very lucky day! Big Bobby...that would be me," he said in a falsely humble tone, brushing at his lapels, "gonna offer you the opportunity of a lifetime!

"Pretty girls like you don't need to beg for money, it should be laid at your feet. You deserve better and I'm here to offer it to you. How does this sound? A nice warm bed to sleep in, meals whenever you feel hungry, and some hot sexy new *couture* to show off those bee-you-tee-ful curves! Man, you ladies are smokin' hot under those oversized second-hand duds! I will guarantee you more dough than you have seen in a long time, and whatever else your heart desires. This is a dangerous place for young ladies like you, you need protection from people who would do you harm. I'm offering you a safe haven from these mean streets. Come on, what do you say, um..."

At this, he offered his large, diamond-ring covered hand. Janie took a step back, but Nicole put out her thin, delicate fingers and he took them, covering her whole hand with his. His smile grew even bigger as he gently pulled her towards him, and she went willingly.

"Hey, no, come on, Nicky," Janie protested.

"Nicky. That's nice. That is a pretty name for a pretty little lady," Big Bobby said, stroking her cheek. Nicole looked up at his bright dark eyes, and the uncertainty on her face melted into a timid smile.

"Nicky," Janie spoke again, with more urgency.

Without looking at her, Nicole said, "Jenny, I'm done with this panhandling shit, I'm done being cold and hungry, I'm done not knowing where my next meal is going to come from."

"That's the way," Big Bobby encouraged her. He looked up and gave Janie his smile again. "Come with us, Jenny. Always room for one more in Big Bobby's heart."

Janie shook her head and watched with roiling emotions as Nicole and Big Bobby walked away. The last thing she heard before they turned the corner was Big Bobby's booming laughter; the last she saw of Nicole was her slight frame overpowered by his huge one as they strolled up the street towards Times Square arm in arm.

She stood on the corner for longer than she should have, unsure what to do. Her world was falling apart; again. Things were happening, not to her but around her; and yet they left her with that feeling of being untethered, with no clear direction or plan. She felt paralyzed, and the feeling was alarmingly familiar: *Now what?*

Thoughts swirled behind her blank, staring eyes, her hands hung limp, her feet inside dirty sneakers were planted on the sidewalk like they were glued down. People rushed by, bumped into her, cursed at her, offered her drugs, asked her for money, pinched her bottom; and still Janie stood without moving.

A child's whining complaint brought her back, grounding her to the present.

"Why can't I have another candy, Mom?"

She watched the mother shake her head, vexed and impatient, and respond, "It's almost dinner time! Fine. One more, and that's it. Is that clear? I mean it this time. Okay?"

The little boy nodded with a grin that said, *whatever you say, mom, just give me what I want*. He looked up into her exhausted, stressed face with wide innocent puppy eyes, wrapped his arms around her leg and said, "I love you, Mom."

His mother instantly melted. She gave him a tight hug, said, "Aw, love you to the moon, little man," and gave him three candies. Janie watched them walked on down the street, holding hands.

She turned and went back to the warehouse. She would start by telling Debbie and Will about Matt and Nicole; and then figure out her next move.

When she opened the door, she was met by the sight and sound of a celebration. There were a lot of people in the warehouse; Janie lost count at ten. It was also oddly warmer inside the vast open space, at least just inside the door. She saw Debbie standing with a group and approached her. As Janie came closer, she saw the reason for the warmth. They were standing around a large, rusty steel barrel in which a hot fire burned.

"Jenny! Hey, guys, this is Jenny, one of our roommates, a master of the panhandling universe and, also, an amazing storyteller!" Debbie announced to the whole group.

Most of them ignored her, some looked up briefly, and a couple waved halfheartedly before turning back to their conversations.

"Hey, Deb, can I talk to you?"

Janie tried to give her arm a gentle tug, but Debbie shrugged her off and said, "Later, okay? We're having a party, isn't it great? Joe over there came into a little money, something about a new benefactor, and he decided to share the love; and Will and I offered up our place. It's gonna be a good night! Introduce yourself around, everybody is really nice. Isn't it cool?"

With that, Debbie turned back to the others warming themselves around the fire.

Janie stood in the circle, listening. They were discussing the merits of living out here on the streets as squatters, making their own way and taking what was rightfully theirs versus going back home to live with parents in tedious, noxious suburbs. Voices passionate, most of them called their families "the establishment" who sold their souls to the almighty dollar. They called this life "free" and "gritty, but real" and swore they would die on the street before ever taking a job for "the man" and being a servant to his materialistic gluttony.

Janie listened as one of the older ones spouted quotes that led to more ardent and intense discussions.

"'*It is preoccupation with possessions, more than anything else, that prevents us from living freely and nobly.' Henry Thoreau.*"

"Yes!" one of the young men yelled. "It's just stuff, and stuff holds you back from living your real life." The others cheered and gave that statement a few minutes' discourse.

"'*Experience demands that man is the only animal which devours his own kind, for I can apply no milder term to the general prey of the rich on the poor.' Thomas Jefferson,*" the philosophical one intoned, to more applause and comments.

"'*We tend to forget that happiness doesn't come as a result of getting something we don't have, but rather of recognizing and appreciating what we do have. Frederick Koenig,*" he continued as soon as the conversation from the previous quote began to die down. The rest approved of this statement by clinking their beers and discussing all they had right here on the streets with likeminded souls.

Janie stayed for a while since it took her mind off her own looming dilemma; but then bored of the diatribes and left the warehouse.

She wandered aimlessly for an hour. Her thoughts swirled in her head, none finding purchase; and when she felt the first shakes overtake her, she panicked. She was far from the warehouse, and she knew where this was going to go. She had to find a pop quickly.

Looking around, keeping her terror at bay, she realized she did not know where she was. The block she was on was abandoned, dark, seedy with burned-out empty windows, and no sign of life.

She hugged herself and spun in a slow circle, searching for anything familiar. Finding nothing, she walked down the street, listening hard through her tremors for any sound of people gathering. She was concentrating so hard she did not notice the group of men who fell in behind her silently, until one of them stepped in front of her.

"Hi, little girl."

He spoke in a menacing whisper. She startled, looking up, and was suddenly surrounded. Hands touched her, rubbed her, grabbed at her everywhere at once.

"No!" she said, as loudly as she could through teeth chattering in fevered fear. She twisted her body to stop the touching and try to get away, but the men just pushed in tighter against her.

"Looks like Little Girl needs something," the same threatening voice said.

"I got just what you need, Little Girl," a voice behind her said; and she felt one of them push himself against her.

"No!"

Her voice was feeble, and they laughed. An arm went around her neck, holding her, and she felt someone fumbling with the button and zipper on her blue jeans. Then they were down around her ankles, and she felt fingers groping.

Looking around wildly, she spotted someone walking across the street.

"Help! Please," she managed to croak through the strangle hold; but the person walked on without even a sideways glance.

She felt herself being dragged towards an alley, ankles held in place by her own pants. The men were hooting with anticipation, rubbing and pinching her as they went. Just off the street, they threw her on top of black bags of garbage piled against the brick wall. While the others held her down, one of them undid his pants and lowered them, approaching her with gleaming yellow teeth grinning. He positioned himself on top of her.

They were so focused on watching, the crunch of tires slowing down on the trash-littered street did not get their attention. The flashing blue and red lights did.

"Shit! Hit it!" one of the men yelled and they all scattered, the one pulling up his pants as he ran.

Lying on the garbage, her entire body shivering and shaking, Janie wrapped her arms around herself and cried.

"Hey, you okay? Did they..."

A flashlight in her face made her put her hand up to shield her eyes. Two uniformed police officers stood over her. The shorter one bent over, took her arm, and lifted her to her feet.

"Want to pull up your pants?" he said, flashing his light over her body, as they both watched.

She bent to pull at the jeans, the flashlight lighting up her naked bottom half, and fell weakly back onto the garbage bags.

"Come on, up you go, miss." The same officer hauled her up to standing again. "What the fuck are you doing out here anyway? Wait, was that a trick we interrupted? Maybe a little business deal you made to get some smack? The way you're shaking, it sure as shit looks that way."

"No," Janie said, finally getting her pants on and secured around her waist. "I went for a walk and got lost."

"Another lost one, Jim," the taller police officer chimed in. "You're all fucking lost down here these days."

"Can you please just tell me how to get back to the Bowery? I can find my way from there."

"Hey, this one still has manners," Jim said.

"Give it time," the other said. "Do you want to go to the hospital? Rehab, maybe?"

"No, please, I just need to find my friends."

"There aren't any 'friends' out here, girly. Just a bunch of junkies like you. Fine, walk up that way six blocks, turn left; that'll get you back. Watch out for those guys and all the other ones just like them between here and there, girly."

Janie mumbled her thanks, and a half hour later was safely back at the warehouse with a needle in her arm.

When Janie came to in the morning, she was the first one awake. Leaning up on her elbows, she looked around at the prone forms scattered through the room. The fire had gone out, but warmth radiated from the trash barrel, and she rose to her feet and went to stand next to it.

"Hey, Jenny," Deb's voice came from behind her.

Janie turned and saw that Debbie was curled up between two young men, looking pretty cozy. The group of three rose unsteadily, and one of the men got the fire going quickly. Will and four others joined them, huddled together for warmth.

"Where is a quote about the luxury of being warm when you need it?" Will said, shivering.

"How about, 'The beauty of Winter is that it makes you appreciate Spring'?" one of the other young men said. "Not sure who said that, other than my grandmother, but right now I could use some Spring."

"Jenny, let's get some coffee at the mission for everybody, okay?"

Another voice from across the gray cold room, deeper and more authoritative, spoke. "Fuck that, I have enough money still to buy a cuppa at the deli for everybody. What do you say?"

"Joe! Hey, you are the man!" the others said in chorus.

Joe came to join them at the fire. As he pulled a few neatly folded dollar-bills out of his pocket, Janie looked him over. Dark brown hair that came down to his shoulders, just brushing his olive-green army coat; his mustache and beard were trimmed and peppered with gray; his teeth were straight and white inside a mouth etched with smile lines, matching the crow's feet next to his light brown eyes; he wore leather boots under his jeans. While all of the others were gaunt, overly thin and jittery, Joe looked fairly well-rested and relaxed.

He handed the bills to Debbie, looking up and catching Janie's scrutinizing gaze. "Hi, I'm Joe. I remember you were here last night for a little bit. You didn't say much, even when Fred was expounding philosophically on the merits of the situation we find ourselves in here on the Lower East Side. So, what's your story?"

Janie did not respond. Joe smiled and said, "Ah, a girl who needs a cup of coffee to get her engine going in the morning. I can totally relate. That's fine, we'll talk later."

He walked away to a corner to relieve himself as Janie and Debbie stepped out into the fresh, sunny morning.

"Hey, where is Nicky?" Deb asked, just noticing her absence.

"She left with some guy who called himself Big Bobby. She said she was tired of all this, and last I saw, they were heading up to Times Square."

"Oh boy, good luck with that," Debbie said, her head shaking. "That does not usually end well. If it did, I would be up there myself. She's not wrong, this does all suck."

"Philosophy Fred would not agree," Janie said, earning a friendly shove and laugh from Debbie. She almost told Debbie what happened to her last night and thought better of it. What could she do or say anyway? Janie should have known better than to wander by herself, and she was here and safe now. She rammed the memory deep, shuddering once as they walked into the deli.

It turned out that Joe had enough money for pizza, beer, and plenty of smack for everybody to put in their veins. Janie noticed that he did not take the needle himself; although he did drink up some beers and take hits of the joints they passed around the fire that night. The chatter was mostly a continuation of last night's debate about the state of the world ("A corrupt, debauched and unscrupulous mess") and the state of New York City ("Cockroach-infested, diseased-rat ridden, polluted, and dangerous for the free-spirited soul").

Janie mostly nodded her head in agreement when someone looked at her for her opinion, until Joe pointed directly at her and said, "What about you, Jenny? What brings you down to this bastion of the lowly dregs of humanity?"

"Long story," was all she said.

"Lucky for us all, we have nothing but time. And I don't know about everyone else, but I love a good story." Joe folded his arms, with a look of expectation and a congenial grin.

Janie felt cornered, not enjoying the sudden spotlight of attention. She knew she had to say something, so she started with, "I grew up in Forest Hills."

Groans of "poor little rich girl" and "must be nice" came from the others until she added, "Not that part of Forest Hills. We had a rent-controlled apartment near the projects. My father works at Alexander's. I had a brother..."

At this she choked a bit and then corrected, "I *have* a brother; at least I think I still do. He left a while ago; I haven't seen or heard from him in years. I started taking classes at N.Y.U., but I didn't really connect with anything. Got lost one night and wound up here, with Deb and Will."

Debbie and Will lifted their cans of Schlitz in a toast as she finished, "And that is the whole ugly story."

Joe smiled at her and said, "I'm not sure that is the whole story, but we'll let you off the hook for now, Jenny. So, gang, anybody up for a walk? See what's happening out there in our little slice of heaven?"

More groans from the group made him laugh. "Come on, it's a beautiful day in the neighborhood; won't you be my neighbor? I promise we'll be back in time for supper. Might even pick up a little something fun for later. Jenny, I volunteer you to represent this fine group out there; someone has to do it."

The others laughed and pushed her towards the door behind Joe. "Bye, mom and dad! Don't worry, we'll be good while you're out. Have fun!"

He held the door open as she stepped through, bowing gallantly with that friendly grin. Out on the street, he said, "Should we head over to Washington Square Park, see what's happening over there?

She shook her head vehemently. She did not want to chance running in to Rhonda again.

"Oh, okay, how about St. Mark's Place? Maybe check out Thompkins Square Park. It's a nice night, there will be a lot of people out."

She shrugged, and he took that as agreement. As they headed north and east, he looked at her and said, "Jenny, you don't really seem to fit in with the rest of that crew. They are embracing this life on the streets; you seem to be kind of floating through, biding your time. What are you really doing here?"

"Neither do you, Joe," she responded, a bit more sharply than she meant to. "You're older than everybody, you're wearing nice duds and you don't hit the needle. What are *you* really doing here?"

She stopped to wait for his answer.

"Oh, I'm a bit lost, too. My life, such as it was, kind of went to shit and I am at loose ends. I lived on the upper West Side for a while but heard about the action down here. So here I am, end of story."

"I'm not sure that is the whole story, and I am *not* letting you off the hook, Joe; if that is even your real name."

"Suspicious, wary and mistrustful. I like that in a girl," he said, chuckling. "Let's head over to the park, maybe I'll tell you all about it."

He was right, the streets were packed with people enjoying the fresh night. Despite her skepticism about Joe, she was glad to have company. After last night, she was not planning to wander much by herself. As long as they stayed out in public, she was not too worried about Joe attacking or hurting her; and so, she let her guard down and began to relax a bit.

"Do you know much about the history of St. Marks Place?" Joe asked her. When she shook her head, he continued.

"Number four, right there; the Hamilton-Holly House. The widow of Alexander Hamilton lived there for a while. This very mainstay avenue of the punk cultural revolution was once an upscale and desirable address. That was back in the 1830's I think, maybe 1840's.

"And before that, Peter Stuyvesant owned all of this area when it was farmland, around the 1650's. He had his own private chapel right on the site where St. Mark's Church was later built. His remains are actually in a vault there. The church and The Bowery, which Stuyvesant named for the old Dutch word that meant 'farm,' are the only remnants left after the city began its planning in the early 1800's. Pretty funny to think of this as upstate, but that is what it was way back then. They planned a pretty intense grid which included a marketplace, but that was scrapped in order to make the residential area even more dense. Then a descendent of Stuyvesant donated land to create Thompkins Square Park, named after the vice president and former governor of New York. His remains are at St. Marks Church, too."

Janie found herself warming to his stories. It was like people-watching, only she needed to use her imagination instead of her eyes.

"Around the 1850's, just after the city took over this part of the island and began building up the grid of streets, immigration to New York exploded. The Irish, who were coming in droves to escape the famine, mostly settled in Five Points, which is now Chinatown; but the Germans all landed here in this neighborhood. It was even called *Kleindeutschland*, Little Germany, for a long time. All the fancy homes were turned into boarding houses and tenements, and were packed with so many people, they had to take turns sleeping. They did not fare well during the cholera epidemic; I can tell you that."

"How do you know all this?" Janie asked with some awe. "Are you a history professor or something?"

Joe laughed before he answered. "No, just a history-obsessed..." He caught himself, hesitating for a fraction of a moment. "...guy who spent too much time in the public library as a kid," he finished.

Janie caught the pause and filed it away for later. She was hoping he continued, so she did not say anything.

"Want to hear more or am I boring you to death?" he asked. She nodded and he began again.

"Look at number 12 St. Marks, see that cement inscription? *Deutsche-Amerikanische Schützen Gesellschaft*, was a German beer club for men. But things around here really changed in the early 1900's, after a huge disaster. The neighborhood families went on a Sunday church outing on a steamship on the East River, and it caught fire. Over a thousand men, women and children died onboard. There's a memorial stone to those children near a playground in Tompkins Square Park. You know, I've never actually seen it, maybe we'll look for it when we get there. So, after that, other immigrant groups took over the area, including Leon Trotsky who lived at number 80, right over there."

After that, Joe fell silent as they approached the park; but it was a companionable silence and Janie began to look around more closely. Just like last time, there was a balance of hippies and punks and homeless people, sitting on stoops or standing in small clusters expounding on theories about the state of the world and politics. As they walked into the park, the strumming of guitars and pounding on drums wafted through the air. A lonely saxophone wailed from one direction; a soft rock song floated in from another. It was like changing the radio stations on a dial, with some of the tunes fading as others took over.

Something about this area always pulled her thoughts towards her brother; and she was startled when Joe said, "What did you say your brother's name was? What was he like?"

"I didn't say his name; and what do you mean 'was'?" Janie became instantly suspicious of Joe again and stopped walking.

"Whoa, sorry," Joe put his hands up in apology. "I didn't mean to upset you; not really sure why I thought of that. Maybe it's all these guys hanging out here. I mean, look at them, right? Who are they, where did they come from, why are they here, you know? Kind of made me connect to what you said about him."

Still wary, Janie looked even more closely at the young men around them. Each face seemed to tell a story of sadness or strife or purposeless wandering or unfettered elation or utter abandon. Her eyes settled on a bearded one, barely out of his teens, sitting on a nearby bench and staring aimlessly around.

"See that young one, with the scraggly beard?" Janie said. "He got in a fight with his father just last night. They live in Staten Island, in the neighborhood called Tottenville with all their fellow *paesanos*. His father is low level mafia and is ashamed of his hippy son. The other mafiosos call him *'fricchettone'* which means freak; and last night at the dinner table, his father got up, pulled a pair of scissors out of his pocket, grabbed him by the hair and tried to cut off his beard. The kid ran right out of the house and took the free ferry to Battery Park and walked here. Now he is trying to figure out what the hell just happened and what he is going to do next."

When Janie stopped talking, she looked at Joe and found him staring at her in astonishment.

"What? I like to tell stories, too. It's just that mine are made up instead of historical facts. I mean, it could be true; we'll never know."

"But maybe we will know," Joe said.

He walked over and began to talk with the young man. Janie stayed where she was and watched. After about ten minutes, Joe pulled a couple of dollars out of his pocket, handed them to him and came back to where Janie stood.

"You weren't far off. He's Jewish, from Long Island, dropped out of college in his first semester, got in a fight with both his parents," Joe told her. "You're good at that," he added with admiration.

For some reason, that made Janie feel good about herself, and a bit better about Joe. For the next couple of hours, they wandered the park; and Janie made up stories about everyone who caught her eye.

A homeless, very old man had once been a multi-millionaire who lost his entire fortune on one hand of poker; a weeping young girl, sitting alone in one corner of the park, just found out she was pregnant a week after her boyfriend dumped her for her twin sister; two men sitting together were having an intense discussion, which Janie decided was caused by one confessing his love for the other who was fighting his desires and trying to live a straight life in Christ.

Joe laughed, shook his head and generally enjoyed the storytelling; until he turned to her and said, "This is so good, you have some imagination. What about me, Jenny? Come on, tell me my story."

Janie looked into his face, undecided about whether or not he was joking. His smile was friendly and expectant and curious. She took a small breath before beginning.

"You're divorced, obviously; fairly recently, too. You still have a faint mark on your ring finger, and you're well-fed. No kids, but you lost your really nice apartment in the settlement and decided to hobo it for a bit because you don't really know where you want to go next; and you like adventure. You grew up in New Jersey, played football in high school and barely passed your classes, except history, of course. Married your high school sweetheart, and we see how that turned out. Drank some and smoked some pot, but not enough to get lost in it all. Your wife threw you out because you kept going back to your old neighborhood to hang with your boys and wouldn't grow up. You have a pretty good job, or *had* a pretty good job, that's how you have money to throw around. Not a lawyer, too nice and too friendly. Not an accountant, too loose with money; or a college professor, you already said. Also, not in construction with those clean hands...wait, you're a cop!"

Janie suddenly backed away. "Are you a cop? Are you a Narc?"

The emotions on his face were startling in the rapidity with which they changed: shock, then self-anger, then an attempt to laugh off what she was saying with an appeasing smile; and finally, a bit of alarm and dismay.

"It's not what you think, Jenny! Come back to the warehouse with me and we'll have a good laugh, hit that needle you all love, and drink the night away. You're a good storyteller, Jenny, I will give you that."

While he was still talking, she spun around and ran. For a moment, he stood, undecided about whether to chase her; then he turned and walked quickly in the other direction.

Janie stopped to catch her breath when she realized he was not following her. Moving into the dark shadow of an abandoned store front doorway, she tried in vain to slow her racing thoughts. Joe, which was likely not his real name after all, was a cop. He was casing the warehouse, getting ready to bust it. All the kids there were going to jail. All except her;

because she wasn't there, and they would not be able to find her, and they thought her name was Jenny. Did she owe Debbie and Will for taking her in when she was lost, and all messed up? That would mean she should at least go try to warn them. Or were they going to get what was coming to them for hooking her on junk and fucking up her life? The debate swirled in her staggered mind, finally settling on the old familiar and unwelcome question: What now?

She decided to try to warn the other kids, and then take off. They were almost certainly very high by now; she herself was beginning to feel the shakes coming on. So, they would not believe her and even if they did, would not be able to respond with any decisive self-preservation. But that was not in her hands; once she told them, she was done with any obligation she might feel. Then she needed to find a safe place and some junk to quell the growing earthquake inside her. Tomorrow she could begin to figure things out.

Decision made, she walked quickly down the street towards the warehouse. Foul catcalls, kissing noises and whistles came at her from out of dark corners, startling her; and she began to run. Janie was out of breath, blowing hard and shaking as she rounded the corner to the door of the warehouse. She almost ran into the cop car that was parked diagonally across the sidewalk, blocking the entrance. Its red and blue lights were spinning, casting bright flashes on the front of the building. Four other police vehicles, including a paddy wagon with its rear door flung open, stretched down the block, their lights spiraling in dissonance and turning the world in front of her into an eerie imitation of that night at the club that had led her here.

It froze her completely, paralyzing her, until Debbie's scream pierced her brain. The police officers were inside the warehouse yelling for the kids to freeze, and in her mind, Janie saw them with their guns drawn, handcuffing the drugged and panicked group, and dragging them towards the street. When the door of the warehouse banged open, an officer in plain clothes was backing out, pulling a struggling Will towards the paddy wagon.

Janie gasped as she recognized him. *Joe!*

As if he had heard her, he looked up and caught her eye.

"Jenny, get over here!"

She turned and ran.

Making her way back to Avenue B, she headed north, not stopping until she was just past Thompkins Square Park. She collapsed in a hard-breathing heap on the corner. Leaning on the overflowing metal trash can next to the stoplight pole, she put her face into her hands and wept. Loud sobbing tears ripped out of her.

The past couple of days welled up and overwhelmed her. She cried so stridently, so loudly and so painfully, that she alarmed herself. Yet, she could not stop. Her body was so wracked with clamorous aching agony that she thought it might never end. She moaned, howled, cursed, and wailed unintelligible words, rocking herself like she had as a little girl alone in her room.

Interminable time passed until the sobs quieted a bit. She was still weeping and whimpering when she felt a hand on her shoulder.

"Hey, hey, little one. Hey, now, what could be this bad?"

The kindness in the voice was an instant salve; Janie hiccupped and sniffed a few times, wiping her eyes on her sleeve before looking up. A couple was standing over her, benevolence and compassion radiating from them and blanketing her in warmth. Janie's thin face, swollen and unhappy eyes, and turned-down mouth pierced them.

"I'm Kathy and this is David. We own this café right here behind you. Come in with us, have a cup of coffee or something. It will make you feel better."

"Have a bowl of Kathy's famous vegetarian chili," David said. "Manna for the soul; at least that's what everyone says."

Janie looked down at her dirty shoes and sniffled quietly, "I don't have any money."

"On the house," David said. "We never let anyone go hungry at the Life Café. Come on in...what's your name?"

"Janie," she responded.

"Janie! Come on in, Janie! Get some hearty food in you and meet the gang."

It felt so good to hear someone say her real name after all this time. She stood up a bit wobbly, shaking and beginning to get feverish. As they each took one of her elbows to steady her, Kathy and David exchanged a knowing look over her head.

Inside, a bustling and buzzing energy engulfed them as they walked to one of the few tables that had an empty seat. David went to get a cup of coffee for Janie, as Kathy introduced her to the others at the table.

"Janie, welcome to the Life Café!"

"Hi, Janie!"

"Hey, Janie. You look like you could use a bowl of Kathy's famous chili!"

This made her laugh in spite of herself, and she answered, "That's what I heard."

Hearing her name over and over again in this positive atmosphere and with welcoming love built her up in a way that chili, no matter how good, never could. She quelled her feverish quivering, but she knew it was a temporary repression, and the earthquake would come back with a vengeance, sooner rather than later. Sipping the strong, rich black coffee, feeling its warmth spread down into her body, she looked around the large room.

The first thing she noticed was color. It was everywhere, splashing and wiggling and cavorting up the walls, across the floor and even on the people themselves. Paintings of fantastical animals played harmoniously with abstract wire and metal sculptures of towering heights and vibrant hues.

All the men and women seated at the tables wore tie dye, or Kente-patterned dashikis with matching caps, or multi-colored flowy dresses. They were chatting amiably, drawing directly on the tables with colored pencils and chalk, and shoveling food into their mouths.

Janie had never seen anything like it. She knew she should feel overwhelmed at this vivid, dazzling, lively oasis in the darkness; but found herself awed instead. She looked at each of the people around the room, and found herself beginning to wonder about their stories, when her thoughts were disrupted by a tinny repeating noise.

A man in a long bright green skirt and Army boots climbed onto his chair, clinking two forks together to get everyone's attention. The chattering in the room diminished and it became silent, the air pregnant with expectant energy. Janie did not know what to think, but sat up straight, holding her coffee mug in both hands, and waited with everyone else.

He looked around slowly, giving every pair of eyes a personal moment. He seemed to hold Janie's for an extra beat, smiling benevolently as if he knew about her; knew *her*. She could only muster a small, exhausted smile in return.

Long but comfortable moments passed, until he raised his hand, palm up, and opened his mouth to speak.

"Brothers
Brothers, brothers, brothers
And
Sisters
Sisters, sisters, sisters
The very air is alive
Vibrating
Beating as a heart beats
Can you feel it knocking?

Let it in
Let it in
Let it in
I say
It calls to you
It connects you
It makes you
Feel
What does it mean?
To feel
To feel the air
To feel love
To feel what
Your brothers and sisters feel
Their feelings
Are your feelings
Their air is your air
Their love is your love
They
Are you
My
Brothers and sisters

He sat, as the listeners let his words sink in. Raucous applause broke out, amid yells of "Yeah, Sparrow!" "We love you, Sparrow!"

Janie sipped her warming coffee as they cheered, just beginning to relax and feel some sense of hopefulness, when the first earthquake struck her. The ceramic cup flew out of her hand and crashed onto the table, breaking into several pieces.

Only the young woman sitting right next to her heard the clatter through the merriment, and put her hand on Janie's back, which was beginning to spasm. She turned her head and whispered to two young men, who stopped clapping and nodded their heads. The three of them helped Janie up and gently walked her out the back door into the dark alley.

"Hey, Janie, can you hear me? We are going to give you a little pop to steady you out, okay?"

Janie forced her shivering head to nod assent, tears leaking down her cheeks at the betrayal and shame of her craving. They sat on overturned plastic milk crates and one of the men pulled out his works while the other used a Bic lighter to melt the powder on a spoon.

The young woman held Janie in a comforting hug, murmuring, "It will be okay. We get it; all of us. Right, guys?"

They both nodded, as they tied the rubber tube around Janie's upper arm and slid the needle into a vein. Janie felt relief flood over her, and through tears managed to whisper, "Thank you," before her chin rested on her still heaving chest.

When she became conscious a short time later, she found herself leaning into the arms of the young woman. The men were gone; and the rocking and comforting motion made Janie fight to control the sobs that threatened.

"I want to stop," Janie said. "I want all of this to end, and I need to find a way out, but every time I try it's too hard and it hurts and the only way to make the pain stop is to..."

"I know all about that, Janie. I've been clean for a couple of months, and it wasn't easy. Still isn't. My name is Julie, by the way; although everyone calls me Chupa, like that new lollipop. You know, Chupa Chups? It's pronounced *chooo pah* because the candy comes from Spain, originally. Have you heard of it?"

Janie nodded her head, leaning into Julie's warmth.

"The funniest thing about Chupa Chups is their ads. '*Smoke Chupa Chups*' and '*Stop smoking, start sucking*' and '*Sucking does not kill.*' They're trying to get everyone to quit cigarettes and start eating more candy."

At this, Julie laughed, and Janie let out a little giggle herself. She found Julie's inane chatter distracting and comforting.

"That's better!" Julie exclaimed. "Hey, do you have a place

to crash? A bunch of us hang out in a warehouse a few blocks from here. It's pretty nice, actually; there's no heat but we use the offices for apartments so there is some privacy. You can stay with me until you get back on your feet. I would love to have some company."

"I would love that," Janie whispered with genuine gratitude.

The warehouse was huge, several stories tall, and it seemed like there were a lot of people living there. Everyone welcomed Janie and introduced themselves as soon as she walked in.

Some of them were messengers for the businesses nearby, sharing a couple of rusty bikes to make their deliveries. A few were musicians who got together around the garbage can drum fires to jam, before heading out to look for money-paying gigs. There were twosomes that lived together in their office spaces, including one married couple that was expecting a baby, and two men, one of whom was suffering severe symptoms of that same disease that took Matt to the hospital.

Julie showed her the place she had put together. It was like a tiny studio apartment, with a hot plate for its kitchen, a rickety table with two folding chairs and a Queen-sized mattress on the floor. The hot plate was connected to a long orange extension cord that snaked under the door and disappeared across the warehouse floor.

"We are pretty lucky here. Most of the other warehouses don't have electricity and working toilets. There is even a shower, although it's mostly lukewarm at best. It's a matter of time before they shut off the power to this place, everything around here is being sold to big money investors; but for now, it's home sweet home!"

It turned out that Chupa was also Julie's stripper name. She got ready late that night to head to the Ambrosia Club for her shift, donning fishnet stockings and impossibly high, clear plastic heels. She blew Janie a kiss and said, "See you in the morning, roomie!"

Janie wandered to the open central space where the twangs of the guitars and the beats of the drums floated up and disappeared into the air of the high ceiling. She warmed herself for a while around the trash barrel fire, thinking. She needed money, she needed a plan, she needed some clothes since she ran from the other warehouse with nothing, and she needed a hit to stave off what she knew would be coming. As she pondered, the door opened and four teenagers came in, laughing and waving around six packs of beer and a baggie of brownish powder.

"The party is here!" one of the girls hooted. "Max is getting good at picking pockets. The poor sucker never knew what hit him!"

"You hit him," the one she called Max said, laughing. "After you banged into the old man and said sorry with that simpering look, I could have pulled his pants off and he wouldn't have noticed."

"Teamwork!" she responded, giving Max a handshake of such complexity, with high fives and low fives and fists thumping and finger snaps, Janie was impressed.

Max caught her look and said, "Don't worry, Annette will teach it to you." Then he passed her a beer and went to grab his needle works from his room.

When Julie got back hours later, morning light was pushing the darkness to one side. Janie was already awake and, again, thinking.

"Good morning, sunshine," Julie called, slipping off her heels. "I had a great night! The place was packed; must be a convention in town. Check this out!"

She held a wad of one dollar bills out to show Janie. "I think I made like forty bucks in one night. I wish there was a convention every night. Most nights, I get about twenty though; so, it's not terrible."

The neatly folded stack of money got Janie's attention. "What's it like? I mean, at the club. Do you have to make a dance routine or something? Do you have to be really good at dancing? Or do you have to...?" Janie did not want to say aloud what she was wondering.

"Fuck for money?" Julie said it for her, with a nonchalant shrug. "You definitely can, some of the girls do it and make a ton of dough. I only do that if I'm really hard up for cash, like it's been a bad run of a few days and I need food money. Then I'll do a hand job in the bathroom or even a b.j. in the alley. But I don't like to."

Her casual tone astounded Janie, but it also gave her an idea. "Can I come with you tonight just to see? I mean, I need money for everything; and panhandling is no fun either."

"Sure! I'll lend you something to wear. I'll introduce you to Tony, who runs the place, and tell him you're new around here and maybe looking for work. This will be so much fun!" Julie gave her a hug, and then stifled a big yawn.

"I'm going to catch some z's, Janie. Take a couple of dollars and get us both some coffee and breakfast. The Life Café opens early and has really yummy blueberry muffins. Mmmmm, yes, a big warm muffin and a large cuppa regular would be so great," Julie said, laying her head down and immediately falling asleep, with a smile of anticipation.

Around midnight, Janie stood wobbling in a black mini-skirt and a pair of sparkly heels, while Julie, with an amused smile, helped her learn to walk in them. Her hot pink sequined top, which would have been skintight and showing cleavage on Julie, hung loosely over her slim build. They walked the few blocks, Julie keeping a hand near Janie's elbow, just in case; and by the time they arrived, Janie was fairly steady.

Standing outside the door of the club, with its glittering

marquee and black painted windows, a large man chomping a cigar was looking over the patrons who entered the place. One man tried to get past him with drunken swagger and a stream of boozy profanities. The security guard pushed him into the street and told him to get lost.

"Hi, Gus!" Julie tittered coquettishly to the bouncer as they approached the club. Still giving him a flirtatious smile, she whispered to Janie, "Gus can make or break you around here; always be nice to him."

"Gus, this is Janie. She is new around here and wants to see if she might come dance at Tony's place. Is that okay?"

Gus shrugged without looking at them. "Just stay out of the way."

Blowing him a kiss, Julie escorted Janie into the club. The darkness inside was near total. A reddish glow came from spotlights on the sprawling stage, and from the bar where the bartender was mixing up a dozen drinks at a time. The bass vibrated the floor as two girls danced around poles to the current hit, "Never Gonna Give You Up." Men sitting at tables below the level of the stage whistled and stomped and called the dancers over to tuck dollar bills into their G-strings and try to cop a little feel before they danced away, shaking their barely covered breasts provocatively.

"I'm almost up. Stand over here by the dressing room, Janie. You can see everything from there and won't get in the way, okay?"

Giving her a quick hug, Julie bounced off, swaying her hips suggestively through the room as she made her way to the D.J. booth to tell him which tracks to play for her first set.

As soon as the song ended, the two dancers scooped up the bills from the floor, still managing to look seductive as they bent over from the waist and wiggled, to the men's hoots.

The lights went dark as they ran offstage, and then a single red spotlight clicked on again. Julie was standing directly underneath it, her back to the audience, hands clasped in front of her, head slightly bowed. The song started off slow and sultry, and then shattered the quiet suddenly with a jarring crash of cymbals.

Julie turned on the first explosive note, her legs and hips moving in quick and perfect synchronicity with the beat of the music, as the tempo picked up to a rapidly pulsing throb. Her body seemed like it was being moved by the erotic lyrics and seductive beats; and then it seemed like it was producing the music; and then it seemed like it was the music itself. The men went wild.

The first song melted into another, and Julie did not miss a beat. Dollar bills rained onto the stage. Julie rewarded their adoring worship with personal moments and red-lipped kisses sent through the air and sultry passionate gazes. After about twenty minutes, the last song ended on a loud and abrupt note, swallowed by the raucous cheers of the men throughout the club, as Julie gave a sexy wiggle before running off the stage.

She was holding a stack of dollars and breathing hard when she got back to where Janie was standing. Janie threw her arms around her.

"You're amazing! The way you move, like you're part of the music, I could never do that, how..."

"Who's this?" A rough, deep voice came from behind Janie.

"Tony! This is my roommate, Janie. She is new and wants to maybe work here."

Tony looked Janie up and down. In Julie's skimpy outfit and heels, she felt exposed, on display, vulnerable.

"She got no tits. I ain't hiring a girl with no tits. No money in it. Go get some tits and come back and maybe we'll talk. Give it over, Chupa." This last he said with his hand out. Julie handed him the money, and he walked away thumbing the bills.

"I have to serve drinks for a while and then I have another

performance. I'll be here until five or six, do you want to hang around?"

"I've seen enough to know this is not for me, Julie. I'll see you back at the warehouse. You blew my mind though. Wow, you should try out for a Broadway show or something with your skills."

She gave Julie a hug and walked back as steadily as she could on the stiletto heels. It was a relief to get out of Julie's clothes and back into her jeans. She lay on the mattress but could not fall asleep. She could still hear the music, see the men leering at her friend, hear Tony's derision about her body. Julie seemed to thrive on it all; or at least, to be immune to it and go back every night. Janie spent the rest of the night wondering what Julie's life had been like to lead her here; and had fallen asleep just before Julie came in and fell onto the mattress next to her.

Over the next few weeks, Janie sat around the warehouse while the others came and went. Their generosity kept her fed and warm and gave her enough smack to keep her from getting sick. Their obvious caring for a needy human soul had Janie feeling both fortunate and depressed; she had never pictured herself sinking so low and could not see the way out. In return, she tidied up the common spaces and ran quick errands that kept her close to the safety of the warehouse and her new village of support. When she thought about getting a job or even going out to beg for money, Janie's anxieties overwhelmed her to the point where she could barely get out of bed or eat. The others, often Julie or the teenagers, would talk her down until she could get up the nerve to face another morning.

On a rare day when the Ambrosia Club was closed, shut down for twenty-four hours by a raid because the manager did not pay his vig to the local cops with enough of a smile, Julie and Janie hung around the warehouse together.

"We'll have us a girls' day, Janie! We can do each other's nails and hair, and maybe go out and do a little shopping. Don't protest, I'm flush and happy to buy my new best friend a couple of fun blouses. What's your sign?"

Julie pulled her make-up case out and set all her nail polish bottles in a row so Janie could choose.

"Sign?" Janie asked, at a loss.

"You know, your Zodiac sign?"

Before she could answer, Julie bubbled on, "I'm a Gemini. My astrology book says: G is for generous, E is for emotionally tuned in, M is for motivated, I is for imaginative, N is for nice, I is for intelligent. Geminis are supposed to have two personalities, the one they show the world and the deeper one they keep inside. My book says that Geminis are energetic, smart, passionate, and optimistic; glass-half-full and all that. We are the life of the party, but also like daydreaming when we are alone. That is definitely true for me; I never get bored."

"My sign is Cancer, but don't ask me how I even know that. I don't know anything about it."

"Let me get my book and we'll look it up! You will definitely learn something about yourself. Be right back!"

She was back with a dog-eared copy of "Astrology and You" before Janie could say a word. Yep, Janie thought about her friend, energetic and passionate, all right. She smiled as Julie leafed through the well-read pages.

"Let's see...Aries, Taurus, Gemini, Cancer, here it is! 'Cancer is emotional and intuitive; practically psychic...hates small talk and white lies and has a lot going on in its watery depths. Cancer prefers intimate groups of close friends to big events or parties. Incredibly loyal and needs a creative outlet like painting or reading. They can be intense, but they also have a wry sense of humor and are very good at observing people. Learning how to step up for what they believe in is a lifelong lesson for Cancer; and they know that there is more to life than what we see. Aw, listen to your poem! C is for caring, A is for ambitious, N is for nourishing, C is for creative, E is for emotionally intelligent, R is for resilient.' So, what do you think?" Julie said, closing the book with an inquisitive look.

Janie did not know what to think and said as much. "I mean a lot of it rings true, but I don't know about the 'intense with a sense of humor' thing; I'm more the 'dishrag with a sense of foreboding' type. And so far, the only thing I've been ambitious about is begging for money for drugs. I do like that part about learning how to step up. I just hope one day I find something to step up for."

The girls enjoyed their day, and Julie was giddy about Janie trying on every cute top they found at the stores on Broadway near Canal Street.

The next day went back to normal, and Janie was left alone with her depressing thoughts once again. She dragged herself out to do some panhandling. She was good at it, and it distracted her to make up the stories about people who walked by. She had just scored a five-dollar bill off a middle-aged woman who was strolling home in a good mood after meeting her friends for a three-martini lunch, when two girls and a boy, barely teens, approached her.

"Hey! We've been watching you, what's your secret?"

"Yeah, you don't go up to a lot of people, but you always get something from the ones you do ask."

"Come on, tell us how to do it and we'll tell you where to score some really good junk."

Janie smiled at their wheedling and deal-making, feeling like an older sibling who is holding all the cards. She had not felt useful in a while and found herself enjoying it.

"Fine; watch this." Janie searched the crowd, and it did not take long.

"There, this guy right here; the one with that freshly-pressed but obviously well-worn gray suit and Vitalis V7 tonic slicking back his hair. He lost his marketing job a while back and after searching the want-ads in the newspaper, visiting every business he could think of and charming the shit out of them and getting rejected, he finally landed a job that he would not have considered taking before. But he has been at it for a few weeks, and is feeling pretty flush, now that the money is coming in and he can pay the bills again. Watch, and learn."

Janie walked up to him. "Mr. Grayman?"

The others laughed into their hands.

The man stopped, confused. "I think you might be mistaken young lady; my name is Harry Storer."

"Oh! I'm sorry. You look just like my dad's boss. Well, his ex-boss, I guess. He got laid off last month because business has not been so good. He hasn't been able to pay our bills in a while, and we may lose the apartment. I was going to beg you to give him his job back; but, sorry to bother you. Have a good one," Janie said, and turned slowly away.

"Wait, young lady, wait. I can sympathize with your dad. Things are a bit rough all over. Take this, maybe it will help a little. Good luck to your dad, tell him to hang in there." He handed her a folded bunch of dollar bills out of his wallet before walking away.

The others waited until he was out of earshot to cheer. Janie hung around with them for an hour while they attempted to imitate her approach. They were not very good at it, but they did have fun trying; and Janie was entertained by their antics.

"Okay, come with us, we'll introduce you to the guy with the good H really cheap. Do you want to party with us tonight? You are pretty cool for someone your age."

"Thanks, I think. I have to go, though. Maybe another time."

"Cool. Cool. Let's go score and then we need to get some more dough before party time. Leanna here is preggers; we are saving up to help her out of this mess. It's not mine or anything; her cousin got drunk and knocked her up when he was supposed to be watching her and her little brothers," the boy said.

Janie's shoulders slumped. "That's rough," she said.

She looked at Leanna's face, so fresh and still hopeful. She was a thin waif of a girl, her belly just beginning to bump out; and she smiled and said, "It's fine. We're gonna take care of it. And I know better next time Barry comes over; these guys said they will come to the apartment and keep him away from me."

The other two put their arms around her shoulders and waist, and the boy said, "That's right. We are like the Three Musketeers, looking out for each other!"

Janie followed them to a corner not far away.

"There's a dealer on every block around here, but this guy is the cheapest and has whatever you want," the boy said.

He went up to the clean-shaven but otherwise grungy and scrawny young man who was leaning up against the graffiti-covered wall, and made an exchange. Coming back to the group, he quietly said, "Got our pot for the night. He said he has Horse if you want it."

Janie did. She flashed the dealer a ten-dollar bill, quietly said, "H," and walked away tucking the glassine envelope stamped "red devil" in her back pocket. The kids all gave her hugs before she headed back to the warehouse.

Julie was out when she got back to their room. Janie pulled out her works, tied her arm off with the rubber strap, heated up the powder until it bubbled, and then sucked up the liquid into the hypo. Holding it up to her eye, she frowned at it.

"This is it. You're the last one. Then I swear I'm going to stop this shit and get it together."

Pushing the needle into the crook of her elbow, and depressing the plunger, Janie felt heat shooting rapidly up her arm. It spread over her shoulder and down into her chest. Far from the usual feeling of relief that led to blissful and benign relaxation, Janie felt her heart begin to pound alarmingly fast.

Instead of euphoria and calmness, she felt instantly sweaty and weak, disoriented and distressed. She opened her mouth to shout for help and no sound came out.

She began to breathe rapidly and shallowly through her mouth, air whistling in and out of her constricting throat. She fell back thrashing around on the mattress, the muscles in her back and neck spasming painfully.

Panicking, she struggled to her feet with a rattled scream, and bolted directly into the table, which flipped over and sent her flying into the wall. She spun onto hands and knees, and vomited on the floor, the closed door, the chairs, and herself. Shuddering and convulsing with a throbbing headache, she crawled back to the mattress and sprawled face down, hair splayed messily around her head and covered in slime.

Breathing with effort, her tongue a swollen lump of clay, she lay across the bed limp and helpless. She waited, anxious and agonizing, hoping someone would come and save her, rescue her, fix her, make it all stop and just go away, make everything better. But no one came.

Her sight went to a pinpoint of light, the rest blurred and gray. Her thoughts reeled incoherently, while sour sweat covered her, causing her to shiver in her damp clothes.

And no one came. She listened to her own raspy, irregular breath, the only noise in the room, and it was the loudest sound she had ever heard.

And no one came.

And then, finally, vision and hearing and *now* blinked a few times; and went dark.

■ ■ ■

The rhythmic beeps penetrating the blackness were soothing and comforting. Their echoes gently rang from near and far, sounding, almost but not quite, like music. Odd that there were no other instruments harmonizing with the tones. Where was the beat of a drum, the thrumming guitar, the wail of a saxophone to synchronize with this solitary, unending *beep...beep... beep...beep.*

Listening hard, eyes still closed, she could hear a slightly different timbre in some of the tones, a higher or lower pitch; but it still made no sense to her. Far off the sound of people murmuring, conversing in quiet and intimate tones floated to her ear.

A metallic clank, loud and prolonged and much closer, jarred her. She moaned and tried to scratch an itch on her face; but she could not move her arms. Tugging, gently at first and then with growing agitation, she finally opened her eyes: white light, white blanket, white machines, white ceiling tiles, white straps holding her wrists.

Her arms were scraped and scratched, dried bloody scabs in long runnels covering them. Her throat was parched, her tongue was a warm lump, her lips were desiccated and painfully cracked. She called out, but her voice rasped in a whisper she herself could barely hear. She swallowed painfully, trying to bring saliva back, and coughed at the effort.

From behind the white curtain next to her, she heard a voice.

"Well, you're back! I'm glad. Although you were awfully agitated these last couple of days. I thought maybe you were a goner. I'll call the nurse since you can't. If I can just reach this button here; they probably moved it because they got tired of me ringing them. It takes them a few minutes to show up, busy place, this. If I could get out of bed, I'd get you some water, but these ancient legs just don't cooperate anymore. Getting old is not for the faint of heart, I say. The alternative is not good either, of course. You looked so young when they brought you in; I hope you can get your life together. I overheard them say you took drugs. I never did drugs myself, ladies in my day rarely even took drink and I did not even enjoy that. I know, I have been told I'm a busybody my whole life, but I can't really help it. I'm interested in how other people live their lives. I always think I can learn from their mistakes or their example. Maybe I have and don't even know it! Oh, here is nurse Shannon now! Hi! My roommate is awake, and it sounds to me like she badly needs some water. I hope she is going to be okay."

"Thank you, Mrs. Greenbaum," the nurse said, as she walked into Janie's half of the room and poured some water from the pitcher at her bedside. After untying her wrists, the nurse handed Janie a Dixie cup, which she gratefully upended.

"How are you feeling, Jane? Sorry, that's what we've been calling you, Jane Doe, since you had no identification on you when they brought you in. What is your real name? I hate calling people John or Jane Doe, it seems so cold."

She took several more sips from the refilled cup before trusting her voice to work. "My name actually is Jane. Jane Thompson. Everyone calls me Janie. What happened? How did I get here? Am I going to be okay?"

At this last, her eyes welled up and threatened to spill over.

"Tears! That's a good sign. We can probably take you off the I.V. fluids soon. We have to wait until you urinate a couple of times, but it should be fairly quickly now that you're up and drinking again. You were brought in four days ago in rough shape. We saw the needle marks and assumed you had overdosed on heroin, but you were pretty violent, so we were not sure. Maybe you got a bad batch. It was touch and go for a bit, but your vitals look pretty good today, so I think you are through the worst of it. You will probably feel pretty yucky for the next few days, though. The drug counselor will be in later to talk with you about your options. Do you want something to eat?"

Janie did, and she had to force herself to slow down and not shovel the tepid, nearly tasteless oatmeal into her mouth. The first bite threatened to come back up, but sips of hot tea helped settle it; and she was able to finish the bowl of warm mush.

Exhausted, she dozed again; waking up hours later when Mrs. Greenbaum announced, "You have company, Janie dear."

A man stood at the foot of her bed. His hands were clasped behind his back, and he was rocking slightly onto his toes and heels as he looked at Janie. He seemed to be assessing her without saying a word. His oversized glasses sat on his long, thin nose; and his collared button-down shirt was tucked neatly into belted jeans. Still without talking, he reached down and unhooked Janie's hospital chart, and took a moment to skim it. Adjusting his glasses, he lifted the chart closer to his face, nodding his head as he turned the pages.

"I think you need new glasses," Mrs. Greenbaum said from her side of the room, breaking the silence to Janie's relief.

"Yes, I think you may be right," the man spoke. "Janie, I'm Mark. I'm a counselor that works with the hospital."

"A drug counselor; the nurse said you would be in." Janie waited for him to continue. She was not going to give him anything yet, unsure where this was going.

"I help those who are ready to get clean of their addictions and join the world again. Sometimes, when people land in the hospital, they feel like they have hit bottom; they decide they no longer want the life they have been living. It's my job to help those people get back on their feet and find a new path. Are you one of those people, Janie?

His tone, his posture and his demeanor told her he had done this many times. He was confident but stand-offish, as if he, too, was unsure where this was going; but hopeful.

Janie's response was barely a whisper: "Yes."

Instantly, his manner changed. "I'm glad."

These two words were warm, supportive, and genuine. He approached her bedside, pulling up the green vinyl chair.

"Is it okay if I sit and we talk for a few minutes?"

Behind the separating curtain, Janie could almost feel Mrs. Greenbaum waiting for her answer. She nodded, and he sat.

"I will give you some of the details and options, and I'll be back every day until you are released. It shouldn't be that long. Here is my card, you can call at any time, and they will page me immediately."

The card was white stock and very plain; only his name, the word "counselor" and a phone number. She held it in her hand as the lifeline it was.

"I'll need to know some information about how you wound up here, Janie. I know how difficult it can be to talk about it, so I will bring you a notebook later. You can write whatever you want in it, and then tell me which pages to read. When you get out of the hospital, I will take you to a place in Queens."

At the word "Queens," which she had not heard or thought about in a long time, she visibly twitched.

"Okay, it looks like I hit on something sensitive. The halfway house is in Ridgewood; is that okay? It really is the best place for you, but I can look for somewhere else."

"It's okay," Janie said, not really sure if it was. But she listened to what Mark was telling her with the desperation of a drowning woman.

The counselor came back later that afternoon, with encouraging words and a composition notebook and pencils. Janie stared at it for a long time. Just the black and white pattern on the cover brought back so much. Her neighborhood schools and all her friends and everything she had done and seen before this moment played in her mind as if she were watching a movie of someone else's life: her parents' indifference and Greg's loving attentiveness and subsequent desertion; N.Y.U. and happy, hippie Rhonda; and Taylor, her impactful, if brief, fellow people-watcher at Washington Square Park; the kids at both warehouses, especially Julie; the dark and scary nights.

Her memories spiraled out of control. She placed the unopened notebook on the side table and stared at the white wall until she fell into restless sleep.

It was still dark and, thankfully, quiet from the other side of the room, when Janie woke up. She raised the head of the bed, took the notebook in both hands, gingerly opened it, picked up a sharpened pencil. The blank white page with its light-blue lines and red margin stared back at her.

More than anything to quiet that stare, she wrote five words: *How did I get here?*

And the floodgates opened.

She was still writing when Mrs. Greenbaum woke up and started her daily diatribe. Janie was able to make noises that satisfied the elderly lady, while not listening to a word she said.

Janie wrote through breakfast, eating the toast and bacon and sipping her coffee with her other hand. She was still writing when Mark came in to check on her. He waited until she had finished a page and closed the notebook to speak.

"Great news! You're getting out of here tomorrow. Everything is arranged at the halfway house in Ridgewood, including some clothes from the church that should do for a start. I see you've been writing away; that is really good, Janie. When you are ready, you can show it to me; or at least, tell me about it in our sessions." He gave her a warm smile before he left the room.

"I'm so happy for you, Janie! You get a second chance. Not many people get that, and those that do often squander it. My cousin, Darren, now that's a sad story for you…"

Janie tuned her out again and opened the notebook to write a bit more.

Janie stood at the front stoop of the house, as Mark searched for the keys in his pocket. It was a two-story box of a place, with its front door jutting out towards the street at the top of a set of concrete stairs. It was painted off-white, which was the only thing that set it apart from very similar-looking houses that ran up and down the street, mere feet apart from each other. There was no sign on the door to indicate this was a house for the lost, and Janie wondered who lived in the other places nearby.

Mark opened the door and held it for her. The entryway was dim, and the musty odor hit her nose before he even closed the door behind them.

"It's not so bad when you get used to it, Janie. It's meant to be temporary, so no one works too hard to keep it spotless, but it's clean enough. Your room is up the stairs, third door down the hallway on the left. The donations from the church are already in your chest of drawers, and I will show you the bathroom, the kitchen, and the meeting room where we have both group and individual sessions. No one is here right now, because they are all off at work, but they'll be back in a few hours. As soon as they get a chance to wind down, we'll hold a quick group to introduce you. I know it's a lot to absorb, Janie. Deep breath; the hardest part is getting started."

Janie went up the stairs with her paper bag of belongings, and found her room: blue rug and walls, single bed with a single pillow, a lamp on the nightstand, a chest of drawers, a desk with a folding chair, a small closet. The window looked out at the house next door, so close it blocked out the sun, giving her room a dingy aspect that matched the furnishings. It was shabby, sad; but it was all hers, for now.

She took her notebook and pencils out of the bag and put them on the desk. The extra sweater and jeans in the bag, donations from the hospital's lost and found, she put in the chest of drawers; where she found two more pairs of pants, several tops, and a few pairs of socks and underpants that actually, thankfully, looked brand new. Janie lay on the bed, and putting her arm over her eyes, cried herself to sleep.

It was late afternoon when Mark came into her room to wake her.

"Sorry, Janie, but we are going to have the meeting in a few minutes. In the nightstand, you'll find some toiletries if you want to freshen up before coming down."

"Guess I should have locked the door," Janie said, with a dry smile.

"No locks on the doors here, just to keep everyone safe; you know?"

Janie thought she might. She could hear conversations from downstairs as she brushed her teeth, washed up a bit, and ran a comb through her hair. Looking at her face in the mirror, she tried a smile. It did not reach her reddened eyes or do much for the slack skin covering her cheeks, but maybe with time and practice it would look like she meant it. For now, it was enough to quell the queasiness threatening her lunch as she procrastinated before facing what was waiting downstairs. Hunching and releasing her shoulders several times to alleviate the knots, she took a deep breath and headed down.

She found a small group in the meeting room, standing around nursing mugs of coffee and chatting. When Mark saw her, he called them to the circle of folding chairs. They sat quickly, trying not to stare at the new girl.

"This is Janie, everyone. You all know the drill. Please

introduce yourselves, and then we'll have a quick check-in before you get to dinner."

"I'm Mara, hi Janie," the middle-aged woman next to her said with a smile. "I've been here five months, originally from Brooklyn, I work at the drug store down the street. This place has been a lifesaver for me, especially Mark. Let me know if you need anything, okay?"

"Derek," grunted the young man next to Mara, without looking up. He slouched deeply into the folding chair, arms crossed and long legs reaching towards the middle of the circle. "Been here a month, delivery boy. From Brooklyn, too."

"Nancy. I came here just over two months ago. You would not have recognized me. I was as thin as a rail and looked a hundred years old. There's hope for you, Janie. Believe me, I'm solid proof."

There were two other men, Arnold and Joseph, both of whom gave short welcome speeches, and then Mark asked if she wanted to say something to the group. She didn't; but she knew she should.

"I'm glad to be here, I think. Wait, I *am* glad; it's just that I'm reeling a bit. I'm not sure what happened to me, but I hope that with Mark's help, I can have a second chance."

Mark thanked them all for their participation, and then asked if they had anything they wanted to share.

Arnold spoke first. "I need more private time in the morning in the bathroom. Everyone goes to work at the same time, and I can't even take a proper shit without someone banging on the door. The other day, I cut myself shaving because Derek barged in, yelling about his turn."

Derek jumped up with clenched fists and began to cross the circle to get to Arnold. Mara, Nancy, and Joseph sprang out of their chairs and blocked his way, escorting him back to his seat, where he sat breathing hard through his nostrils and giving Arnold a threatening stare. Janie sat in rocked silence, taking in the sudden change in the atmosphere and holding tight to the chair to keep from running. Only the counselor seemed unfazed, which quickly calmed the room again.

Mara leaned toward Arnold. "You know the rules. We each get five minutes to start, and if you have time, you can get another five when everyone else is done. This is not your home, Arnold, it's a temporary arrangement until you figure out how to live on your own. It's supposed to be uncomfortable to motivate you."

Joseph chimed in, "You could get up earlier, you know. No one else is using the bathroom before six. Take a shit at five, and you can have the whole thing to yourself for an hour."

Nancy added, "We're trying to be fair here, Arnold. You're still not so good at that. No one here owes you anything, even private bathroom time. Remember why you're here, why we are all here; and try a little harder to get along, okay?"

Mark gave the silence that followed a few minutes to see if there were any more comments, while Derek still simmered and Arnold sulked. Janie sat, hoping and praying no one asked her opinion, and was relieved when Mark finally said, "Anything else, group?"

"I'm hungry," Joseph said, and everyone chuckled, lightening the mood. Reminding them about the next group meet, Mark added, "Have a good night, everyone," before heading out the door.

Mara came over to Janie and invited her to share dinner. "I remember when I first came, no money, no belongings, no food, no idea what the heck was happening. It's not much, but I am going to make spaghetti and meatballs, and you're welcome to some. Mark will fill you in on your job, everyone has to work, and you'll start day after tomorrow, so a few of us will feed you until then. Just like with the bathroom, we take turns in the kitchen. I'm first today; are you hungry?"

Janie accepted the warm invitation gratefully. The kitchen

was barely big enough for the two of them, so Janie stayed out of the way and watched Mara cook. The shelves held mismatched plates and bowls, one frying pan and a couple of different-sized pots, a hodgepodge of glasses and coffee mugs; and silverware, none of which were sharp knives. On the counter was a tall aluminum coffee urn, its red light on. Mara, her back to Janie, chatted amiably while she moved around the small space. When she was done, she scooped sauce onto the spaghetti, and washed out the pans. She turned and carried two steaming plates, leading Janie to a long table.

"You have spaghetti sauce on your nose and left eyebrow," Janie said. They both laughed as Mara wiped at her face with a napkin.

"So," Mara said, as they sat. "I won't ask you about your story since you have no reason to trust me yet. I hope you will soon, though. Is it okay if I tell you mine? It won't take that long, and maybe it will make you feel more at ease with your own sudden change of direction. I get it; believe me."

Janie, forking a meatball into her mouth, nodded her head in assent as she chewed.

"Good, thanks. You know, I find the more I tell my story, the less hold it has on me. Strange thing, that," Mara said, shrugging. She twirled her fork in her pile of spaghetti, expertly spinning it until she had a neat roll wrapped around the tines.

Catching Janie's amused stare, she laughed and said, "Sorry, it's the Italian in me. One of those things you learn as a kid, and it just becomes a habit."

Mara watched the sauce drip off her fork and onto the remaining pile on her plate before putting it into her mouth and chewing thoughtfully. She swallowed and looked into Janie's eyes. It was a gentle gaze, and Janie felt instantly comfortable. She ate quietly, waiting for Mara to begin.

"I like to start in a different place each time. I guess it's like writing a story, you know? You revise it every time you re-visit it; and, hopefully, it gets clearer as you go. I was married; actually, I still am but only because I'm waiting for him to sign the papers. He was a good guy, except when he wasn't. The last time he wasn't put me here with you all."

As soon as Mara began to tell her story, Janie saw it all unfold like a movie in her mind.

Mara

"My fault, right?! Always my fault. Let me tell you, you bitch; the only thing that is my fault is marrying you. Should have listened to my mother, she was right about you. No good..."

His fist came down heavily on her ear, as she cowered in the corner with her arms covering her head. The ringing blow was just the first since she had made it into the house from the car, where he had been drunkenly harassing her as he drove them home from the bar.

"Whoring..." another blow.

"Stupid...money-hungry...cock-teasing...piece of shit cunt!"

Each word was accompanied by another punch, until at last he lost his balance and stumbled backwards. He banged against the counter, the only thing that saved him from pitching over.

It also gave Mara time to get up unsteadily, drunk herself, stagger to the bathroom, and lock the door while he bellowed in rage and frustration. Shaking, as he pounded and kicked the door, rattling and pulling on the doorknob, she opened the medicine cabinet. Brown plastic pill bottles were jammed haphazardly on the narrow glass shelves amid the Brill Hair Cream and Jean Naté Eau de Toilette. It was hard to read the labels, between the agony in her head from the beating, and the alcohol still muddling her thoughts and blurring her vision.

Finding the Valium, she turned on the faucet, shook a pill onto her hand, and popped it into her mouth. She used the same hand to scoop enough water to swallow it down and then wiped it dry on her dress.

She spilled several more pills into her hand and looked at them for a long minute. While she did, it became very quiet outside the door.

"What are you doing in there, Mara? Come out now, come on, I was just kidding. You know how I get when I see you talking to another guy. It's just because I love you, you know that. Mara?"

She looked into the mirror. Her face was puffy and splotchy, her eyes bleary, her cheeks blackened from running mascara, her long braid pulled apart. She looked back into the pile of pills in her palm, while Ed wheedled and whined a few feet away. He pounded again on the door, but this time, weakly, almost pitifully.

The small pile of white pills waited to see what she would do. Her whole body waited. Her foggy brain finally said *not today, Mara*. This was not the time; she was not ready still.

Instead, she bent down and pushed the pills underneath the door, where Ed retrieved them. She listened to him make his way unsteadily to the kitchen to get some water. It was the last thing she heard before climbing into the tub and sinking onto the cold porcelain, where she awoke in the morning, remembering little of the night before.

She went to the kitchen and got a bag of frozen green beans, putting it against her aching ear and then on her tender shoulder. She knew they had gotten into it again last night, but she couldn't remember why. Ed was passed out on their bed, his legs hanging off one side, his shoes still on his feet. He snorted once and then snored loudly, as Mara went back to the bathroom to shower and try to rouse her misfiring brain. The steaming spray of water helped a little, as did the two Tylenols she dry-swallowed and the first cup of black coffee she chugged, standing next to the Mr. Coffee machine and staring out the window. She almost never remembered how the fights started when she thought about it the next day; but it had been going on for their entire relationship, and she was getting to her wits' end with it.

She loved Ed; and she knew he loved her, too. When he was sober, which was every day until after finishing his shift at the Standard Motor factory, he was sweet, caring, kind; loving, gentle and hardworking. She knew by now if he chugged his first three beers in under thirty minutes, it was going to get rough; and she would quickly start mixing her vodka and sodas to prepare. Once he moved on to vodka, drinking it like water, the other Ed came out: frustrated, mean, jealous and short-tempered Ed who, in fits of rage, used Mara as a punching bag.

Every day-after, especially on a Sunday like today when neither had to leave for work, they would sit quietly eating eggs and toast, and he would apologize and swear off the booze; and every time, Mara believed him. This morning the nagging voice in her head told her, for the millionth time, he was not going to change. As she poured her second cup of coffee, watching the dark brown liquid flow into the mug and white steam rising into the air, she tried to quell the voice; but today, it seemed extra pushy.

What are you doing, Mara? Doesn't this look familiar? Your mom was weak too, and let this keep happening again and again. You saw it, you grew up with it, you cried every time she crawled into bed with you after and begged you to make sure you found a nice man who treated you right. And here we are, look at this now, you following in her sad, helpless, spineless footsteps...

"At least we don't have kids!" Mara said aloud; and heard the voice scoffing at her and saying, *not for lack of trying.*

"What?" Ed said in a dry, husky voice, coming into the room rubbing his dark, messy mass of hair. "Did you say something?"

He looked like an oversized six-year-old, his shirt pulled out of his pants and his shoelaces untied, eyes closed and cheeks ruddy in his handsome square-jawed face. Mara felt herself melt. The voice in her head quieted for the moment, not completely gone.

"No, honey. Want some breakfast?" She got up and he watched her reach painfully over her head to grab the box of pancake mix. When she turned around, she saw tears in his deep brown eyes, mouth in a frown.

"We got into it again." It was half question, half statement. "Damn it, I'm such a fucking asshole."

He put his hand over his eyes and cried streaming tears, his shoulders shaking. Even red-faced and crying, he looked so good. She went to him and wrapped her arms around him, and they cried together.

They tried, over the next few months, to fix things. Couple's therapy, A.A. meetings, long walks in the evenings to replace the other habit. It was good, very good; and Mara found herself thinking again about children. When she brought it up to him, his eyes watered in emotion.

"We tried for a while, babe, and it never worked. But, yes, let's try again. A baby is just what we need; a real family of our own."

For whatever reason, this time it only took a month of trying; sweet, gentle love they made that gave them both hope and peace. She was waiting for him to get home from work that Friday to tell him the news. Dressed in her favorite skirt and top, hair and make-up done, she had a roast chicken and potatoes on the table, which was set with all their matching plates and silverware. Candles, one pink and one blue, waited to be lit, a book of matches nearby. She had bought a bottle of sparkling apple cider to pour into their wine glasses for the toast.

Five thirty came and went. The sky began to darken as the sun's light faded. The glaze on the chicken became milky and gloppy, and the potatoes in the pan wrinkled as they cooled. When it was fully dark, she put away the dinner and the table settings. She had no appetite for food, nor for what she suspected, *knew,* was coming.

She sat in a chair in the living room and waited. She got up and rearranged the fruit bowl on the counter. She took a dry rag, sprayed some Lemon Pledge on it, and wiped the coffee table, the stereo cabinet, and the shelving unit in the tight hallway. Several times, she heard a car come down the block, its headlights shining into their apartment; and she froze. Then it moved on down the street, and she felt both relief and deeper fear.

She thought about leaving. She thought hard and long about leaving, but in the end knew she had nowhere to go. She would not burden her few friends, who thought they had the perfect marriage. None of them had ever hung around late enough for things to get ugly.

She could never show up at her parents' apartment and admit what was happening. The last time she had seen them, to announce their engagement, her father had come after Ed with his fists up, her mother pleading uselessly for him to stop. Mara and Ed had run out of the door, and were halfway down the block before they stopped, gasping and laughing.

"Your old man is something else, baby!" Ed had said, as he put his strong arm around her and walked her back to his car.

She could just get on the subway and go into the city and find a hotel room. It would cost all the cash she had, but if she stayed overnight, he would be sober by the time she got home. But he would panic when he found the house empty. He might take the car and drive around looking for her. He would never find her, but what if he drove into a tree trying. It would serve him right, she thought; but then she put her hand on her still-flat belly and knew she did not want that either.

Still, she decided it was the best option. In the morning, he would be apologetic and then so happy when she told him the news, and he would get back on the wagon.

Decision made, she went into their bedroom and packed a

few things in a tote bag. She thought about leaving a note but decided he either would not bother to read it or would not be able to, anyway. She thought about looking up a hotel in the Yellow Pages so she would have a destination in mind; and then figured she would just find one once she got off the subway. Fear, sadness, insecurity, dread, and anxiety wreaked havoc on her hormone-infused mind; but her new priority, the one beginning to grow inside her, drove her on. With determination, she opened the front door.

Ed stood there with his hand on the knob, reeling from side to side. A sneer grew on his face when he saw her. It made him ugly; Ugly Ed was back.

"Going somewhere, bitch?" he asked, slurring the words. Before she could back up or push past him or say a word, he swung his right arm back and slugged her with drunken strength, right in the belly.

She stumbled backwards to the sound of nasty laughter and fell over clutching herself around the middle. Lying in a fetal position at his feet, she moaned as cramps overtook her.

He aimed a solid kick at her back as he staggered towards their bedroom, saying, "I didn't think so."

Spasms wracked her entire middle, and she rocked back and forth trying to stop them, to stop the pain, to stop what she knew was happening. Sobbing *no no no please no*, as waves of agony and nausea overpowered her, she managed to roll onto her knees and crawl to the bathroom.

She was curled up on the cold tiles when she felt the first gush of blood rushing out between her legs. Knowing the battle was lost, she screamed out her rage and despair and grief and pain.

An eternity later, it was over.

She lay in the crimson puddle, unsure how to move or if she could move or if she even wanted to. Time passed, and exhaustion and despondency made her want to sleep right there. She felt hollow, in every way. Hopelessness, misery, and futility fought for space in her head, until a thought broke through: *She was ready.*

Finally.

It took great effort, physically and emotionally, to get up. The sight on the floor brought back rage and despair, but she was too depleted to make a sound. It took all her strength to hold onto the sink, open the medicine cabinet and find the bottle of valium.

She held it up to her eyes, and through the brown plastic container, could see, gratefully, that it was still almost full. She turned on the faucet and filled a cup with water. Opening the bottle, she shook as many pills directly into her mouth as she thought she could swallow without choking and poured enough water after them to make them go down. She did it again and again until the container was empty. She decided to see what else she could take to make sure the job was done, but as she was searching the shelves, she became woozy and sat down hard on the floor; back into the middle of the mess.

Her head began to spin, then her whole body began to spin. She closed her eyes and lay on the tiles. The cold was now comforting and calming. It felt good, and the last thought she remembered was, *I'm coming baby...*

Janie

"I woke up in the hospital, Janie. I still don't know how I got there, but the nurse did tell me they would not allow Ed inside. Between the blood, the pills, and the scars, they decided I was better off without him. That was five months ago, and I have not seen him since. I hope I never do again. The weird thing is I still love him, but we are toxic to each other, and we are both better off this way. I am still reeling from all the loss, but this place has helped me so much, Janie. If you work the program, it will help you, too."

Janie sat, fork in her hand, the plate of spaghetti and meatballs congealing and forgotten. It took her a very long moment to speak.

"Mara, I am so sorry all of that happened to you! You seem so strong; I never would have guessed what you went through. I hope I can be as resilient; I feel like what happened to you is so much worse than what I did, but I don't know if I will ever come back from it. I just don't know where I'm going, and you seem to have it all together."

Mara came around the table for a tight hug. "You will figure it all out, Janie. I just know you will."

Janie did not sleep well that night. Mara, cowering on the floor while hell rained down on her, haunted her thoughts; as did Mara's story of recovery and strength. Did she, herself, have such strength? If she did, she could not fathom its source and how to tap into it.

Morning came, and with it, her discussion with Mark to plan the next step. He outlined group meetings and individual sessions, told her about her job assignment at the local grocery store, gave her a packet with information on Narcotics Anonymous and took her for a walk to familiarize her with the neighborhood. It felt good, and also odd, this first day of her new, normal, everyday, like-everyone-else, life.

She slept a little more soundly that night, although she had a dream about showing up for work naked. The worst part of the nightmare was that nobody noticed, and she walked around anxiously, just waiting for the first shriek.

She awoke with the sun on the first day of her new job and took her full five-minute turn in the bathroom to get ready. Mara gave her a comforting, encouraging hug as they walked out the door together and turned in opposite directions.

Training at the Bohack's grocery store took a couple of days, and Janie was a nervous new employee. She could not remember the last time she was responsible for anything but herself; and that had not ended well.

By the end of the week, Janie was stocking shelves at the store. It was mindless work and gave her an opportunity to remember how to interact with ordinary, regular people. She got over her shyness with customers asking for the location of an item, and with the other employees, who were friendly, accepting and patient with her.

Hazel, about the same age as Janie, always offered some of the Yodels or Devil Dogs or Snowballs or Funny Bones or Ding Dongs she carried for afternoon break, with a wry comment about her own obesity and the favor Janie would be doing to take one or two or three.

"Skinny as you are, you should eat the whole box," she would say through a mouth full of chocolate, as she ate the whole box herself. Janie would laugh alongside her, politely shaking her head. On the first day, she had accepted a Twinkie but thought it tasted like sugary Elmer's School Paste and had spit it discreetly into a napkin.

Gary and Harry, twins who always worked together, were the entertainment at the store. They finished each other's sentences, told off-color jokes, and were constantly playing pranks on each other to make the rest of the workers laugh. When a bad-tempered argumentative elderly woman came into the store, Harry would tell her in conspiratorial whispers to watch out for Gary, who was a known thief and would steal the teeth out of her head if she got too close. Watching the lady avoid Gary, holding her large handbag close and giving him the suspicious evil eye, was hilarious even to Janie, who thought it was just a bit unkind to the woman. Gary, in his turn, would tell the most unattractive women or a flamboyantly dressed man that Harry had the hots for them. The flirting that followed had them all holding back their laughter with some effort. The funniest, Janie thought, was when they decided to dress exactly the same, and prank a customer by switching places and confusing the shopper until she or he did not know which way was up. The twins made the days more fun.

Jimmy, a young man with brain damage from oxygen deprivation at birth, worked alongside her, unpacking boxes and stocking the shelves. He did not look her in the eye, and when he accidentally dropped a box of items on the floor, which happened daily, he flew into a rage and threw even more.

The first time it happened, Janie was terrified and bolted out of the storeroom, through the long aisles, past the cashier, Ruth, who was regaling her current customer with tales from the old days, out the front door and down the street. She stopped on the corner, panting and panicked, until the assistant manager came out of the store and found her there.

"Jimmy's all right, Janie. He can't help the way he is, and he doesn't really understand much of what's happening around him, but he wouldn't hurt a fly. He's been with us for a few years; you'll get used to him. Just learn to duck when he starts going apeshit. It doesn't last long. Come on now, back to work."

The ancient lady at the register, Ruth, was her favorite. She had lived in the neighborhood for years and filled Janie's break times with stories of New York City at the beginning of the century. Janie found she could sit and listen to Ruth's spirited tales of a life she knew nothing about and could never imagine; until with disappointment, she realized breaktime was over and it was time to get back to work.

Ruth, always smiling and calling everybody "Shuga" or "Honeypie," enjoyed an audience and found Janie to be a very good one. From the first lunch break that they shared in the employee lounge, Ruth entertained Janie with her Deep-South accent and amusing anecdotes; and Janie delightedly soaked them all up.

Ruth

"No 'lectricity, no cars, and not much in the way of running water, neither. My family come up from down south and landed in Harlem, and laws, what a time to be 'live; you young'uns have no idea!"

Ruth slapped her knees with both hands and the smile on her face told Janie she was seeing it all as if it were happening right then.

"'Course it's easy to look back now and say 'oh what happened back then!' But Lawd have mercy, I wish you could really see it how it was. Joy on the street, work for everyone, and the art and the music! Comin' up from where we come up from, we all thought we was in heaven. Up at the Abyssinian Baptist, Reverend Powell used to preach about findin' heaven on earth, and I al'ays thought we did, right there.

"We lived near the Lafayette Theater and I used to love standin' across the street watchin' the stylish ladies and the classy gentlemen gettin' outta they fancy automobiles and walking in there like kings and queens. White folk and Black folk all together; moseyin' and sashayin' into that ritzy place like they didn't have a care in this ol' world. I swear I never seen the like.

"You know that painting called 'Evening Attire" by that James Van Der Zee?"

Janie shook her head and made a mental note to look it up at the nearby library.

"Well, the model for that picture was my very own auntie Vi. That Mr. Van Der Zee sees her walking up the street and says 'I just got to have you pose for me!' It inspired Auntie Vi so much, she became a artist her own self; took instruction from Augusta Savage herself!"

Janie made another mental note and shook her head again

as she realized there was a whole other history of New York she had never even heard of.

"We was just po' folk at first; coming on the train with so many others, right around 1915 if memory serves. Our worldly belongin's fit in two burlap bags. But my daddy and my momma had everything they needed in they heads and they hearts, and hit the ground running soon's we got off that train!

"I was just a little thing, 'bout four when we arrived; and I didn't know nothing about us bein' poor; 'cause there was always joy in our place. Ever' night they was singin' and testimony all up and down the hallway; so many of us so glad to be alive and free! Our first apartment was in one of those tenements; rats and roaches and such a ruckus of babies crying. We had to walk up four flights of stairs, and that is one of my earliest memories 'cause with my little legs it was like climbing a mountain ever'time! But we didn't stay there long, 'cause Daddy got a job right away.

"My daddy worked in the tunnels they was digging back then for the new subway. Them men spent they lives digging through rock, clay, sand, and water; called theyselves 'sandhogs' and it was a hard job they did. I overheard him some nights tellin' momma about men drownin' and being pulled outta quicksand and bein' crushed by cave-ins or almost dyin' from gas that would leak into the tunnels and cause a strong man to just fall right to the ground. Some of those stories haunted my dreams for a long time, I tell you, Shuga! He used to sing me this song at night that the men sang in the tunnels, let's see if I 'member...

"*Oh, Joe! Come on let us get this job done, ugh bam. Oh, Joe! Come on let us get this job done, ugh bam.*

"That was it! Sometimes he changed the words just for fun, *Oh Ruth get yo'self in bed ugh bam,* haha!

"Momma got work sewin,' had her own Singer machine and everything. I used to love watching her hands work the fabric through that bobbin' and hammerin' needle; it was like a song all its own; and it was like magic to me that beautiful blouses and dresses and coats and such could come right out the other side.

"I 'member when we moved into the place I would grow up in; it was right near the park and it had a elevator and the windows were big and bright and all the rooms were sunny and warm; and no more rats and roaches for us!

I was just about fourteen when Momma and Daddy started takin' me at night to the Lincoln theater, named after that president, Abe, who freed my own Grandaddy and Mawmaw; and what a ruckus we raised. All the workin' folks crammed in there to listen to Ma Rainey and Fats Waller. And the dancin,' laws! You heared of the Lindy Hop?"

When Janie shook her head, that old lady stood right up and began to hop herself around the room, kicking her legs out, while the memories ran through her head. "Matty Purnell and Shorty Snowden invented it and there was competitions every week. That is where I met my husban,' my Hubert, and we used to give them other couples a run for they money, I tell you!

"Then bad times happened, everything crashed to a bad ol' end. It seemed at first it was just poor luck a few folk was havin'. But then it was all of us. The theaters closed up, Daddy lost his job, they was no more sewin' work for Momma. It was like someone just pulled a plug and life done changed. Hubie and I got married in the Abyssinian and it gave us a little joy in dark times. Had us a couple of babies pretty quick after, and he thought things might be better outside the city. So we got on the train and come out here.

"Tough goings out here in Queens, too, durin' the Depression and all; but my Hubert al'ays managed to find a way to bring in money. Me and the kids helped out, too. We had us six babies, lot of mouths to feed, and every one of them pitched in, even the littlest one, our baby Jeremiah. It was hard, Lawd knows, hardest time I can remember; but it was also the best of times 'cause we al'ays found time for laughin' and singin.' My Momma taught me to rejoice in the Lawd and find time for joy, and good things will happen. She used to say, 'The Lawd he'p those who he'p theyselves; and she was right!

"Hubert worked at any construction site in the city that would pay him to do whatever they needed. He would get up before the sun and take the subway and just start stalkin' those building sites until he found work; there was so much construction goin' on, all them skyscrapers goin' up. But them was union jobs and they didn't allow no blacks in them unions. Hubie would do the clean-up, the heavy lifting, whatever was asked of him. He came home after dark every night, dirty and sweaty and tired as all get out; but he brought home enough money to keep us from starving."

Each time they shared a break, Ruth would pick up the story right where she left off. Janie felt like she was listening to episodes of a radio show; and sat with an eager look on her face soaking it all in while her cup of coffee went cold, forgotten.

"During those days, the three boys went out together every morning; shining shoes for the rich folk or selling apples or carrying newspapers, whatever they could find. Al'ays brought back a few pennies each day, and some pretty good stories too.

"I 'member one time them boys came home, laughing so hard they was falling all over each other, and little Robert James had wet his britches. They could hardly talk but I finally got the story out of them. They was a man who stopped for a shoe shinin' but he would not sit down on the stoop 'cause he didn't want to get his nice suit all dirty, even though them boys had a nice clean piece o' cardboard for the customers to sit on. He went on and on and on about a speck o' dust on the heel, a tiny scuff on the side where ain't nobody gonna see it, railin' at the boys to shine harder. They said they never worked so hard for a penny and hoped to never again. Used a whole can o' shine on that man's loafers. He didn't want to pay them until he was satisfied them shoes looked better than the day he buyed 'em, and even then he told them if he could give 'em a half-penny he would, never see'd such a poor job of shinin'. Stalked off in a huff and hadn't walked a yard when he stepped in a big steamin' pile of doggy doo right in the middle of the sidewalk. Let out a squawk that would straighten yo' hair and he turned on the boys like they done somethin.' 'Course it didn't help none that they was rollin' on the floor laughing like a bunch o' hyenas. They saw him coming at them and took off for home like they tails was on fire! After that, whenever we saw a angry white man, and in those days they was plenty, we would say, 'there goes another man-ure!' We found funnin' wherever we could."

Janie would check the schedule as soon as it came out to see when their next lunch time together would be; and she would pick Ruth up at the register with an eager, "Lunch break, Ruth!" and escort her to the breakroom to make sure they did not miss a minute. Ruth never disappointed.

"My Junior, the oldes,' he was quite the artist. He made pictures with coal that he found on the street and those pictures still make my heart swell to this day. Mos' of them was drawin's of us making fun after a long workday but some of them were sad enough to break my heart. One of them was of a little boy sittin' in the middle of the street with his head down, lookin' like he was waitin' to be saved or killed by a streetcar, didn't much seem to matter to him. Junior sold those drawings much later to a museum in Harlem that did a exhibit on children's art during the 'Great Depression,"' as they call it now. I was such a proud mama of that boy. He went on to be a real artist, went to Paris and everything; never thought I'd live to see the day!

"Me and the girls found work cleaning houses for those rich folks who didn't lose everything in the crash. Some of them ladies was so nice, even said thank you when we got done and would give us a bit of food with our nickels at the end of the day. I 'member one lady, a little spitfire of a thing; her husband owned some kinda factory and they was one of the lucky ones and I just 'member her being so kind.

"But some of them white ladies, they was just downright mean. Treated us like it was still slave time, barking orders and even raisin' a hand at my girls if they missed a spot of dust. And some of them husbands..."

At this memory, Ruth stopped a moment to take a breath.

"Some of them husbands did not keep they hands to theyselves. We had to leave more than one job 'cause of that. The worst one coulda got me arrested, but I wasn't 'bout to let no man force hisself on my child!

"I had left Letitia, my oldest girl who was thirteen, in the kitchen to finish rolling out the biscuits and took the little girls outside to hang the sheets on the clothesline in the backyard. Them little girls just loved rubbing they faces on those damp wind-sweet sheets, and I had to scold them all the time; but it made me laugh, too.

"Any ways, on that day, I heared a noise coming from the open kitchen door, and it sounded like a scuffle goin' on. First, I thought may be it was the man and his wife, and I wasn't goin' anywhere near that. Then I heard my Letitia sayin' *no* and my head 'bout exploded, and I couldn't get in there fast enough. Near tripped over the laundry basket and scared the little girls to death. The sight I seen I will never be able to erase from my eyes, Lawd forgive me. He had Letitia up on the table, her skirts was pushed up around her and he was trying to get his belt off. The things he was sayin' I won't repeat 'cause ain't nobody should be talkin' to a young girl like that. I grabbed the rollin' pin off the counter and swung it at his back with all my might, and I was a strong young woman back then. It got his attention and he turned around all red in the face, fists balled up like boxing gloves. I brought that roller up between his legs and he hollered like the devil bit him. Guess maybe I done taught him a lesson with that one, 'least I hope so.

"Grabbed all my girls and went out into the livin' room. The lady was sitting on her fancy couch with all her fancy friends holding a cup of tea and when we came charging into the room, she dropped that cup right on the floor. All them ladies was lookin' at me like I done lost my head, coming through the front room like that; but that wasn't nothing 'cause I let loose on her.

'Your man was tryin' to get under my girl's skirts! Ain't no man gonna do that no matter how much we need the money. If I was you, I would start wonderin' how many high yeller babies running around after he got done with the maids you had before we came, and mayhaps the next one should be old or ugly. I will thank you for the day's pay, ma'am, and then you won't never have to see us again."

"I never see'd the color drain out of a face like that; I never see'd anyone turn so white that was already so white to begin with. She didn't say nothing but pulled out her purse and held out a dollar bill with a hand so shaky I thought it might plumb fall off. I almos' didn't take it, nobody never gave me that much for a day's work and I didn't like the idea of taking it after what just happened. But then I did and said, 'thank you ma'am, good luck to you.' And we went on right out the front door like we was guests at tea. After that, I never left any of my girls alone in a room."

Janie thought her own mother would not have survived any of what Ruth had been through or been strong enough to protect her daughter from harm. Her mother certainly would not be telling this story with wonder and awe in her voice the way Ruth was sharing it. It was clear that surviving, making sure that her family survived together, gave Ruth the strength to carry on, to thrive even. Janie's respect for her grew exponentially.

"I heard tell of children leavin' they families and wanderin' the country by theyselves so they mama's didn't have to feed 'em or worry about 'em, thousands of 'em. Junior thought about it for a hot second until I got wind of it and tol' him ain't no way; we was stickin' together come hell or high water! And that was the end of that."

"Somehow, we made it through that tough time. We was one of the fortunate ones, praise the Lawd. Our chil'run did well in school, ever' last one of 'em. Now they's nurses, doctors, teachers; one runs a auto mechanic shop not far from here and one even became a union carpenter! Three of our grands go to Howard University, future leaders, all three. We are blessed, Janie, we are blessed. I lost my Hubie, bless his soul, a bunch of years back; miss that big smile ever' day. I don't need to work for money now, but I do enjoy the socializin' and it gives me a reason to get dressed every morning.

"Lookin' back, I believe it was our faith, both in the Lawd and in ourselves, that guided our good fortune. That, and a whole lotta singin' and dancin'!"

Janie absorbed every one of Ruth's stories like rain on dry grass. At night, some of Ruth's little gems swirled around in her head and she thought about her own life. Once again, as she had after listening to Mara's story, Janie realized her own troubles were on a different scale than those of her new friends. They were inside her and not coming from things outside her control. To her, they had always seemed insurmountable; but maybe, after all, they weren't.

Janie

Over the next two months, Janie began to adjust to her new routine. She found herself jumping up eagerly at the alarm to get ready for work on weekdays. The newfound focus on normal everyday life gave her a feeling of contentedness she had not felt before. Even the meager celebrations they did at the halfway house for Christmas and to ring in 1982 felt pretty great.

On her breaks, as soon as the weather got warmer, Janie walked over to nearby Klein Park, although calling it a "park" was a bit of a stretch. It was just a grassy triangle with painted wood slatted benches facing the street; a perfect place for her to play her old people-watching game, and she relished every minute there.

She watched a beat cop, the same one every day, stop to talk with the homeless men who sat on pieces of cardboard surrounded by their worldly belongings. He was a paunchy middle-aged man with the telltale red-purple nose and cheeks of a heavy drinker; but seemed caring and kind as he gently placed a quarter in a paper coffee cup or chatted up the forgotten people. One day, he brought a pair of shoes, scuffed but clean, to a barefoot, filthy drifter, whose tears of gratitude traced runnels through the grime on his cheeks. Musing from the lack of a wedding ring on his finger and his plump middle, she guessed that he was divorced because of his drinking habits and mostly ate McDonald's sitting in front of the television set in his studio apartment, watching Three's Company until bedtime. He seemed to look forward to this daily social contact with people who appreciated his attention.

A teenager came to the small green space every day at the same time with two feather-tailed Irish Setters, shiny red coats and high-stepping legs showing off their ditzy and delightful personalities. Janie could not help but smile every time she saw them. The boy was tall and skinny, his jeans hanging on his narrow waist. His pimply face was always smiling patiently at the antics of the two happy-go-lucky dogs, as they pranced around at the end of their leashes. Janie guessed he was a paid dog-walker, since most teenagers did not enjoy the chore of walking the family dog. But there was something else in his demeanor and his cheerfulness that made her curious; and one day, as Janie watched, a model-hot petite young woman came running up to him, gasping an apology.

"I'm so sorry, Steve! I got hung up, but I rushed here as soon as I could. I hope I didn't make you miss your orthodontist appointment; your mother will kill me."

Instead of handing her the leashes and sprinting off to the dentist, his smile grew even bigger, and he reassured her. "It's fine, Isabel. They usually run late at the dentist's. The dogs already did their business; I'll walk back with you and then head out."

He walked next to her with his shoulders straight and an elated smile as she chatted animatedly; and Janie realized that he was completely in love with her, in the way only a teenage boy can be infatuated with an oblivious young woman a few years older.

On another lunch break, she watched a boy, around six, pushing his younger sister in her stroller. They were singing the alphabet song together, and she was making adorable mistakes that made him laugh. Janie felt warm love emanating from them and it brought back a strong memory of that same feeling between herself and Greg. It had been a long time since she had thought of him, and she enjoyed the memory with a bit less heartache than usual.

She realized it had been even longer since she had reached out to her parents. This unwelcome attachment to her nostalgic musings bothered her enough that she decided to call them right now before she changed her mind. Her optimistic side thought maybe things would be different now; after all, *she* was different.

Plugging a dime into the pay phone slot, she dialed the home phone from memory: *TW7-0877*. Funny how some things just stick, she mused. The phone was picked up after three rings. Her mother's *"Hello?"* was hard to hear with the vacuum cleaner going in the background. Funny how some things never change, Janie thought.

"Mom? It's me, Janie."

"What? I'm sorry, I cannot hear you. Let me turn off the Hoover."

It became oddly muted on the line as Janie waited for her mother's return. "Better. Now who did you say this is?"

Janie almost hung up.

"It's Janie, mom."

"Oh, Janie. Hello, dear, how are you?" She could have been speaking to any of the neighbors or someone she met in a grocery store, for all of the enthusiasm and interest in her voice.

"I'm fine, mom. How are you and dad doing? It's been a long time."

"Yes, it has! Nothing ever really changes around here, you know. Your father got promoted to floor manager last year, so that is good news. The neighborhood is still the same, but some of your school friends are married already, and that little Benjamin across the street with the handsome big brother just had a baby; I heard he married a girl who is also a student at Cornell. Your little friend Deidre from around the corner has two kids with two different fathers. I heard she started doing drugs and drinking before graduating from high school, got mixed up with a bad crowd."

This last news made Janie very sad; but she supposed if

anyone knew what she herself had been up to the past two years, it would make them sad too.

"Are you married yet, Janie? Are you calling to tell me that I am going to be a grandmother? Because if so, let me tell you I am not that excited. Some women can't wait to be grandmothers at my age, but I am not in a hurry. Raising you and Greg was hard enough. I'm enjoying my life now that I have time to do what I want. This is what you have to look forward to, Janie. You have to find enjoyment wherever you can, like your father and I do. Before you know it, you'll be saddled with a lot of responsibility, and everyone else will come before you."

Really?? Janie thought. She had not known what to expect out of this call and got exactly what she should have figured anyway.

"Not having a baby, not married, so you can relax. Have you heard from Greg at all?"

"Oh, Greg, no, not a word. He probably joined some hippie commune in California and is strumming away on a street corner, asking for money. That boy was almost the death of me. It's a good thing we had you, dependable and a good student. If you're not married yet, what are you doing for money?"

"I have to go, Mom; my work break is over."

"You're working! Good for you, but don't forget to wear makeup to work, dear. Men like a pretty face. Sooner is better than later, Janie; if you wait too long, the better men get all snapped up. So nice to hear from you, dear. Goodbye."

The dial tone let Janie know her mother had hung up. It took her a moment to do the same; and then she walked back to the store to finish out the afternoon.

On another morning while she sat on the bench, a short, plump middle-aged woman came towards her, wheeling a shopping cart overloaded with groceries and laundry; and trying, for all the world, to keep track of a four-year-old boy who darted away and dashed back to her yelling about something he had seen, ignoring her admonishments to stay nearby.

Grandmother, Janie thought; and then, *no, babysitter. The neighbor lady who had no kids or grandkids and could use a few extra bucks to watch this little angel while his parents worked.*

They were walking by Janie when the fire bell from the station on the corner wailed loudly and suddenly, making them all jump.

"Holy shit!" the boy yelled, grabbing hold of the woman's leg.

"David!! We don't speak like that!" she reprimanded, giving Janie a *what's the matter with kids today* look.

"Fine! Wwooowww! Is that better?" the little boy said, rolling his eyes at her.

She turned to Janie. "I would tell his parents when they get home from work, but that's where he learned to say such things, so it's no use. What is this world going to come to?"

The woman took David's hand firmly, while he squealed and complained and tried to wriggle out of her grip, and walked away.

As Janie sat day after day, watching the people who went by, she grew calmer and, somehow, more confident. She had come to feel that every person she closely observed left her a bit changed.

Over time, she began to participate in group sessions at the halfway house more enthusiastically; even offering Nancy, who was also recovering from heroin addiction, words of encouragement.

On a night when Nancy, in tears and shuddering, spoke of how much she wanted just one more hit, Janie put her hand on the shaking shoulders.

"I know what you mean, Nancy. I sometimes feel like it was

so good to just go numb and have no worries in the world. That waiting after the needle pinch while you could feel the drug working its way up your arm into your head, and then just, ahhh, nothing. And it felt so nice."

Mara, worried that this was going in the wrong direction, opened her mouth to speak; but stopped when the counselor put his hand on her arm and shook his head.

Nancy was nodding in agreement and stopped crying to look at Janie like the kindred spirit she was.

"When I feel that way, Nancy, I force myself to stop that tape; like when you grab the cassette out of the recorder so fast, the tape gets stuck and pulled all out of shape. It's not a real thing, that thinking, it's a lie; and it's not really you, it's the drug lying to you. When I'm weak, when I want to listen to the lie and believe it and do what it says and forget this hard stuff, this real stuff, this real life, I picture myself ripping up the cassette, throwing it on the floor and stamping it into dust. Because I remind myself about the day after, Nancy. I remember how you come to, after being numb, and how loud and bright and hostile everything is and all you can think of is getting another hit; and then it's just a vicious cycle that ends with you in the hospital or dead. Any time you need, even in the middle of the night, when that tape starts playing, come and find me and we'll stamp on it together, okay, Nancy? Because you can't do it alone; that's another lie. You can't get through this life alone if you want any chance of happiness and..."

Nancy threw herself into Janie's arms and sobbed so loud and long, the men became very uncomfortable and began to clear their throats and squirm in their chairs.

After Nancy had calmed down, Mark said, "If there's nothing else tonight, I think this is a good place to end the meeting. Nancy and Janie, could you stay for a couple of minutes? Good night, everyone, and as usual, good work!"

At other meetings, there was nothing Janie or anyone else could think to say to Derek. His anger simmered on the surface constantly. He sat through group, sullenly morose, arms crossed tightly, lips pale, eyes narrow. Arnold, the bathroom-hogger and constant complainer, was often the object of Derek's rage in their group meetings. One night, he boiled over.

"I'm sick of people using my favorite coffee mug and then putting it back in the wrong place," Arnold whined at one of the sessions. "You all know it's mine, and you take it anyway. It's bad enough I have to live with you misfits, and drink lukewarm water that tastes like someone threw a brown crayon in the pot; the least you can do is leave my coffee mug alone."

Derek sprang out of his seat like he had been touched with a live wire. He ran into the kitchen and came back with the offending cup in his hand.

"You mean this mug, you sleazy douchebag asshole dick?"

He swung the coffee cup hard against the wall and it shattered, leaving him holding a jagged edge with a handle. Arnold jumped up in outraged fury and ran towards Derek, who raised the razor-sharp piece and tried to ram it into his eye. In the split second before he succeeded in blinding Arnold, Mara, Joseph, and Mark dove into the middle, barely making it in time. As Janie and Nancy watched in stunned horror, the counselor threw himself against Derek and knocked him off balance. Mara pushed Arnold back into his chair and yelled, "Call 911!", spurring Janie into action.

Shouting to Nancy, Mara pointed at the panting and pouting Arnold and said, "Watch him!" as she went to help Mark and Joseph wrestle on the floor with Derek.

He was still holding the broken mug and trying to cut them. Mara stepped on Derek's hand and, while he shrieked in rage, kicked the sharp ceramic piece across the room. She sat down on Derek's kicking legs, while the other men overpowered him.

Mark subdued Derek with calming talk until he was back to slow simmer; and they sat on top of him until the police came and handcuffed him and took him away.

Mark made them all come back to the group circle and debrief. He had to find Nancy in her room, where she had jammed a chair under the doorknob and was cowering behind her bed.

"I'm sorry that happened to you," he said, looking each of them in the eye. "Derek obviously has issues with anger and was easily provoked. Does anyone have a comment or question or feeling they want to share?"

"Is he coming back?" Nancy asked, hugging a bed pillow she had brought down from her room.

"Absolutely not. He will be placed in another group home far from here, and with much more support."

"Why did he attack me?" Arnold whined; and the others looked at him, shaking their heads.

"Because you are so fucking annoying! When are you going to get it that you're not the only important person in the room, idiot? The biggest surprise is that none of the rest of us have attacked you yet. Ignoramus!" This from Joseph, who sat with his arms crossed, glaring at Arnold.

Janie spoke quietly and earnestly. "Thank you for acting so quickly, everyone. I just sat there like a dummy. He could have really hurt someone, and I did nothing to stop it."

Mara came to give her a hug. "You called 911 right away, Janie. Give yourself some credit."

Janie hugged her back, and spent another sleepless night, her mind restlessly replaying the event.

In the morning, stocking shelves with PacMan cereal boxes and six-packs of Squeeze-It Chucklin' Cherry juice alongside Jimmy, Janie's thoughts wandered. She had begun to think maybe her parents were right and all this was happening to her because she could not accept her lot in life. Was she, in fact, fighting against her own nature, causing this unhappiness, and leading her down rabbit holes? Her parents had always scraped by, and although not outwardly joyful, ever, had seemed adequately content. Was it enough, or was there more? Was her discontent and restiveness opening new doors, or shutting them? Was she actually going somewhere, or just going in circles?

These thoughts swirled around until Jimmy, having trouble reaching a top shelf, let out a growl of frustration and threw an entire case of Planters Cheez Balls onto the ground. Janie slowly backed away and around to the next aisle to wait for him to calm down and pick everything up.

At group session at the end of that week, Janie brought up her worries. "I think maybe this is really it for me; and I just have to accept that."

Mark leaned forward in his chair. "No one here is judging you if this really is your level of capacity, Janie, but..."

"Everyone judges me," Arnold interrupted querulously.

The group groaned in unison and Joseph replied, "We don't judge you, Arnold. We just don't like you."

Over low chuckles, Mara leaned towards Janie. "I think Mark is saying that if you are satisfied, then don't worry about what anyone else thinks of your choices. But are you, Janie? Are you satisfied?"

Janie shrugged her shoulders; she had no ready answer to that question and sat back as Arnold's complaints took up the rest of the meeting.

It kept her up at night, thoughts turning and arguing in her head. If this was it for her, why was it bothering her so much? Did the fact that she was struggling with herself mean there was something more that she was after; something she herself did not understand yet?

Her mind wandered to Greg, rare and dangerous territory. He had been so restless, searching for his way against all odds, even to the point of leaving everything he had known to reach for his dream; so young and yet so driven. Growing up, he had always had a way of rising above and seeing clearly; it was why she had depended on him when she felt lost or sad. When he left, even though he had explained it plainly and patiently to his whining little sister, he left a void she had yet to fill in a healthy way.

For a long time, she had felt abandoned. She had begun to recognize that this had led her to the path she was on. Now she had to own it, be responsible for herself, take on the mantle and find her own dream. But did she have one? And what in the world could it be?

In the dead of night well before dawn, she knew she was once again losing the battle to get any sleep, when an odor wafting around caught her attention. She sniffed carefully, then sat up slowly, covers falling to her waist.

Puzzled, she took a few more inhalations through her nostrils; and was rewarded by a coughing fit that confirmed what her brain had been trying to tell her: *smoke!*

She tried to jump out of bed, but the covers twisted around her legs, and she fell to the ground. She untangled herself and ran to the door. When she threw it open, silence and darkness greeted her; but the smell was much stronger.

She went down the hall and knocked loudly on Nancy's door. When there was no answer, she opened it and could hear Nancy's gentle snoring.

"Hey, Nance, get up. I smell smoke. I think we should get out of here and call the fire department. Nancy? Hey, wake up."

Nancy rolled over and blinked hard to open her eyes. Janie's words reached her slumbering brain at the same time as the smell of smoke; and she jumped out of bed, suddenly alert. Janie had a split second to feel envious of Nancy's deep sleep before Nancy yelled, "Smoke! Fire! Everyone get up!"

They ran down the hallway, opening doors and yelling. Arnold's stood ajar, and his room was empty. Within a minute, Mara and Joseph had joined them and they headed down the stairs. They all wore pajamas except Joseph, who had grabbed a towel on his way out and wrapped it around his bare waist.

As soon as they reached the first floor, they could see gray smoke dancing and spreading along the ceiling. It was coming from the kitchen in rolling waves. The telephone hung on the wall just inside the kitchen door, and Janie ran towards it as the others ran out the front door. The heat seared her face as she reached for the receiver, which was already warm in her hand. She could see flames licking the counter tops and climbing the cabinets; and she could see the source: the toaster was plugged in, two blackened pieces of bread ablaze in the slots.

The dial took forever to return from the nine; long enough for Janie to think *hurry hurry*. The one-one took a couple more seconds and then a tinny voice said, "9-1-1, what's your emergency?"

Janie yelled the address into the receiver and, dropping it so that it dangled swinging against the wall, ran to join the others. Arnold had a jacket on over his pajamas and was wearing shoes on his feet. It was clear he had run outside as soon as he realized there was a fire in the toaster.

Mara dashed to the corner two blocks away and pulled the fire alarm on the red box; within minutes they could hear the first sirens in the distance. They moved down the block a bit and watched the first floor of their home burn.

Janie sat still in her galley kitchen, pondering for the millionth time where she had come from and where she was going to go next.

She had not been back to Bohack's since that awful day Arnold had set the house on fire, abandoning everyone to save himself. It had been two months since she had earned a dime, and she was just thankful she had enough saved up to pay the hundred dollars rent-controlled monthly cost in her new place.

She was also grateful for Mark's weekly check-ins, relying on them for her only real contact with the outside world. He calmed her and let her know he was ready to help her move forward as soon as she was settled. She knew he meant it was time, past time, for her to get back out there; she just could not do it yet.

The anxiety caused by the sudden event ending her time in the halfway house with her new friends and support system had thrown Janie into a tailspin, from which she was still digging out. Mark had helped them all find new places to live, Nancy into a rehab facility and the rest of them into apartments; but none of them could afford a phone so there had been no way to stay in touch.

The last hug with Mara had felt like tearing the bandage off a still bleeding wound, even though Mara had, as usual, said all the right things.

The first night in her new place, a six-story building on a busy street a mile and a world away from the halfway house, had been fraught with fear. She had tried to sleep, but every siren blaring and horn honking, every banging of a sanitation truck lifting dumpsters and then dropping them back onto the concrete, every curse yelled by people who either slept on the street or did not sleep at all, made her twitch and pull the covers up tighter.

When dawn brought light through her thin curtains that first morning, she got up and, shivering more from distress than from cold, took a hot shower, got dressed in the clothing Mark had given her, and sat at the kitchen table, missing the urn of coffee at the halfway house.

Later that morning, she ventured outside and made her way to the Ridgewood Church where Mark had explained she could find anything she needed. He was right. Struggling to carry a large black garbage bag filled with a Mr. Coffee machine, a couple of mugs, plates and pieces of silverware, and enough clothes to last a week, she made her way back to the apartment. Once inside, she set the bag down and sat for a moment, relieved to be safely back in her own place. It took hours for her to get up the nerve to leave again and get some groceries.

Now it had been two months since she arrived at this place. Janie listened to the sound of the normal world, the one where people had a daily routine: get the kids ready for school, get dressed, go to work, come home, make dinner, watch T.V., go to bed; repeat.

After an hour or so, the noise level reached a crescendo and then began to lessen incrementally, punctuated by a parent hollering in a rage, "You are going to be late to school! Get the fuck out the goddamned door!"

A furious pounding of feet followed, disappearing as quickly as it started and leaving a muted silence behind.

Still, Janie sat in her folding chair, listening. She knew Mrs. Franklin from apartment 3E would be the first person to begin the next wave. The rattling of the old woman's large set of keys as she secured the door locks behind her would be followed by the painfully slow long squeaky song of her shopping cart wheels as she made her way past Janie's apartment to the elevator.

As if they were set on a timer, Mrs. Franklin's singular noises appeared, and before she made it to the elevator, several other doors opened and let out the rest of the elderly neighbors to begin their missions of making it through another day. Mrs. Davis in 3G, with her white wispy hair and pursed lips, pushed her mother's wheelchair through the door; but since it was a tight fit, there was the usual banging as she fought to get it out. Janie saw it all in her mind's eye as it was happening in real time outside her apartment door.

Finally, around nine, quiet. She plugged in the Mr. Coffee, remembering the fateful toaster fire that had brought her to this place. She measured a scoop of coffee out of the nearly empty can and poured it into the filter, which was still wet from its first use yesterday. The machine made complaining noises as it began to heat the water. Janie realized that she would have to look for another one when the Ridgewood Church of God had its monthly giveaway.

Her grocery store calendar from Bohack's, held to the wall with a flat silver thumbtack, reminded her today was June 13th, 1982.

She did not always notice this melancholy anniversary when it came around on the calendar. It was hard to believe it had been five years since the day that had caused a rift in her existence, caused the careening that had led her here, to this life. Sometimes it felt like yesterday; other times it felt like so much longer, or that it had happened to someone else. For just a moment, she allowed herself to wonder where Greg was at that second, what he was doing. But the thoughts led her to dark fears that maybe he was just *not* anymore; and she stuffed them deep.

Now, after a short time on her own, she had developed a routine that kept her anxiety to a minimum; wake up, take a shower, drink coffee and eat breakfast, read for a couple of hours, leave the apartment to get something only if necessary, eat lunch, do a little tidying up, make dinner, go to bed.

It was beginning to feel like a trap of her own making.

She knew she should do something: find a job, develop a hobby, make a friend, but just the thought of any of that gave her the willies.

The strident blare of cars honking in rage at each other out on the street brought Janie out of her reverie. She looked down at her watch, another good find at the Ridgeway Church, and thought, "Shit! I've been sitting here for hours. Come on, get a move on!"

Even though it was a warm Queens Day, she put on a long-sleeved shirt, jeans, and sneakers. She had, only once, made the mistake of wearing a tank top into the store, exposing her arms. The looks of sympathy from some shoppers at her needle scars, and outright antipathy from others, had caught her off-guard; and she had left her shopping cart in an aisle, hurried home, gotten into bed and stayed there for three days.

It was still, thankfully, silent in the hallway when she stepped out the door and made her way to the elevator. If there was someone in there when it came, she would mumble an excuse and take the stairs instead. The residents were not mean; that was not why she avoided them when possible. In fact, they were mostly elderly and lonely, with a few single mothers mixed in. It was the small talk, the questions, the probing curiosity that she could not handle.

She was finally getting better despite this emotional setback, she could tell that; but she did not want to have to delve into a story about how she got here, to rent-controlled housing. They all had stories; she did not want to hear them either. It was all too much for right now.

The two-block walk to the pharmacy, to pick up the valium the doctor had prescribed for her when she finished her course of methadone, was noisy with traffic and people. Older models of cars, dented and beat-up, honked impatiently at intersections as if this would magically make people get out of their way. The ubiquitous squeegee men, taking advantage of the stuck cars to wipe their windshields with a filthy rag and then beg the already irate drivers for money, were out in force on this mild morning.

She felt grateful for the anonymity this city offered her; she was invisible here on the crowded, busy street. She thought about it as she walked. She had not always felt that way, but then she had gone to that Bar Mitzvah party and met Jerry.

That night had swung her in a direction that led her here. She always told herself she had gone this way to punish her parents, to assuage the lack of love, as revenge. But maybe it had always been in her, and all the other stuff was an attempt to cover it up. It didn't really matter; she was here now.

The line towards the back of the drug store was not too bad; there were four people ahead of her. First in line was a young woman; a *very* young woman, Janie noticed, when she turned slightly to look down at the baby in her carriage with a mix of irritation and worry on her face. Janie wondered if the baby was sick, or if the young mother were here to pick up birth control pills. Either way, she radiated a wish to be somewhere else; maybe even *someone* else. Janie knew how she felt.

Right behind the young mother, a short stocky man wearing the uniform of blue-collar workers everywhere, belted jeans and button-down flannel shirt, stood firmly with both feet planted and his arms at his sides. The patience of Job, Janie thought, slightly amused. Maybe picking up his elderly mother's medication for urinary incontinence, or his wife's Librium.

After him, Janie noticed an elderly man and woman she recognized from another floor in her building. They were arguing about the cost of the Baby Ruth candy bar he was holding with obvious yearning. In the end, he reluctantly walked off to put it back.

The person just ahead of Janie caught her eye. It was the red leather pumps she wore, with a matching bag, that made Janie zoom in on her. Her dress, obviously expensive and well-made, might have been worn to a gala luncheon at the fancy Tavern on the Green on Central Park West. Stylish and tasteful, it touched just at the knee, showing, below, the stockinged legs with perfect modesty. The white gloves on her petite hands came to the wrist, and as the line of people moved towards the counter, she removed them and placed them carefully inside her purse. Her fingers, wrinkled but neatly manicured, held several rings that bordered on gaudy, but were somehow still classy.

When the lady got to the counter, she spoke so quietly the cashier had to lean over to hear her. He handed her the white-paper bag holding her prescription and took the cash she offered. Janie saw the elderly woman shake her head in a bit of ire as the cashier took a long time to figure out the change. Then she turned around and caught Janie watching her.

Her make-up was way overdone. The blue eye shadow, penciled brows, and bright red lips distracted momentarily from the crow's nests by her eyes, the deep lines furrowing her mouth. But her hair was perfectly coiffed and before she stepped away, allowing Janie to take her place at the counter, she smiled with yellowed aged teeth.

"You look so beautiful," Janie said to her, in spite of herself. "Your dress is gorgeous, and the matching shoes and purse are perfect."

"What is your name, dear?" the elderly woman asked.

"Janie Thompson," she responded, not really knowing why.

"Well, Janie Thompson, dear. You have made my day. Thank you very much."

It seemed to Janie there was an overwhelming emotion just underneath the surface that the woman was tamping down as she spoke. Sadness? Loneliness? Janie could not tell. Without another word, the lady walked elegantly away and out the door into the world.

On a whim, Janie grabbed a Baby Ruth bar and added it to her purchase. The June sun, and the people rushing by on their personal missions, and the pigeons cooing as they searched for crumbs, pulled her to a nearby bench. She took the candy bar out of the white paper bag and tore the top off the wrapper. Pushing the chocolate-covered peanuts, caramel, and nougat through the opening, she took a bite and closed her eyes to focus on the sweet and crunchy taste as she chewed. She had forgotten what this was like: to be in the world, part of the fabric, one of the crowd, just another member of the neighborhood. She opened her eyes to take it all in, as she took another bite. Janie sat for a half hour, relishing the warmth, the taste, the sound, the sights. She finished the candy bar with a satisfied smile before heading back to her small but cozy refuge.

Two days later, just after the hallway had gotten quiet and Janie was filling her second cup with coffee, she thought she heard a knock on the door. Deciding it was probably coming from a nearby apartment, she ignored it.

The second knock was slightly more insistent; enough to convince Janie that, in fact, someone was standing at her door, looking for her and wanting to speak to her for some reason. Mark had just come a few days before, so it could not be him. She stared at the door, willing whoever it was to go away; hoping they were mistaken and at the wrong apartment, and would realize that without her having to tell them and would just leave.

The third knock told her that was not going to happen.

She had two choices: she could open the door and deal with whatever was on the other side, or she could sit here and wait them out and hope they would not just come back later and the next day and the next until she finally got up the courage to let them in. The thought of spending every day and every night wondering, waiting, and worrying made her get up. Better to confront it now, than to agonize and still have to deal with it anyway.

Her hand was shaking the tiniest bit as she unbolted the locks, leaving the security chain latched, just in case the intruder tried to ram his way in and murder her.

She was stunned silent when, through the three-inch opening the chain allowed, she saw standing there, holding a white bakery box sealed shut with red and white striped twine, the elderly lady she had spoken to at the pharmacy.

"May I come in, Janie Thompson? You do remember me from the other day, I hope?"

It took a moment for Janie to find her manners. She mumbled, "Of course;" then closing the door briefly to unlatch the chain, she opened the door wide and stepped aside.

Grateful that she had cleaned the apartment just the day before, she led the elderly woman to the living room and offered her a seat.

Before sitting, the lady held up the white bakery box and said, "I thought we could have some coffee to go with this coffee cake from my favorite Jewish bakery down the street. They make the most delicious cookies as well, but I thought it was a tad early in the day for that. Maybe next time, if we meet in the afternoon, I will bring hamantaschen, which they make all year around. Have you ever had the poppy seed? It's so tasty, I don't know how they do it. Probably a lot of butter, which at my age, I should be watching but, at my age, I think I should be able to enjoy whatever I want. Of course, you are too young to understand what I mean, Janie, dear. Shall I help with the coffee?"

This last she said pointedly, since Janie still stood trying to process that she had a guest standing in her living room, a nearly complete stranger, who seemed to expect they would now have a relationship where they met again on another afternoon to chat and eat poppy seed hamantaschen.

"No, no, please sit. I will get it. I was just having my second cup and there should be enough in the pot for one more. How do you take your coffee?"

"Milk and sugar, dear. Again, it goes against doctor's orders, but that is the way I have always taken it, and I am not going to change at this stage of the game."

Janie scrounged through the cupboard to find a presentable

mug for her guest. Her plates did not match; and a knife and two forks, also unmatching, were all she had; and she brought everything to the coffee table. She suddenly felt a bit embarrassed at her living conditions but had to shake it off. The lady did not seem to be judging her; in fact, she seemed grateful to be there.

Janie was intrigued as she sat next to her, cut up the coffee cake and gave them each a slice. The odor of cinnamon and brown sugar and butter wafted around them; a comforting scent that complemented the rich smell of fresh-brewed coffee. The elderly woman picked up her plate, took a modest bite of cake, sipped her coffee, and sat up straight with a contented smile.

"That is just perfect, Janie. Thank you for inviting me in. I hope we will become great friends. I truly think things happen for a reason, and if I had not worn my red pumps that day, you might not have noticed me at all! And yet, here we are; isn't it marvelous?"

Janie, enjoying her own first bite of the moist coffee cake, nodded her head politely.

"I am eager to hear what a nice girl like you is doing in a place like this; but you are probably wondering the same about me. You are also probably wondering how I found you. Well, I should be embarrassed to tell you, but that is an emotion best left behind as one ages; so, I'm not. I followed you home from the pharmacy! You did not make it easy, stopping like you did. I'm intrigued; what were you doing? You seemed like an invisible apparition sitting there, watching the world go by as you ate your candy bar. By the way, that is how I knew you would like cake.

"I'm not the type of person who normally stalks others, just so you know; but I found you fascinating. Most people do not see me, do you know what I mean? At my age, I'm merely an unimportant presence in the fabric of their daily lives. It's one of the reasons I get dressed up when I go out; hoping someone will notice and engage; and there you were! By the way, how do you like these pumps? They have the silver threads running through that match my dress, my handbag, and even my necklace!"

At this she paused, and Janie spoke to fill the expectant silence. "You look even more beautiful than the other day. And I do know what you mean about not being seen. The truth is, I actually like that; watching people is usually better than talking to them."

The elderly lady clapped her hands in delight. "Well, now I am honored that you chose to speak to me in the pharmacy that morning! Like I said, it must have happened for a reason. So, if I may, I will tell you my story; and then you can tell me yours!"

She gracefully took a small sip of coffee, and then began.

The Lady

Her name was Mrs. Dorothy Geraldine Wechsler Thomas.

Back in the day, at the beginning of the century, she had affectionately been called, "Dot." It had suited her perfectly when she was a girl. With her petite frame, button nose, and infectious smile, she had skipped into many drawing rooms to the refrain of, "Oh look, here is Dot now!" followed by the offer of sweets and confections.

No one would think to call her Dot now; would not even associate such an infantile moniker with the Mrs. Thomas of today. Of course, there was no one left who would call her at all; so, there was that.

"This was once an enclave of single-family homes and rowhouses, very WASP-y as they called it, where everyone knew everyone else. This part of Queens has a history that goes back to Peter Stuyvesant's time, did you know that? The Dutch and British established separate towns right next to each other. The Dutch created Bushwick, Brooklyn; and the British founded Newtown, which was the original name for this neighborhood. My husband William traces his lineage back to those days and was very proud of that fact his entire life. Later, many German families overtook the area after having settled in Little Germany on the Lower East Side of Manhattan. Apparently, things became untenable down there after the cholera epidemic and a horrible boating accident that killed a thousand men, woman and children just enjoying a Sunday church outing. Are you okay, dear?"

The mention of the history of St. Mark's Place gave Janie a terrible start; it brought back strong unwelcome memories of that evening with the police officer "Joe" and the bust at the warehouse. She shook herself, took a sip of warming coffee, and nodded. She found she was losing herself in the story Mrs. Wechsler Thomas was weaving; and hoped she would continue.

The elderly woman took a bite of the coffee cake, and then a sip of coffee, before warming back up to her story.

"A huge underground water source was discovered here, and suddenly breweries were being developed at such a rate that at one point, there were over thirty within a couple of square miles! Right here, where we are sitting, they developed park lands for picnics and beer gardens and racetracks and amusement parks. I think it must have been such a grand and gay time to be alive!

"Anyway, the Germans built many of the two- and three-story row houses that are still here today; and once the Queensboro Bridge was finished in the early 1900's and connected this area to Manhattan, well, it really exploded out here! The population of this neighborhood has always been very diverse; but there was a small group of wealthy families, like the Thomases, who built single-family homes on the farms that were still left in the 1900's. Those children went to a small private school exclusively for them, and it was at a dance between my school and William's that we first met. I know it is hard for you youngsters these days to imagine, but we married less than a year after that first dance. I was fifteen and he was seventeen; don't look so shocked, some of my classmates were married with children by then! He was already working with his father running their cutlery and tool factory after school. Oh, he was so handsome, and he used to tell me I was the prettiest thing on two legs! You know, it was the last thing he said to me before he passed, ten long years ago.

"When we were courting, we loved nothing better than going into the city. Sometimes we just walked around and gawped at the people; those poor immigrants down in lower Manhattan lived in such squalor and the wealthy ones in midtown in such splendor, it was hard to reconcile. At one point there was so much disease in the tenements that the schools were held outside year-round to try to mitigate the spread of tuberculosis. Those poor children, wrapped in bags and shivering to keep warm through the dreadfully bitter winter; it's a wonder they learned a thing.

"There were model yacht races at the Conservatory Lake in Central Park, and the zoo there used to put on shows for us. One time, we watched a zookeeper put his whole head into the mouth of an enormous hippopotamus. My heart almost stopped! We would ride the street trolleys up and down Fifth Avenue for hours, just having a grand old time of it.

"Once we married, we lived with his parents in the home where I still live, just about four blocks from here. The house was big enough, and it was not uncommon then for married young people to live at home. Thank goodness, William's mother was a kind, dear soul; I heard nightmares about mothers-in-law from many of my school friends.

"The Great War, what they call in school World War I now, was coming to an end, but it brought on a dreadful disease they called the Spanish flu that killed so many people around the world; and many right here in Queens succumbed. It was a very dark time, and we spent much of it close to home. I hope to never live through such a thing again; entire families died, one after another in a matter of days, and the horse-drawn death carts rumbling through the neighborhood stopped at the houses of the poor and the wealthy indiscriminately."

Here Mrs. Thomas stopped for a moment, caught up emotionally in her own storytelling. Janie was just about holding her breath; it felt like the white screen at the theater that happened when the projectionist in his room was inexpertly changing reels in the middle of the movie. After a pause, Mrs. Thomas turned and put her gnarled hand over Janie's smooth one with a smile.

"The time period that came right after we now call the Roaring 20's; and did we roar! F. Scott Fitzgerald once described the 1920s as 'the most expensive orgy in history,' which may shock you; but after everything we had endured, we certainly had earned a bit of fun. Now I have been talking forever! I hope I've not bored you, dear."

Janie shook her head vehemently. She had nowhere to be anyway and was disappointed when Mrs. Thomas stood and said she would take her leave now and not overstay her welcome.

"I hope I may call on you again, Janie, dear. It is so nice to have someone with whom I can share stories." With that, she allowed Janie to show her out.

The silence in the apartment after Janie closed the door behind Mrs. Dorothy Geraldine Wechsler Thomas was a dense vacuum; and Janie hoped the elderly storyteller would return sooner rather than later.

Exactly a week later, when Janie heard the gentle first knock on her door, she opened it with an eager smile. Mrs. Thomas, wearing yet another exquisite outfit and holding up another white bakery box, said, "Hello again, Janie dear! I brought the hamantaschen!"

Janie quickly set the Mr. Coffee to perk and brought plates to the living room table. Before she even settled herself, the woman began talking.

"Let's see, where did I leave off? Oh yes, the twenties! Oh my, you young people have no idea how much fun we had in those days. And you should have seen my closet then; the sequins, the tassels, the matching feathered headpieces! I was in my glory. We often went to the Lower East Side to the back of Ratner's Restaurant where, by the way, the blintzes were heavenly; and you entered the nightclub through a bookcase! That was to keep it secret from the police, you know; drinking alcohol was not allowed, and mixing blacks and whites was still frowned upon. But the Jazz music, and the dances, and the celebrities and even the gangsters; it was so very exciting. They say the mafia organization Murder, Inc. was born in that back room. I don't know about that, but I did see Meyer Lansky, Lucky Luciano, and Bugsy Siegel there more than once. They had the best table in the place, and everyone knew who they were. It just added to the intrigue and the excitement!

"In the middle of it all, we had our first baby, a boy we named William Junior. He was our pride and joy; but he died when he was just under a year old. It was very mysterious; he just went to sleep and never woke up. It was not that unusual in those days, but you never think it might happen to your own perfectly healthy baby."

She stopped for a moment to gather herself. Out of her handbag, she drew a neatly folded linen handkerchief embroidered with a fancy script G.D.W.T. on one corner. She blotted her eyelashes, quietly blew her nose with it, and held it in her hand instead of putting it away.

Looking at Janie, she gave a sad smile and said, "Just in case. It has been an entire lifetime, but some things never really go away, even when they are well-buried."

For a moment, the two women sat companionably sipping coffee. Janie took a bite of the poppy seed pastry and closed her eyes, appreciating every chew. When she opened them, she saw Mrs. Thomas watching her with satisfaction.

"I had a feeling you would enjoy those, Janie. Anyway, to continue my story, William's family business was doing very well through this time. Everyone needs knives and sharp tools, you know; and they treated the employees like family. Every summer, we held a picnic for the workers and their children; and my William and his father never forgot a birthday; and the factories were closed on Saturdays, Sundays, Christmas, and New Year's Day. They were ahead of their time; and the employees had great respect for them. When the economy crashed hard, and so very many people lost their jobs or took their own lives in despair, the Thomas Cutlery Company managed to keep on going.

"Those were very hard times, even for those of us who were relatively fortunate. Hundreds of people lined up outside the factory every day looking for work or begging in shame for a penny to feed their children. I saw our workers with my own eyes, giving away the food out of their own lunchboxes, the coats off their backs, the hats off their heads, anything they could spare as they came to work in the morning. Those poor unfortunates who had lost everything built shanty towns they called Hoovervilles in the city parks just to have a place to live; and every night around dinner time, they would come to our back door with tin plates asking for our leftover food. Their sad, ashamed, and sometimes angry eyes haunt my dreams to this day.

"And yet, even in the midst of the horror of daily life, an amazing thing was happening in New York City that just goes to show the strength of the human spirit, Janie. It was during this time that the Empire State Building, the Chrysler Building, Radio City Music Hall, Rockefeller Center, the Waldorf-Astoria Hotel and so many more of today's famous New York City landmarks were being built. You may have seen the photograph of the eleven laborers taking their lunch break sitting on a steel beam of the RCA building in Rockefeller Center, more than eight hundred feet above the street; it's a pretty well-known one. I do love that picture; it captures the times in so many ways.

"Once that terrible time finally ended, life went back to a semblance of normal; although after the previous twenty years, I do not think there was truly a normal to go back to. In any case, people found work again and routines set in and, for a couple of years, anyway, life settled down. Yes, there was a war going on in Europe and we heard a few bits of news about things that were happening in Southern Asia as well, but it did not affect us here. William and I took advantage of the calm and went to see the new shows on Broadway; so many of them came out in 1940, it was hard to keep up! And the music was such a delight: Frank Sinatra at the Hotel Aster in the city; the Glen Miller band and the Dorsey Brothers upstate at the Glen Island Casino in New Rochelle. Billie Holiday captured it all with 'I Hear Music,' which became such a hit. It was a wonderful, if quite short-lived, interlude and we enjoyed every minute."

A police siren that suddenly blared outside broke the spell that Mrs. Thomas had woven in the room.

"Oh, goodness, how I do go on! Let's just sit and enjoy our little repast and each other's company for a while."

They did, chatting about the neighborhood, and the weather, and rehashing the story of how they first met.

After a while, Mrs. Thomas stood and said, "Janie, if you are agreeable, I would come back next Wednesday again, and continue to tell my story. But please let me know if I am boring you silly; a lonely old lady like me does not always know when to stop."

Janie's smile let her know that she welcomed the company and her stories.

Over the next several Wednesdays, which Janie began to look forward to so much she cleaned the apartment and bought flowers on Tuesdays to make the place a bit more cheerful, Mrs. Dorothy Geraldine Wechsler Thomas told the rest of her story.

"It is hard to believe all the events I lived through, looking back now. The bombing of Pearl Harbor led to our involvement in the second World War and changed our factory into a body armor and airplane-parts manufacturer for quite a while. They brought us thousands of pounds of metal removed from some of the most famous hotels in the city to melt down.

We worked around the clock then, and there was more work than the employees could handle, since so many of the young men had signed on to fight overseas. We even hired women to take their places, unheard of in those days! We had nightly dim-outs, where all outdoor lights in the five boroughs were turned off. It was eerie and made the far-off war seem much more real, but the stars during those dark nights were quite a brilliant sight. When the war finally ended, New York City just seemed to break out of a long, dark, hard shell. There were parades, and all the marquees were lit up again, people crowded the shops and restaurants; there was such a sense of relief and merriment, it seemed like the difficult times were soon all but forgotten.

"It took many years of trying, and I had all but given up hope; but we finally had another baby, another son. In fact, I was a ripe old forty-three when he was born, nearly unheard of in those days. Some of our friends were grandparents by then! We named him Wechsler, after my family; Wechsler William Thomas, a good and strong name for our boy, who was a happy, fat baby that made everyone smile just to look at him. As he grew into a handsome little boy, his favorite thing to do was to go to the factory with his father and visit with the workers. He would try to help them, carrying finished pieces from one part of the factory to another on his chubby legs, to everyone's delight. He did well enough in school; not a natural book learner, you understand, but a very hard worker and so he managed to keep up. I never saw him frown or cry or look upset, even when things did not work the way he wanted. In this way, he was just like his father and his grandfather; and we all knew he would take over the family business one day and make us all so proud.

"After high school, he attended City College to get a business degree. Every morning, he would get up with the sun and walk a mile to the subway; and every evening he would come home after dark, eat his supper, and tell us all about his day and the new people he was meeting. It was the 1960's, you understand, and the youngsters were something else! It made me so happy to see him embracing the times, much like we did at his age. He never grew his hair like some of the boys did, and as far as I know, he never did the drugs that were so popular. But he enjoyed the music and the political marches and the nights sitting in Washington Square Park or Central Park just 'hanging out,' as he would say. There were girls, of course; he was so handsome and kind. But never one special girl, even though we kept hoping.

"Wechsler graduated and started working at the factory full time. He insisted on starting out on the floor with the employees, to get to know all aspects of the factory business. He even brought one of his best friends from City College to the business, and together they worked hard and entertained everyone with their stories of the hippies and life in the big city. I know, Queens is one of the city's five boroughs, but most of us in the other four always call Manhattan 'the city,' it's just one of those funny things.

"Wechsler stayed in touch with his group of friends for years, and often went into the city on weekends to 'hang out' with them. One night, he came home and told us about this music festival that his friends were planning to attend. They had gotten him a ticket, and he was very excited about it. I guess all their favorite musicians were going to be playing over the three days, and they were going to take a train up and camp in tents on the big farm that was hosting the concert. I'm sure you have heard of it; it was called Woodstock, and it turned into something much bigger than the original plan. It made me very happy to see him so enthusiastic about it.

"The news stations broadcast live video feed from the concert in the evenings, and my, the place was just an ocean of young people! William and I almost pressed our noses to the television screen during the news hour, playing a game of 'Spot Wechsler.' It was rather funny looking back, how we would yell, 'There! That's him!' every time we saw a young man in the crowd who looked like our son. One time, I *did* see him, and I never said a thing to William. He was stark naked and swimming in a huge mud puddle with other naked people!"

She stopped to laugh at the image she recalled; but then her voice broke as she continued.

"If I had known it would be the last time I would see my son alive, I might have told William. Even though he would have been shocked, at least he would have known our son was happy and having fun.

"We expected him home on Monday or Tuesday. After seeing the crowds, we thought the trains might be a bit overwhelmed and it would take him longer to get back; so, we did not worry. I was just looking forward to hearing the stories he would tell when he got home!

"Early on Wednesday morning before William even left for work, the home phone rang. Thinking, believing, it was Wechlser, I picked up the receiver and said, 'Hello you crazy Hippie!'

"It was silent long enough for me to think maybe the connection was not good; but then I heard weeping on the other end. It was one of the girls from Wechsler's group of friends, a Wendy whom we had met on several occasions. A very nice girl, she was. When she could finally speak, I did not interrupt what she was saying. I just couldn't. William came over and I put the receiver between both of our ears so we could hear together.

"'Mrs. Thomas, Wechsler was in the hospital for two days. I know we should have called you, but it was such a crazy scene; it was a tiny hospital and there were hundreds of people there trying to get help after the festival ended. There was no food or water at the farm; and a lot of people got sick. Wechsler didn't seem that bad as we were leaving to head back to the train station, but we had to walk and wait for hours, and he collapsed right into my arms. It took a long time to get an ambulance to take him and a long time for a nurse to even see him when we got there. By the time they got to him, they told us that he was severely dehydrated. They put those I.V. bags up, you know? And they tried to revive him, but...'

"My hand still held the phone receiver loosely between our ears, but William paled frightfully and sat on the floor. I'm sure I looked just as dreadful, but I held on long enough to hear Wendy say, 'I'm sorry, Mrs. Thomas. He didn't make it,' before I dropped the receiver and sank to the floor next to him. I remember how it swung there and I could hear Wendy's tinny voice saying, 'Hello? Mrs. Thomas?' She began to sob again and then I heard the click as she hung up and it was the loudest sound I had ever heard."

The handkerchief had somehow come out of her handbag, and she held it to her eyes. Janie's own eyes were streaming freely, and she wiped them on her sleeve. Feeling helpless, Janie did not know what to offer the woman except herself, which she did, moving closer to her and gently holding the gnarled hand while Mrs. Thomas contained herself. When she finally did, she looked up at Janie with ancient, tired eyes.

"That took the wind out of William's sails for the rest of his life. Oh, he kept the company going; it was the only thing that got him out of bed in the morning, you know. But his heart was broken, and his spirit was broken. Like many kind and gentle men, he held me when I cried and soothed me when I was sad, but he never, after Wechsler's funeral, spoke of his feelings. In the end, I think that is why he only lived a few years beyond that; keeping your feelings inside allows them to destroy you. Somehow, I was able to go on, get through that horrible time and keep living this life. Even after I lost William, I kept on living. It sometimes keeps me up at night, pondering why things have happened the way they have; and my conclusion is: they just do. Not very helpful, I know."

Her smile was tinged with both sadness and irony.

"Janie, dear, you are an exquisite listener. I was never so fortunate as the day you spoke to me at the pharmacy and then invited me into your home. But it's your turn next week; I have spoken enough and now I want to hear your story. We can see each other next Wednesday; and as usual, I will supply the baked goods that we both seem to enjoy very much."

With that, they stood and walked to the door; and for the first time, Mrs. Dorothy Geraldine Wechsler Thomas turned and gave Janie a hug. Janie felt that embrace in her heart.

Janie

Mrs. Thomas never returned.

The following Wednesday, Janie waited the entire day for her, sitting on the couch in the clean-smelling apartment, arranging and re-arranging the flower bouquet and listening with her entire body for the now-familiar gentle knock at her door.

It never came, and when the sun was low in the sky, Janie began to rationalize her absence: *She just forgot, being eighty-something; she had an appointment she didn't tell me about; she did not sleep well and needed to rest.*

As Janie lay down in bed that night, she fully expected to hear Mrs. Thomas knocking at the door early the next morning with her usual chattiness: *Silly old me, I thought yesterday was Tuesday, well, here I am dear, with more pastries!*

But there was no knock the next morning, or the next, or the next.

The following Wednesday, after coffee and toast, Janie tidied up the kitchen, waiting. She wiped out the refrigerator and re-arranged the spice rack and moved the rickety table a few inches to the left to see if it looked better there. When the knock on the door did not come, she left the apartment and went outside. Janie stood in the shade of the doorway looking up and down the street for the sight of a fashionable elderly lady holding a bakery box hurrying towards her with a smile.

After an hour of standing there straining her neck and eyes, Janie began to walk. *Just about four blocks from here,* she remembered. But four blocks in which direction? She knew she was looking for single-family homes but, after living here for only a few months, she did not know where those might be. And what would she do when she found them, knock on every door asking, *Do you know Mrs. Dorothy Geraldine Wechsler*

Thomas? This was Queens after all, no one knew most of their neighbors; but maybe she would get lucky. As she grew more worried about her friend, she knew she had to try.

She decided to use the grid of streets to guide her search. Up *five* blocks in one direction, just in case; across one and back down five blocks in the other. In this way she zigged and zagged herself into exhaustion and hours later made her way back to her apartment. Closing the door behind her, she burst into frustrated tears. After all that, she had only covered a quarter of the area that was "just about four blocks" from here.

The next morning, she set out to cover the grid in a different direction; but was met only with low-rise buildings and store fronts with apartments above them. The same thing happened over the next two days; and the look she got when she asked a police officer if he knew where she could find single-family homes or an extremely well-dressed elderly woman drove her home in despair.

The worry gnawed at her sleep that night, and before the sun was fully up, Janie had finished coffee and a light breakfast. *One more try*, she thought; and as soon as the neighbors had finished their morning exodus, she got into the empty elevator, still smelling vaguely of perfume, cigarettes, sweet milky coffee and sweaty children. She walked several blocks in a diagonal, realizing she had missed entire areas by using the grid.

For two hours, she wove her way back and forth through the neighborhood. She found a row of single-family homes that looked old but very-well appointed; and her heart leapt in her chest. It was just the type of place she had pictured in her mind as the elderly lady had spun her stories. In her mind, Janie could see the forty-year-old Thomas couple pushing a perambulator proudly down the street; Mr. Thomas and his little son heading to the factory, Wechsler's chubby legs hurrying to keep up with his tall handsome father; the college graduate returning home, ready to take up the reins his family had prepared for him; and Mrs. Thomas herself, alone but not bowed and beaten, walking in her finery to some nearby destination.

She stood on the corner for hours, watching people come and go on the block; but none of them was the indomitable, spry, well-dressed woman of advanced years she was searching, waiting, hoping for.

The impossibility of this task hit her then, and she walked back a few blocks towards her apartment, heart sinking, and found a bench to sit on.

Watching people amble or hurry by, she made herself breathe deeply and rhythmically, the way the counselor at the halfway house had taught her. Just as she felt her heartbeat slow a bit, an elderly woman in a pretty dress walking briskly in the same direction as Janie's apartment caught her eye and gave her a start. She opened her mouth to yell, "Mrs. Thomas!" but then the woman turned for a moment and Janie could see that it was not her friend; and she sank back down on the bench.

The visual and auditory cacophony melted into the background as Janie remembered the last afternoon she had spent with Mrs. Thomas; how she had told the sad story about the end of her husband's and son's lives, and her own reflections.

It made me so happy to see him embracing the times, she had said, referring to her son. What Janie would have given for a mother like that; one who lived life to the fullest and found joy when her son did the same. One who found delight and wonder where others, like her own mother, would have seen a brick wall.

Keeping your feelings inside can destroy you, she had said. And this one Janie knew intimately. It had led her into darkness from which she might never recover fully. Stuffing her worries about her brother, her resentment towards her parents, the shock of her roommate's suicide, the betrayal of Joe the narc that led to the arrest of her friends and pushed her further into the murky and seedy life she had carved to numb herself; the caustic and destructive things she told herself in reflective moments, all had led to nowhere.

No, that was not completely true. They had led her to Mara, to Ruth, to Mrs. Thomas, to people who, by sharing their own stories, taught Janie to get outside her own head and be more perceptive, more aware, more awake. She kept going back into her pessimistic ruts; but truthfully, was it not a little less every time? Was she not changing just a bit, maybe growing up and out; becoming a different Janie, a better one, a stronger one?

Why do things happen? Mrs. Thomas had said, and then: *They just do.*

It was such a simple acceptance, and yet Janie thought she herself might never get to the point where she could think that way. But maybe she would; maybe she should start right now and stop driving herself crazy trying to find Mrs. Thomas, who, for some unknowable reason, did not want to be found. Janie should just go home and go on, she finally decided, and began to get up off the bench.

It was then that she noticed the row of neat storefronts just before her, each with a different colored awning: a Chinese restaurant, a dry cleaner's, a German deli, a fruit market with baskets of oranges, apples and melons displayed out front, and right in the middle of the block, a small store called "Bonanza Gift Shop." The place was mostly plate-glass window, the door an afterthought. From where she sat, she could see that the window was cluttered with a jumble of items for sale; and on the side closest to the door was a hand-written sign: *Help wanted, inquire within.*

She stared at the store and its sign, everything and everyone around it blurring. People hurried past the gift shop door, which was held open invitingly by a wooden triangular block wedged in the bottom. An occasional woman or child stopped to admire the offerings crowded onto shelf displays in the window. As Janie sat there watching, two women pushing strollers went inside, struggling to fit into the narrow dim space. They left a few minutes later, each carrying a shopping bag and looking very satisfied with their purchases.

A middle-aged woman in an apron, carrying a push-broom and dustpan, followed them out and waved her thanks as they went up the street. She began to sweep the sidewalk in front of her place, pushing the litter into a small pile and then onto the dustpan before walking to the nearby trash can and dumping it in. Wiping a fallen piece of hair out of her eyes and stretching her back, she gazed around at the busy avenue and went back inside to wait for the next customer.

A voice in Janie's head, familiar and clear, made her jump: *Janie, dear, what are you waiting for? And what are you afraid of? Go on now, go see that nice lady about a job.*

She knew arguing with this particular voice was useless, but still she sat there long enough for it to repeat: *Go on now, dear.*

Janie began to argue with herself: *I don't really need the money yet, I'm doing okay...What if the store gets really crowded, I will definitely panic and run out of there and never come back... I didn't come out here today to look for a job, I came out to look for my friend.*

That last one made her get off the bench and turn towards home; but her feet took her directly into the little store.

The sunlight coming through the large plate glass window warmed and lit the tiny space. Crowded shelves lined the walls, and ancient ceiling fixtures added a musty yellow tinge of light; giving Janie the feeling of having walked into the near past. The dry dusty smell took Janie back to her childhood roaming in the humble mom-and-pop stores on 108th Street, a young girl fascinated by the many, varied and unusual offerings lining aluminum shelves and hanging on metal hooks.

The store was well named. There was actually a bonanza of items vying for attention: greeting cards, candles shaped like owls or large red mushrooms, lava lamps, coffee mugs, macramé hangings, knickknacks, cuff links, silk flowers; pogo sticks, troll dolls and mood rings; hair bands, dog collars, kitchen towels and matching aprons; an array of items that insured a person could find something they wanted if they would just come inside. It was brilliant, and Janie could not help smiling with delight.

The middle-aged woman was seated on a stool behind the huge old-fashioned cash register counting receipts. She smiled widely when she looked up and saw Janie.

"Good morning! What can I do for you today, young lady? Do you need a birthday gift for someone, or maybe a little something for yourself?"

"I saw the sign in the window," Janie began in a quiet voice.

"Sign? Oh! Yes, oh good! You're here about the job!"

Janie nodded, and the interview began.

"What is your name, sweetie? And why do you want the job?"

"I'm Janie Thompson. I live nearby, and I have worked in stores before; since I was in high school, actually. I attended N.Y.U. for a bit, and... then, I worked at the Bohack's not far from here before there was a fire in the house I lived in, and I had to move."

The woman nodded her head in encouragement, so Janie continued. "I have not had a job since then, but only because I was still...adjusting to the change. Anyway, I was really just out for a walk and saw the sign and thought I would come in and see what it was about."

"I heard about that fire! It was in one of those homes the kids go to when they need a bit of help finding their way. I was so glad to hear that everyone was okay; my nephew was in one of those a while back, and he is doing great now. I'm so sorry that happened to you, Janie; but maybe fate brought you in here today because my last girl just moved away after working here for years. The store is usually quiet, and I could really manage by myself, but I do well enough and enjoy having company. Why don't you fill in the application; although it is just a formality because I am good at reading people, and you can have the job if you want it."

"I can't work on Wednesdays, though, if that is okay," Janie said, still holding out hope that one of these Wednesdays, a familiar knock would return to her door. "I also don't have a bank account, so if you could pay in cash, that would be great."

"That is all just fine! My name is Wilma, by the way; and I am so happy you came in today! Can you start tomorrow?"

Janie's shy nod made Wilma smile and clap in delight. She came around the counter and gave Janie a warm hug.

"Welcome to the Bonanza family, Miss Janie Thompson! I will see you in the morning, we open at nine."

When Janie left the gift shop, she walked a block towards home and then stopped short.

What just happened? she asked herself; and after a moment, she shrugged and continued home with a lighter step, looking forward to tomorrow in a new way.

She found herself smiling as she stepped into the lobby of the building. The elevator was there, so Janie ran and just made it; and did not even mind, as she usually did, finding someone already inside heading up.

A woman, smoking a cigarette, was standing behind a stroller that she might have found in a garbage can. Its fabric was ripped, one handle was missing, and the wheels looked like they might fall off any minute. Squeezed into the seat was an adorable cherub-faced boy who looked too old to be in a stroller; he had to be five or six, Janie thought. He gave her a big gap-toothed smile and she wiggled her fingers at him.

"What the fuck are you looking at?" the woman said, blowing a huge cloud of smoke into Janie's face. "Mind your own fucking business. And don't talk to strangers, Bobby, how many times I gotta tell you that?"

She cuffed the child on the back of the head and his eyes dropped immediately to his knees.

Janie got off the elevator on her floor, coughing and waving the smoke away as the door closed and it continued on its way.

Before she lay down that night, so keyed up she did not know if she would be able to sleep, she carefully set her alarm for six; even though the usual ruckus inside and outside the building woke her before that time every day. She did not want to be late for her first day on her new job.

She was standing outside the Bonanza Gift Shop when Wilma came to open the store just before nine. The owner of the shop smiled delightedly and said, "I knew when you came in yesterday that I was going to like you, Miss Janie Thompson!"

After Wilma showed her how the cash register worked, Janie shyly asked, "Would it be okay if I straightened out the shelves a little bit?"

She spent the rest of the day, between customers, organizing the sale items in engaging and eye-catching ways that brought nods of approval from Wilma. But Janie found that helping the customers was actually fun, and not one shopper left without a purchase after Janie spent time with them.

That night, she slept better than she had in a long time.

Over the next few weeks, Janie worked every day, except Wednesdays, of course. Wilma never asked about her need to take that day off, and Janie never offered an explanation. There was a nearly immediate uptick in sales at Bonanza, and Wilma was quick to offer praise to her new employee.

"Janie, there is something about you that every person who walks into the store likes! You seem to just look at them when they walk in, listen to them, and ask the right questions, and always find just the perfect thing for each one. Sweetie, you have a gift!"

Janie gave her a humble thanks and went to attend to a group of junior high school girls that had just wandered in, all braces and hair and giggles.

Every Thursday, a truck pulled up in front of the store and unloaded the latest goods that Wilma had ordered. Janie helped the driver carry in boxes and place them in the back room, while Wilma supervised. Then, companionably, Janie and Wilma unpacked the items and found room for them on the shelves. Pulling out a Chia Pet kit, Wilma laughed.

"I don't know if these will really sell, but the commercial on T.V. says 'ch-ch-ch-chia!' and it's catchy, so let's see what happens."

"I think these slap bracelets will be a hit with the teenagers, and the Walkmans, too," Janie said, placing them together on a shelf.

She opened a box of refrigerator magnets with kitschy quotes and stuck them all over the back of the large ancient cash register. One caught her eye and gave her a moment's pause: *People come into your life for a reason, a season, or a lifetime.* She thought of those people who had come into hers, so very many of them; and knew that Mrs. Thomas would have loved that saying.

Wilma broke into her reverie, ripping open a large box by pulling a pair of scissors across the packing tape on the top.

"I bought these diaries and journals because I remember my daughters always keeping their darkest deepest secrets in them when they were growing up; especially their puppy love crushes on Michael Jackson and Danny Partridge," Wilma said, stacking them by the register.

"Not so secret, if you knew about it," Janie said, smiling and pulling one out of the box. "What is this one?"

"That is a blank book journal for grown-ups, I think; for people who just jot down their thoughts. I like that it's called 'The Nothing Book- Want to Make Something of It?'"

Janie read the rest of the book cover aloud, "'For poets, cooks, travelers, writers, diarists, students, comedians, brides, grandparents, kids, tourists, doodlers, secretaries, list-makers, forgetters, artists, sketchers, businesswomen, businessmen, leaf-pressers, gift-givers, minimalists and all of us who ever wanted to do a book.' I think that about covers everybody. Maybe I should buy one for myself. I wrote some of my thoughts when I was in the...before I moved to the halfway house; and I think it helped."

"I will make it a gift to you, Janie, for all of your hard work and impressive skills with customers." Wilma gave Janie a quick hug before getting back to unpacking the rest of the boxes.

When she arrived back at the apartment that afternoon, she placed the Nothing Book on the coffee table where she could see it, but it sat there unused.

On her walk to work in the morning, thoughts chased each other through her head: *She had a job! She was good at it, and she liked it. People liked her; lots of people; normal people. She was sleeping better, making a bit of money, she was...happy!*

She walked right into a child who was skipping down the street towards her, paying no more attention to his surroundings than she was.

"Oh, so sorry! Are you okay?" She put out a hand to lift the boy off the sidewalk. He smiled up at her, the angelic toothy smile familiar.

"Wait, aren't you...Bobby? Right? We met in the elevator in our building a few weeks ago. Where's your mom, aren't you a little young to be out here alone?"

"I'm nine!" Bobby said.

Janie was too shocked to speak; he was the smallest and most immature-looking nine-year-old she had ever seen; a rib-thin waif of a young man.

"What's your name?" he asked her.

"I'm Janie. Don't you go to school, Bobby? I mean, it's 8:45; is today a holiday?"

"I go to school sometimes, when mama makes me. I don't like it much. The kids make fun of me. They call me sissy boy or baby boy, and don't want to play with me. But mama's still in bed today, she drank a lot last night; so, I snuck out. I have to get home now, 'cuz if she catches me, she's gonna give me a whoopin.' Bye, Miss Janie!" and with that, he took off at a gallop towards their building.

A few mornings later, she saw Bobby again, scampering towards home with a bit of a limp. He stopped when he saw her, breathing hard with a beaming smile for her. "Mornin,' Miss Janie! I got to get home, but I always like seeing you!"

"Are you limping, Bobby? What happened?"

"Oh, mama gave me a good shove when she found me trying on her sparkly high heels. She calls them her 'club' heels, but she says she can't go out and have fun anymore because of me. I thought she was sleeping when I snuck into the closet to put them on, but she wasn't 'cuz she jumped out of bed, called me a 'fagboy' and pushed me into the night table. That's why my leg hurts. What's a fagboy, Miss Janie?"

Janie's heart hurt for this sweet child. "It doesn't mean anything, Bobby. But maybe you should leave your mother's shoes alone if it makes her really mad."

"Oh, I can't resist those pretty shoes! Sometimes, when she leaves me alone in the apartment, I try on her club dresses, too. I just like the way they look; you know? Gotta go, Miss Janie, see you again!"

She raised her hand in a wave, but he was already down the block. On the rest of her walk, her thoughts turned to Bobby. She wanted to help him, but his mother had made it clear that she was to mind her own business. She worried about what his mother might do to Bobby if she found out Janie was interfering, but a little boy should be in school; and, she thought with a twinge of memory about her own cold upbringing, should be loved.

Janie was distracted at work that day, and when Wilma asked her about it, she smiled sadly and said, "There's a little boy in my building who lives with his mother. I'm a bit worried about him; she has a temper and takes it out on him. I'm just not sure how to help him; or if it might make things worse to even try."

Wilma gave her a hug and said, "Janie, you will do the right thing for this young man, I am sure of it!"

Over the next few months, Janie met secretly with Bobby as often as they could manage without getting caught. She gave Bobby her apartment number and he came down to see her whenever his mother was passed out or had left the apartment for a while. Deciding that the best thing for Bobby would be to just listen to him and encourage him, she mostly sat while he chatted on in his bubbly way. Realizing quickly that Bobby was smart and liked to learn, she persuaded him to attend school regularly; and helped him through the worst of the bullying.

"You are going to school for yourself, Bobby. These kids are just cruel and they pick on you, but it doesn't mean anything. I know the teachers and principal didn't do anything when you told them; and I am very sorry about that. But now, you need to find a way to deal with it. It will eventually stop, but it could be a while. What do you think you could do?"

It turned out that Bobby had a knack for making people laugh, and he learned to charm enough of the other kids to keep most of the bullying at bay.

On one afternoon, as Janie was getting Oreos and milk and an apple for Bobby, he asked her about the Nothing Book on the table.

"Oh, that's a journal that Wilma gave me. I thought I might

write my thoughts in it, but I just never really was able to get started. Wait, why don't you take it? Maybe it would be something good for you!"

"I could never take it to my apartment, Miss Janie. If mama read my thoughts, I don't think she would like them much. Could I do it here? You could read it if you want. I know you won't hurt me no matter what."

"Of course, you can, Bobby. And I would never read your personal thoughts. If you want, you can read some of it to me and we can talk about it."

Bobby did, often coming in and writing in the book while he ate his snack. Then he would share his thoughts and Janie was always astonished at how creative, sweet, and thoughtful they were. He loved his mama, despite the way she treated him; forgiving her even though she did not ask for forgiveness or seemed to feel she needed it. He had a few friends at school, mostly girls who liked the same music and television shows he did. He did not have a clue what he wanted to do when he grew up, but did not seem to worry about it, either. He loved poodles, fads, and pastel colors, and anything sugary; and he was learning to cook, having become tired of reheating frozen T.V. dinners every night. Janie enjoyed his visits, which happened two or three times a week. She looked forward to hearing Bobby's latest notion or whim.

Janie was beginning to realize she enjoyed interacting with other people; and that she was good at it. A conversation with Wilma confirmed it when the woman reiterated how sales had gone up the day Janie started to work at the store; and how well they had done through the holiday season. Wondering what she could do with this newfound idea about herself, she was intrigued to find, among the usual junk in her mail slot, a course catalog for the City College of New York. It was addressed to "current resident," but Janie thought it could be a little sign; maybe from Mrs. Thomas, as she remembered that

Wechsler had been a student there.

Looking through the offerings, she stopped when she saw the section called "Counseling and Psychotherapy." Over dinner, she read carefully through the information; and decided then and there to give the college a call the next day to speak to someone about it.

For several days she walked past the pay phone on her way home, slowing down as it called to her, reminding her that she should reach out to that college. It took almost a week for her to stop with a nervous sigh, insert her dime and dial the number for the registrar's office.

Her hand and voice both shaking, she inquired about the cost of taking one undergraduate class in the Spring semester that was about to begin, how to register and what the schedule would be. On the advice of the woman at the registrar's office, she followed up with a call to the department of Psychology. The advisor she spoke to was warm and encouraging; the call went on so long, Janie ran out of nickels and promised to call back the next day.

During that second call, as she plugged coin after coin into the slot, he gave her information that led to her decision to go back to school. She would begin by getting an Associate's Degree in Substance Abuse Counseling; and then maybe continue on to a degree in Psychotherapy.

Over deli sandwiches the next day, she told Wilma of her plan.

"Oh, my goodness, Sweetie, what a perfect idea! You will be so good at counseling others who are going through what you went through, and lucky patients who will have your wonderful empathy on their side. If there is anything I can do to support you, please just ask! You can still work here and take evening classes if you want. Oh, Janie, how exciting!"

Janie smiled and agreed. It was very exciting, and nerve-wracking and terrifying and daunting; and it was time she pulled on her big girl pants and went after a dream. Even if she failed, a nagging worry that tried to discourage her, at least she would know that she tried. She walked home from work that day with an extra bounce in her step.

She told Bobby her plan that afternoon, and his enthusiastic hug told her he approved. "You always encouraged me to go to school; now I can do that for you!"

Through the biting cold days before the new semester began, Janie found herself in high spirits. Even underneath a wool hat and scarf, her face took on a beaming radiance that attracted people on the street to stop for a moment and engage her in conversation. To celebrate her newfound purpose, Janie took herself ice skating at Wollman's Rink in Central Park and thought that a steaming cup of hot chocolate had never tasted so rich and creamy.

A few days later, there was a knock on the door at Bobby's usual time. It sounded so different than his familiar cheery rhythms, Janie did not think it was him at all. The sight that met her eyes when she opened the door left her speechless. Through the three-inch gap that the security chain allowed, the figure in the hallway was unrecognizable. One eye was swollen nearly shut, and the other was neatly made-up with sparkly blue eye shadow, black liner and skillful mascara applied to thick, beautiful lashes. Tears tinged with black make-up traced down his face. His cheeks were both rouged, but one had a nasty dark bruise underneath the pinkish powder. His lips, painted bright red, were split with drying crusting blood.

"Miss Janie," Bobby whispered. The sound of his voice slapped her to action, and she unlatched the chain and pulled him in to the apartment.

He stood just inside the door and quietly spoke. "Mama caught me trying out her make-up. She got furious and said I would never be a real man until I stopped acting a fool, and she was going to teach me a lesson I wouldn't forget."

With that, he crumbled into her arms and sobbed. Janie held him tightly, not knowing what to say that could make it better.

As soon as he could speak again, he told Janie, "I know you want to call the police, but that would only make it worse. She doesn't mean to hurt me, Miss Janie; she really wants me to be good. And I am trying..." and he broke down again.

When he was more composed, Janie helped him carefully wash the make-up off his face, avoiding the bruises and cuts; and gave him ice to put on his eye, cheek, and lip. Even with the mean purple swelling, he gave her a sweet smile, tinged with sadness. A few minutes later, he handed her the ice, gave her a long tender hug, and left.

The next morning when she was having her first cup of coffee and staring at the Nothing Book on the table feeling helpless, she noticed a piece of paper that had been slipped under her door.

Unfolding it, she read: *Dear Miss Janie, mama is asking where I went last night, and is very suspicious about who helped me. I swore to her the police were not called, and I lied to her and told her I went to see a friend from school. She told me not to leave the apartment again or I would get "what-for" so I will probably not be able to visit you for a while. At least she is letting me go to school, as long as I tell everyone I fell and hit my face on a table. Anyway, I want to say thank you so much for being a friend to a lost little soul like me. You have no idea how much you helped me. Maybe we can run into each other on my way to or from school! Hugs and kisses, Bobbi. P.S. I like this spelling of my name so much better, but I can't let mama see it!*

Janie held the note for a long time, feeling a laundry list of emotions all at once. She tucked the folded paper into the Nothing Book and put it on her nightstand so it would remind her to say a little prayer, or what passed for one since she had never really learned how to pray, for Bobbi every night.

Janie did occasionally run into Bobbi out on the street, and he would chat animatedly about school, while looking around to make sure they did not get caught. Every once in a while, Bobbi popped into the store to admire some of the merchandise and give Janie a quick affectionate hug before scooting back out the door to get home. He was always so upbeat despite the obstacles; it gave Janie hope and optimism that she had not felt before.

It was his positive attitude that buoyed her as she stood outside the CCNY campus on the first day of classes. She had arrived hours before her class was scheduled to begin, so she could wander and orientate herself and work up the nerve to go inside. The stunning gothic architecture of Shepard Hall held her gaze for long minutes. It was completely different than the glass and concrete buildings of N.Y.U. and gave a completely different feel to what she was about to do. The students buzzing by on their way to or from classes seemed to feel it too; they reverently lowered their voices as they passed the building. She decided to go inside to look around before finding the location of her first class.

The inside of the building was every bit as magnificent as the outside. A large bronze plaque near the entryway caught her eye, its inscription containing a quote by one of the founders of the original college, which had been called The Free Academy. Horace Webster, a man who apparently was a force to be reckoned with in the mid 1800's had said, *"The experiment is to be tried, whether the children of the people, the children of the whole people, can be educated; and whether an institution of the highest grade can be successfully controlled by the popular will, not by the privileged few."*

Janie felt her shoulders straighten as she turned to wander this impressive building. She approached the Great Hall with awe. The marble floors and imposing columns drew her in, and the grand pipe organ installed above her head in one of the walls grabbed her attention. Then she turned to take in the massive mural at the end of the hall, entitled, "The Graduate."

She stood for a long while observing with growing delight the meaning of the painting: surrounding the man who was graduating were an abundance of people from all walks of historical life, including Galileo and Isaac Newton; Shakespeare and Beethoven; and dozens of others, all of whom were gazing meaningfully upon the new graduate.

The message of Shepard Hall was clear: here was a place where learning was not only possible, it was expected, fostered, supported, and nurtured. Janie wiped a tear from her eye and went to find her first class with a new sense of purpose.

That feeling dissolved when she tried to enter the classroom. Her step faltered and the young woman directly behind Janie bumped into her when she stopped short.

"Oh, sorry," Janie breathed, stepping aside as the student gave her a look.

All the other students seemed so young, so determined, so committed to this path they were on, Janie felt overcome and out of place. She stood outside the door for long minutes, checking her watch to see that the class was about to begin. Her feet wanted to turn and run; and just as they began to take over, the professor stepped in front of her.

"Good afternoon! Are you looking for Introduction to Social and Cultural Anthropology? Professor Anne Billen? That's me. Come on in, we're about to get started."

The teacher held her arm out to indicate that Janie go ahead of her into the room; and Janie went.

As soon as Professor Billen shared the syllabus, Janie felt her tension ease. At the very top of the thick stapled packet, she read a description of the class: "This anthropology course provides a broad and integrated perspective on human behavior, sociocultural diversity, and human evolution. Such a comprehensive focus begins an excellent preparation for careers in a wide range of settings including health, international affairs, public service, education, law, management, and industry."

Just reading these words made Janie feel stronger, motivated and ready to become part of the river of learning into which she had thrown herself. That first day's discussion on the effects of current social norms on human behaviors had Janie participating with knowledge and maturity her fellow students still sorely lacked, and they all quickly looked to her in admiration. When the class ended, Janie sat for a long moment in the empty classroom, marveling at how much she had enjoyed herself.

Her second class, English Literature of the Twentieth Century, was just as enjoyable. Once again, the few years she had on the other students showed in her perceptive contributions and responses to the works of Kipling, Kafka, Woolf, and O'Connor.

For her mid-semester response project, Janie chose Shirley Jackson's short story called, "The Lottery." It had given her chills when she read it the first time; and she did not sleep well that night.

Janie stood at the front of the room after passing out mimeographed copies of the story, still smelling faintly of chemical duplicator fluid, and gave her classmates a moment to skim it. She held the notecards, on which she had jotted key phrases, bulletin points and a few quotes she wanted to highlight, tightly in one hand.

Despite rumblings in her stomach as she waited to begin speaking, she found herself enthusiastic and started off with impassioned energy.

"Shirley Jackson has captured a piece of the human spirit in this short story that really forced me to ask myself about group mentality and the normalization of tradition; even when that tradition is destructive and vicious to members of our own community. She begins the story like any small-town gathering that people look forward to."

Janie picked up the first note card and read a quote.

"'The morning of June 27th was clear and sunny, with the fresh warmth of a full summer day; the flowers were blossoming profusely, and the grass was richly green. The people of the village began to gather in the square, between the post office and the bank, around ten o'clock; in some towns there were so many people that the lottery took two days and had to be started on June 26th. But in this village, where there were only about three hundred people, the whole lottery took less than two hours, so it could begin at ten o'clock in the morning and still be through in time to allow the villagers to get home for noon dinner.'

"You think, okay, this is some kind of annual thing everyone in the country does in their own towns and cities; a special event in which someone wins a lottery. You start to picture what it might look like in other places, and how they could handle it in a city like New York. Shirley Jackson also immediately makes it sound like some people could be ho-hum about it; wanting to get home in time for noon dinner.

"To further normalize the event, she goes on to describe what the townspeople were doing while they gathered waiting, and how the lottery is run by the same man who is in charge of the teen club, Halloween and square dances. She makes it clear that these three hundred residents know each other's lives intimately. She shows very little information on the beginnings of this tradition; making a point of saying that few people really knew how or why it started and some people thought it should no longer be done. It made me stop and think about all of the traditions I always took for granted without wondering how and why we do them: Halloween, Valentine's Day, Mother's Day, Memorial Day and Labor Day, which I always mix up..."

The class chuckled here, a few people saying, "Oh my God, me too."

One young man yelled out, "Yeah, what the heck is up with

Groundhog Day?" followed by more laughter.

Janie continued. "The lottery finally begins, and the head of each family goes to choose a piece of paper out of the special box. During this time, there are side jokes and conversations that, once again, make everything seem so normal. And we still don't know what the lottery winner gets, although there was some slick foreshadowing of the boys grabbing stones. It is only towards the end of the story that it becomes clear that the lottery is in fact a death sentence. The victim of this year's lottery is one of the mothers. Her neighbors and friends, and even her children and husband, pick up stones, form a circle around her and throw them at her until, presumably, she is killed.

"Shirley Jackson's story made me ponder so many things about human behavior. First, the horror that people could make murder a traditional, mundane event; but then I thought about the death penalty. Now we hide the killing in a tiny room, strapping someone into a chair with few witnesses and very little media coverage; but up until fairly recently, people were hung in town squares or shot by firing squad or even burned at the stake. I imagine people then would also be concerned about getting home in time for supper, and it makes me shudder.

"Second, I wondered why a town would think it's a good idea to kill one of its members every year. Every person in the town had an equal chance, including the final victim's son who was so young he needed help from another member of the community."

She read off another note card.

'"Remember," Mr. Summers said. "Take the slips and keep them folded until each person has taken one. Harry, you help little Dave."

Mr. Graves took the hand of the little boy, who came willingly with him up to the box.

"Take a paper out of the box, Davy." Mr. Summers said.

Davy put his hand into the box and laughed.

"Take just one paper." Mr. Summers said. "Harry, you hold it for him."

Mr. Graves took the child's hand and removed the folded paper from the tight fist and held it while little Dave stood next to him and looked up at him wonderingly.'

"This particular part seems innocuous until you get to the end of the story and find out what happens to the lottery winner. I went back and read it again, and I think it may be the most horrifying part of the whole story. Davy is acting just like any two-year-old, not understanding what is going on, but wanting to participate like everyone else. Once I read the whole story, I realized it could just as easily have been him that 'won,' and that it is likely in other years that a two-year-old did get chosen and the thought of the townspeople cold-bloodedly stoning a baby..."

Janie had to stop for a moment; the air in the silent classroom was thick, as the others thought about what she was saying.

"And finally, the way the 'winner' acted was so sickening, I started to wonder if Shirley Jackson hated her family."

The class laughed at this, and it was a relief to them all.

"Mrs. Hutchinson starts screaming that her married daughter should be counted as part of their family and take a ticket too. I could not believe that a mother could want anyone, let alone a daughter, to face the horror they all now had to deal with. But then again, I thought about my own mother and decided she might do the same. She was not a warm, caring person, and honestly, I am not sure how she would act in the same situation. But the truth is, maybe none of us really know how we would react to something like this."

She paused again to let them think about it.

"Shirley Jackson's story is an extreme example of societal customs based in ancient rituals of human sacrifices to the gods, but the behavior she illustrates, condoned murder, happens constantly in present-day society, at least in our own little piece of the world. Organized crime is a clear example. Within the organizations, murder is the way they cull the herd and try to stay king of the mountain, and from the outside, when we read about yet another hit job we think, 'well, of course, that's what they do. It does not affect me because I'm not in the mob.'

"But more commonplace cases like teenage drug use due to peer pressure, or physical abuse of a wife or children where the police say it's just a family matter, or discrimination based on race or sexual orientation that leads to, in the best case, poor treatment, and in the worst, outright murder; all of these are present-day human behaviors based on group mentality and socially acceptable customs.

"Shirley Jackson published this story in 1948, and it was not well-received by the public. When asked about it in an interview, she said, 'I suppose I hoped, by setting a particularly brutal ancient rite in the present and in my own village, to shock the story's readers with a graphic dramatization of the pointless violence and general inhumanity in their own lives.' Instead of being shocked by the premise of her story, they were instead shocked and outraged at *her* for writing it. Maybe now, thirty-five years later, we can read it with the mentality that it is truly a warning about ourselves. Maybe if we all thought about how badly people behave without questioning things, we can prevent the fall of our own society somewhere in the future. One can only hope!"

The other students began to call out questions, and a lively discussion ensued. Janie fielded the queries and managed the discussions like she was born to it. The professor sat back with a smile and let it all happen; and after the other students cleared out still chatting about her presentation, she gave Janie high praise.

Janie thought she had not felt this good and this strong since she could remember; and she carried that feeling through the rest of the day, and on through the semester.

The cohort of students became tight and bonded as they forged through the program, often going out at night for drinks together. They always invited Janie, and she always politely made excuses, although she did join them for an occasional lunch or after-class picnic on the grass at St. Nicholas Park.

Two of the men and one of the women from the group had privately asked her for more than friendship. She had been taken aback by each of them; attractive, younger than her and genuinely interested. She told them with complete honesty that she just was not ready for any kind of relationship, that she was still trying to find herself; and they accepted this with grace, for which she was grateful.

On a Friday afternoon during Spring Break, one that just begged for her to stay outside after ending her shift at the store, Janie stopped by the apartment to pick up her mail from the rusted metal slot in the lobby and walked to the park bench to enjoy the sunny warmth. For a long while, she sat with her eyes closed, a contented smile on her sunlit face; but the sounds of other people enjoying the day was too much of a draw and she began to do her favorite pastime of people-watching.

The first thing she noticed was that everyone, every single person from the tiniest to the oldest, was smiling. It awed her to see how the warm bright light of the afternoon helped everyone forget troubles and embrace the moment.

What a gift such a day is! Janie thought as she waved back to elderly women and small children and bike messengers and groups of young mothers pushing strollers who greeted her and each other as they went by.

This never happens in Queens, she thought, laughing out loud and drawing four children, who had been running by, to her bench. Hearing her laughter, they buzzed over to chat her up before darting away to play.

After an hour of soul-enriching delight, she remembered the stack of envelopes in her hand and gave them a cursory glance. Janie almost never checked the mail slot in the lobby until it became so full that the carrier left the slot door hanging open. It was always crammed with flyers, catalogs, ads for deals from the local pizza place or Chinese take-out, and envelopes from charities asking for donations with large type print yelling, "DO NOT THROW THIS OUT! YOUR COMMUNITY NEEDS YOUR HELP!"

Junk…junk…junk…She sorted through the pile, tossing each unwanted piece into a mess on the bench next to her, to be thrown into the corner trash can on her way home. About halfway through, a white envelope fell out facedown onto the ground. Another politician asking for a donation, she thought. She nearly threw it on the pile without flipping it over but thought to at least give it a glance.

Samantha Buchanan, Esq., Estate Planner, Granger, Lehman, Schmidt and Bernstein Law Offices, 26 Park Ave, New York, New York, it said in very official-looking letters on the return address sticker. It was addressed in neatly handwritten script to Miss Janie Thompson at her current residence.

For a moment she only stared at it, fear creeping up her legs to her stomach, through her constricting throat and lodging in her brain, freezing her. The sounds around her, still joyous and completely oblivious to the drama on the park bench, muted into white noise competing with the loud buzzing in her mind.

Don't open it, just throw it out. Whatever it is, you don't need it. Open it right now! It looks really important. It's probably bad news that is going to ruin everything for you. Open it!

She tore the top off the envelope and the folded paper inside almost fell onto the ground. She caught it clumsily in midair. A smaller paper fell out from inside the fold and landed face down. She picked it up and turned it over.

And froze.

Her name was printed clearly on the line that said, "Pay to the order of." Puzzled, she looked at the tiny box to the right of her name and almost dropped it again. Ten thousand dollars. A one, followed by six zeroes, with the necessary comma and decimal point in their correct places.

It must be a mistake. The only people who might have money to leave were her parents and they had no way of finding her. Her hands shaking, she opened the folded paper and saw the lawyer's letterhead followed by typical business format, and then two very simple lines of typed print.

The amount on the check was left to you by Mrs. Dorothy Geraldine Wechsler Thomas in her will. Please call me as soon as possible to discuss the rest of your inheritance.

Below this, the lawyer's name was illegibly signed; her full name and title typed at the bottom.

It was the last thing Janie saw before she fainted to the ground.

Part 3

Adversity doesn't build character; it reveals it.
-James Lane Allen, novelist (1849-1923)

Introducing Jane

A wet handkerchief dabbing her face brought her back. Janie opened her eyes to see a crowd gathered over her. The owner of the damp cloth was leaning in close, and as soon as Janie blinked, she stood up straight and announced to the crowd, "She is okay, just fainted, thank the Lawd. You can go on your merry ways now! Give the poor thing some room to breathe."

Her authoritative tone compelled the others to obey, and Janie was left alone with the woman, who was elderly but large enough and strong enough to lift her back onto the bench like a small child. Still holding onto Janie's arm to make sure she did not slip back to the ground, the woman peered closely into Janie's face.

"Are you okay, honey child? You turned ashen gray down there, gave this old Mawmaw quite a scare, to be honest."

Janie nodded, not sure if she could trust her voice. After a moment she said, "I'm okay, I just had a shock."

She held up the letter. She had been clutching it so tightly, she never lost hold of it when she passed out.

"I just found out that a friend died. And she..." Janie could not finish and began to weep.

The woman folded Janie into her breast with a comforting embrace such as Janie had never experienced. It made her give up everything in heaving sobs; a soul-cleansing cry that came from somewhere deep inside, over which Janie seemed to have no control. The woman rocked her gently until it subsided.

"Looks like you needed a good cry, honey-pot. We all do sometimes. I am sorry about your friend; but she is now in God's glorious hands, and once you get past your grief that thought will make you glad. We don't always know or understand His plan, but you can trust there is one, that is what pastor Matthew always preaches. Maybe your friend knew you still have work to do, and it was just her time. Do you think so?"

Janie nodded, not knowing what she believed, but wanting to please this warm and loving lady.

"Do you want me to walk you home, Miss...."

"Janie," she said. "My name is Janie Thompson. I think I'm okay now. I'm going to sit here for a minute and then head back."

"Well, I'm Ethel Teasdale, but most people call me Auntie E or Miss Ethel or just plain Mawmaw. I will send a prayer up for you and..."

Miss Ethel gently took the paper from Janie to read the name, then handed it back. "And your friend, Mrs. Dorothy Geraldine Wechsler Thomas, at church tomorrow morning."

Janie gave her a tight hug and said, "Thank you, Miss Ethel. For everything."

She watched the woman walk down the street, waving back when Miss Ethel turned one last time to check on her. Janie read and re-read the letter, emotions clashing in her head, before heading back to her apartment. She hung the check, the letter and the envelope with refrigerator magnets where she could see them every time she walked by the kitchen that weekend.

On Monday morning before work, Janie stopped at the Manufacturers Hanover Trust bank and opened her very first ever savings and checking accounts.

She was waiting when Wilma arrived to open the store, and as soon as they entered and turned on the lights, Janie told her, "I can work on Wednesdays now."

"That's just great, Janie..." Wilma started to say, until she looked at her young employee's face and stopped. "Oh, dear. You can explain it to me if you want, but you don't have to."

Janie looked down for a minute, and then simply added, "I

have a bank account now too, if you want to pay me with a check."

Then she got right to work.

That afternoon, Janie stepped into the phone booth on the corner, called the Bell Telephone company and arranged to have a phone put in her apartment; and she stopped by the shop down the street to buy herself a small Phillips Magnavox color television complete with a rabbit ear antenna set. With mixed feelings, she placed the television in the living room, remembering her afternoons with Mrs. Thomas.

She still had not decided whether to reach out to *Samantha Buchanan, Esq., Estate Planner;* but when the phone company came the following week to install her light blue tabletop push-button telephone, it was the first call she made.

The secretary answered with a nasal greeting and then a "Please hold for Ms. Buchanan, Esquire."

The voice that greeted her was strong and professional. "Miss Thompson, thank you for contacting me. Mrs. Thomas thought you might not call, and she gave me strict instructions in case you did. You will need to come into my office in midtown to hear the rest of the will. When can you make it? I am here every day, including weekends, from nine to nine."

"I don't know, I don't really want anything more from her, the ten thousand dollars is much more than I need and was so generous. What happened to her, please? I did not even know she died until I got your letter."

"She said you would say exactly that about the money," Ms. Buchanan gave a laugh before continuing. "She fell ill and was taken to the hospital by ambulance. The diagnosis was basically old age. She called me from there, demanding that I come to see her and bring a notary so she could change her will. When we arrived, she knew I was checking to see if she was mentally fit enough to make such changes, and she barked at me, 'I am sound of mind, but not body, Samantha. I do not want to be one of those rich widows who leave their belongings to a cat or a random church. Janie was so kind to me and gave me so much joy at the end of my life. I never thought to feel that again.'

"She dictated a letter to you that I will give you when you come in; and I am not to give you any more details until you come to the office. She said distinctly not to take 'no' for an answer. I do not know the nature of your relationship with her, and I do not need to, either; but she made herself completely clear, which should not surprise you."

It was Janie's turn to give a small laugh in agreement.

"You can call my secretary to make an appointment, but please consider doing it sooner rather than later. It is always best to take care of estates as quickly as possible."

Janie agreed and hung up the phone. Sitting alone in the silent apartment trying to sort out her thoughts and feelings, Janie realized that Mrs. Thomas, *Dorothy*, had been her only friend since she left the burned-down halfway house. Now, she was to respect the woman's final wishes, and go to the lawyer's office to read her letter and hear the reading of the will. She reached for the handset and dialed the law office once more to make an appointment for the following Saturday morning.

Before she even left her apartment that morning, her stomach was flipping and threatening to expunge breakfast all over her best blouse and shoes. She stood staring at the door in front of her, breathing the way Mark had taught her. Four deep breaths calmed her down enough to get her resolve back and put her hand on the doorknob.

The long walk to the subway station under the morning sun gave her spirits a lift. Whatever was about to happen, she thought, she would handle it.

The tall, fancy building on Park Avenue where the lawyer awaited gave her pause. The doorman, in his flawlessly pressed uniform, opened the door, stepped through and said in a jaunty tone, "Good morning, Miss! Beautiful day today. Can I help you?"

He walked her to the bank of elevators, guided her to the correct one, and pushed the fourteenth-floor button for her when it arrived. Doffing his hat to her, he went back to his post. Janie had time to notice there was no thirteenth floor in the building before the doors slid silently open into the intimidatingly bright, busy, and beautiful reception area of the law offices.

The secretary with the nasal voice called Ms. Buchanan's line to announce Janie's arrival and then escorted her, in stunningly high stiletto heels and a very tight-fitting short skirt, down the wide hallway towards the lawyer's office. They passed a large conference room in which a half dozen impeccably suited men were smoking cigars and toasting some obviously good news with short glasses of amber liquid.

"Hey, Carla, come sit on my lap, we're celebrating in here!" one of the younger attorneys yelled as they walked past, to the randy laughter of the others. Carla, obviously the secretary's name, stopped long enough to smile flirtatiously and respond, "Maybe later, Mr. Durney; work, work, work!"

As soon as they were out of sight, Carla's face turned flushed and hassled, but she did not say a word to Janie.

Ms. Buchanan's office was small but impressively decorated. Her degrees from Columbia University were prominently displayed above a bookshelf filled with volumes of law and judicial decisions. She hung up the phone while Janie looked around. Indicating Janie should sit in the leather armchair in front of her cherry-wood desk, she templed her fingers and gave her client's beneficiary a once-over. Janie, in her turn, looked at this striking, confident woman, not much older than her, with a bit of awe.

"Please, call me Samantha," the lawyer said, leaning across the desk to shake Janie's hand with impressive firmness. "Mrs.

Thomas told me you were a little shy, and to try not to intimidate you so you would not run away. It looks to me like you might just need some self-assurance; maybe you had a rough go up to now, she was not specific. By the way, I love your blouse and your earrings."

Janie sat up a bit straighter, suddenly feeling a little more confidence in herself without knowing why.

"Thank you, Samantha. Mrs. Thomas was literally my only friend those few months; and I guess maybe I was also hers. I miss her."

Janie's eyes threatened to water but she blinked them hard. "I did not know about any of this, and I am so grateful to her for leaving me more money than I have ever seen in my life. I am not sure what else she left in the will, but honestly, I don't need any more."

Samantha opened the manila envelope in front of her, marked clearly with Mrs. Thomas' name, and pulled out a single sheet of paper, a typed letter. She passed it to Janie and sat back to allow her time to read and absorb it.

April 13, 1983

My Dear,

Since you are reading this letter, it means that I have passed on. Do not spend too much time mourning me. Know that I am at peace and reunited with my beloved sons and husband, probably dancing a Lindy Hop and eating pastries from whatever passes for a Jewish bakery up here.

Janie let out a laugh and her eyes overflowed at this point. Samantha pulled a small box of Kleenex out of a drawer and slid it across the desk. Janie sobbed into a tissue for a moment and then was able to continue.

You know from all the stories with which I bored you, that I led a fortunate life despite some of the tragedies I suffered. These last years, however, had been so lonely I believed I had outlived any chance of further happiness; until the day you gave me a compliment standing there in line at the pharmacy. I do not know what you believe, I really do not know what I believe myself, but if there is a God, he put you there to give me one last joy before my time came.

You were the granddaughter I should have had, and for that I go to my grave ever grateful. My only regret is that I did not have a chance to allow you to tell me your story, Dear. I could tell it was a sad one, and I can tell you now, via this letter, that you deserve more; and that you have so much more to give to others.

I told you once, and I want to tell you again so that you will really hear it and think hard on it: you are a very good listener. You made me feel heard and seen with your undivided attention and your empathy. This is a gift that most people do not have; and I want to help you reach your potential so that you can share it with others, who like me, just need a good ear.

Therefore, I leave everything in my will, which Samantha will read now, to you. I hope you will consider taking this gift as a sign of the confidence that I have in you that, with proper guidance and training, you can be the beacon of light to others that you were with me. Some of us, most of us, just go through our life's journey with our eyes shut, feeling like we are on a trajectory not of our choosing and not in our control. I offer you, with the utmost respect and yes, even love, the opportunity to take your voyage to hand and use it for good.

Most sincerely,
Mrs. Dorothy Geraldine Wechsler Thomas

*P.S. Enough with the infantile moniker! Just as I outgrew "Dot," surely you have long surpassed the time of your childhood nickname. From now on, I hereby proclaim you officially "Miss **Jane** Thompson." May you live a long, happy, fruitful, and thoroughly liberated life.*

After Samantha saw that she had read the letter several times, she spoke: "She dictated that letter to me just a few days before she passed, peacefully in her sleep. The nurse even said she had a smile on her face when they found her in the morning. Let me read you her last will and testament, and then, if you want, we can talk about your options."

Last Will and Testament
Of Mrs. Dorothy Geraldine Wechsler Thomas

I, Mrs. Dorothy Geraldine Wechsler Thomas, of Ridgewood, Queens, revoke my former Wills and Codicils and declare this to be my last Will and Testament.
Article I: Identification of Family
All predeceased; no family or next of kin remain living.

Article II: Payment of Debts and Expenses
I direct that my just debts, funeral expenses, and expenses of last illness be first paid from my estate.

Article III: Disposition of Property
A. Specific Requests
I direct that the following bequests be made from my estate:
All of my accrued wealth, all of my jewelry and anything of value, and my home and furnishings to be given to Miss Jane Thompson, also of Ridgewood, Queens. She may dispose of the items of value in any way that she sees fit. She is to occupy said home for a period of no less than five years; at which time, she may sell the residence at her will and pleasure.

Samantha stopped reading. Jane felt the room spin momentarily and gripped the edge of the cool desk with her whitened hand, but then it quieted and righted itself.

"Are you okay, Jane? There is more but it is mostly legal

mumbo jumbo, eleven pages worth; I will read it if you want."

Jane shook her head, not trusting herself to speak just yet. It took her a moment to gain control of her emotions.

"I just enrolled in school this semester." Jane's voice held a measure of wonder. "I am studying to be a substance abuse counselor and then, maybe, a psychologist. I guess Mrs. Thomas saw something in me before I saw it myself. I hope one day I will live up to her confidence in me and hopes for me. I never thought I could, but maybe I was wrong. No; I *was* wrong."

Samantha nodded her head in agreement. "Mrs. Thomas most definitely recognized something in you, Jane; and even though I do not know you at all, I feel it too. I will give you my card, which has the office phone and my home phone number so that we can stay in touch. I want to offer you my support; we all need someone in our corner, and I would like to be in yours."

Jane took the card and a copy of the will. Her own handshake was both stronger and more resolved than it had been when she came in.

Samantha smiled at this and said, "Atta girl! Call me any time, Jane. I mean it."

Jane called Samantha a few times, to help with closing on the house and ending her lease on the rent-controlled apartment; and to just chat. Samantha always made time for her, offering encouragement at every turn.

The week she moved into the house, Jane reached out to her friend.

"Samantha, can you come to the house for dinner? I know you're really busy, and I know you don't come out to Queens very often, but I would love to cook dinner to celebrate and thank you. Without you, without your support and your friendship, I would not be where I am today, literally."

"I don't normally eat dinner, but for you, just this once, I will make an exception. That is how much I like you, Jane. I'm going to take a car service all the way across the East River and eat a homecooked meal. The sacrifices I make for you..."

They both laughed. "Honestly, I'm not promising you anything worth all the trouble, Samantha. I'm no Julia Childs. More like the Galloping Gourmet's forgotten younger sister; but I think I can manage not to poison us both, anyway. Sunday, around 5?"

The friends agreed on the date, and Jane managed to put together a salad and a roast chicken without injuring either of them. It was a lovely evening; the best one Jane could ever remember.

"I feel like such a grown-up," she said, sitting down at the table after bringing out all the food.

"And I feel like the Queen of Sheba," Samantha responded. "I don't remember the last time I sat in someone's dining room to eat a personally prepared dinner. To you, Jane," she said, raising her glass of Perrier.

"To you, Samantha. My friend."

They toasted and enjoyed the rest of the evening in companionable conversation.

A year later, on her way to the city for her classes, she heard a soft, familiar voice.

"Miss Janie?"

Turning, she found herself looking at a thin young teenager. Dressed in a short skirt, tank top and Keds sneakers, the teen had beautifully done make-up and was wearing earrings with matching bracelets.

"Miss Janie, you don't recognize me? It's Bobbi!"

"Oh goodness, Bobbi!!" They hugged tightly. "You're all dressed up, and you look so happy! Are things better for you now?"

"Mama has a new boyfriend and spends most of her time at

his place, so I am on my own and yes, it is so much better! I am on my way down to the Village, I have so many new friends down there that are just like me; it's amazing!"

Remembering Jinxy standing on the corner with other drag queens, Jane became a bit worried. "Please be careful, Bobbi; when I lived down there not that long ago, there was a lot of danger on Christopher Street and on Sixth Avenue. Please tell me you are watching out for yourself."

"Oh, I am! And my friends are helping me a lot, I just love them! Are you walking to the subway, too? Can we walk together?"

They chatted all the way, Bobbi doing most of the talking. Jane did manage to get a word in, telling Bobbi about her new address and plans to hang a shingle outside: "Jane Thompson, Drug and Behavior Counselor. I'm getting there, I have a real live patient coming soon; with my advisor's help, of course."

"I will help you hang that sign. And I can be your first client!" Bobbi exclaimed, stopping to hug her again.

"Well, technically, my advisor at CCNY has to arrange and supervise all that. But you can drop in any time, Bobbi. I'd love that."

They parted ways at the subway station, with Bobbi effusively promising to come by soon.

"I have a lot of nicknames for myself."

Jane's first patient in her new home office settled onto the couch. "I call myself Dark Dina, Dina Downer and Doubtful Dina, depending on my mood. Now I can add another one: Druggy Dina."

The woman, in her early thirties, looked into Jane's eyes with a challenging gaze. She had just gotten out of a rehabilitation hospital and was sent to Jane, since it was near her apartment. She seemed to be assessing whether this young woman had what it would take to keep her in line so she did not fall back off the wagon, like so many times before.

"Maybe now you can change that one to Sober Dina," Jane said. "Doesn't have the same ring as your ideas, but I like the sound of it. Do you?"

"Yeah, I guess that is going to be the new Dina. It will take a lot of work on your part. Can I call you Jane, instead of Dr. Thompson? Easier for me if we feel like friends a little."

"It's not 'doctor' yet, and may never be, but 'Jane' is fine."

"Good. I'm a piece of work, Jane. Have been for a long time."

Jane took out her notebook and a pencil. "I hope you don't mind if I write down my thoughts. It helps me think about things later."

"Write away, Doc. Oh wait, not a Doc, at least not yet. Write away, Jane."

"Let's begin with you telling me more about these nicknames, Dina. Many times, when someone is addicted to drugs, it is something that actually began long before they started bingeing. Not always, but often. In my own case, I'm still not exactly sure how I wound up down the rabbit hole, or why; so, I might be a case study for an exception to that rule. Still working that one out in my mind."

Dina stared at her. "Wow, Jane. Thanks for the honesty. I've been to shrinks and counselors before, and none of them ever shared their personal history. It gives you something; like you're one of us and you get it. Cool...Anyway, I know exactly why I chase the lightning. I've been doing drugs since I was, oh, probably nine or ten. I was raised out in Arizona, and my family was really loose about sex and drugs through the sixties; so, growing up, I did a lot of both. It seemed all right to me then; I thought all families did stuff like that until I was in high school and started seeing how normal families lived."

Jane interrupted gently. "Well, 'normal' is a very curious word when it comes to people and families, Dina. I am not really sure there is such a thing. I would say my own family wouldn't qualify, even though a lot of people outside looking in would have thought so. It sounds to me that you started to realize the way you were growing up wasn't always in your best interests, though."

"Yeah, that way of looking at it works. It was too late, though. I was all twisted up in my head. I started having these really weird dark thoughts in my teen years, a lot about sex, like bondage and S&M stuff. Thing is, I tried it all, and didn't like it. But that didn't make the thoughts go away. Weird, huh?"

Jane gave her an encouraging smile. It was one of the things her supervisor told her was a gift she had; being able to withhold judgement and even shock when patients bared their deepest shame or demoralized, punishing thoughts.

"Anyway, it's not just sex. I think of horrible things that could happen to people. Not like murder, you know? I'm not one of those psycho killers like that guy behind the shower curtain. It's more like unspeakable accidents or horrifying fates that befall everyday people. Sometimes they keep me up at night. It's not that I am wishing it on someone or even worrying about it happening to me or to people I know; it's more like, well, really bad things happen even to good people. That's just how it is. And I guess I sort of fantasize about it. Probably doesn't help that I love Stephen King books." She laughed out loud.

Dina spent the rest of the session in stream of consciousness sharing. She was all over the place with her anxieties, her upbringing and, most of all, her unsettling thoughts. She left Jane's office with a look on her face that told both of them she did not know if this was going to work out.

Jane spent the week re-reading her notes and thinking intensely about Dina's dilemmas. She spoke to her supervisor about them at length and read up on possible ways forward for her patient. It kept her up at night and disrupted her schoolwork. She badly wanted to help this patient; and she wanted to succeed in her new profession. When Dina arrived at the next appointment, Jane nervously told her she had an idea.

"Dina, you shared in the last session that the biggest trigger that takes you back to drugs and alcohol is the fantasy thinking of horrible things that happen to ordinary people. You said it worries you that you are a bad, or "weird" person and that you can't control these thoughts. So, here is my idea."

Dina sat back, listening but not expecting to be impressed. Jane took a breath, and plunged in.

"Have you ever written down your thoughts as stories? Fictional stories can be about anything; and I think if you write them down, they may feel less threatening and abnormal. Writing is an art, you know? If you look at some of the most famous paintings at a museum, many of them examine the darker side of humanity. Why couldn't you do that with your thoughts? I mean, Stephen King is very popular, and his stories are all about misfortune and catastrophe happening to 'normal' people."

Dina had been reclining on the couch, sinking into the cushions with one leg crossed over the other, her arms folded across her chest. She suddenly sat up and gave Jane a dumbfounded look.

"Write stories? You mean, like take these weird and dark thoughts and make them happen to characters? Other shrinks have told me to keep a journal, but no one has ever suggested I write out my weird shit as short stories. It almost sounds like fun..."

Dina mused silently for a long moment, while Jane sat very still and let her ruminate over the idea. She watched Dina having an inaudible conversation with herself that went on for several minutes. When Dina looked up at Jane, it was with some excitement.

"I'll do it! I friggin' love the idea! I don't know if people will like the stories or if I even can actually write, but I'll bet even Stephen King wasn't Stephen King at first. I have always loved stories; so, why not? Jane, you are a genius, a natural at this counseling stuff after all, and I know we still have more time on the clock, but I really want to get started right now!"

Jane went into her office closet, pulled out a new spiral notebook and a pencil, and handed both to Dina, who gave her a tight quick hug and nearly bounded out the door.

The next day, Jane stopped in at her supervisor's office for her weekly guidance and check-in. Dan, a psychologist who had been overseeing budding therapists for many years, gave her a welcoming smile.

"How did it go with your idea for your first independent client, Jane? There are bound to be ups and downs on both your parts; and some self-doubt on yours. Most counselors hide that uncertainty from their clients, but I have a feeling you share yours. It is one of the things that makes you relatable and easy to talk to."

"I'm almost afraid to say how well the recent session went, Dan. When I told her about my idea, she loved it so much, she could not wait to get started. I know that won't be how every patient's treatment will go, nailing it on the second day. And I know that, even for Dina, the idea could fizzle or even backfire later; that's what we learned in our training. But honestly, it felt good and I'm just going to enjoy that for what it is. If things go downhill quickly, I will come running back to you for help, you can count on that!"

The following week, Dina came in with her notebook in hand.

"I've been working on a story since the minute I left here, Jane. It almost got me fired from my job at the hardware store, and it kept me up every night until dawn. But I am going to leave it with you, if that's okay. I would really love to have you read it and then we can talk about it at another session."

She carefully tore the pages off the spiral binding, and handed them to Jane, biting her lower lip while her eyes shone with eagerness. Jane put them carefully into a manila folder, on which she wrote Dina's name.

"It's called 'Lightning Larry.' I warn you, it's a bit dark."

Jane wrote the story's title on the folder and placed it on her desk. "Thank you so much for trusting me, Dina. I don't know if you know that you're my first real client here in the office; and I am happy that you liked my idea. I still have so much to learn about how to really help someone."

"Are you kidding me? If you can read me that quickly, I have no doubt you were born to do this, Jane. I think at today's session I want to spend some time on how I wound up at rehab again; it was my third go-round, but this time felt different. I don't know if it's because I'm older now, or if I'm just tired of repeating the same old pattern; but maybe if I figure it out with you, I can really make sure this is the last time."

The hour went quickly and ended when Dina gave Jane a hug and said, "See you next week!"

In the evening, over dinner, Jane opened the folder with Dina's handwritten story inside. Thankfully, her printing was as neat as a teacher's, Jane thought, as she began to read.

<u>Lightning Larry</u>
By Dina Merant

Larry lay sprawled across his bed the way only a sixteen-year-old boy can: on his stomach leaning on bony elbows, long legs thrown haphazardly behind him, oversized feet hanging off the edge. Tightly drawn curtains blocked out the brutal Southern Arizona sun. The slammed door, which had neatly cut off his mother's ranting, was as forgotten as the small cardboard box tossed carelessly onto the floor. With a tight smile of anticipation, Larry began to re-read the carefully clipped, but dog-eared, newspaper articles spread out on the bed before him.

All right, so I'm a little obsessed, he thought to himself. *Who isn't obsessed with something? At least I'm not out there doing drugs or anything.*

And then that thought was forgotten, as the familiar headlines took hold of his attention: "Lightning Strikes Golfer" screamed one; "Bolt from Clear Blue Injures Swimmers" stated another; "Strike Three, You're OUT!" His personal favorite.

"Lightning Larry," as the kids at school called him right to his face, had been fascinated for as long as he could remember by the crack of blinding white light and the echoing explosions of the monsoon storms that infected the desert like clockwork two months out of the year. He was aware that other people had four seasons to give the year its rhythm; Larry had February and July.

He so clearly remembered the very first time he truly noticed the lightning, he could smell the ozone in his nostrils.

Just five years old, he had heard the slow rumble followed by the boom which shook the house, as he was dipping his Oreo in a blue plastic cup of milk. The sound galvanized him, but not the way it might any small child sitting alone in the kitchen. Instead of screaming in fear, Larry let his cookie slide forgotten into the milk and float forlornly there; and walked in a trance towards the front door. He had felt it in his chest, in his blood, in his *bones*, and it had drawn him outside.

The monsoon storm was typical for a desert July: ferocious, violent, fierce, black, apocalyptic. The dazzling flashes that turned his world white-purple, and simultaneously exploded that world with deafening detonations, electrified his tiny body. He stood in the midst of the tempest, and something in him changed permanently.

Looking back now, he supposed it was like your first kiss. Although he had yet to experience said kiss, he thought it might be like that- transforming, altering the course of life forever.

After that day, every afternoon during those two months half a year apart, Larry stood outside the house scanning the sky for the telltale black clouds rolling in over the Santa Catalina Mountains. He watched them gather and grow with a tightening in his chest that was part fear but mostly rapture. The darkness came at him with breathtaking speed until he was enfolded by it. He would stand in the sandy yard as the lightning burst around him with random rhythm in a crashing display of line and color that stunned him. He began by counting slowly to five after each flash, and then he couldn't even get to three; and then his mother would holler for him to *for Chrissake get inside and close the door.* He would run inside and drag a chair so close to the large picture window that his nose touched the glass; until his mother made him move back *exactly three-and-a-half feet so that lightning don't jump in through that window and knock you on your hind parts. I swear to Jesus I don't know what's wrong with you!*

How could he explain to her that this was exactly what he wanted?

Over the years, Larry's fascination had grown into something more, something stronger, something...real. Sometime over these last months, Larry went from watching the brilliant and thunderous display to wanting, *needing,* to touch it. To feel it, to participate in it, to be part of it; that was what he craved. He knew it would be dangerous, and also knew that the danger was part of the whole thing. Some people get a thrill from the bogus scare of a roller coaster; well, this was almost the same, only not fake. To experience the electricity passing through his body, to become one with such an untamed energy force; he had to find a way. So, he began to scan the daily newspaper for articles.

And his mother had said, "Lookatcha, reading the paper. Trying to find a job? Good idea, keep you out of trouble."

To avoid any more prying from her, he waited until she threw the papers in the trash bin before he snuck out a pair of scissors and snipped the articles to put in his cardboard box. Since last February there had been eight reports in the newspaper of lightning strikes, and Larry had practically memorized them all.

"Lightning Riskier for Livestock Than for Humans" was the most bizarre headline. According to the National Lightning Detection Network right here in Tucson, which tracks almost all of the millions of cloud-to-ground strikes in the U.S. every year, lightning often hits cows, horses, and other livestock animals. 250 pigs were killed by a single bolt in Thailand, 835 sheep died in a Utah mountain strike and 85,000 chickens on a farm in Florida met the same fate.

That was Larry's first try. He'd had to take a bus across town and walk five miles north to the ranchers' area to find cows, and then he'd spent the afternoon among the stupid bovines waiting for that afternoon's storm. The cows lumbered slowly among the cholla cactus, snuffing for something edible and often coming up with a snout full of prickles. When the storm came, the lightning bolts all struck the mountains to the east and Larry got nothing but drenched. He arrived back at home in a bad mood.

"Lightning Strikes Woman at Fence," read one of the articles. In this story, a Florida woman had been standing near a chain link fence. When lightning hit the metal it jumped to her, knocking her off her feet. Larry had tried that too. He had walked up and down the road in front of his house while the storm raged around him. He paced slowly because every yard on the block was surrounded by connecting chain link fences and he figured if any of them got hit, he would feel it. When the storm passed on, not a single bolt had struck anywhere near him. Larry walked home in a foul mood.

"Storm Leaves One Injured When Lightning Strikes Barbecue Grill at Park"

"Lightning Hits Man Under a Tree"

"Clearwater Beach Lightning Strike Injures Three"

He would have loved to try that one, but he did not know where Clearwater was, and had never actually been to a beach anyway. Maybe the town pool would do, but he had never heard of it getting hit by lightning.

"Gardener Shovels Voltage in Freak Accident"

That was just luck, thought Larry. The poor sucker was digging holes in his garden in the foothills of the Colorado Rockies when the lightning started bouncing around him the way it sometimes did there. It even had a name, "ball lightning," and it was the damndest thing. Larry had, of course, done his research. One time, a young girl was inside an ice cream shop minding her own business when the glowing blue ball came through the door, burst right above her, singed her hair, melted the ice cream to nothing, burnt the cone and left her shoulder paralyzed for 2 weeks. Maybe I should move to Colorado, he mused.

Larry had tried everything in those news articles.

He had found the tallest tree near school, not very tall considering it was the desert, after all; but still the tallest one around. That day, the storm had been relatively calm and missed him completely.

Another afternoon, during a pretty good storm, he had run around like a nut touching every grill he could find in the park. In the pouring rain, singing Chi Coltrane's hit, "Thunder and Lightning", he joyfully raced in erratic circles around the picnic area. When that one ended without success, he actually felt inexplicably good.

The closest he came was when he stood on the pitcher's mound at Hi Corbett Field and waved a metal bat over his head, taunting the clouds. "Three Strikes and You're Out! Come on, pitch me a good one! Hey, batter, batter, batter!" A bolt sizzled through the air throwing purple sparks way above his head and struck the chain link fence bordering center field about 300 yards from him. For a second, he thought he might have felt a tingle, but then the thunder crashed down and Larry swore he heard it chuckle.

When he got home that day his ten-year-old brother, Gary, was sitting on the floor in the hallway by the front door putting the finishing touches on a Lego tower. Their little sister was playing with her dolls nearby. When Larry opened the door, Gary looked up at the sour-faced and dripping teen and teased, "Lightning Larry, Lightning Larry. What's the matter, didn't strike gold today?"

Larry stomped by him, barely slowing down as he delivered a vicious kick to the Lego building. The banging of his bedroom door was not enough to block out the rising wail of his brother: "*MOOOOOOMMMMMMM*" and the simultaneous "*Goddamit, Larry!*"

He calmed himself by re-reading a page he had ripped out of a library book at school. He savored the first sentences that always rekindled his feelings of hero worship: "Roy Sullivan may be considered the luckiest or the unluckiest man in the world; depending on your point of view (*Lucky*, Larry always said to himself). The Virginia State Park Ranger has survived being struck by lightning seven separate times over the course of a 35-year period. According to the Guinness Book of World Records, Sullivan has the distinction of being the most lightning-struck person in history. The first lightning strike shot through Sullivan's leg and knocked his big toenail off. Then in 1969, a second strike burned off his eyebrows and knocked him unconscious. Another strike just a year later left his shoulder seared. In 1972 his hair was set on fire and Roy had to dump a bucket of water over his head to cool off. In 1973, another bolt ripped through his hat and hit him on the head, set his hair on fire again, threw him out of his truck and knocked his left shoe off. A sixth strike in 1976 left him with an injured ankle. The last lightning bolt to hit Roy Sullivan sent him to the hospital with chest and stomach burns in 1977."

All of that, any of that, to Larry seemed like a small price to pay.

Larry imagined himself in Ranger Roy's place, each strike increasing the size of his muscles until the last one turned him into...*Kid Flash*! He knew how Marvel Comic Book that sounded (actually, DC Comics if we are going to be picky), but he smiled to himself and decided to head down to the kitchen for a snack.

His little sister sat on her knees on the cheap kitchen chair at the Formica table, dipping Oreos in a cup of milk. When she smiled at him, her white dripping mustache and cookie-covered teeth made him laugh out loud. He patted her on the head as she sang, "Hi Larry!" with a mouthful of crumbs that sailed all over her bright pink t-shirt and onto the pile of Barbies on the table.

He chuckled to himself as he headed back to his room with a handful of graham crackers and a banana. He had to make a plan that would work, and it had to be tomorrow because the monsoon season was already winding down. He did not know how he would be able to make it another six months like this.

That night he found an article in the newspaper about lightning rods and how they worked by re-directing the electricity along a wire and into the ground. He ran down to the hall phone table and grabbed the Yellow Pages business phone book. His finger scrolled down the short, alphabetized list under Lightning Protection Equipment: Alton's Lightning Rod Company, Lightning Protection Inc, Strike Zone...that one caught his eye and he read the accompanying ad: *"Above All, You Need Lightning Rods"*. That was a good one. He wrote down the number and stuffed it in his jeans pocket.

In the morning, Larry called Strike Zone and got directions. He took the bus to the south side of town and walked into the small dark showroom. The stout man behind the counter offered a meaty hand: "Bob Meadham, son. What can I do for you?"

"How much are the lightning rods?" Larry asked in a voice he hoped sounded serious. He looked around the cramped space and saw little but some odd hardware and several poster-sized photos of house rooftops.

"Well, installed, they can run anywhere from your basic rod system, that's kind of like an antenna on the roof like in that photo there, at about three thousand dollars. Then they go all the way to your top-of-the-line protection system at around $10,000. That one comes with a guarantee or your money back."

Larry could barely find his voice and made some mumbled excuse as he backed out of the storefront.

On the nearly empty bus, he sat with his chin tucked firmly in his hand, mouth turned down in disappointment and frustration. He gazed out of the bus window as it headed north in the line of rush-hour cars. The vehicles came in all shapes, sizes, and colors, but something about them was nipping at his consciousness as he mentally crossed another failed idea off his list.

Then he realized what it was: antennas. They all had antennas...which were just like lightning rods. That was it! Tonight, he would be Lightning Larry for real. With his own lightning rod, A.K.A. mom's car antenna, he would be sure to attract a good strike.

Instantly his mood changed, and a vacant smile of satisfaction and triumph turned his frown upside down. That was the perfect phrase for it, he thought: thank you, Mrs. Rodriquez. His third-grade teacher was famous for her happy little sayings.

He did not think his mother would notice the antenna missing for an hour tonight. The kids would be keeping her busy enough and he should be able to get it back on before she even saw that it was gone.

Tonight, tonight, tonight would be it; he was sure of it, he felt it in his bones.

****

The storm was a monster. It overtook the area with a murky blackness completely devoid of light except for the intermittent flickering blasts of lightning. Larry stood trembling on the highest hill at the neighborhood park, watching its approach. He felt, he *knew*, that this was it; and so, he began to wave the antenna over his head.

Softly he began calling to it, "Come on I'm here waiting for you...come here, come here, come on..."

Then it was there, and lightning crashed in zigs and zags with no pause between the flash and the crash. Bolts, fat and thin, long and short, multi-tined forks shooting in all directions came and came and came, exploding the world purple, pink and unnatural white. Booms echoed around him and through him until his heart beat to the irregular claps, rumbles, cannon shots, cracks and snaps. It went on for so long that Larry's crooning turned into a moan and then a scream that rose up and up and was lost in the wildness.

Fifteen minutes after it arrived, the storm walked off across the park on spidery lightning legs, leaving a deadening muteness behind as if the park waited to see if it might change its mind and come back. Larry crumpled to the ground sobbing, soaked with rain and sweat; the antenna still clutched in one hand. It took great effort for him to stand, and he swayed as he gazed dismally at the now-distant rumble and flash.

He shuffled, head hung low, down the hill and out into the neighborhood. He did not know how his feet were moving; it was as if they were not connected to the rest of him, like they knew to take him home because he was not capable of making that, or anything else, happen right now. The thought of another failure, a big one, tried to knock on his consciousness, but found utter numbness there and gave up. He realized he was back on the sidewalk when a dog barked at him; he could not even muster up the energy to snarl back at it.

As he turned the corner onto his street, flashes of light caught his attention and for a bewildered moment he thought the storm was coming back. But these lights were red and white, and they spun rhythmically, throwing widening, rotating spots on the houses...fire trucks...ambulances...police cars. Right on his street, right in front of his house...

His house!

Smoke lazily rose out of the place where the roof had been, and sparks still flew like orange fireflies up and out into the night sky.

Larry stopped as the scene seeped into his stunned awareness, and then suddenly he bolted into the crowd that was held behind the yellow police tape across the street. He shouldered his way to the front and roughly grabbed the arm of the man next to him.

"What happened?" he managed.

"Lightning," answered the man, tsking. "Such a shame..." He shook his head and looked with detached distress at the sight across the road.

Larry turned and saw. Three white-sheeted forms lay on stretchers on the sidewalk in front of his yard: one large, one medium and one very, very small.

The scream that grew out of Larry's mouth made everyone step away, and turn all of their attention on him, one spectacle that grew out of another.

The words he shrieked could barely be understood: "ME! ME! I said to hit me you son of a bitch, not them; ME!" He repeated the words until they became a keening wail that brought the EMT's and police officers running.

The last thing Larry saw as he was wheeled into an ambulance, strapped tightly to a stretcher and still shrieking, was a whitish cloud in the sky above his house. It seemed to be grinning at him.

Jane finished the story, holding the sheets in one hand, and her first thought was: Well, yes, it was pretty dark. Her second thought was: it was also pretty good. She gave it a second read and wrote some notes on her notebook to share with Dina when they met again the following week.

"I see what you mean about these kinds of shocking gruesome thoughts," Jane said at their next session. "Your story was macabre and chilling, but at the same time, it appeals to that same morbid sense people have that makes them stop to look at bad car accidents, you know? I really think it's healthy and therapeutic to write them down as fictional stories, even if you never publish them. I think you have a talent for it."

Dina laughed. "I always thought Stephen King must have terrible dreams, but I'll bet he's great fun at parties, especially around a campfire. I've been on fire with writing since that first session, Jane; and I have never felt better in my life. When I make my first million on my best-seller, I will dedicate it to you!"

At a meeting with her supervisor, not long after she began to work with Dina, Jane sat reflecting on her new path.

"Dina says I really helped her already; in fact, she even said I am a natural at it. Her words were, 'born to do this.' I don't know about all that, but I will say that I really love doing it. To be completely honest, I never thought I would find something I love this much. I never thought there was anything out there like this for me."

Dan smiled at Jane. "Most people come into this practice because they have been told that they are good listeners or give good advice, or because they like hearing people's stories, or because they have a story of their own that led them to this course of action. You have all of those, Jane; it's what makes you very good at it. I have another client in mind for you if you think you are ready. I will warn you; this is going to be a tough one. Her name is Angela. Her story is similar to yours, but she seems much more lost than you ever were. I think it's a good match and maybe speaking with someone who did find her way will be what she needs. Of course, I will be there to support you however you need, but it is up to you."

The office, small and comfortably furnished, became very quiet as Jane gave the idea some thought. Dan sat back and waited.

Finally, she said in a soft voice, "I would like to try, Dan."

He nodded his head and said, "I thought you would, Jane. I will set up your first session here at school, and then if it goes well for both of you, you can move the rest of the sessions to your office in Queens."

Jane loved the sound of "your office" and left Dan with a smile.

"Really? What the fuck do you think you can do for me? Cute little girl with a savior complex, out to rescue the people of the world from themselves. Let me tell you, much smarter people than you have tried and failed. So, good luck."

Jane, hiding her startled reaction with great effort, took a silent breath and waited.

"What, not going to say anything? Oh, I get it, you're one of those 'let 'em talk' shrinks. I've seen it before, you let me go on and on until I get tired of spouting off, and then you offer some bullshit cliché that is supposed to make it all better. I can play the game too. I'm not going to say another thing until you talk."

With that, the young woman tightly crossed her tattooed arms over her chest, sat sullenly back into the armchair, and glared at Jane.

"I was once like you, Angela" Jane started.

"The fuck you were."

Jane tried again. "No, you're right, that was a stupid thing to say. I don't mean that I even know what you've been through really, other than what's in your medical chart, which is all clinical and cold. I just mean I wasn't always a cute little girl with a savior complex."

Angela hostilely pushed a lock of her dyed blue hair out of her face and re-crossed her arms even more tightly.

"Can I ask you some questions?" Jane asked.

"No."

"Do you want to hear my story? I am happy to share it with you."

"No."

"Do you want to end the session? We could try again next week at my office in Queens."

"Yes. And there won't be a next week."

The scowling young woman pushed herself up and stalked out of the room. Jane sat staring at the slammed door for long minutes, before writing a few scant notes, and then getting up herself, and heading home.

The following Thursday afternoon as the appointment the supervisor had made for Angela approached, Jane's stomach was unsettled. She fidgeted with everything on her desk while she watched the clock. She thought Angela might not show up and found herself actually hoping that she would not.

The doorbell buzzed loudly at exactly two o'clock, making Jane jump. She did not get up right away to answer it. Its harsh ring came a second time, and still she sat there. It started buzzing again and did not let up until Jane took a deep breath and walked through the waiting room to open it.

"Sorry, I was just—"

"Bullshit. You're afraid of me. How do you think you can help someone you're terrified of?" Angela stood defiantly on the stoop, her hair now orange, her lips painted black. She pushed past Jane and sat defiantly on the couch.

Taking a deep breath, Jane closed the door and walked into

the office. She sat in an armchair near the couch and said, "Honestly, Angela, I don't know if I can help you, or if anyone could. You're so angry..."

"I *am* fucking angry. Good job, you must be the number one counselor at that college. They should give you a medal for your astute brilliance. You might be an actual mind-reader, for fuck's sake."

"Can you tell me why you're angry? That might be a good place to start."

"Because the world sucks, this city sucks, my life sucks. Oh, and you suck too. Is that helpful?"

Jane sat quietly for a moment. She was not sure what to say next, and then realized it did not really matter.

"How do I suck? You don't really know me."

"I might be a mind-reader too. Let me try: You grew up somewhere around here, left for a while, maybe went to the big city to escape mommy and daddy, you're wearing long sleeves on a warm day so you have needle marks you're hiding, failed at everything, got a broken heart from your asshole boyfriend, came back to Queens and decided it would be good to have a job where you get paid to do nothing except sit there and dole out bullshit platitudes to the poor lost souls in this dirty old world. How did I do?"

Despite the tension that pressed the very air in the office, Jane burst out laughing.

"What the fuck?!"

Jane reached over to her desk, grabbed a tissue out of the box and dabbed her eyes while trying to stop herself. "I'm sorry. You just reminded me of someone from a long time ago. You're very good at reading people, you know. That story is pretty close to the truth."

Jane rolled up a sleeve and showed Angela the faded needle marks on her arm.

"That's nothing, I have tracks between my fingers and toes

and between my legs. I even put one right in my neck and it almost killed me. I was disappointed when I woke up from that one. And you ask why I'm angry. That word does not begin to cover it, Miss Therapist. Not even a little bit."

Angela assumed her crossed-arm position and did not say another word for the rest of the session. But the following Thursday she was back. This time her hair was purple and her lips blue.

Jane pulled on all her training and her tricks to try to reach Angela. Building on last week's session, she asked about the needle in the neck that almost killed Angela; and got a short, quick, emotionless response. Jane shared intimate details of her own upbringing and was rewarded with one derisive word from Angela: *"Princess!"* She mentioned attending N.Y.U. and feeling disconnected and detached from the whole scene. Angela almost started to share a thought about that but caught herself and clammed up tight.

Jane's suggestion to write stories was met with, "The world is not ready for that. May never be."

When the hour was up, Jane walked Angela out and sat for the rest of the afternoon in pensive thought, feeling like a failure. At her next meeting with her supervisor, Jane shared her feelings of inadequacy in dealing with Angela.

"Of course, you can stop any time, Jane. You would not be the first to find her impossible to reach. I think you might consider giving it more time, since we don't always know, as therapists, when we do start to get in. But it is completely up to you."

She was glad she decided to stick it out when Angela showed up the following week. Her hair was blue again, and it was the first thing Jane said when they sat down.

"Oh, you like the blue, huh? I change it to match my mood. This week I'm deep blue, so there you go."

"That's pretty cool, Angela. I never thought to choose a

color to wear, or dye my hair, to match how I feel. I should try that."

"What color would you pick right now?" Angela asked in a challenging tone.

It took Jane a bit of time to give the question serious consideration. "You're going to hate this, but I think white. It's a blank color, you know? And when I think about working with you, I just feel like a big blank."

After she spoke, she became anxious about how Angela would react to such a statement.

It was Angela's turn to burst out laughing. "That might be the most honest thing anyone has ever said to me."

The rest of the hour, they chatted about what the colors could mean.

Angela warmed quickly to the topic. "Most people, except for hippies who just fucking love a rainbow, wear black. They say it makes you look slimmer and all that garbage; I just think it means they are too lazy or too scared to let color be their freak flag. Even when I was little and people asked me my favorite color, it changed every day. Guess even then I was a trouble-maker." She gave a rare smile.

"You're an artist!" Jane exclaimed. "I mean, I've never met anyone who thinks about color the way you do; it's almost like you see color as emotion and emotion as color."

Thinking of Dina and how she had found herself through writing, Jane offered a cautious suggestion: "Have you ever thought about expressing yourself through color, either by painting or maybe photography?"

Angela pointed at her hair. "Pretty sure I already do that. No, I'm no artist in the sense you mean. It's all in my head and it will probably stay there. When I was little, I thought I would be a fashion designer; I used to spend hours drawing models in all kinds of crazy outfits. My mother grabbed my sketchbook in a drunken rage and ripped it to shreds and beat the shit out of me. She told me to stop being a stupid fucking idiot with no better sense than a cockroach; and I should stop thinking I would be somebody some day because I was going to amount to nothing, just like my father. I never drew again."

Jane felt like she had made a slight in-road that day; and looked forward to the next session.

When she opened the door the following week at Angela's time, she was shocked to see that the young woman's hair was black; her lips were black; her nails, with their bitten and bloody cuticles, were black; and her shirt and pants were steel gray. Her eyes, already dark, were lined with kohl and simmering with rage. She stalked in and stood in a corner, face scowling, arms crossed.

"Angela, hi, I'm glad to see you," Jane began cautiously. "I can see all the black, and it tells me—"

"Tells you fucking what? Did you believe all my bullshit about color last week? What a stupid fucking sap you turned out to be. Just like all the rest. Figure out what makes Angela tick. Find the magic wand and wave it over her and voilà, she's fixed! Made whole! A fully functioning member of society ready to take up the yoke and do her part! Fuck you, fuck society, fuck color, fuck me."

Jane was taken aback by the fury for a split second and then asked Angela if she wanted to sit down. In response, the seething young woman turned her back and faced the corner.

"If it's okay with you, I'm going to sit."

"I don't care if you take a shit or fly to the moon."

Jane was encouraged that Angela was responding to her at all. She had no expectations that Angela was going to calm down in the next forty-five minutes, but at least she was here, and she was safe. Jane could not fathom what had set her off, but wanted to keep her talking, even if she was cursing and being aggressive.

"Did you take the subway down today? I know sometimes

you walk—"

"Stop trying to engage with me."

Jane waited a long moment. "Is there anything you want to talk about today? Anything at all?"

"No. Fuck you."

Jane let fifteen minutes of silence go by. She sat listening to her own breath, the birds chirping outside the window, the slow whir of the ceiling fan. Just as she was about to say something, not really knowing what but hoping it would not piss Angela off even more, the young woman exploded.

"Coming here was stupid. You almost had me, with your cute little face and your sincere little eyes. You almost had me thinking maybe I found someone who cared, someone who might get me; might help me. But you can't, no one can and my mother was right, I have no more sense than a nasty dirty hateful fucking primitive insect. It was a waste of time to come here. I don't know why I bothered. You don't know me, and you will never get me. The idiot at the college thought we might be similar in some way. Why, because you punctured a few veins? You are nothing like me. Whatever pathetic little dilemmas you faced in your laughably woeful life don't hold a candle to my shit. You might be able to help other poor sad unloved little girls, but you got nothing against my demons. I suppose in some weird way I should thank you; I finally get it. The spotlight is on and it's showing some serious, permanent ugly."

With that, Angela stamped back out the door, slamming it so hard a book fell from the shelf, knocking a small glass vase off the table and spilling water all over the floor. Jane was shaking as she cleaned up the mess and did not sleep well that night.

As soon as class was over the next day, she made her way to Dan's office to tell him what had happened and ask for advice. She had already decided she could not help Angela; and although it made her feel terrible, she knew it would be a disservice to continue trying.

The supervisor was standing, leaning over his desk, and just finishing a phone call as she walked in. He sat wearily, both hands on the desk, head shaking, looking suddenly older; and then he noticed Jane waiting in the doorway.

"Come in, Jane. Sit down, give me a minute."

She sat, uneasy, and waited.

After several minutes, he looked up at her. "Jane, this job we both have chosen can sometimes be very hard. We try to help people in any way we can, often getting emotionally invested in our clients, even though it's Psych 101 to stay detached. The very good ones often cannot help it."

Jane's feeling of unease notched up to anxious, and then dread, as she sat there.

"Angela was a very hard case," he continued.

"*Was?*" she interrupted, now in full distress.

Dan passed a hand over his eyes and took a breath.

"Angela has taken her own life, Jane. She was found this morning. She hung herself in the restroom of her halfway house. I understand she did not leave any note of explanation."

Jane felt rumblings in her veins and bones, an earthquake of conflicted pressure that had her stomach churning and threatening. Her breath stopped somewhere between lungs and throat; her hands did not know what to do with themselves. Dan came around and sat in the chair next to her. He put his arm over her shoulders, which were stiff as a marble sculpture, and let her digest the news. She finally managed a sob and the flood gates opened. She reeled out of control, scaring herself.

She tried to speak.

"I didn't know...she seemed...it was all so...I tried..."

"I know you did, Jane. I know you did your best, as you always do. Some people are lost beyond our ability as therapists to reach. Angela was very troubled; she may have attempted suicide before. No one was ever able to crack through her defenses in all the years of trying. I can tell you that she liked you, though. She went back to you more than to any other counselor."

This made Jane weep harder. Dan pulled a box of tissues near her, and she grabbed several, trying to gain control and mop up her face.

"I'm sorry, Dan. This is not very professional of me."

"Nonsense, Jane. We are human, never forget that."

Dan sat with her for another half hour. As soon as she could stand steadily, she said a quiet thank you and left the building. In the sunny warm day, which Jane found ironic thinking of Angela with a belt around her neck in a cold tile bathroom, she wandered aimlessly for hours.

Passing by Morningside Park, where the roof of the cathedral of St. John the Divine peeked over the tree line, she made her way south on autopilot. The late afternoon brought out crowds of people getting out of work and kids getting out of school and tourists transitioning from their afternoon adventures to the coming city night. Jane weaved her way through them like a ghost.

She entered Central Park just past the Museum of Natural History, where people wandered Strawberry Fields by the nearly completed John Lennon memorial. She passed the frisbee players on the Sheep Meadow, and exited onto the hectic, busy Fifth Avenue; seeing nothing, hearing nothing but the buzz in her head.

St. Patrick's Cathedral, Rockefeller Center, the stone lions in front of the public library, the Empire State Building, Union Square Park, the Cube at Astor Place; she passed them all in a trance of emotional turmoil.

As the sun began to set, she looked around and realized where she was: Thompkins Square Park. In shock, she took in how much the scene there had deteriorated since she had left just a few years ago.

The grassy areas were teeming with rat-infested garbage and make-shift tents; needles and glass pipes and glassine envelopes were strewn everywhere. Emaciated men and women were passed out on benches, on the grass, on the concrete walkways. There was no music playing; no joyful chatter; no toddlers dancing with long-haired barefoot mothers. The energy in the air was angry, wretched, chaotic, drug-fueled, and hopeless.

Jane walked into the middle of it.

Instantly, young men came out of the shadows and surrounded her. *"Crack, H, bennies, poppers, crystal, weed, whatchuwant, I got it..."*

She stopped short. A familiar craving crawled up her legs, made her scars ache, gave her brain a tight squeeze. Memories of the smell of a match heating the spoon, the pinch of the rubber tube on her upper arm, came flooding back to her senses like a long-lost friend.

How easy it would be.

"Come on, girl. Whatchuneed...looks like you want somethin,' like you need a little something...maybe a good pop, good for what ails you...come on, little girl, it's all here..."

How easy it would be.

The days of feeling no pain called to her. The nights of cold outside but warm, so warm, on the inside knew her name; and it was Jenny.

Jenny, who lived day by day, in the moment, grounded in a gritty reality of surviving by her own wits. She had been popular with the others living in the same world; and she now recalled with nostalgia their words of praise. They had been friends after all; maybe the closest friends she had had since high school, bonding over their shared street life.

She looked back on that life with the eyes of a very different person; and wished with all of her soul that she knew then what she knew now. Life out in the "real world" was hard; too hard. Those conversations the last two nights in the warehouse before Joe had...before the end, had been right. True freedom was being your own person, living on your own terms.

Jenny had no stress beyond cadging money off strangers to get her next fix; no responsibilities except to herself; no pressure; no expectations; no silly aspirations and dreams to reach for; no... no...

"NO!"

Jane let out a cry and shoved her way through the tightening circle of pushers.

She ran, shaking and sobbing, back to midtown, never slowing down for the whole two miles; not seeing or hearing any of the city night's medley of sights and sounds; not feeling the gasping and wheezing of her own lungs, until she reached Park Avenue and slid down the wall of the familiar, tall, fancy building to the sidewalk, next to the startled doorman.

Recognizing her, he rang Samantha's office. The lawyer came down in a hurry, escorted Jane upstairs to an empty conference room and sat down next to her on a leather couch.

Jane blurted the story to her friend, and as she spoke, the hysteria in her voice began to slowly abate until she found a drained quietness taking her over.

"I almost lost everything, Samantha. I was one tiny plastic baggy away from giving up everything I have worked so hard for, all up in smoke, literally. Mrs. Thomas would be so ashamed of me if she could see me right now. This is who I really am, Samantha; not who you thought, not who she thought, not who, for a second, even I thought. I can't help anyone, what a stupid idea; I obviously can't even help myself when things get too hard. I don't know what I am doing."

"Look at me, Jane," Samantha said; and the tone in her voice left Jane no choice. "What do you see?"

"A strong, successful, driven, smart woman who believes in herself and does not let anyone get in her way. That makes me feel worse, Samantha. I will never be you, or even close to you."

"No, you won't. Because what drives me is different than what drives you; because my strong is different than your strong, because my smart is different than yours. I was fortunate to be raised by a modern woman who gave me confidence and taught me to thrive in a man's world. It has not been easy; you see how they treat my secretary, Carla, like a piece of meat. But I could never have survived what you survived, Jane. And, I don't have the patience for most people's problems, but you see right through them. It's because of what you have been through, what you obviously are still going through, that people can open up to you. That is why Mrs. Thomas opened up to you. She would not be ashamed of you in any way, Jane. She would tell you to pick yourself up and get back at it. Think about it; you know I'm right."

Jane did know she was right and could hear the old lady's voice telling her to do just that. She looked up into Samantha's face, humiliated.

"Don't you dare apologize, Jane."

Jane clamped her lips to keep the words she had been about to utter inside; and smiled wearily at her friend.

"I hope one day I can be there for you the way you have been for me, Samantha."

"I hope the day never comes that I need you to, but you have already done more for me than you could know. I'm not one who makes friends easily. Shocking, I know."

They both laughed a bit, and then stood. Jane gave Samantha a quick thank you hug, knowing it would make her friend uncomfortable to overdo it; and promised to make a lunch date soon.

She made her way home, took a scalding shower, and

crawled into bed until morning.

It took a couple of weeks for Jane to approach her supervisor and tell him she was ready for another client. Dan introduced her to a young man who had been out of rehab for a year and needed support to maintain his progress. He was a grateful, cheerful patient who was well on his way; and he was just what Jane needed to regain her confidence. Between him, Dina and the continued visits from Bobbi, Jane felt she was getting back on her track.

On a warm morning before her first appointment, she took her coffee outside to sit on the front stoop and watch the world go by. Her old game of people watching had taken a back seat to actual interactions with actual people; but she still enjoyed observing those who went by and wondering about them.

She had just sat herself down and was taking her first sip of steaming coffee when she heard a rustle in the bush beside her. Thinking *Squirrel...or...Rat!*, she made ready to jump up and run back inside.

The rustle came again, this time accompanied by a barely audible squeak. Before she could stand to investigate, a tiny whiskered nose poked out of the bushes; then a small round gray face, large yellow eyes and triangle ears, and a paw that seemed to wave at her as it played with one of the branches in front of its nose. It squeaked again, and then noticed Jane. It came ambling towards her, falling on its face and rolling over in a somersault. Jane laughed so hard her coffee splashed onto her shirt and startled the kitten, who darted back into the bushes.

"Kitty, kitty, Pssss, psss, here little kitty, don't be afraid."

She put the mug down and crouched on hands and knees in the grass to see under the bush. She was rewarded with a little paw in the face, which made her roll back in surprise and almost do her own somersault on the grass. As she lay there, the kitten sprang out of the bush and landed on her. She remained still, and the kitten began to purr and knead her stomach. Tentatively, she reached out her hand and lightly touched its head; it rubbed against her palm, purring louder. Gently, she sat up, cupping the adorable ball of fur in her arms.

"Where did you come from, little one?" she spoke softly to it.

Jane stood carefully and looked around for a crying little girl searching for her lost kitty, or a Missing Cat sign, or even a mama cat with other babies. People walked by, obliviously single-minded on their way. No one seemed to be searching for this fuzzy, sweet little thing, so Jane took it inside.

She poured a small amount of milk in a plastic bowl and put it on the floor. Watching the wobbly stance of the kitten as it lapped with its pink tongue, Jane fell instantly in love. When she picked up the kitten, milk dripping off its whiskers comically, it licked her hand. It was clear that it was just as smitten as she was. She lifted it up to look under its tail, feeling badly about thinking "it" and saw that it was a female.

"Hm, what should I name you, little girl? I mean, if no one comes looking for you, I guess you're stuck with me."

She sat on an armchair with the kitten curled up asleep on her lap and still purring. The gray fur on her body held an undercoat of striped tabby. Her ears were pointy, one dark and one light, and her tail was ringed like a racoon. What a mess, Jane laughed; and that was when she noticed the kitten's front paws.

"You have extra toes! Aw, it looks like you are wearing mittens. You're too cute. Should I name you Smoky? Smudge? Daisy? Buster? Squirrel?"

Nothing seemed quite right. She picked up a tiny paw. "You and these little mitts. Hey, how about Mitzy! I like that, do you like that? Hi, Mitzy, I'm Jane. Welcome home."

She lifted Mitzy, still sleepy, to her face and gave her a gentle kiss on the pink nose. They sat in companionable quiet until the bell rang for Jane's first appointment of the day.

The cohort lingered after class on a warm day in mid-May. It was the last day they would have together as a group. Every one of them had made it through the program, and the professor emotionally told them that in all her years, she had never had a group that supported each other, buoyed each other, and helped each other reach this goal the way they had. She had put together a telephone and address list so they could stay in touch and continue to foster their connections.

She went to each student to hand it over personally with a warm handshake. She told the group, "The relationships you make here will continue to be your lifeline as you grow in this profession. Remember each other when you have doubts or questions or just need to chat. Best of luck to you all, and I will see those of you who are continuing on in the Psychology Bachelor's program."

She left the room, but the others stayed, not wanting to be the first to make the exodus to begin their next chapter. The air hummed with elation, euphoria, melancholy and angst over this achievement. Jane felt all of those as she hugged each classmate; then, at last, she and several others walked out the door into the sunshine.

On the subway ride home, Jane's thoughts turned to the patients with appointments coming up. She took out the spiral notebook she always carried and reread her notes, jotting down ideas and plans for them. She was so engrossed, she did not hear the muffled indistinct announcement that her stop was coming up, and it was only when the man next to her stood to get off the train that she realized where she was. She dashed for the door as it was closing and had to jam her shoulder in and push it back, saying "Sorry," when everyone nearby groaned impatiently.

When she walked into the house, Mitzy stood and stretched

herself into an arch, padding the sofa a few times before jumping off to rub against Jane's ankles.

"It's a special day, Mitzy and this calls for a celebration!"

She opened a can of Chicken of the Sea tuna fish for the cat and made herself a grilled cheese sandwich and tomato soup. Licking tuna juice off her whiskers, Mitzy gave Jane an inquisitive look as she carried her plate and bowl to the table.

"What?" Jane laughed, as if Mitzy had asked her a question about her meal choice. "This makes me happy; it reminds me of good times. Sue me, I'm a simple girl."

And she thought this childhood favorite had never tasted as good.

She showed her eleven o'clock appointment to the door with her usual encouraging, "See you next week."

Sitting on one of the chairs in the small cozy waiting area was a man.

"Oh, I didn't think I had another appointment today," she said.

He stood up, tall and thin. His crow's nests were beginning to appear, and his smile lines were almost hidden by his neat beard and mustache. He gave her a smile, a sad smile she thought.

And then he said, "Janie."

She froze, felt her heart skip a beat.

Smells are supposed to trigger very strong early memories in people; but the sound of a voice, long buried, can do the same.

"I loved you when you were brand new and…"

She ran into his arms.

Greg, her big brother Greg, held her close for a long time. Still clinging to each other, they sat on the couch, knees touching and holding hands. She did not even know where or how to start. But he did.

"I should have taken you with me."

"Paths not taken," she said.

"Spoken like a true therapist," he smiled. "Kind of reminds me of the Choose Your Own Adventure books we both loved growing up. I remember reading them to you and you always agonized over every choice you had to make."

"I still do," she said, laughing. "How did you find me?"

"I've been combing the white pages for years, even called the operator a bunch of times to ask her to look for you, but no luck. Finally, I got the brainstorm idea to look for you in the Yellow Pages business phone book and there you were! Jane Thompson, Drug and Behavior Counselor, Ridgewood, Queens. I can't wait to hear how all this happened, Janie. I hope it wasn't too bad for you after I left."

"It was not an easy time, Greg. But none of that is your fault. I think if you would have stayed, it might have been worse for both of us. You know, I did not think to look for you in the phone book; I didn't know if you were in California or Vermont or maybe even if you were..." Her voice broke but she continued. "When you left, you said you would let me know where you wound up and when you didn't, I just kind of...kept living."

Greg wrapped his little sister in his arms, the apology communicated directly from his heart to hers.

After a moment, she said, "I'm done for the day; do you want to come into the house and have a cup of coffee or something?"

"My wife and son are..."

"You married!"

"Her name is Glory."

"That sounds like an artist's name," she said.

"Worse," he replied, and in their mother's voice, "One of those *hippie* artists."

They both laughed.

"What about you, Janie? Any big love in your life?"

"I go by Jane now, Greg. A good friend told me it was time to let go of infantile monikers, to quote her in her own words; and she was very right. As for your other question, I'm still working on being my own big love. Once I get a grip on that, maybe I will be able to handle someone else; but right now, Mitzy gets all my extras."

"Mitzy?"

"My cat," she said with a smile, and they laughed again. And it felt so very, very good.

"Jane." He rolled it around in his mouth, tasting it, making himself get used to it instantly. "Jane Thompson it is, then. My little sis is all grown up. I'm just sorry I wasn't there to see it."

"Guilt doesn't look good on you, big brother. And it doesn't do either of us any good. You can't change the past; and anyway, what happened back then helped shape who we are today. But now you're here. You're here! And that means we have a whole lot of new memories to make. Together."

They hugged again, making up for lost time.

"Glory and Dylan are back in the city in our apartment, and I promised to bring you there. Is that okay? Little Dylan really wants to meet his Aunty Jane. And Glory made a cake, red velvet, her best one. What do you think, ready to meet your family?"

"I think you should wait here; it will take me just a few minutes to get ready!"

She looked in the bathroom mirror. Her eyes appeared bright and happy, her cheeks healthy and glowing. Her face broke into a laugh when Mitzy jumped up onto the sink, did not quite find a place to land and fell back off, taking the toothpaste, soap, and hairbrush with her.

"You little nut!" Jane picked her up and nuzzled the sweet cat. "I'm going out for a while, but I'll be back, promise. I'm going to meet my sister-in-law; can you believe it? And my nephew! Mitzy, we have a family, and I think things are going to be okay. Maybe better than just okay; maybe things for us are going to be really good."

She gave the pink nose a kiss and put her down on the neatly made bed, where the cat walked in tight circles until she was satisfied that she would be comfortable, plunked herself down, and promptly fell asleep.

Jane walked to the bureau and opened the second drawer where she kept her folded shirts. The scars on the inside of her arms were now barely visible and she pulled a cute tank top over her head. She stepped into the handmade skirt she had bought from her favorite boutique, Jeorjia Clothing Shop, and smoothed it out over her hips.

With one last smile at herself in the mirror, *Hi Dylan, I'm your Aunt Jane*, she gave Mitzy a wave, stepped out the door and headed to the office space. She walked downstairs, anticipation making her steps lighter and smile wider.

She opened the door to the waiting room to find Greg gone.

Her heart sank into her stomach. Her mind churned, not able to accept what her eyes were telling her.

He wouldn't, *couldn't*, do this again. Would he? Had she said something; been too assertive or forceful in some way? Maybe he thought this had been a mistake, and that his life was better off without her after all. She just did not know if she could make it through this again.

When he had left the first time, she had been so young, so afraid, so vulnerable, so full of doubt, so shocked. Now she was none of those things and she needed to do something about it. She would not allow this to happen; she needed him and, even if he did not realize it, he needed her too. All those years of love, before the day he walked out the door of the cold apartment they grew up in, meant everything to her. She had to make him see that. Maybe she could stop him on his way to the subway and beg him, demand of him, not to leave her. Again.

She walked towards the front door numbly but resolutely, put her hand on the knob, turned it, pulled the door towards her, stepped outside.

He was standing there on the sidewalk, looking up the block and waiting. For her.

A rush of relief, a release of the breath she had been holding, and a last shudder rid her of the distress and panic that had taken her over. She stood for a moment watching him.

Her brother, standing on the sidewalk, could have been anyone; no one; someone she had passed by without noticing. Just like all the barely distinguished people around her all the time; just like she herself must be to those same people.

But *this* one, this man, this was her brother; the one person who had meant more to her than the millions that had occupied the same space she had over these many years. Even while he was gone, even while she had buried him deep so she could make it through each day; still it was Greg's love that had carried her to here. And now, it was Greg's love, and Glory's, and Dylan's and her own, that would carry her onward.

She smiled, inside and out, as she took the first step towards him.

Note to the Reader

Thank you for reading my latest book, and for taking an extra moment to peruse this little personal reflection. I seem to like sharing my insight with you, Reader; a bit of after-thought that might wrap up the story you just read in a nice gift bag with a pretty bow. I think of it as an alternative to sitting and chatting with you about my intent for this novel, or at least as a preface to such a conversation.

As I listened to my friends and family and readers share their thoughts about my first novel, <u>Woven</u>, one theme kept coming up: they wanted more. Some wanted more about the characters in the book; an entire novel featuring Lillian, for example. Some wanted me to dive deeper into the parts of the book where time jumped ahead too quickly and left many questions. Others wanted more about the historical periods in the book; in particular, more about New York City in the 60's and 70's, to see how the attitudes and events of the time affected people's lives.

They say it takes a village to raise a child and I would argue the village should not stop there; we grown-ups need our village too. Out of the gentle nudges of my supportive community, Janie Thompson, an ordinary girl, was born.

The term *sonder* is another story about my village. I get countless gems from my writing groups; and "sonder" is one of those. It was a "Word of the Day" that struck such a deep chord in me, I started writing this novel that same morning.

I have been a people watcher for quite a long time. My husband and friends and I often amused ourselves during our college days by making up stories about the people we saw. It was fun to get as outrageous as you could with the tales, a competition whose prize was the admiration of close friends. I highly recommend it for its entertainment and creative values, or as a distraction from daily life. You can use Janie's people-watching fictions as a model if you need one, panties optional.

It was only later in life that I truly started to *see* the people around me, to wonder about their lives; and to learn more about my own, through the wondering. Growing up a city kid, it was survival to turn off the visual noise in order to get where I needed to go. I learned not to make eye contact and invite unwanted attention; in effect to be as invisible as possible, but also to make others around me invisible. When I finally stepped outside myself, when I truly realized I am but one speck in the human universe, I began to appreciate, empathize with, and raise up the other people I meet and see.

<u>Sonder</u> is both a journey of survival and a peek at the life of an unremarkable human being you might barely notice as you pass by. As the definition of the term says, she lives a "vivid and complex" life; one of the infinite epic stories we may never hear. It's my hope, reader, that Janie's story makes you wonder about the richness we have all been missing by not stopping and engaging with the extras in the movie of our lives.

Of course, I must thank some of the members of my village whose criticisms and suggestions shaped this final version of <u>Sonder</u>. My husband and children, my beta-readers, both the hired ones and the volunteers, and my writing workshop groups all gave imperative feedback, and for that I am ever grateful for their support and patience.

Peace.

Maureen Morrissey
March 2022